The Riverbed

ATOPON BOOKS

Atopon Books
907 15th Street
Santa Monica, California 90403
United States

Publisher's Cataloging-in-Publication data

Name: Mattessich, Stefan, author.
Title: The riverbed / Stefan Mattessich.
Description: Santa Monica, CA: Atopon Books, 2023.
Identifiers: LCCN 2022943413 | ISBN: 979-8-9862104-7-6 (hardcover) | 978-0-578-95179-9 (paperback) | 979-8-9866109-4-8 (ebook)
Subjects: LCSH Friendship--Fiction. | Santiago Creek--California--Fiction. | Orange (Calif.)--Fiction. | Bildungsroman. | Fantasy fiction. | BISAC FICTION / General | FICTION / Magical Realism | FICTION / Fantasy / Contemporary | FICTION / Coming of Age
Classification: LCC PS3613.A8439 R58 2023 | DDC 813.6--dc23

Cover Image: *El Cielo de Salamanca* (detail), Fernando Gallego (1494) / Alamy stock photo

Printed in the United States of America

For my parents

*T*he headwaters of the Santiago Creek form high on the tallest mountain of the range stretching from the San Bernardino Pass southeast to the San Diego County line. In its upper reaches it falls through rugged gorges, cascading over rock shelves and scouring alcoves into cliffsides. Eventually it evens out in flats of alders and sycamores, threading the main canyon as far as the broad central basin of present-day Orange County, where it meets the Santa Ana River on its way to the sea. Braided rather than meandering, the creek finds its equilibrium in a constant instability, deforming and splitting flow, widening and deepening channels, crossing, uncrossing, and recrossing its ancient beds. Also ephemeral, it tends to flood in rainy seasons, percolate into groundwater forebays, and disappear in times of drought. Never settled in itself, it runs its fitful course less like a single creek than many creeks super-imposed on one another, caught in cycles of perpetual revision. An errant design or simply an error in design, it testifies to nothing so much as God's unaccountably awkward hand in His Creation.

Early settlers called the mountain Old Saddleback because of the curved sandstone ridge that joined its two peaks into one metamorphic mass, but it's had other names as well. The native peoples of the Santiago, the Tongva and Acjachemen, associated it with a cave where the star-chief Chinigchinic made his abode. He was a favorite deity but not the first. In their origin story, the two creators of the world were in fact not gods but imaginary phantoms, and they messed up not only places and things but people, too. The son they begot in particular left a lot to be desired. He failed to give good advice on harvests, to provide rain, and to protect from disease, and he became a feckless tyrant who had everyone eating clay. When he died, Chinigchinic descended from heaven and promised to do everything over. He reformed the people into proper human beings, gave them laws and rituals, and taught them how to maintain themselves on the acorns, berries, fish, and game he added to the landscape. His handiwork wasn't perfect either; he was more an improver than an innovator; but at least people were able to live in greater harmony with their sketchy creek than they had before. His cave, located fittingly enough between the two peaks not far from the sandstone ridge, they called Kalapwa, which was how they also referred to the mountain itself.

In 1769 a soldier in the service of Gaspar de Portola, who first expropriated the land from the Tongva and Acjachemen for Spain, mislaid his blunderbuss, or trabuco, somewhere in the main canyon. As it was a matter of honor, like Greek heroes with their shields, to keep the weapon within reach at all times, he conducted an exhaustive search that proved as futile as his pride was unshakable. The trabuco would not be found. In the end its loss enslaved him. He deserted his post to wander through the watershed looking around boulders, behind fern brakes, or in riparian grasses, bemoaning that thorn of accident on which his mind had caught. He would spend the rest of his life on the mountain in a state so distracted the early Californios commemorated his obsession by calling it Sierra del Trabuco.

In 1888 Madame Helen Modjeska, one of the most famous tragediennes in Europe, built a summer home by the banks of the Santiago. She attracted a host of actors, poets, divas, histrions, conjurors, mimes, and saltimbanques to festivities that were notorious for their outlandishness. Guests in exotic costume roamed the grounds she christened the Forest of Arden, mistook each other's identities, picked wild grapes, or climbed naked onto outcroppings of serpentine and pretended they were Adam and Eve. Masques were performed in glades strung with Chinese lanterns while Bohemians sat sipping green absinthe at metal cafe tables. Lovers consummated their trysts under rustic arbors of pungent wisteria, adventurous mortals pursued their pagan gods into caves and pools. Her scandalized neighbors, too conventional to join in, were nonetheless appeased by the air of glamor she conferred upon their workaday lives, and they named the mountain Modjeska's Peak in her honor.

Don José Antonio Yorba and his nephew, Don Juan Peralta, petitioning the Governor of California for a grant to the entire watershed in 1809, christened both creek and mountain the Santiago, after their patron saint. They saw a good source of water and land excellent for grazing, and in the following year they drove the first herds of Spanish cattle into the foothills. They built roads in the canyon, abattoirs and vats for rendering tallow, and a resplendent adobe in what is today El Modena. The ranch centered around the making of leather goods for trade with Yankee ships that sailed around the Horn, and oxen regularly drew carreras laden with hides to the embarcadero at San Juan Capistrano. For over thirty years the ranch prospered, even though the place to which the dons had come worked mysteriously to wash out their ambitions and desiccate their sympathies. They never felt at home by that desultory creek. Things happened that could not be explained. Much-cherished family heirlooms locked in chests were found repeatedly in water troughs or cold storage sheds. A priceless first edition of Don Quixote, a book José Antonio consulted like the Bible, disappeared from its glass case only to turn up in a hayloft, transformed from the literary classic of Cervantes to a forgettable knock-off penned by someone named Alonso Fernandez de Avellaneda. One night during a storm Bernardo Yorba, José Antonio's son, was seen on the zanjas cursing the Santiago for its caprices, at the same time fifty guests would swear they sat down to a dinner of steak and frijoles with the affable don.

It was again as if the world had not been properly put together along the Santiago, and from the small rift it formed all reason fled. No one bothered to survey the land, markers seemed to move and shift in men's fickle minds, and boundaries were kept like words of honor among thieves. Livestock, ranging freely in the foothills, grew clever in their attempts to outwit the vaqueros. They would lure them into dense thickets or up steep ravines, stranding them in dead ends while they slipped away down some spur no more accommodating than the eye of a needle. Once a whole herd vanished before the very reliable eyes of Juan Peralta himself in the Cañada de Los Bueyes, only to reappear the next day calmly chewing their cud in the cordgrass fens at Newport Bay twenty miles distant, an event so miraculous it drove the venerable patriarch mad with the thought that his stock had grown wings and flown away on the fierce Santa Ana winds.

As a sense of the literal atrophied in the Yorbas and the Peraltas over the years, and they began to neglect the business of the ranch, letting brush reclaim the roads and fences fall into disrepair, unscrupulous outsiders took advantage of the situation. Bandits hid in the branch canyons and raided wayfarers on the nearby El Camino Real. Squatters laid claim to vast stretches of territory that, according to the official property registers of New Spain, did not exist at all. Horsethieves also took refuge there, and gypsies rolled their caravans into apocryphal meadows. In the days leading up to the Mexican War the Santiago came to be known far and wide as a veritable no man's land.

After the war, American homesteaders poured into the Santa Ana River basin. They were sheepherders and beekeepers from Mormon settlements in Utah, or flinty Scotch Presbyterian farmers who had set off across the Great Plains in search of New Jerusalem. An optimistic, iron-willed people who would never succumb to the fatalism of desert streams, they came with the authority of the U.S. Land Office behind them, subdivided what remained of the ranch after James Irvine finagled the bulk of it away from its Yorba and Peralta heirs, and built their miniature ranchos with wishing wells and tidy English gardens. They began at once to transform their surroundings. Small dry-grain farms were started. Roads were squared and straightened. Miners sunk shafts into veins of coal and hauled it down in six-horse teams to feed the engines of the Southern Pacific Railroad. When Hank Smith and William Curry found a piece of blue quartz that looked like silver in 1879, five hundred prospectors appeared almost overnight to stake claims on or around the Santiago. They pierced the hillsides with tunnels and drifts. They blasted rock walls under powerful hydraulic head in the hope of uncovering whole ledges of silver ore. Then placer gold was allegedly discovered in Mustang Canyon, triggering an exodus not seen since the Gold Rush. For a while the Santiago was famous throughout the United States, and the camps set up on its shores grew into bustling towns with wide-awake saloons and post offices. Only oldtimers from before the war, men like Aramente Hernandez, a retired vaquero who had been raised in a mission settlement, predicted the creek would never cease its dissembling. As he said to a reporter for The Santa Ana Sentinel on March 7, 1880, "There is nothing to the Santiago, I tell you, nothing but sand. The Santiago is a creek like the devil is an angel—that is, not really."

But if Aramente Hernandez was right and by 1882 the towns had become ghost towns, with the mines abandoned and not a single gold flake found, he was wrong about the Santiago. Other profitable operations took over: limestone fired in kilns, gravel quarries, cement plants. By the last decade of the nineteenth century Orange County's first water companies had applied for patents. Citrus groves were planted in the desert east of Yorba Linda, and the new boom of oranges commenced. The Santa Ana River and its main tributary were replete with water moving in seiches through the underground strata, enough by 1920 to support one of the largest industries in

California. Artesian wells were drilled into even more underlying aquifers, pumping stations were established, and systems of pipe were built out to the burgeoning groves.

With the boom came fresh influxes of people, and population in the region soared, swelling the communities that had sprung up on the coastal plain. An old problem took on new dimension with these demographic shifts: rainy season floods that choked the riverbeds and washed into the new streets. The Army Corps of Engineers stabilized the bank lines and added catchments to contain runoff. At places where excessive scour had taken place, they filled in the bed with rip-rap. Where build-ups of silt threatened to block the watercourse, they excavated the bedload. Dams were constructed above the Santa Ana Narrows and on the Santiago at Villa Park after the worst flood in recorded history breached the levees in 1938. The Santa Ana River changed its course altogether, flowed into an abandoned channel right through the middle of Anaheim, and discharged into coastal lagoons near Seal Beach, moving the river mouth over three miles north from its present location. Once more it reverted to its old wild extremes, its old flexuous surprise, invoking a primordial right to elude itself.

After the completion of the dams, both the Santa Ana and the Santiago flowed through Orange County only insofar as it was necessary to replenish the groundwater basins or power the hydroelectric turbines. They were dispersed into storm drains, canal headworks, and spreading grounds. A naturally cyclic storage system for subsurface water was enhanced and made more efficient; runoff was routinely reused two and three times, and hardly any of it emptied into the ocean at Huntington Beach. Indeed, hydrologists determined that, due to aggressive upstream pumping, groundwater in the lower forebays of the Santa Ana flowed away from the Pacific Ocean after 1948, inland over alluvial cones, sucked back into the system of circulation from which it had just escaped. The Santiago became once again what it had always been: a creek only by implication, devious, passed over, winding behind slumpstone fences through the housing tracts, land-use districts, and low-rise mini-cities of a suburbia grown so outsized it would swallow the very orange groves that made it possible.

In the end suburbia swallowed the Santiago, too. It overwhelmed the creek's productive capacities with its voracious sprinklers and swimming pools, forcing the purchase of more water from the Colorado River to add to the reservoirs. What water the creek could supply deteriorated in quality *due to agricultural waste and brine from nearby oil fields leached into the aquifers, and the water companies were forced to abandon their wells. The creek more or less died below the Villa Park Dam after 1965, transformed into yet another no-man's land, this time by virtue of the same forces that had civilized it. So maybe Aramente Hernandez was right after all. The Santiago was not really a creek but an angel become a devil, or a devil become an angel, a place for which there were only avatars—a place, anyway, at the empty center of all intention, where no one went but a few miscellaneous misfits and nothing happened but the things they invented.*

1

Logomachy

Fox Solis was a solitary and self-contained person. He learned early to tread lightly on this earth. He hadn't had much of a choice. His father, who disappeared before he could remember, left him and his mother Sylvie, a seventeen-year-old high school dropout, to fend for themselves. Fox's earliest memories were of unfamiliar rooms with clocks that ticked as if he wasn't there, long lines in lobbies of social service offices, checkout girls impatiently waiting while his mother pulled out wads of food stamps. She always seemed to be working jobs a long bus ride away, fighting with landlords and avoiding creditors. Things would get so bad she couldn't stand it anymore and they'd just bolt, hoping for a new start someplace else. After a while running from troubles became their path of least resistance, and they rarely stayed anywhere long. Fox used to drag with him a box of ragtag things, a photograph of a Native American man, a colored paper lamp, and so on, hoping they'd connect each new wall or bare light bulb with what came before. They never really did. He went to bed most nights sensing around him ghosts of other people just as temporary as he was.

But things had started to turn around for them. His mother, graduating from a technical school with a degree in business administration, landed a good job as an agent at an escrow company in Orange. It meant more money than she'd ever made in her life. They moved into a two-bedroom apartment on the upper story of a duplex, which gave them four whole walls to themselves, just as in a house. A massive bougainvillea bush stood outside the kitchen window and shaded a back porch big enough for a cafe table and a barbecue grill. The building had its own washer and dryer so they wouldn't have to go to a laundromat anymore, and it came with a carport. The landlord even allowed them to have a cat. All together it spelled a welcome reprieve from their former skittish existence, maybe even an end to the rootlessness that had been their lot for so long. Fox for one wouldn't have minded making forays out from the brakes and hedges of his heart every now and again.

Central to this prospect would be his friendship with Axel Acher. They met on his first day at Peralta Junior High, where he arrived, as usual, right in the middle of the school year. The principal presented him to his new home room, and the teacher, Mr. Disher, assigned him a desk opposite Axel. The rest of the class laughed under their breaths at this apparent misfortune. Axel was clearly a pariah. Tall and unco-ordinated, with a head the shape of an adze tapering through a gaunt jaw to a chin almost grafted onto his Adam's apple, large hands and pale skin, he cut the perfect image of the gawky loser no one wanted to be, prompting a hatred that Fox could tell was instinctive and without remorse.

When he sat down Axel was hunched over a frayed, much fin-gered paperback of Tolkien's *The Two Towers*. He wore an English flat cap made of faded black-gray herringbone and a suede jacket tagged all over with words. They were drawn in ornate cursives, cuneiform wedges, and stenciled serifs, and swarmed so thick on cuffs, sleeves, fronts, and pockets that they didn't look like themselves anymore, but gaseous nebulae of torn and mashed together letters.

Fox, fearing to disturb his new classmate's concentration, eased his desktop open and carefully stowed his notebooks and pencils beneath. Axel didn't bother to look up.

That morning the class went on a field trip to the beach. Mr. Disher drove in his own car, leaving his wards to the supervision of a bus driver named Bert, an anxious man with shifty eyes and a resentful personality. No one allowed Axel to sit or even stand near them on the bus, and Bert refused to let him cross the yellow line by the front door. He had to shuttle up and down the aisle for the entire trip—a fate to which it appeared he was no stranger. Bert was also his regular bus driver and some of the other kids had made his exile a customary practice.

They arrived at Crystal Cove State Park, a stretch of open coast-land between the towns of Corona del Mar and Laguna Beach in southern Orange County. From a parking lot the class walked along a wood-plank pathway through a meadow to the crest of a cliff. A slowly descending trail led them to the beach. They headed to tide-pools nestled in the grooves of an exposed reef, where Mr. Disher held forth on the biology of hermit crabs and sea anemones.

At lunchtime they were allowed to wander off on their own. Most kids sat on a stone outcropping studded with clam borings and pre-historic shell deposits. Presently Axel appeared on the beach below carrying a piece of weathered driftwood he had found. It was nine feet tall and wound about with kelp like a caduceus. Ignoring the amphitheater of kids behind him, he dug a hole in the sand expan-sive enough to accommodate its more bulbous extremity, once a root system of some kind. It took a while but eventually he got the whole thing to stand upright. He then sat cross-legged inside a circle he drew around it and faced the ocean, eating his lunch out of a paper bag.

Before long Fox noticed his hunched back begin to convulse with laughter. He made a series of gestures that accompanied an agitated apostrophe to the sea. This was too much for the others.

"What a retard!" a boy yelled from the outcropping.

"You're freaking my funk, dude!"

Axel pretended not to hear what they were saying.

"Dork!"

"Dick-wad!"

"You're ruining the view!"

Danny Kemp, a hormonal prodigy with five o'clock shadow and hair on his chest, took matters into his own hands. He jumped down and stalked across the sand toward Axel, who sprang to his feet and cried out in bizarre parody of medieval English:

"Cross not this circle where I am herborowed, infidel!"

"Just go somewhere else all right, jerk-off?" said Danny, closing in.

"Come not one toad's length more, cretin, or I shall wreak upon thee great servage and pilling!" He pulled out the driftwood and pointed it at his adversary.

Danny halted. "What did you call me?" A glance over his shoul-der brought a number of other boys, like eager members of a gang, leaping down the rocks to his side.

"Beware this fiendish serpent!" cried Axel, struggling to hold up the driftwood.

The boys surrounded him. To keep them at bay Axel swung the driftwood in broad sweeping circles. The other kids cheered on his assailants, who darted in and out with big grins on their faces, looking for openings. Axel turned and turned, growing dizzy, until finally he succumbed to exhaustion and collapsed.

Danny grabbed him by the lapels of his suede jacket and lifted him to his feet. No one called him a cretin (whatever that was) and got away with it. He shoved the offender and punched him in the stomach. Axel fell doubled over. Everyone erupted in hoots and catcalls. They gave in to the kind of collective impulse, furtive and vaguely licentious, that incited kids to do unspeakable things when they thought they could get away with it. Another boy kicked Axel in the back. Others spit and poured sand on him. Everyone might have taken their turn were it not that Bert lumbered down the beach to call them back to the tidepools. He broke up the proceedings before they could gain much momentum, although not because he liked Axel any more than the rest of them. Only the accidents of age and authority, Fox suspected, kept him from chiming in on that wavelength of primitive spite, even adding a kick or two of his own.

People tore themselves away from the spectacle and left Axel crumpled on the beach. Sand infested his clothes and clotted the tears that streaked his face. Only Fox stayed behind. He had stood by as usual, keeper of distances that he was, too self-conscious as the new kid to interfere. He didn't know what to think of Axel's willful provocations, but it touched his heart to see him clutching his knees and staring off like a marionette doll tangled in his strings. He knelt down on the sand and inquired if he was all right. Axel said nothing.

Fox decided the best approach would be the honest one. "Why did you do that?" he asked him.

Axel sat up and grabbed his cap, which had fallen off. He startled Fox by how completely he forgot his former humiliation. In a moment Fox saw how little other people mattered to him.

"Do what?" he said, fitting the cap back on his head.

"You know, draw attention to yourself that way."

Axel pondered the question, squinching the lean muscles of his face into a frown. At last he scratched his temple and said, "I didn't think anybody could see me."

"But everybody could see you!" Fox exclaimed.

Axel nodded. That really seemed not to have occurred to him.

Bert came huffing down the beach a second time, his gelatinous belly sloshing around his broad hips. "Move your butts!" he commanded, and, under his breath but still loud enough to be heard, he couldn't resist adding: "You little shits."

Fox helped Axel to his feet, and together they started back to the tidepools. An offshore wind refreshed their faces, and the blue day sparkled all around them. Axel was still trying to sort out the mystery of his own insensibility as they went.

"The world isn't what you think it is, is it?" he observed.

"It can surprise you if you don't watch out."

"What's inside is not the same as what's outside." Axel paused, gazing over the ocean, lost in vague dissatisfaction with this thought. A mass of cumulus clouds sat above the ridgeline of a hazy Catalina Island. Walking there like Admiral Peary to the North Pole, he murmured, "Sometimes you have to step out of your own mind."

Fox wasn't so sure about that, but he let it stand without comment. It gave Axel an idea. He picked up a piece of chert from the sand, ran back to the base of the stone outcropping, and began to scrape against its porous surface. Fox came up behind and watched him inscribe the letters *L-O-G-O-M-A-C-H-Y*. He had no idea what that meant. When he asked, Axel said, "A war with words."

2

Ambuscado

Axel soon invited Fox to the principal arena of this war he waged, the Santiago Creek winding through the neighborhoods where they both lived. One afternoon he led his new friend to a gate built into a chain-link fence behind a drug rehab center on Tustin Avenue. Axel mumbled some sort of incantation before opening it and led Fox down a rough dirt bank into the channel. They walked past the construction site of a new offramp on the adjacent Costa Mesa Freeway. Big earth-moving machines were busy grading and smoothing the embankment below a half-completed retaining wall, encased in falsework. Further on they encountered a rusted-out hulk of metal that once was the chassis of a car and a pile of rimless truck tires.

Fox noticed that these features of the landscape were to Axel far from ordinary. They were sites of old battles and scenes of high romance. They were markers of remembered stories, monuments to what he called "the spirit of elder days." Where Fox saw junk or weeds, Axel saw trolls turned to stone and the cairns of evil druids.

"You're crazy," was all Fox could say.

"No," Axel replied with a dismissive wave of his hand. "I'm a knight-errant."

He'd been messing around in the riverbed since he was a little kid, populating it with the figments of his hyperactive imagination. He made up kingdoms, mapped territories, gave names to places and things like Adam did in Paradise. Hikes became journeys, hours stretched into years, the past turned into the future and made Axel a seer. Locusts would blight the land and plagues afflict whole nations. Epochs passed with the rapidity of pages in a flipbook. One day Axel might be the hoary and bent old king of a dying dynasty, another the horned spawn of a demigod. He was a general or a foot-soldier, a villain or a hero, depending. He cast fear in people's hearts or he saved them from calamity. He left home for perilous climes, only to return possessed of melancholy wisdom. He slew griffins, harpies, and hippogriffs. On one occasion he was consumed by fire when a dreaded giant named Beleagar laid waste the Plain of Jars; but pitied by the gods, he arose imperishable from the ashes and turned Beleagar into a wild pig, hunting it to its ignominious demise.

Fox, curious and more than a little awed by this strange person, started coming on other riverbed adventures, and soon they were stalwart companions. He never played along in the same spirit. He lacked the same stores of make-believe. An old dinged hubcap Axel called a bronze breastplate remained for Fox just a hubcap, puncturing the illusion with the sadness of all discarded things. It was with them that his allegiances lay. But still he brought a spirit of his own to those adventures, one more in keeping with his reserved nature. He liked the riverbed for its emptiness and repose. He took comfort in its anonymity.

Of course, Axel's predilection for acting his fantasies out was often provoking to someone as discreet and fastidious as Fox. He could handle his friend's antics when it was just the two of them alone in the riverbed, but it got harder when other people were involved, and Axel continued to have a problem remembering that the world wasn't what he thought it was. Fox would never forget the first time he really crossed this line.

On a bright summer day some months into their friendship they went to the Santiago Golf Course for what Axel characterized as a "reconnaissance mission." He had made the golf course into a kingdom called Norn, and its denizens, the Norns, had been his enemies from time immemorial. Like scouts ahead of some battle they crept under an overpass to the adjacent third hole and peered through a curtain of wild dill, dry and rattling with last year's seed, at the flat green. No one was there, but they crouched and waited for a group of men to arrive from the fairway that ran along the bank and down to the dry channel. They could hear the men's speech mingled with frequent bursts of birdsong, the racketing of cars on the street above, and the soughing leaves in the high branches of the eucalyptus trees that formed a grove upon the opposite bank.

Behind them, a brief declivity of jagged earth fell into a still pool cluttered with slabs of broken concrete and black algae thickening in the water like ganglia. Skeeters flitted over the taut tension-surface, and a lone frog croaked forlornly in the shelter of a cattail stand. On its far side a massive pier and a dirt glacis receded one hundred feet to a tilted V of glaring light.

After a while Fox sat back, crossing his legs and rolling out the tension in his shoulders. He twisted around and noticed a flattened soda can in the pool. The chill interior of the overpass smelled of bacterial metabolisms sucking oxygen from the still water. He imagined a cold liquid filling up his insides and bloating his body, turning him, too, into a kind of shale. It was a way he had of feeling like he blended in.

Axel continued his keen-eyed surveillance of the putting green. Heads soon jutted over its edge and balls began popping into view. Axel stirred, his lips pursing revealed a mind full of stratagems. Fox's breath caught when an old man drove a cart onto the green and parked it quite close to their hiding place behind the dill.

One by one the other players appeared. They wore plaid kilts and argyle knee-highs above brown and white alligator shoes, T-shirts printed with logos such as *Golf, It's a Way of Life*, baseball hats with *Angels* written in wavy tangerine letters across the top, and white silk tassels that hung from large-buckled leather belts. They seemed unaware of their outlandish appearance. They might have dressed in such crazy clothes all the time. Fox surmised they must have been celebrating some Scottish holiday or festival. He looked to Axel for confirmation of their oddity, but with the Norns nothing surprised him. Their barbaric ways surpassed all understanding.

Fox could hear the voice of the man in the cart very distinctly. He was recounting a story about his experience as a ball turret gunner on a B-17 bomber plane during the Second World War. He was older than the others, with a bald head sunburnt and peeling, florid cheeks and washed-out blue eyes. He remained seated, his hands on the steering wheel, his arms extended straight out in front of him. As the others went into their routines, assessing lies and choosing clubs, he didn't seem to mind their inattention. He spoke less with any certitude of a captive audience as from a deep-seated will to tell, to disclose, that in the end would not wait for listeners.

Axel's disdain for the men was palpable. He hated the fraternal plot being hatched on that green. He saw in their game no ordinary diversion from humdrum life but the proof of a dark sorcery it was his duty to thwart and undo.

Some men fell to the ground and eyed the terrain, others practiced their swings, curving their knees and hips in clipped, awkward torsions. The tassels swayed gracefully in the folds of their kilts.

One player pitched his ball in a high backspinning arc up onto the green. It dribbled to a halt about five feet from the hole.

The old man, meanwhile, had turned to an account of his "smash eighteenth mission," when the Germans shot him down. "It was the 2nd of January, 1945," he said, "and we drew the big B: Berlin. We went after a synthetic oil plant, but the lead bombardier decided not to make his bomb run because of antiaircraft fire. God they were shooting the hell out of us. . ."

He went on to relate how, after dropping their bombs on a secondary target, the Germans blew out one of the plane's engines and disabled the hydraulic lines that controlled the still open bomb bay doors. More alarmingly, he said, they had cut the oxygen supply to the cockpit, which meant the pilot and his crew would soon asphyxiate. The gunners, trapped in the main cabin, felt the plane begin to descend. They didn't know what to do. "The only way to get to the pilot was to cross the walkway over the bomb bays," the old man explained. "But the walkway was so narrow you couldn't wear a parachute and squeeze between the V racks that hung on either side. Everybody was yelling at each other, we had to bring oxygen to the pilot fast, and one of us had to go across that hole without a parachute."

Absorption in the story was beginning to take hold among the listeners, all of whom stood on the green by this time, exchanging mashies and niblicks for putters and analyzing their shots. Just then a blue moth fluttered through the laminar waves of heat on the green, drawing Fox's eye in its wayward wake to a place even more overlooked than he was.

"So what'd you do?" somebody asked.

"I snapped on a walkaround bottle," the old man said, "with maybe nine or ten pounds of oxygen in it, and went across that bomb bay at twenty some odd thousand feet."

"Bet you got a medal for that."

"Bet they turned you in for a Silver Star," said another man.

"I've seen it," said still another. "I've seen that Silver Star on your mantelpiece, Mitch."

"That's a big deal, a Silver Star."

Mitch sat up tall in his seat and rotated his shoulders into wing-like volutes. He didn't mind basking in the honor and pride his bravery conferred, but still he kept the focus on his story. There was neither honor nor pride without that to convoke them.

"I made it to the cockpit and revived the pilot," he went on, "who took the plane down to where everyone could breathe again. A second engine gave out, and we knew the plane was a goner. We strapped on our parachutes and gathered around the emergency hatch. One by one we all took the plunge."

There was an almost atmospheric change on the green now that Mitch was sailing into the sky like Icarus with his wings. Axel, scorn curling his lip, found the ritual binding of men together in companionable fellowship sinister in the extreme. The men played strokes, the balls converged with slow fatality on the hole, the clarified day breathed and shimmered.

"When you jump out of an airplane," Mitch told them, "you hear a big rush of wind, and then everything gets so still and quiet you can't even feel yourself falling. I turned around on my back like a man relaxing on his sofa and looked up toward the airplane as it banked away. The last thing I remember thinking before I pulled my rip cord was how it seemed like somebody had taken a can opener to it, it was so full of holes."

Fox observed the golfers relax into that sofa, that featherbed feeling of free fall, and plunge right along with Mitch through a few stray clouds and a sudden whiteness of cloud cover. When they all emerged out the other side again, there was a vast patchwork earth rushing up to meet them.

Back in 1945, Mitch landed in a field covered with snow, not knowing which way was which or even what country he was in. "I hid behind a bush until nightfall and then ran through a forest of pine trees. By morning I was so hungry I could hardly think straight. I wandered and wandered without meeting a soul. It was strange, how empty it was. For all I knew I was the only person in that forest. I happened on a recently harvested cabbage patch and ate the stalks. For water I ate snow. I was starting to feel a little crazy, like Robinson Crusoe on his island, when later that afternoon I came to a field that looked familiar. I stood there breathing in the cold air as it dawned on me what had happened. Damn! It was the same field I'd lit into the previous day. I'd come full circle."

The last stroke played, the men set their sights on the next hole, down another fairway that bisected the dry watercourse and skirted the eucalyptus trees on the far bank. They poked their tees into the green and chose their drivers as Mitch told of how he was eventually captured by German farmers while asleep in a haystack. One by one the men squared up and took their turns, and the sound of each stroke as it sliced the air recalled the action of some heavy blade falling.

They finished and headed off for a low wooden bridge that spanned the central channel to the fairway on the other side. Mitch followed after in his cart, yammering away.

When they were gone, Axel stood up and began to clamber into the Santiago after them. Fox grabbed him by his jacket.

"No!" he said. "Let's go. Leave them alone!"

Axel turned to look Fox full in the eye, silently urging him on. It was a dare, a call to arms, and it struck a chord somewhere between shame and care in Fox's sanctuaried heart. He let go of the jacket and followed Axel into the riverbed.

They crossed the concrete channel and ascended to the other bank, entering the eucalyptus grove. A tall narrow space like the nave of a cathedral opened before them. They walked over ground thickly strewn with leaves, deadwood, and mentholated seed pods. Axel was careful to avoid unnecessary noise but keen to gain on the men. Midway down the fairway he was stalking them like a hunter in the vicinity of prey.

The eucalyptus trees began to thin by the edge of a rough. The men were spotting their balls and hitting them toward the next green. Axel relinquished his cover and sprinted into the open, forcing a discombobulated Fox to follow after. On a slight rise stood a clump of four slender cypress trees commanding an excellent view of the entire golf course. The small interior they enclosed also afforded an ideal hiding place just off the green. They came upon the cypresses from behind as the men swung past. Once again they heard Mitch, now recounting his experiences at a POW camp in Frankfurt.

What Axel did at this point gave Fox quite a jolt. He produced four eggs from the pockets in his jacket, two in each hand. Worse, maybe, he had gone to the trouble of drawing on each egg networks of black spidery lines with a felt tip pen. That made them look like small grenades.

Axel held two of them out for Fox.

"No!"

"Yes!" Axel insisted.

"They'll catch us!"

He foisted the eggs on Fox and said, "They'll catch you anyway."

Seeing this rather puzzling remark meant his friend was going through with the attack regardless, Fox gave in. With a strong sensation of disbelief, he, too, threw his arm back, bracing himself for the shock of engagement. On a count of three they both lobbed the eggs, two at a time, in high parabolas out over the green. Just as they slipped inside the cypress trees the eggs splattered around their targets.

Pandemonium ensued. The men, livid, demanded of each other which way the eggs had come. They turned in helpless circles, scanning the horizon, or craned their necks upward in the improbable likelihood of a plane. The absence of an aggressor unnerved them all.

Inside the cypress trees the two boys stood stock still and waited. They heard solemn oaths of vengeance give way to reasoned discussion. "It isn't possible those eggs came from nowhere," said Mitch. "Whoever threw them must still be around."

"That's right," someone else chimed in.

All speech petered out. The two boys listened to the silence until a nearby crack of twigs alerted them to an emergency. The men were sifting through the weed-filled rough. "I wouldn't be surprised if they were hiding in these trees right in front of us," they heard. Terror expanded through Fox's whole body and pressed against his ribs. It was all Axel could do to gasp as a pair of hands brushed the prickly foliage:

"Run!"

They burst from their hiding place and fled broken field down the sloping grass and across the fairway. Shouts went up as they saw the group of men in two lines like a ripplewake flow down the slope beside them. They headed straight for the golf cart that Mitch steered at them, curling around either side and veering toward a sand trap. Two men gave chase directly, another fell back to block any escape in the direction of the third hole, and two others fanned out toward the clubhouse, which was also where Mitch headed at full speed. As Fox and Axel cut across the golf course, swerving down into the channel of the riverbed and bisecting another fairway, the two men who had fanned out turned in wide loops to confront them in their path.

They deviated up the far slope to the second hole, breaking in on another game. Their pursuers yelled, "Stop them!" The players dropped their clubs and splayed their arms, ready to tackle. The two boys went into a weaving pattern. They dodged one golfer, then another, and emerged miraculously on the other side of the green, followed now by five men, five stout clansmen with their tartan kilts billowing in unison around their thighs.

Fox and Axel curved away from their pursuers, cut obliquely across the riverbed a second time, and headed for the culvert to one side of a parking lot. Keeping a little ahead, Fox saw Mitch in the cart angling for the culvert, too. He beat the old man to the semi-circular opening beneath the bridge, but Axel's cap flew off his head into the fairway and he went back to retrieve it. Mitch interposed himself between them as Fox leapt onto a concrete abutment. Axel picked up the cap, did some fast thinking, and took off toward a cinder block fence that wrapped around that stretch of the golf course. Mitch chased after him in the cart. Axel ran for the fence as if he intended to plow right through it. But just as Mitch gained on him, he planted his foot and cut sharply across the front end of the cart. Mitch turned, slewed, and the shift in gravity lifted the cart on two wheels. It hung balanced for an instant as Axel froze in his tracks, pointed the cap at Mitch, and screamed, "Thou art slain! Thou art slain!"

Mitch stared, caught in a skew of abruptly shifting force, and heard himself saying "What in Sam Hell does" just as the cart, toppling over, yanked the last words from his lips.

Fox called out from the abutment, and Axel ran over as the rest of the men headed for the overturned cart, attending to Mitch where he lay sprawled on the grass. Fox led Axel through the culvert to the riverbed on the other side, and together they vanished into a forest of tall bamboo plants growing thickly between the banks.

3

Axalax

Axel had always been a preternaturally intelligent kid. The first word he ever spoke, at the towering age of thirteen months, wasn't *Da* or *Pa* or *Ma* but *Pleroma*. His parents, Blaise and Maude, who were devoted Christians, taught him to read the Bible at four, and by six he was reciting whole passages and stories by heart. He'd inherited the confident spirit of a preacher from his grandfather, who had been a well-known evangelist in Southern California for decades. At eight Axel was delivering his own sermons from a makeshift podium he'd erected in their living room. He went on the television show *Christian Jeopardy* at ten, beating out much older contestants with his uncanny command of the gospels. His parents were so impressed they began to wonder if Axel wasn't some sort of latter-day saint, another Joseph Smith tapped by the Lord to spread His Word in the end-time. Just in case, they dedicated themselves to helping their son walk with Jesus.

But then Axel began to talk like the Bible even when he wasn't interpreting the story of Lot's wife or Joseph's dreams. He asked for chocolate chip cookies or a second helping of chicken wings in high King James style. He admonished his parents about their foibles and shortcomings in the exact jargon of Saint Paul. It was as spooky as a ventriloquist's doll. Alarmed that they may have flipped a pathological switch in their son, they stopped the ritual of the sermons and took him to baseball games instead. Eventually they withdrew him from a private Christian academy for prophetically gifted children and sent him to the local public school, encouraging him to be like everyone else, a normal Orange County tract-house kid.

These attempts to straighten the curve in their son's character only backfired. He preferred to stay in his room with the many books he liked to collect, cutting himself off from the outside world. He had next to no social graces. When he didn't shun people, he got on their nerves with his eccentricities. He might laugh right before someone came to the punchline of a joke, answer simple questions with long and pointless disquisitions, or begin walking like a Beefeater for no conceivable reason. Such displays, however innocent or unmeaning, also had something personal about them, and he easily left others feeling that they'd been insulted or mocked.

By the time he met Fox, however, his antics weren't all that innocent or unmeaning. He was consciously fighting higher powers, though not always with entire clarity about just what those powers were. This had to do in part with him not having connected them to his parents' Christian values. He shared them as he believed in God himself and even though his logomachic struggles were a way of slowly breaking free from his Christian world. He just didn't know it yet. Fox played a part in this break as the first friend he'd had who wasn't from that Christian world. Fox had no idea he was playing a part and never purposely did anything to help the process along, but he contributed what he could: the tolerance that comes naturally to someone with a soft touch and an open mind. Even when Axel went too far with his crazy play-acting, Fox took him as he was and not as he ought to be. It wasn't hard for him either. Having no particular allegiance to normal tract-house kids and plenty for the ostracized and the lonely, he knew where he stood as unswervingly as Axel did, if not on all the same levels or with the same antinomian fervor. Axel appreciated this principle in him, too; it assured him, whatever the differences between them, that they were on the same side.

But the real turning point for Axel wasn't his friendship with Fox. It came when disaster struck right around his fourteenth birthday, one year after they had first met. His uncle Gary was driving him home from a church retreat when a tire blew out on the freeway and sent the car skidding across five lanes of traffic. It rammed into an earthen berm, overturned, and tumbled violently along a swale until it hit a silt fence installation. Axel, hurtled through the windshield a distance of over thirty feet, split open his skull and broke both wrists, his shoulder, and several ribs. They rushed him to a hospital where he passed the night in a coma.

He had what doctors afterward told him was a near-death experience. He remembered walking up a vast slope covered in tall windblown grass. The sky was vivid and infrared, streaked by rapidly moving clouds. Through the grass he saw other children wandering toward a precipice. At the crest of the cliff stood a man dressed all in black, like a hooded figure of death from old paintings, only he had a shepherd's crook rather than a sickle in his hand. A line of children snaked to his feet, and one after another they went to the edge, paused while he blessed them, and jumped into the airy deep. Axel took his place in the line and finally came before the dark figure. He looked out over a wide sea to a beautiful ship carved in the shape of a swan, all inlaid with mother-of-pearl. On the ship he saw a mariner so radiant he seemed to be made of light. His limbs and torso rippled like liquid glass as he patiently pulled a closely reticulated silver net from the scintillating water. On his head he wore a silver winged helmet. At length the mariner paused and looked back at him, and with a force beyond words to describe, beyond the power of sinew or bone to hold together even, Axel felt himself shattering with the discovery that it was *his* face he saw across the expanse. Then, as if caught in a riptide, he was drawn down the slope again, away from the precipice and back into the world. He awoke shortly after that.

This experience revealed a divinity in the broken vessel of his body that Axel had never so much as glimpsed in the Bible or anywhere else. It brought on a crisis of faith. Why did sin negate God's image everywhere but in Christ, he asked, when he had so plainly observed it in his own heart? Why did salvation depend on atonement through outward belief, when he had his own luminous inner pilot to guide him? Such questions posed themselves so insistently that he lost his purchase not only in his parents' authority but in God's. He began to see why the book in Paul's hand was usually closed and he held a sword in the other. He didn't want anyone to have their own relationship to the Word. Paul had always puzzled Axel because he called the angels "rulers of the darkness of this world." But he didn't see how the angels could be lords over corruption when they were made of light. They didn't belong to the earth any more than they belonged to heaven. They were in between, not one thing or another but mixed and volatile, inconsistent and vicarious intermediaries of an ecstatic spiritual reality; they helped people, through the contact with this reality, to know their perfection in self-transcendence, in expelling themselves from themselves. That angels were also demons, capable of twisting or blocking this knowledge, only further underscored the ambiguity that made attaining it a matter of one's own discovery and interpretation. How could Paul think this ministering activity was wicked, he wondered, unless he had no feeling for the worship God asked of us or, worse, for the restiveness with which He sojourned among us? Unless Paul was not a stranger on this earth? Unless he served a different God, a false God? Axel, putting two and two together, concluded that he had to be a lord over corruption.

In the months of convalescence following the accident Axel grew keenly interested in angels, their names, their hierarchies, their properties and powers. He poured over every book he could find touching on the subject of angelology, and he often burdened Fox with detailed accounts of archangels, principalities, thrones, and virtues; this or that angel's evolution from Zoroastrianism to Christianity; angels before Saint Paul and after, according to Pseudo-Dionysus or Saint Thomas; angels as Gnostic aeons or angels as demiurgic archons. He spoke of nothing else. Fox could never keep the names straight. Jacob, Uriel, Israel, Elijah, Sandalphon, the giant Adam—they seemed distinctive yet interchangeable to him, signifying first one thing and then another, pregnant with meanings that never seemed to be fixed. In the end they became a jumbled mess in his head, just like the words on Axel's jacket.

He couldn't always be sure if their incoherence were his or Axel's, but in any case it reflected a change that had come over his friend. His mind worked more quickly and attained to states of greater concentration than before, and a new gravity permeated the riverbed dramas that resumed once he stopped having to wear a neck brace. Everything became interconnected. Places were settled in their mythical associations, events fit into a definite narrative order. Once the last casts on his hands came off he began to write all sorts of texts, chronologies of kings, fragments of epic sagas, ethnographies of local folklore and customs, descriptions of fake flora and fauna. He filled notepad after notepad with the things he made up and recited them to Fox in the various secret camps they had established in the riverbed.

At one point Axel developed the vocalic habit of tensing the *Oh* of Orange into the more uvular *Ur*-ange. He would not refer to it any other way. One day that good township became, in some metamorphic process known only to the alchemist in his brain, the Ur-angel, a creature, he informed Fox, resembling a huge turned-out asshole with wasplike legs and six wings, backed by the caudal segments of an enormous swishing tail. This archfiend governed all things profane in a vast empire called Ur, peopled by men who, slaves to their most fallible urges, thought only of their own survival and loved only the death they feared. According to Axel they blighted everything marvelous. Meanness of spirit was their spirit.

Fox went along with the introduction of Ur and the darker cast it gave to their exploits in the riverbed without thinking about it too much. After almost dying in a car accident he didn't wonder that Axel's outlook would darken. But he had to admit it was harder even than it used to be for him to take part. He tended to demur not because he wasn't interested but because he felt his own imaginative shortcomings so strongly. It was difficult for him to trust himself. On one level Axel's obsessions seemed more honest, or at least more vital, than his own brooding reflection on the webs of actuality in which he was caught. But on another they filled him with foreboding. He didn't understand how Axel could have so much confidence in that angelic realm when its indemonstrable nature left him so tongue-tied. It seemed to Fox rather in the irresolute that the unseen exerted its influence, sometimes beneficent but just as often malign. For all that he came to admire the courage in Axel's imagination, and even wish some of it for himself, he never shook the feeling of the proverbial fox who, leaving his hole for the world at large, promptly returns chastened to its safe confines once again. This, of course, only had the effect of winding his inhibitions into yet more tenuous coils.

Before long Axel's logomachic struggles became so involving he literally forgot himself in them. He became possessed by an alter ego to whom he even gave a name: Axalax. Born in the year of the Empire 9372, he fled as a child into trackless wastes after his parents were poisoned by an evil priest. Raised an outcast among orphans and wolves, he grew up in fierce rebellion against the men of Ur. Alone or with his trusty comrade he harried their outposts, sabotaged their roads and bridges, infiltrated their star chambers, and otherwise undermined imperial authority every chance he got.

He appeared at first as a character in Axel's stories. Only gradually did it dawn on Fox as he listened to them how Axalax was merging with his author. There were instances when the story would end yet Axel keep on speaking in the same archaic manner. There were stretches when Fox asked himself just how long he could keep it up, and well before the fact he was privately wagering on just when a whole riverbed sojourn would pass in the company of Axalax. The day that happened was already too anticlimactic to be anything special, and soon enough it became the rule rather than the exception.

Fox missed Axel when Axalax was around. It seemed his flights of verbal fancy and elaborate mummery could very well go on without either of the two humans on the scene. This appurtenance Fox felt in the riverbed had him thinking twice about not only Axalax's bravado but what they were both really doing there. As a result he lost his bearings more easily. He forgot the reasons for their peripatetic wanderings and escapades. Maybe it was just a sign of growing older, more unsettled in boyhood pastimes, more intent on breaking out of his shell. Or maybe he was afraid of the limit he sometimes bumped up against in the riverbed, an extreme point in play where the whole world took on that same superfluous quality, and he retreated all the more within himself. Either way he couldn't help feeling that it might be time to put away childish things.

4

The Whirling Wheel

One day Fox and Axel lay flat on their backs in the riverbed, spread-eagled on a square flat of weathered asphalt that had been laid down for reasons long forgotten. The wash, desolate as usual, scintillated in its own wild abstraction. Sunlight glowed lustrously in a nearby tussock of pampas grass. Crusts of alkali slowly crystallized in the grooves of old planetary wheel tracks that scored the hardpan. The place in its stillness seemed to be remembering a former turbulence, vortices around the exposed roots of a willow tree, runnels in the branching cracks of marbled sediment. Flow was memorialized here in windrows of brittle sycamore leaves, there in plastic bottles snagged on cow thistles, caught as if in the throes of some once purgative flood.

They were enjoying the intermittent spectacle of four Blue Angel fighter jets as they flew in diamond-shaped formation back and forth, up and down, in circles and swoops across the sky. The planes zoomed in perfect silence across the riverbed, their shadows like wraiths flitting from fence to riprap to shrub. Then, following in their wake, came a tinny whine blossoming into a thunderous boom. Sound was split from its event. To Axel this marked a break from the natural order of things, resonance preceded by echo, echo without source, pure echo: a message from the invisible world, bodiless yet primitive as the subvocalizations of flesh, susurrating blood, the all-enveloping vibrations of atoms, molecules, and crystals. They were angels, sounding bodies, manifestations of the noise from which the Word first came, trembling and terrible.

Fox considered the likelihood of angelic visitation as the fighter jets arched high into the sky, froze for an instant and fell through one twist of a spiral to become four black dots headed straight at them. Fear gripped him, fear of attack, fear of visions, fear of angels, he didn't know. But he would just as soon they stayed in their heavenly spheres and stopped blowing their trumpets in his foxhole.

The planes bellied up on their approach. He noted the rockets that hung tucked into the jointures of the wings. He imagined them igniting and shooting over the A-frame roof beyond a cinderblock fence that stood upon the bank, a Church of Jesus Christ of Latter-day Saints, to engulf the riverbed in blood-orange plumes of flame. Angels for Fox were often angels of destruction.

All went quiet again. They lay still, their mouths open, their jaws relaxed. Their heads rested gently on the asphalt square. Minutes passed this way, and it looked as if the planes had left for other skies. Fox for one was glad to be alone with the filarees and petty spurge, the sowbugs and lacewing flies of the Santiago.

After a while Axel sat up and grabbed a tall lacquered stick, his "staff," scored with devious lines, runes and blazons. "What next, my liege?" he asked. "Shall we hunt the fire-breathing worms of Gothrap, or shall we wile away the day in the woods of Bland, telling tales of valor and great deeds?"

That was Axalax.

"We could head to the place we found the sofa in," Fox offered.

"The caves!" cried Axel. "Our inner sanctum. Where outlaws go in dead of night to brood on counsels deep! Let us hither, my suzerain, before the sun descends to its watery bed. I follow you with all my heart."

"Oh brother," Fox murmured.

They set forth down the wash, braiding their way through strands of chamise. Up ahead loomed the Newport Freeway overpass. For Axel it was a mountain spotted with howling jackals, and in its granite depths were carved the dolven halls of a dwarf city, Doria, long abandoned to the dragons who had plundered it for gold. The two teenagers passed within and walked in darkness. The roar of cars above, incessant movement, incessant destination, echoed through the overpass.

Near the far end they came upon a round pier on which a message had been scrawled in red spraypaint. It said: "For inhuman head call Heloise 666-6969." Frightened pigeons fluttered out from their perch in an expansion joint between two bridge beams as Axel pondered the secret significance of the words.

"It's a warning," he decided. "It means in code the triple-tongued dragon Sidereal knows we are here and comes up from his den to incinerate us with his breath. There he is!" He pointed back over Fox's shoulder. "Fly! Fly before all is lost!!" With that he took off and left Fox looking back through the overpass. He sighed, muttering, "I don't see a dragon." The thought struck a plaintive chord in him. Beginning to run after, he said to himself as the shock of each footfall jarred his body, "Where's the dragon, Axel? Tell me how to see the dragon. Tell me how to see it like you do."

Once in the open air he looked out upon a swale covered in granite boulders roughly the size of soccer balls. Axel was visible in the distance, brandishing his staff at his dragon, wobbling over the uneven terrain with enough recklessness to have Fox worrying about the broken shoulder and ribs, however nicely healed they appeared to be. Not running this time, he hopped onto the first boulder and followed more gingerly in his friend's wake.

Terrain reverted to bar tail and ripple on the far side of a low dam. There four rusted pipes like horizontal smokestacks jutted from the bank and emptied into a dried-out crater. From its edge a phalanx of poisoned hemlock marched down the riverbed. Fox found Axel in its midst decimating the white stalks with his staff, whole rows of them at once. He was as usual surrounded by enemies, in danger, fighting for his life. As Fox looked on he almost saw in Axel's repeated blows, and in the bent shapes of the hemlock, the bodies of his adversaries in their death throes, their agonies of thwarted hate.

But the next moment, hastening past the sense of emergency, he returned to the riverbed, to an acknowledgement of its beloved vacancy, and felt nothing of Axel's forsaken plight. He sat cross-legged upon the ground and waited for exhaustion to set in with his friend, to bring him back to the flows of dust and glare, the slow drift of distracted time passing for Orange on any given day. Eventually Fox went to pee underneath the horizontal pipes. He felt with the emptying of his bladder a pleasure that spread so voluptuously through his secretive loins it made him blush.

On buttoning up his pants, he turned to see Axel grinning at him as if he knew just what he was feeling. A suspicion came over

Fox that his friend had telepathic powers. But it passed immediately as Axalax leaned on his staff and squinted at the sun. After a long beat he drooped his head to one side, overwhelmed as if by some private grief.

"I'm thirsty," Fox said. "I—" Axel stopped him with a sharp monitory look.

"Be careful, my liege."

Fox paused in mid-breath, searching for some upwelling of disinterest or reverie, but nothing came.

"—could sure go for a Big Gulp," he finished, hoisting himself onto a pipe and straddling it.

Axel glowered at him. He was slighting the high drama that had just unfolded there. With an incredulous lift of the brow he trailed an upraised hand across the destroyed hemlock as if the scene might speak for itself. Fox gazed on it, conned it for the figures of an inscrutable text he could not read, and felt not for the first time ashamed of his incompetence, his persistent infirmity, without knowing what to do about it.

"An Orange Crush," he went on. "I could drink Orange Crush forever."

"And still not find the bottom of your fizzling lust," averred Axel, standing now by Fox's dangling feet. "Avaunt! Avaunt! Such noxious exhalations waft from these infernal pipes." He placed the palms of his hands on either end of the one next to Fox's and stuck his head inside. "Into what weird creature's lair do they inwardly gape?" he mused. "Who lives in there stirring his cauldrons of boiling sugar water? Ach, sssss! Be cautious, my preciousss. Who are you indeed, *gollum, gollum?*"

He squeezed his narrow shoulders all the way into the pipe, making guttural noises in his throat, and Fox saw him for an instant he could almost call real not as Axel stuck in a pipe but a pipe with legs drilling into the bank.

Shadows bulged and grew denser in the riverbed. A breeze was felt. Presently they clambered up to a rutted path that ran along the crest of an embankment. They followed it to a blackberry bush and lingered picking the berries. Axel grew solemn, absorbed in the catch of thorns on his jacket sleeve and the squish of pulp on his palate.

A bend in the riverbed at that juncture curved and looped back on itself, enclosing a topography of dunes and sinkholes that municipal authorities had left to the Santiago. From where Fox stood, he could see boys riding mountain bikes along paths worn into the badly eroded ground. They went at it with verve, grinding their front tires into the dirt and sailing off plywood ramps.

Suddenly Axel stood by his side. "Men," he sneered. "Urlings, hard at work on their schemes of savage excavation. Great wrong have they done us, Fox." Mischief was now in his eyes. He tucked his staff under his arm and pointed it in their direction. "Them will I encounter or else lose my life forthwith." And before panic canceled one beat of Fox's tremulous heart, Axel charged the mountain bikers with a loud holler.

One boy, about twelve, angling for his ramp, pumped the pedals of his bike for all he was worth when Axel bore down upon him. As he sailed into the air Axel's fewtered lance loomed into view, scaring him half to death. He leaned away, turned his wheel, and landed on his side with a yowl. Axel, meanwhile, headed up the path toward a second rider, who skidded to a halt.

"Away, varlots!" he shouted. "You do violence to me and mine. For I am Axalax, and rightful master of this befouled tarn."

The boy stared hard at Axel as the others congregated by his side. They were not happy.

"Get thee gone," he cried, less sure of himself now. "Or I will unlock my word-hoard, and blight thee with poetic plagues."

The kid who crashed his bike stormed up the path, bleeding at the knee. He was also husky for a twelve-year-old.

"What the fuck do you think you're doing?" he cried.

Axel glared at his new adversary. "Stand back, Sir Sauceyes," he commanded, "for I am passing wroth, and postehaste will smite thee with this spear." He raised the staff over his head. The other kid was just angry enough not to care if Axel was serious, and, as knights do, they rushed together. There were sundry strokes, helms were cloven, stout buffets sustained, and by the end of it Axel lay winded on his back. The bikers remounted their steeds and once more began riding along the loopy paths.

Fox picked up Axel's cap from where it fell during the fight and, kneeling beside him, handed it over. Axel's face was smeared with sweat and dirt. A bruise had blossomed upon his cheek.

"Are you okay?" Fox asked.

Axel raised a hand in the air and said, or recited, because that was what it sounded like, "Such are the fortunes of war, Fox, that betimes we suffer indignities, setbacks unexplained, and some dread enchantment thwarts our dearest actions and most noble cause." He sat up, fixed his cap upon his head, and dusted off his jacket. "'Tis the work of that baneful sorceress Mimema, by my troth. She neutralized my amulets and set those rogues upon me."

Fox thought it was the other way around but said nothing. He had never heard of Mimema before. She must have been a new character in one of his stories. "Let's get out of here," he urged, "before they come back."

They returned to the riverbed and headed toward a thicket of tightly intertwined willow trees: one of their many safe houses in the dangerous Empire of Ur. They skirted its edge until they found a vine of white morning glories trailing in branches notched with withered catkins. At that point a cleft in the mass of leaves opened into a passageway wide enough to crawl through. Axel clumsily dragged his staff behind him into the tunnel. Fox followed behind. At one juncture the tunnel widened into a sort of ventricle lined in stained cardboard. Candles melted down to barest nubs stood in small recesses, and an inflated condom hung on a string from a branch, staring balefully back at them. Further in, a chamber almost the size of a room had been hollowed out and furnished with a moldy vinyl sofa.

As they approached the chamber, expecting to find it empty as usual, they heard instead a voice. Axel's aroused look meant they would have to explore the situation further. They eased nearer, sliding on their bellies to an antechamber formed around the trunk of a willow tree, and positioned themselves as close as they dared.

Seated on the sofa was a man with blasted eyes, long matted hair, and a thick, coarsely textured beard. He wiggled the toes of his extended bare feet, bulbous with corns. A purple birthmark ran from the center of his forehead down across a temple, bisecting one eye socket. Bizarrely, his yellow fingernails were so long they curved around the tips of his fingers. His hands looked like a buzzard's talons.

He was telling some invisible interlocutor about a vision he'd had of a "whirling wheel." "I swear to God," he said, "way up in the sky this huge whirling wheel, with eyes on it and lions, eagles, angels and shit, and inside it were other wheels, wheels inside the wheel. . ."

Shadows blocked up around the man, silvering his outline. He seemed to hover there like a specter in the dim light. Just then Fox was startled by the sensation of a hand resting on his shoulder. Horrified, he whipped around to see whose it could possibly be, but no one was there, which made it even worse.

"This old guy stepped out from the center of the wheel," the man said, "and he was made of brass, brass all over, from head to toe. All he talked about was famine, doom, pestilence, war, wrath, wickedness, junkies and whores." The man paused. "He said, 'I am a sign to you.' 'No shit?' I said. He said, 'Fuck you, you fucking pathetic renegade son of a bitch! Who do you think you are?' Who do I think I am?" He gave a derisive snort. "A 'Son of Man,' that's who the fuck I think I am, and you can kiss my ass, too." He darted wild glances through the tangled reaches of willow trees. "You can all kiss my ass."

The sound of a branch cracking under Axel's knee startled him. He didn't like sharing that space with anyone else and started to slide off the sofa. "That old dude was one bright motherfucker," he muttered as he grabbed a duffel bag and crawled toward another passageway snaking into the brush. "One shiny bright motherfucker. . ."

Fox, watching the man leave, marveled at how like a dream he was, a shared dream and so not actually a dream, but something else denser and more tangible, more real than a dream could ever be. This, he supposed, was that mythic dimension in which Axel lived and breathed so lustily. He wondered if he, too, might now be moving in its same heady atmosphere of passion and belief.

Axel disentangled his staff from the brush and scrambled into the passageway after him. Fox backed off, inadvertently squishing a slug with the palm of his hand as he maneuvered into a different tunnel. Revolted, he tore a sprig of willow leaves from a branch and paused to wipe the guck off.

The man didn't acknowledge their pursuit except to show an unsuspected agility, gaining speed as they did, keeping ahead, beating them out of the thicket. This elusiveness only added to his mystery. Once outside Fox half-expected to find him crumpled on the hard bottom of the riverbed, his knees melting into his chest as his head shrank into his neck. A part of him even hoped to see the man morph into a turkey buzzard, the long black tailfeathers shooting out of his rump, the talons clenching at air, the wings unfolding from his shoulders. And he hoped to stand side by side with Axel when this bird-man took off at last in gangly flight, joined to a world of miracles whose passwords did not escape him.

Of course, when he found Axel shading his eyes with a flat hand and gazing up at the sky, the man nowhere to be seen, another part of him rested easy. It wasn't sure just how much corroboration of mythic dimensions he could in fact handle. But on following his friend's gaze he saw, to his astonishment, a turkey buzzard swerve over the riverbed as if in their vicinity it had detected a corpse it might feed on. It circled back to drift sideways toward a large sign fixed on two poles to the roof of a low tin building up on the bank. The sign said "Stop Casting Porosity," and the raptor disappeared behind it, out of sight and out of mind as far as Fox's other part was concerned.

5

Fox at School

The first-period bell screamed through the main building of South Orange High as Fox, a sophomore by this point, slipped behind his metal desk in Mrs. Ludwig's keyboarding class. Around him people settled into the rows of seats and snapped on their computers. An electronic hum slowly filled the room. He braced himself for the ensuing two-minute keyboarding test.

Mrs. Ludwig swam up to the front with the attendance sheet in her hand, slurring her words horribly through an elaborate mechanical contraption that she wore in her mouth. She'd had an accident last year on Katella Avenue; her teeth and gums had to be reconstructed and her jaw wired to her skull. When she spoke, saliva tended to glisten and pool at her lips, and every now and then she had to spit into a cup she kept on her desk. This, coupled with the horn-rimmed glasses through which she peered with eyes made tiny in the thick bathyspheric lenses, left her students collectively thinking of a Creature from the Black Lagoon.

"Cheung, Borittthh!"

"Here."

"Clark-Kent, Melittthha!"

"Here."

She went down the list. Fox looked up at the light filtering hazily through the Venetian blinds on the windows and thought of the comet that had recently begun streaking through the skies above Southern California.

"Muttthhgrove, Morrittthh!"

He had gone with Axel one night to the riverbed and looked at the comet through binoculars. There were rumors that an alien spaceship followed in its tail, but Axel dismissed them on the ground that the sun's gravity was pulling the tail forward and it preceded the comet, not the other way around. It was more likely that the comet followed the spaceship, he said.

"Tthholittthhh, Fokttth!"

"Here."

"Ttthhuttthhman, Tthharah!"

Fox imagined a race of Mrs. Ludwigs piggybacked on that comet, jumping off at the point it came closest to earth and floating down through the atmosphere to further infiltrate the Orange public school system. It baffled him how a person could end up as Mrs. Ludwig. Or any teacher for that matter. Home Economics teachers, PE teachers, cosmetology teachers, shop teachers, English teachers—they all seem like inmates in a loony bin. If students were crazy, and Fox concluded soberly and from long experience that they were, teachers were only crazier. He remembered the old adage about the blind leading the blind, and that when they did both ended up in a ditch.

Mrs. Ludwig finished the count and turned her attention to the stopwatch. It was not working again. Billy Walker, a first-class apple polisher with whom Fox had the misfortune to share three classes, came up to help. The two of them stood at the front of the room fiddling with the stopwatch while Fox stared into the depths of his blue screen. It almost literally hurt his brain when Mrs. Ludwig's voice wrenched him free of its hypnotic allure with the command to start practicing for the test. He ran through the alphabet on the keyboard, repeating each letter twice.

"We're ready now," sang Mrs. Ludwig. "Thitthh tthhtopwatch itthh tthhho troubletthhome!"

She passed out the test, comprised of a paragraph on the virtues of studying human resources management. When everybody was ready, she gripped the stopwatch in her left hand, tucking her elbow tight into her ribs, and leaned against the wall by the door. On a count of three she cried "Tthhhtart!" A fierce mutter of computer keys sucked the capacity to act from Fox's fingers. He appealed with his eyes to Mrs. Ludwig, who was watching the second hand sweep across the dial of the stopwatch as if the outcome were somehow in doubt. Clearly she wasn't going to be of any help unfreezing him. He fought through panic and tried his best to key in the words, but it was no good. He couldn't focus.

After Mrs. Ludwig splattered "Tthhtop!" over the heads of the people seated by the door, he calculated his score to six words a minute, which was about the mean for him. When he took the test by himself he could get that up to more like twenty-five, but it never came easy to him. He had a problem with words. When he first learned how to read, he noticed that the letters got all confused. They spun or turned inside out as if in a mirror. Like the comet with its tail he was always getting things backward. It made sense since he was left handed as well, which meant he had to use scissors with the handles flipped around and sit in desks with the tabletop angled to the other side. When he started learning cursives his teacher even made him write upside down so he wouldn't smudge the letters with the palm of his hand. He quickly fell behind, and the experience sharpened a sense of inadequacy. At eight he was diagnosed with dyslexia, and tutors helped him adjust to its extra fold in his brain enough to be able to catch up. He could read well enough now, but it still took him time and effort to arrange words and sentences in the right way, especially when he was nervous or tired. The problem worsened in times of stress.

At the end of the period he flitted into the long hallway and merged with the flow of people. He talked to no one, kept his eyes lowered, and wondered about the shame it always made him feel to be at school. He couldn't fathom it. He was forever on the verge of saying sorry. Worse, no reasoning with himself seemed to shake the certainty of this feeling. He *was* guilty. The very walls and lockers rebuked him as he went. The fluorescent ceiling lights, reflected at regular intervals on the marble floor by his feet, were so many sentences passed on the mere fact of him being there. Even the rancid odor he caught through the cafeteria entrance was somehow his fault.

He spied the door to Pedro Freyre's social studies class, his next destination, and was about to dart diagonally for it when he saw Sasha Dobrovolsky, the weirdest kid in school, appear like an apparition in the throng. He was dressed entirely in white, with white beaded slippers, white stockings, quilted white breeches, a white knee-length tunic drawn in at the waist and opening at the chest onto a white satiny undergarment, a white cravat at his throat, and a woman's white picture hat with a white gauze veil billowing around his pale chalky white face. Padding regally down the hall, slender and delicate, he seemed to carry with him the rarefied atmosphere of some utterly foreign world. This was not the first time Fox had seen Sasha in his getout. He'd been wearing it to school every day since the year started. But now the half-cracked vision of loveliness he made stopped Fox in his tracks. He couldn't say exactly why, but it struck him that Sasha, too, was grappling with a sense of shame. It seemed to be the point of his whole performance. He was staging some sort of botched Immaculate Conception for everyone to see.

Fox at length shook himself free from Sasha's spell and entered the classroom. Pedro Freyre stood by the chalkboard gripping his shoulders tightly and waiting for everyone to find their seats. He was another crazy teacher. Wiry and intense, with wigged out hair that shot up from the V of his receding hairline and a goatee on his sharp chin, Pedro (he let his students call him by his first name) was famous for whipping himself into such a pitch of outrage about the slave trade or the atomic bomb dropped on Hiroshima that he became completely unintelligible, following out random trains of thought, contradicting himself, arguing with his students, reproaching them for their complacency and himself for reproaching them. He liked to show black-and-white movies that had nothing to do with anything, read poetry aloud, and bring in friends of his to talk about being an accountant, a schizophrenic, or an Elvis impersonator. Pedro was all over the place. There was no method to his madness, and no one ever quite knew what to expect next.

Today the plan was to play a song by the rapper Ice Cube. Pedro handed out copies he'd made of the lyrics to skeptical students. They weren't buying his attempt to be relevant, and besides, the song was around a thousand years old. It was about police helicopters that chased people through the neighborhoods of Los Angeles County. It started with the sound of a tropical bird cawing over a drumbeat, and it segued into spoken rhyme. Ice Cube called the helicopters "ghetto birds" and told how they terrorized people by hovering over their houses and beaming searchlights into their windows.

The song ended, and Pedro asked the class what it thought. When nobody said anything, he launched into his own convoluted interpretation. He said the idea of the ghetto as a jungle suggested that the helicopters were symbols for "civilization," for law and order, but at the same time they didn't come to civilize the savages who lived in the jungle because they, too, were "birds," and so also belonged to the jungle. The helicopters, that is, brought the jungle with them. The jungle wasn't there before the helicopters, and for this reason the helicopters were just as savage as the people they claimed to civilize.

"But the song doesn't say anything about a jungle or savages," said Angel Melendez suspiciously. She wasn't sure she liked the way these words were being bandied about. "It just talks about cops chasing people in the 'hood."

"That's true," conceded Pedro. "But the fact that the helicopters are birds does make you think of a jungle, right?"

"No."

"Sure it does," he said. "Where else would big birds like that come from?"

Another student piped up: "But if the helicopters are birds in a jungle, and the helicopters symbolize law and order—"

"Then the law is a bird in the jungle, too," finished Pedro. "The law is. . .lawless, savage."

Universal protest. Pedro repeated his hypothesis, but he heard himself through his students' ears this time and faltered, losing his confidence.

But actually Fox did get what Pedro was driving at, in a way, so after an awkward silence he ventured a timorous comment. "You mean it's reversed."

"What?" said Pedro.

Capillary dilation in Fox's cheeks disabled all higher brain functions, and he just managed to say: "Reversed. The order. Like the comet."

"The comet?" said Pedro, fearing a practical joke.

"Its tail," Fox stammered. "It doesn't follow behind. It comes first. Because the sun is pulling it forward."

Snickers ran through the classroom, prompting from Fox pained glances at the offenders.

"Right," said Pedro slowly. "No, that's right. Because it's not that first there's a jungle and then the helicopters come to civilize it. First there are helicopters *and then* there's a jungle. It's only there because the helicopters invent it *in order to civilize it.*" He nodded. "Yeah. That's good, Fox."

"But if the jungle's not real," said Angel, "then why are we talking about it?"

"It's not real until civilization is there to think it up," said Pedro. "It's a preconceived notion, an idea in somebody's head. People say, 'this world's nothing but a jungle,' only they do things as if it really was a jungle, instead of just a metaphor in their heads. They forget that that's what it is."

"So what's there if not a jungle?" asked Angel.

"A neighborhood," said Pedro. "Where people live, and do things."

Most of the class sat idly by listening to this irritating exchange. Jungles, birds, helicopters, law and order—it all got jumbled together. That was the way a Pedro Freyre class always went. Nobody knew what was happening, not even Pedro. Students sat there spinning wheels, not learning anything. Fox wasn't sure what even he thought about that, but he granted it was more interesting than any other class he had, whatever that might mean when every other class pretty much bored him silly.

Next period he sat on the bleachers in the gym, taking advantage of a lazy PE teacher who'd left his charges to the supervision of a couple of basketballs and some jump ropes to engross himself in *The Fellowship of the Ring.* He was at the place near the end when the Company left the forest of Lorien and floated down a river into a narrow gorge where there were two big statues of kings from the ancient land of Numenor. Boys were shooting baskets in front of him, sweating in their clothes and cussing at each other. Down the bleacher from where he sat a group of Latino kids played music from a boom box. Angel was there arguing with them about rap, and through the sharp shelves and rock chimneys above the Sarn Gebir rapids Fox heard her sparring with her friends.

"All that bitch and hoe shit in rap is way sexist," declared Angel.

"You don't have to listen to the parts you don't like," said one guy, whom Fox knew as Jason. "They're just singing about people having a good time with their old school homeboys, chillin'."

"All they're doing is representing us," said another.

"They're not representing *me,*" said Angel.

"Who is, then?" said Jason in a challenging tone. "All that watered down shit they play on the radio, is that who's representing you?"

"No," said Angel.

"That's right," said Jason. "Because the real authentic barrio is not watered down. It's tough, it's mean, it's the mean streets. It's macks and vatos and bitches and hoes. We got to be able to tell it like it is."

"Never forget your raza, Angel."

Fox was borne toward the towering pillars of stone with other members of the Company on elf-wrought boats, the river's current quickening beneath him. Far above, the crannied eyes of the two kings peered out beneath crumbling helms, and their left hands were raised palm outwards as if in warning.

"Besides," said one of the other girls there, "just because the song talks about hoes doesn't mean *you're* a hoe. That's just a particular kind of girl. It's not the only kind."

"That's right," said Jason. "A hoe you take to bed, a girl you take to your mother."

"Which am I then?" said Angel.

They all laughed. "I guess you're neither," Jason said, thinking about it.

"That's right!" she cried. "I'm not your girl or your bitch, your virgin or your whore, and that's the way I like it, because all they are are ideas in your head. Metaphors. And I'm not here to be your metaphor. I'm not here to help you chill."

"That's cool," said Jason, "that's cool. You can do that. The music'll let you do that. You don't have to listen to the parts you don't like."

"It can't be analyzed," said another. "It's music. You feel it, that's all."

"I don't analyze nothing," said Jason. "I just like the beats."

"I've heard that before," cracked Angel.

"What?"

She pulled from her knapsack a scrapbook of newspaper clippings she carried with her. She used it for weekly competitions in extemporaneous argument put on by the school debate club, which she had helped to organize. Her database included information on such topics as the destruction of gray whale breeding lagoons in Mexico, water wars in Bolivia, child abuse by priests, predatory payday lending scams, opioid epidemics caused by greedy pharmaceutical companies, and so on. She flipped through it until she found the article she wanted.

The river, pent up between narrow cliffs, opened out suddenly into a vast oval lake called Nen Hithoel, rimmed by gray hills clad with trees. In the distance Fox heard a great roar where the lake spilled mightily over a waterfall.

"You remember that skinhead who killed the Vietnamese kid?" she said. "Bob Bush was his name, and he'd also shot two Latinos in a bar near Manteca the month before."

"Aye chingada-madre!" growled Jason.

"It says here, 'Bush, whose body is covered with white-power tattoos, told the court that he was drunk when he stabbed Toi Minh Ho twenty-four times in a Tustin playground. His lawyers maintained that the killing was not racially motivated.' Then it says, 'When Bush was asked about his tattoos, he responded by saying, "Everyone's entitled to his beliefs."'"

"He better not be spouting his beliefs around me," fumed Jason. "I'll mess him up good."

"Racist punk-ass skinhead," added one of his friends.

"I feel you," said still another.

"'During his trial,'" Angel read, "'Bush admitted that he carried a cartoon in his wallet quoting Adolf Hitler and that he hung a white supremacist poster on his wall. But he refused to admit he was a racist. When he was asked why he listened to racist Death Rock music, Bush responded by saying, "I just like the beats."'"

The Company drifted on the current that flowed into the center of the lake. Shadows deepened in the vales and on the slopes of the westward hills, and the red sun sank below the horizon. Stars squeezed out from the darkling sky, and night was laid on the surface of the water. Paddling meditatively in his gray-timbered boat, Fox watched the comet where it streaked through the northern sky. The tenth day of his journey from Lorien was over, and the chapter came to an end. He turned the page and began the next chapter, "The Breaking of the Fellowship." The Company spied a tall island called Tol Brandir and headed for a green lawn sloping down to the water, where they drew up their boats and made camp. They set a watch, fearful of roaming Orc bands on the eastern shore, but the night passed without stir.

Fox noticed abstractly that the argument over rap music, after taking on a distinctly shriller tone, had broken off along with the music they were playing, and the only sound was the tinny bounce of the basketballs on the gym floor. When he looked up he was startled to discover Angel had climbed the bleachers and was standing over him with arms akimbo, a curious expression on her face.

"Why are you always reading?" she asked.

He reflected. "I don't know," he said. "I like it, I suppose? It's fun?"

Angel's nose wrinkled on one side when she smiled or frowned, and he couldn't quite decide which she was doing now. She was long-limbed and thin through the shoulders, with jet black hair tied back in a braid, dressed in jeans and a white T-shirt. He lowered his gaze back to the page he was reading. But again she interrupted him.

"That's all I ever see you do," she said. "Read. It seems like you prefer books over people, because I never see you talk to anybody or hang out with your friends."

He steadily regarded his book. Frodo took a walk to the summit of Tol Brandir and sat on a stone chair, wondering if he should go to Mordor and destroy the Ring of Power in the furnaces of Mount Doom. Some of the letters on his page, Fox noticed, were also beginning to spin and jump.

"Except that one guy," said Angel. "What's his name? He wears that jacket that's tagged all over."

"Axel."

"That's him. The guy who talks to himself."

"No, he doesn't."

"He does!" cried Angel. "I saw him once walking past the Rite Aid on Chapman, saying something about battles and fire and smoke."

Fox knew that could be true about Axel, but he didn't react or look up.

"The two of you are like Tweedle-dum and Tweedle-dee," Angel observed, intent on getting a rise out of him. "Except you're short and he's tall. Have you ever noticed how short people and tall people end up being friends a lot? I think it's because the feeling of standing out is the same for both even though they're opposites."

Fox fought an urge to scratch a rash on his neck. He'd started shaving and hadn't gotten the knack of doing those places with more angles and tougher whiskers.

"Anyway, you're like twins," Angel said, "the way you walk around together, always in step. It's funny."

She mimicked their peripatetic style by locking her elbows and knees, lapsing into a dreamy stare and lumbering forward and back on the aluminum bench where she was standing. She awaited his response to this comic display. When none was forthcoming, she grew confused.

"What's so interesting about that book?" she pressed.

"I don't know," he said with irritation this time. "I can't explain it."

The PE teacher appeared in the gym and blew his whistle, signaling the end of third period. Relieved, Fox gathered his things, said "So long, Angel," and descended the bleachers. She stayed behind, her nose wrinkling once more into that ambiguous blend of a smile and a frown.

He met up with Axel for lunch on the school football field. They sat under a goalpost and munched their sandwiches while soaking in the sunshine and smelling the fresh cut grass. Axel was subdued, a state as usual for him at school as it was unusual for him anywhere else. He had a much harder time of it even than Fox. The teasing and the insults were constant. He dealt with the opprobrium by sinking further into his own private worlds, but this just seemed to make matters worse. It was his ability to live inside himself that people hated most.

Later, Fox stood in biology class dissecting a hairless mouse that stank of formaldehyde. The others in his group watched over his shoulder as he cut with an exacto knife vertically along the mouse's sternum and pried the ribs apart to reveal the little brown organs packed tightly together. At the sight of the mouse's viscera, his lunch did strange things to the various organs, tracts, and ducts of his own. He handed the exacto knife to the girl next to him and said, "Your turn." She took it from him and handed it to the next person. "No, it's not," she said.

Mr. Blick, the biology teacher, sat behind a tall counter cluttered with bunsen burners, alembics, retorts, and a stuffed owl. He spoke methodically to the class, walking them through the steps of the dissection which he recited from a book. His high nasal drone dovetailed in near mystical ways with the formaldehyde smell and the opened bodies they were now pinning at four corners to pieces of cardboard. He instructed them to pick at the intestines with their knives and tease them out until they were stretched to full length. Then he asked them to probe daintily for the kidneys and the liver.

Fox felt a tap on his shoulder, and he turned to see the bullfrog face of Billy Walker at close range. He'd taken the extraordinary liberty of leaving his own group and accosting him in full view of Mr. Blick, who, however, was too busy reading the steps from his book to notice.

"Guess what I heard?" said Billy.

"Leave me alone," Fox said.

"Apparently Angel Melendez is mad at you for disrespecting her. Apparently you said insulting things to her, and at lunchtime she called her brother Julio and told him about it."

"She did?"

"Do you know who Julio Melendez is?" inquired Billy.

Julio Melendez was a legend at the high school. He played on the wrestling team and was so good his senior year he went as far as the district finals, competing for the championship in spite of a broken foot. While he lost, this indication of insane athletic commitment gained him the respect of everybody except Principal Castranova, who expelled him the next day for smoking marijuana in the parking lot. Julio had since then gone on to an illustrious career in a street gang called Los Fuckers, and he had a reputation for extraordinary brutality that Fox had no reason to think was exaggerated.

"But I didn't say anything!" he protested.

"She says you made lewd sexual remarks about her," said Billy.

"I was just reading my book!"

This did rouse Mr. Blick from his recital of the dissection, and he ordered Billy back to his group. Fox felt tentacles of fear shoot through his body. He tried to think fast, but couldn't. He was a slow thinker or he was nothing. It occurred to him that Billy might be inventing the whole thing out of some strange desire to come across as helpful; he wouldn't put that past the guy. Or maybe Angel put him up to it. . .or just asked him to relay the message. . .in which case it *was* true. Then he reasoned that, even if Angel had told her brother such a preposterous lie, it didn't mean her brother was going to care. Julio was not in school anymore, and he'd hardly leave whatever important thing he might be doing in the real world to bother himself about a nobody like Fox, when he didn't even do what Julio thought he did, whatever that was.

These reflections settled him down enough to remain standing by his horribly gaping mouse until the bell rang. Out in the hall, however, word seemed to have spread that he was in trouble with the fabled Julio Melendez, because people were looking at him with a mixture of sympathy and derision that reminded Fox of the heightened expectations of wolves before a killing. He was hopeless in fifth-period geometry, incapable of hearing the rambling disquisitions of Mr. Ashland, who stood like a stick figure beside his overhead projector and wrote the latest proof onto transparencies. And in his final class of the day, Spanish, Billy sidled up yet again and said with relish:

"Julio's been sighted in the parking lot. Students flock around him like he's a hero or a god, and they all want to know if he's going to kill you."

"But I didn't do anything!" Fox cried, at the end of his tether. "I'm innocent."

"They say he has a knife," Billy went on in a low voice. "The kind with a button you push to make the blade come out. A switchblade. He's going to wait for school to end, and he's going to come looking for you. He says it's a matter of honor."

"Honor?!" Fox echoed hoarsely.

"Honor," confirmed Billy. "His sister's honor. Which is to say, Julio's honor, and the honor of the whole Melendez clan. The Melendez family honor."

"What can I do?"

"Go to Principal Castranova," advised Billy. "Tell him what happened. Offer to make a public apology. Demand a police escort home. But whatever you do, *don't go out the front door.*"

Billy was so untrustworthy an ally that Fox's first impulse was to leave through the front door, but he thought better of that and instead planned out a devious path through the locker rooms in the basement of the gym, under the football bleachers to a cyclone fence that he'd climb over to oleander bushes lining the street on the other side. From there he'd sprint the long two miles across Orange until he reached the apartment he shared with his mother and their cat, Pinky.

He marveled at the sheer absurdity of his situation. One second he was an ordinary kid in an ordinary school, and all things were as they should be, magisterially ordinary; the next, he faced a gauntlet of death and the terrible fury of Julio Melendez. And why? Because he, who never had a sister or much of a family to speak of, had violated the honor of both.

When the bell rang he marched straight to the basement, where a hallway cluttered with ventilation ducts and asbestos-covered pipe led underground to the gym. He passed through a musty storage room filled with old weightlifting equipment and issued into the boy's locker room. From there he peered cautiously across a paved stretch of ground toward the football field. He never thought he would feel so reluctant to leave the boy's locker room. But he took the plunge and sprinted for the bleachers, threading a path through the rods that held up the seats in back.

At the fence he climbed over into the shelter of the oleander bushes and reconnoitered. A few students dotted the sidewalk in either direction, unconcerned, secure in the peaceful suburb they thought they inhabited. Deciding the coast was clear, he stepped into the open and waited for traffic to subside enough to cross the street. At that moment a kid rounded a corner and spied him. He let forth a loud yawp and gestured to others coming up behind.

Fox tried to cross Blithesdale but couldn't. The flow of traffic was steady because of the cars streaming out of the parking lot. He took off running, followed now by the kid on the corner and one or two others. He emerged from the shadow of the main building in full view of the front entrance, where students were loitering on the steps or boarding the busses that were parked in front. Right away another shout went up, and he watched in horror as nearly everyone turned and pointed. Through the crowd he detected a number of guys heading toward him, and there was Julio, short and stocky, dressed in baggy pants about four sizes too big, a Pendleton shirt, and seven or eight gold chains crowded around his neck.

A police car was parked up the street, and Fox considered an appeal to Officer Palin, the cop who stationed himself in front of the high school every day. His car was an arsenal of various gadgets: liquid stun guns, disabling net launchers, the console to a gunfire location system whose microphones had been mounted in undisclosed spots throughout the school. But he had no clue about the event of Fox's possible demise happening right in front of him because he was too busy maneuvering his radar scanner onto his shoulder at the same time as he trained his remote frisking camera on the students lining up before the busses. Unless Julio had a gun or fired it in the air before he killed him, Officer Palin wasn't going to see the problem until it was too late.

Fox ran along the sidewalk, followed now by a host of other teenagers. A small gap between the cars at last afforded him an opportunity to cross. When he did he couldn't believe what he saw. Flowing in reticulate streams through the traffic were at least thirty people intent on the chase. He wondered if the whole school wasn't after him, since he noticed many types and nationalities: Laotians who hung out in gangs and didn't speak English, white guys in steel-toed Doc Martens and flight jackets, girls with cosmetology department sweatshirts and their boyfriends' names tattooed on their forearms, football players with no necks and volleyball players with necks as long as giraffes, tanned surfer dudes and hyper-professionalized student council members. He wondered if there weren't a couple of teachers in there as well, maybe a coach or a vice principal, even a janitor or two, to round out the ridiculous picture. People tagged along out of some irresistible rubbernecking impulse, sensing disaster in the making, and that disaster's name was Fox Solis.

He ran down the middle of a residential street, past palmettos and blue palo verde trees, mailboxes on erect chains, ornamental rocks in yards, coiled garden hoses, sprinklers making rainbows, hopscotch squares drawn in pink chalk on the sidewalks. He began to weave, incapable when afraid of keeping to straight lines. As he did the space around him took on a dreamlike sheen. In the very force of his exertions he felt a slackening of tension, a repose, as if he wasn't running anymore so much as gliding. It was a lightheaded feeling but also a durable one, like gaining a second wind. The muffled pounding of his feet on the pavement and the smooth rush of air through his lungs suggested he might run this way forever. Perhaps he always had been running this way. He'd gotten pretty good at it over the years.

He continued through the neighborhoods, past the houses with their rhyming eaves, gables, driveways, and manicured dichondra yards hinting at still more ominous patterns in the suburban universe, orders beyond the visible it would take all his wits to safely negotiate without injury or death. At length he saw Axel by a fence smothered in waxy-leaved ivy, waving him over and pointing to where the fence receded along the property line between two houses. A red globe hung from his left hand by a fine silver chain, and it emitted a faint blood-colored glow. He seemed to understand just what was happening and know just what Fox should do. He swerved out of the street and followed his friend into a long dark tunnel that narrowed gradually as he went, its obsidian walls closing around him until the aperture was no wider than his head. And still he kept following Axel's red globe down that tunnel, leaving the upper world behind. Pretty soon the path was no bigger than a grain of sand. He wasn't sure how they could keep going down into the infinitely small like this, but they did, and soon a door appeared before them, an arched postern in a brick wall. Axel pushed the door open and suddenly Fox found himself in the riverbed near the spidery Garden Grove Freeway overpass. The glare bouncing off the massive deck, piers, and gunnite-clad channel was so bright it put his eyes out.

6

Cloud City

Axel's other main interest, apart from the riverbed and the many stories he invented for it, was his book collection, which grew by leaps and bounds. He haunted used book stores, library sales, garage sales, and fleamarkets to buy as many as he could. Strangely it wasn't just books he liked that drew his attention. Mostly it was; he had very defined interests and read into them all the time. But Fox also saw him pick books that had no interest for him whatsoever. Axel owned a biography of a sport legend, a political tract by an ex-rapist turned radical, a lesbian pulp novel, a self-help carpentry book, a training manual for weimaraners, among other choice examples Fox had noticed cluttering his shelves. The pleasure in these books seemed to consist of getting and storing them more than anything. It hinted at a side of Axel's character that had often puzzled Fox. He could be driven and agitated yet also aimless and haphazard at the same time. Firm intentions drifted or went nowhere as if on purpose, as if he was trying to run his actions into the ground, or his consciousness into the ether. This paradox caught well enough the spirit of his fabulations: maniacal devotion to a purposeless splendor. But Fox didn't always know how to square that with a guide to wildflowers in the Dolomites written in Cyrillic.

Axel's parents, alarmed by this and other of their son's unusual proclivities, kept trying to steer him toward pastimes they considered normal. He only became more intransigent and now on religious fronts as well. He fought them over prayer at dinner time, Bible study, church meetings. He embarrassed them once by heckling a Good News Club teacher in the ancient tongue of Noldorin, gleaned from appendixes to *The Silmarillion*. He ended up driving her in tears out of the hall. On another occasion their pastor, Palmer Arkwright, whose evangelical ambitions had him preaching via satellite television all over the world, delivered a sermon before an audience that included a few nationally prominent apostles of faith. Axel, recruited to help the sound man make sure the microphones were properly placed and live, carelessly lowered a boom right in front of the podium just as the pastor came to the most crucial part of his text, the dry bones parable in Ezekiel. This discombobulated him and he lost his place, having to stop and recompose himself while the apostles waited impatiently in the pews. Given the pastor's perfectionism and leonine temper, Axel's parents feared excommunication from the church for that, or worse.

Once they forced him to dress up in a suit and go door-to-door asking people if they ever thought about Jesus Christ. They hoped that would jog him out of his rebel moods. But he hated it. People slammed their doors in his face, yelled at him for invading their privacy, chased him off their front porches with brooms. The first person he did manage to persuade, a kindly old piano teacher from Hungary, invited him into her living room and gave him cookies to eat. But he betrayed the cause. He told her that the God they called Jehovah was not really God but an imposter, a demiurge, who'd usurped His place and ruled in His name. What Christians called the Creation was actually the Fall, and salvation through Christ was a conceit designed to keep people imprisoned in the Vale of Tears. The real God down in Hell was called Satan, the Angel of Light.

This didn't sit well with Pastor Arkwright, who already had a reason to see Axel as a troublemaker, and his parents withdrew him from missionary work. It was a moment of stalemate. When they tried to reason with him, Axel invariably found ways to confound their thoughts and twist them into things they didn't mean. It could be particularly exasperating when he quoted Scripture back at them. Force wound up being the only effective means of discipline, but it came with the unhappy consequence that he resented them for it. Sullenness was added to the list of his antisocial traits. His parents had to admit they no longer knew how to communicate with him. This resulted in an uneasy truce that worked for neither side. Axel grew yet more intractable while they dug in to inflexible beliefs about what was proper behavior for their son.

One day in this stretch Fox took the bus to Axel's house because his dad had promised them they could borrow his car for the afternoon. Having just become eligible for their first driver's licenses, they wanted to drive up the Santiago Canyon for a hike above the Villa Park Dam, a region of the creek they'd not as yet explored.

A dense radiation fog, gray and still, shrouded the ranch house where Axel lived. A side yard led to Axel's bedroom window, which he had covered in black paper. A step had been roughly fashioned out of two-by-fours at its foot, and on either end of it were ceramic candleholders shaped like trees with old men's faces in them. Candlelight welled through the glass marbles that served as their eyes. Fox knocked on the window and at once it slammed open, ready to swallow him into Axel's crypt.

The walls on three sides were lined with tall bookshelves, one of them blocking the door that led into the house. Skeins of white webby crepe hung from a ceiling plastered with photographs of skulls, and in one corner a bubbling red lava lamp surmounted a Doric column about five feet high, its white paint peeling. Over a chestnut brown IKEA desk hung a poster-sized map of Middle Earth framed by painted scenes cut away from old *Lord of the Rings* calendars. The surface of the desk was piled high with the notepads Axel filled with his stories and other miscellaneous texts. From a boom box came the pointy sounds of a harpsichord and the music of Scarlatti. Various odd-looking fish floated and bubbled on the screen of his computer.

Axel flopped back on his bed and stretched out, propping the book he held on his breastbone. "Hebrew,'" he read aloud, "'is the language of the angels.'"

Fox sat on the edge of the bed. "Who says that?"

"Regiomontanus Martyrus, a priest of the Early Church."

"What are you reading?"

"*The Old Testament Pseudepigraphia*," he said. "It contains books that were not allowed into the Bible."

"Why not?"

"They had too many angels in them, and angels were heretical to the scribes."

It was a musty old volume with covers that had been embellished with gilt and marbled to look like leather. Fox saw the name Ben Solomon printed below the title.

"I'm reading the story of the patriarch Enoch, who became an archangel called Metatron. When he flew to the Throne of Heaven in a chariot and looked in God's face he exploded in sparks. His flesh became a Garment of Light, and he swelled to fill the whole universe in what they said was a perpetual Resurrection. Some of the angels didn't like him because of his human stain. Once a rabbi accused him of trying to take God's place, and that made God so angry He punished him for his pride. Metatron got sixty lashes of fire for that."

"*Was* he trying to take God's place?"

"Well, yes and no. Enoch was this guy who was born in the Maccabean era, but as Metatron he existed outside time and space. So he's always with God, immortal, but he's also a mortal, with a body and a life. He served as God's spokesman or standard bearer, sometimes even His double, or stand-in. Some commentators called him the lesser Yahweh, others the archangel Michael, still others Adam Kadmon or Anthropos, the Divine Man. He was also associated with the True Prophet, or Christos, the Angel Christ. I guess he's a lot of things at once."

That didn't surprise Fox or encourage him to understand much of what Axel was saying. He picked up another book from the floor: *Harmonica Mundis* by Johannes Kepler. He hefted it in his hand as if gauging its weight might help him to a sense of its appeal. "We should go," he said. "It's getting late."

Axel sprang up and checked the time on his tarnished silver pocket watch. "Right you are!" he cried in a jovial spirit. He was excited for the trip.

They exited through the window and walked back around to the front door in search of Axel's father, whom they found in the living room reposed upon a Barcalounger opposite a television, slouched way down until his chin rested upon his red paisley shirt. His long thighs lay athwart the glass coffee table and his crossed cowboy boots dangled out into the middle of the room. In this improbable position he managed to hold a guitar against the round protuberance of his belly. He was in the process of tuning it.

"How now, good my lord!" declaimed Axel. An instantly irritated Blaise glowered at the television. Fox followed the vector of his gaze. All he saw on the screen was the face of Pastor Arkwright in closeup, talking, discoursing. He had a head flattened at the sides, with a jutting jaw, deep-set eyes and prominent, shiny temples. His mouth was puckered. He reminded Fox of a halibut.

"Fair knight, well be ye found!" said Axel, again waiting for a response.

Blaise plucked a note and turned a knob on the neck, tuning to classic pitch. He didn't like what he heard. "Time for a new set of strings," he muttered.

Axel turned to his friend. "By my troth, Fox, methinks I see the dour Sir Blaise Saunz Pité. He it was who smote Dinadan the Haut Prince in the lists of Aftergut, after he had lost the covering of his shield—"

"Cut it out," barked Blaise. "I hate when you do that. What do you want?" Fox's attention shifted to an open sash window, and he absorbed himself in the formless white fog outside.

"Sir," said Axel with a crisp military stamp of the foot, "I pray you, grant me the boon I did ask of you anon."

"What?"

"Our celestial journey to the citadel of Roche Dur, aerie of the broad-winged hawk and haunt of the false-hearted gull."

Blaise stared, head cocked like a dog trying to puzzle out a sound. All he could say was, "What?" a second time.

"Ah Jesu, succor me!" Axel cried. "How can one of honor so vast not recall the promise he did make?"

"Promise?" said Blaise. "Why didn't you say so then."

"I did."

Blaise turned away. "I don't remember making any promises, Axel."

"You promised by your faith and by the faith you owe to God, that we your golden chariot could take to the flinty crags of Roche Dur."

"I'm not talking to you unless you speak English," said Blaise.

"Your chariot of fire, gentle lord," said Axel.

Blaise plucked another exasperated note, but he was getting it now. He meant his car, a vintage 1960 Buick Electra, black on black, with whitewall tires, a split windshield and the original V-8 engine. He doted on it. "I said we'd see about that."

"You lie!" cried Axel. "You lie like a Christian!"

"Christians don't lie," said Blaise reproachfully. "I didn't promise anything. I said we'd see."

"Beguile me not with your shameful non sequiturs," said Axel, "for by my hand many a false knight has seen his last!" He raised the appendage in question with the palm turned inward.

"I don't trust you with it anyway," said Blaise.

"Why not?"

"Because you're a teenager, that's why not. You're not supposed to trust teenagers. You'd probably drive it into that stupid riverbed, given half a chance."

"Blackguard!"

"I don't like you going there anyway."

"Blaguer!"

"It's a silly thing for a fifteen-year-old to do."

"Son of a Whoreson!"

"You can't have it," intoned Blaise coolly.

"I can!"

"You *can't*. That's English, Axel. You understand English, don't you?"

Shortness of temper could not do justice to what followed this largely rhetorical question. Fox knew how it felt to be on the receiving end of Axel's anger. Once he had made the mistake of plucking the cap off his head. He told himself he was only being playful, but in his heart he knew it was a stranger impulse than that, especially knowing how much the cap mattered to Axel. Change and scraps of paper he stored in its torn satin lining flew all over the place, and he bellowed as if someone had broken his arm. Unnerved, Fox ran away with the cap, and Axel chased after him with the relentlessness of a bounty hunter. All Fox wanted to do was give it back, but such were Axel's awful wails and solemn promises of retribution that he didn't dare. Finally he dropped it on the ground and kept going. Axel still held a grudge against him for that.

This time he railed at his father, who, tuning his guitar as calmly as he could, was nevertheless rattled.

"Now you really can't have it," he told him.

"You said so!" shrieked Axel.

"I said, maybe, if I didn't need it for anything else, and now it turns out I do. Your sister's going to Family Retreat for a sleep over. I have to drive her."

Fox took refuge in the television. Pastor Arkwright was mad at somebody off screen, a technician. Something had apparently gone wrong during his sermon. The pastor's eyes glowed with a fiendish luster, bleaching pixels on the screen. "The only thing that matters in this ministry is respect," he fumed. "Respect for God's leadership and respect for the pastor, His chosen apostle on this earth. . ."

"It's not fair."

"Who said it had to be fair?" Blaise countered. "I'm the dad. That means I'm the boss around here, the jefe, the head honcho, the mover and shaker, God's apostle on this earth. What I say goes."

"Base lout!" Axel cried. "By God's Passion how the devil hides behind the cross!"

This made Blaise mad. "You know what you need?" he asked in a menacing tone.

"A sword, a sword, to cut your faithless heart in twain!"

"Discipline, that's what. Discipline. Someone to set you straight about a few things, like who's in charge here at the Acher ranch."

At that opportune moment Axel's mother appeared, a large matronly woman in a gray linen dress, which was the only thing Fox ever seemed to see her wearing.

"Hello, Fox," she said warmly.

"Hello, Mrs. Acher."

Leonora, Axel's twelve-year-old sister, skidded in just behind her mother. She wore a black dress with the blood red embroidery of a rose on the front. She watched gravely as the argument unfolded.

"We made a deal," Axel told his mother. "Fox and I have been planning this for days."

Fox watched the television. Pastor Arkwright was saying: "I'm not ministered to, I minister, understand? Either you keep behind me or you hit the road. Humility before honor. Spiritual authority. *I'm* your self-anointed. . ."

"Let's talk about this in the other room," Mrs. Acher urged. "Blaise, will you please come into the kitchen so we can iron this out?"

"Don't indulge him, Maude," Blaise said. "A father's word is law."

"But he never keeps his word," protested Axel. "How am I supposed to respect the law if the lawgiver breaks his promises?"

"I didn't promise anything, dammit. You're putting words in my mouth."

"Fox, will you excuse us?" said Mrs. Acher. "We'll be right back. Blaise?"

"Aw hell," cried Blaise, pouncing to his feet with a gawky agility and striding out of the room. Axel and his mother followed behind. Fox drifted to the television and stood over it.

"Paul told his congregation, 'I preach the gospel of Christ crucified,'" said the Pastor. He directly addressed the camera like a captain in the middle of a mutiny. "If you don't have the guts to go it alone in Christ crucified, then you better stop your yapping and let someone who does lead the way. Now cut to music." He stared liquidly into the camera for a few seconds and glanced hard across his shoulder. For an instant he seemed trapped in the television. "*Cut to music,*" he repeated. "When I say cut to music, I mean cut to music. Good God Almighty am I surrounded by imbeciles?!"

The screen, after blanking out for a second, showed aerial images of antennae, power lines and radar dishes shot from a helicopter. It curved slowly around a red and white radio tower on the top of a mountain. A phone number appeared, and a sentimental Glen Miller tune came on. Just then Fox noticed that Leonora was standing behind him. She had chalky skin and bluish circles under her metallic gray eyes.

"Hi, Leonora."

She protruded her lower lip and squinched her nose. "I have a canker sore," she told him.

Fox nodded. Her expression was blank enough to be inanimate. "Oh."

"Do you have a cat?"

"Yes."

"Does it remember you?"

"I don't know."

"Cats don't remember anybody," she said. "It says so in this book I'm reading."

"What is it?"

"It's called *One Hundred Years of Solitude*. It's pretty good. It goes in circles."

Leonora inspired unease in her forthright manner of address, so Fox cast around for something else to do and noticed a clutch of photographs arrayed on the mantelpiece. Most were of Blaise as a young man. Following in the footsteps of his father, Blaise was a child prodigy in the field of evangelism. He grew up helping his dad preach the Good News of the Lord all over Southern California. Fox picked up a picture of him playing banjo in his dad's traveling evangelist band. His shoulders were draped with Christmas lights, and the fingers on his left hand blurred over the frets on his banjo, caught in between chords. He looked happy.

"Blaise used to play in a Christian rock band," Leonora told him. "That's how he met Maude." He'd noticed before how she and Axel sometimes called their parents by their first names, but he'd never thought to ask why they, or any kid, would do that. "She answered his ad for a singer, and they went on tour all over the Southwest. They even had a Top 40 Christian rock hit once, *Deliver Me Now*."

The next photo to catch Fox's eye was a 3-D postcard with a full-length picture of a teenager in a sky-blue jacket, white slacks, and square-toed patent leather shoes. He extended one palm out as if he wanted to give you something, and in the other hand, raised above his head, he held a black Bible.

"This is your dad?"

"Yeah."

He picked the postcard up, scrutinizing the face. Blaise's long sloping nose and adze-shaped head confirmed a strong genetic resemblance between father and son. Across Blaise's feet, floating in the grainy mucous-colored depth of the card, he read the words "I've got a message for you!"

"Tilt it," said Leonora.

When he did Blaise dissolved and Jesus, with wavy brown hair and a goatee, wearing a gaudy yellow shirt and a blue cloak, appeared in his place. "Praise the Lord!" was written across Jesus's chest.

Fox tilted the postcard up and down, transposing Blaise and Jesus Christ, Jesus Christ and Blaise, "I've got a message for you!" and "Praise the Lord!" On the television the camera dwelt lovingly on the radio tower while Glen Miller sang *Over the Rainbow*. Axel was still yelling in the kitchen, and he could tell by his stridency that they wouldn't get the car like they had hoped. He put the 3-D postcard back on the mantelpiece and picked up an old photograph of the Acher family. Blaise sat in a wicker settee next to his wife and held baby Leonora in his arms. A three-year-old Axel sat on his mother's lap. Blaise wore a bowling shirt with the words "Aftergut Box Factory" emblazoned on the front. He didn't look so happy this time. Fox tuned back in to the conversation in the other room.

"It's that stupid riverbed!" Blaise was complaining. "That's what started all this. I don't want you going there anymore."

"You can't stop me!"

"You see if I can't!"

"Go to hell!"

A door slammed. Leonora ignored it, as unflappable as ever. Fox heard Blaise talking irately about God's pastor and Mrs. Acher's murmurous but placating voice. He peered around the living room as if it might tell him what was happening. Pastor Arkwright had resumed his sermon on the television. He went on about God's anointed and shepherds and how a guy named Eliezar slew the Philistines in the lentil field.

"Do you believe in God?" Leonora inquired.

"I never thought about it much," he replied. "I don't go to church."

"They used to call people who weren't believers 'heathens.'"

"I guess that's what I am then."

"There's a special place for heathens in hell. It's called Limbo. But to go there you have to've been born before Jesus. Those heathens didn't believe in God, but they didn't know there was a God either, so how could they have sinned? They weren't bad or anything, and they really didn't deserve to go to hell, but they couldn't go to heaven either because they weren't baptized. If you're not baptized you have to go to hell. Were you baptized?"

"I don't think so."

"Hmm," said Leonora. "That's a problem." She nodded to herself, thinking through various options for saving him from damnation. Then she cast her eyes up as if receiving a message on her own private frequency and said: "Axel's gone."

"He is?"

"He went out the back way." As some explanation for how she knew this seemed to be in order, she added: "He always does when he's mad."

Mrs. Acher walked into the room and stopped short on seeing him.

"Oh dear," she said, "you're still here. Axel's left, Fox. I thought you went with him."

"No." He took note of a plain silver cross resting on her neutral bosom. That always seemed to be there, too.

"I thought he'd come around to the front and get you."

"He didn't."

"Oh dear," repeated Mrs. Acher. An awkward silence passed between them.

"I guess I'll be going then," he said at last.

"I'm sorry," she said, opening the front door for him

"That's okay. I'll catch up with him later. Bye, Leonora."

He slipped into the fog. It was so dense he could hardly see past the cars parked on the street. He heard a radio talk show coming out of some nearby open window, or maybe a number of them, since the voices attended him down the sidewalk. An RV, a telephone pole, a century plant loomed wraithlike into view, gray on deeper gray.

He headed for a nearby elementary school where a sixth sense told him he might find Axel. Just past the school entrance he cut across the front lawn toward a gate in the chainlink fence that surrounded the playground. A row of large magnolia trees followed the street inside the fence. He couldn't see the first tree until he was close by it. No one was around. He walked underneath its leafy canopy to the trunk and touched the bark. He called out Axel's name. The fog lifted his voice into the air and carried the syllables away. Almost immediately, carried back as if in echo, he heard his own name, "Fox!" He made for the sound, crossing onto cement scored with painted lines, boxes, circles rimmed with numbers, hopscotch grids. He came on a basketball hoop and called out a second time. Again he heard his own name relayed back to him.

"Faaaahhkks!"

He searched the fog with his eyes, imagining bodies come forward in the flash of their evaporation. An army of ghosts might have been marching through there. He pushed on and presently heard a *clink* of steel against steel, repeated at regular intervals. Before long Axel materialized in the mist before him, standing beside a tetherball pole and holding the clip at the end of the rope that hung from the top. He was banging the clip against the pole and appreciating the bell-like tone it emitted. He kept his ear as close to the pole as possible, feeling the strands of his hair damp resonance as they grazed the steel.

"I'm sending a signal," he explained.

"Who to?"

"It doesn't matter."

"What's it say?"

"Just one thing." Axel turned his other ear to the pole, banging it in sync with the monotone of his voice. "No. No. No. No. Over and over again." He struck the pole a final time and listened to the sound fade away.

7

Sift

On a hot day in the riverbed they stopped for the coolness at a
70-inch drainage pipe that jutted from a rip-rapped embankment.
Axel clambered up to sit in its concrete mouth, pulling his knees
to his chin and lacing his bony fingers together at his ankles. In this
pose he perused the depths of a brackish pool below. Fox knelt by
the pool's edge, too allergic to the smell of rotten eggs he caught
from the pipe to join his friend. He dipped a stick into the water
and poked at a splotchy red alga that grew on a rock.

"There's a man in this pond," Axel observed presently, rubbing his
chin against his knee. For once he wasn't wearing his suede jacket. His
pale white elbows flared slightly at his sides, and his clavicle, visible
above the misshapen collar of his T-shirt, made sculpted shadows
on his skin. He had Fox thinking of a famished frog perched on a
rock and looking for flies.

"If you stare at the oily films, you'll see a thigh and long hair
and bits of lip twisting in the water," he said. "You have to come up
here to see it."

Fox reluctantly climbed onto the pipe beside him. Their shoulders touched as he, too, studied the filmy streaks of dark color in
the water.

"See the face in that purple swirl?" Axel said, pointing. "Its cheek
is bloated and blotchy."

"There's a closed eye, too."

"No, it opened!" Axel cried, suddenly energized. "Did you see
that? It winked at us. Before it smiled and floated and shot dreamy
looks through the water. Now it wants to destroy us."

He jumped back to the riverbed and started picking up heavy
stones. One after the other he hoisted into the pool.

"Don't let the water touch you!" he called out. "If it does, Gorgoth will have you in his thrall!"

He aimed a stone nearer Fox's dangling feet. Just as he scrambled backward into the pipe a hand of water reached up, slapped at him, and soaked the concrete where he'd been sitting. Axel swung still another stone at the base of the pipe before he could get out.

"The Fox is cornered," he cried. "The famous Fox, outfoxed!"

"Cut it out, Ax."

"Loud roared the thunderous waters in ghastly torrents rolled!" he went on in the midst of his exertions.

"You don't know when to stop, do you?"

"Take that!" he cried, casting one last stone into the water. "I banish thee, Gorgoth, to eternity in thy filmy fastness."

Fox's irritation seeped into the loose ground of his own insecurities, so secretly addressed by Axel's excesses. As usual he didn't know what to do with them, so he deflected attention to something else.

"Who's Gorgoth?" he asked as they resumed their vagabondage down the riverbed.

"A sorcerer who fought in the Wars of Elves and Men."

"What were they?"

The two of them walked side by side, Axel making exaggerated use of his tall staff, Fox popping Lemonheads straight from the box into his mouth. Lizards scurried frantically before their advancing feet.

"The riverbed," said Axel, warming to an explanation, "is only the remnant of a much greater land that once stretched from the western reaches of Faerie to the Black Mountains in the east. It was called Illyria, a place where both mortals and immortals lived together on the Plane of Indwelling, that the gods of the Vala called the Hexis."

Mostly when Axel spoke of such matters Fox blanked out. He might try to follow along, map the territories he described or keep the plots and names straight, but after a while it didn't seem worth the failure that most often rewarded his efforts, and not least when, as now, what he heard was new to him. He contented himself with vague half-hearing.

"But according to the chroniclers," Axel went on, "some among the mortal races fell prey to Treb, master of deceit, enemy of all that lives."

"Treb?"

"Bert backwards," said Axel drily.

"That bus driver at Peralta?!"

"Yes."

"He called us 'little shits.'"

"A viler man never lived."

"So you turned him into this evil guy in Illyria?"

"No one knew whence Treb came," said Axel, going full Tolkien on him now. "Some thought he was a lesser spirit fallen from grace in the time of the Numen-Ithil, when the Vala first built the Hexis. But others thought he was a demon from the Aerial Void, come to destroy the work of the Vala, and especially their first begotten children, the Elvennesse. In cunning forms wondrous to behold he passed into the Mortal Kingdoms and sowed seeds of distrust in the hearts of men. He praised the elves to all who would listen, but in secret he spoke lies to poison men against them, saying they, too, could have immortality, if not for the elves who kept from them the elixirs of everlasting life."

Fox could tell by the way Axel heard himself speak how perfectly formed it all was in his mind. He didn't exactly trust this mimetic impulse in his friend; but he also never assumed what he didn't understand was for that reason unintelligent, so for the most part he gave Axel the benefit of the doubt. Maybe it was all perfectly formed in his mind. Maybe he, Fox, just needed to learn how to hear it.

"Treb it was who incited the men of Norn to steal these gemstones, the Silifeana, filled with an unsullied magic," Axel said. "They belonged to the House of Hithlum, the noblest elven dynasty in Illyria, and they shone with a light taken from the gardens and fountains of Faerie. The elves of Hithlum prized those jewels above aught else, and when the Norns refused to yield up their bounty, they went forth in strength to take them back. So began the First War and all that followed after, too full of grief ever to be contained in song or tale."

Showers of white down fell in drifting clumps around them, shaken free from shrubs somewhere up on a bank. A blue jay lit with a flurry of wings in a nearby thicket of reddening poison oak, cawing imperiously, rousting a couple of towhees into halfhearted flight.

"What happened?" Fox asked.

"The Anfauglith," said Axel gravely. "The Twilight of the Elves. Many were the wars that defiled Illyria then, and many things that were fair passed away forever. The crystal citadel of Phorus shattered on the Plain of Jars. The circular towers of Ix, where seven mages took turns burnishing the hologram of the world, burned in the Battle of Tarn. The Vala looked on in wild dismay, for they saw that Treb had taken the Silifeana for himself, and some part of their power had passed to him. He proclaimed himself the Dark Lord of Illyria and built a fearsome city called Archolon, which spread a pall of black smoke across all the land."

They had passed onto a hardened and cracked stretch of alluvial fan. Both banks were gunnite, and that made the riverbed as hot as an oven. Shimmering convection waves bent and distorted light on the horizon, cast shadows of rolling air, blurred color and form to make them see things that weren't there: black smoke, crystal citadels, armies massing for battle.

"Then the Vala knew that Treb would soon make all the world a wasteland," Axel said, "seeking to reduce all living things to his own shadowy likeness. The Vala grew wrathful at the terrible destruction, and in their wrath they altered the Hexis. Time and space shifted, and the world was plunged into cataclysm. A gulf opened between Faerie and Illyria, into which mountains of water poured. Faerie receded beyond the reach of those who stayed behind, and only the Sundering Sea remained. Treb was struck down in the moment of his triumph and banished back to the Aerial Void. He became a wraith doomed to endless craving for the existence he never more could have. His minions, too, frozen in their own reflections, longed for a body to call their own. Gorgoth was such a one."

Axel knelt beside a hole from which the pointy snout of a mole jutted briefly before vanishing again inside its burrow.

"So that was the end of the wars?" Fox asked. "No more Treb?"

"Alas, no," sighed Axel, digging his hand into a mound of finely sifted dirt. "That was only the beginning. Now the world was changed, and one by one the lights of Illyria went out. Trees became mere trees, flowers mere flowers, mountain peaks mere mountain peaks. And the warlike men who fought in Illyria ceased to see or believe in the elves who wandered still in their midst, searching for the woodlands and green valleys they once knew but now could scarcely recognize."

Fox picked a lone dandelion from the ground and blew the pappus from its seed head, listening.

"And even though Treb was no more, and the leaguers of his dominion crumbled into dust, he lived on in the minds of men exalted like a god. They rebuilt the towers of Archolon and made that infernal city the capital of their new empire, Ur."

"I was wondering how that came into it."

"Everywhere the elves went they found only avatars of Treb, or Ur-angels," Axel said. "Some resisted, hoping against hope that Illyria might yet bloom again. But others despaired, yearning for the life they had lost, and the Vala, hearing their lamentations, dispatched swan-prowed ships to take those who so desired back to the land of Faerie. At that point many began to leave, migrating westward to the firths of the Sundering Sea, there to depart from this world forever."

Axel, spying a line of large black ants, broke off his story and set about exterminating them with his feet. The transition from one activity to the other struck Fox as seamless, suggesting analogies he felt rather than understood. It went on long enough to bother him.

"Why do you do that?" he asked.

"I don't like them. They have no cortexes."

It occurred to Fox that he should join in, that in this simple activity of death he might approximate Axel's same avidity in himself. But he didn't want to kill the ants. He was okay with letting them be in their own ant world, forming their mindless geometries in stubborn interaction with dirt clods and silt wavelets, grabbing, dragging and accumulating without end. It might have been different had they been in his kitchen, but even then they had a right be what they were without too much interference.

Axel appeared to guess these thoughts in Fox, for he had stopped massacring the ants and turned his gaze upon his friend with a new interest.

"What?" Fox said, rattled.

"Nothing."

They stood in silence for a moment, awkward with one another all of a sudden.

"I don't see why you have to kill them, that's all," Fox said, sensing an explanation was in order. "It seems, I don't know. . .mean-spirited, somehow."

"I hate the natural world," Axel admitted sheepishly. "It's a trap, a prison house."

Fox didn't know what to say to that. He supposed he agreed with the second statement more than the first. He might not always like or feel comfortable in the natural world; he might fear or flee its confinements with all the guile he had in him; but he didn't hate it either.

They started up the riverbed again. Axel spoke more about the Wars of Elves and Men, and about the Anfauglith, the disappearance of the elves. This time, though, it struck Fox that his friend was trying to address, through his story, whatever reservation about his character he thought Fox had been harboring. At least Axel wanted him to know that his story wasn't entirely crazy, that it had *some* foundation in reality. They actually were living in the empire of Ur, he seemed to be saying, and it actually was a bare and literal place, or naturalistic prison house, ruled by warlike men. And it was cut off from another richer, more figurative domain that one recovered in storytelling. Fox did make this connection, especially when Axel introduced a new character named Sift, the last of the elves from old Illyria. He had spent aeons wandering the wastelands of Ur, Axel told him, in forlorn allegiance to the higher powers that had once passed through them. But he had lost his faith in men. They were so wholly given over to domination and fear that he could no longer bear to be near them and yearned to follow his brethren back to the land of Faerie. Unfortunately, the opalescent ships had stopped coming, or Sift had forgotten how to find them, and forsaken he had no choice but to go on haunting the desolate spaces of human habitation.

They had reached a hoary sycamore tree and halted in the shade it offered. Yellow moths fluttered in the canopy of brittle leaves, and a woodpecker made its intermittent tattoo somewhere in its upper reaches. Under the canopy there was a stone ring with the charred remnants of a fire. Someone must have used the spot as a campsite. Fox squatted on an upturned bucket while Axel sat crosslegged on the dirt and produced one of his spiral notepads from the leg pocket in his cargo pants. It turned out he'd written the story of Sift down and hoped Fox wouldn't mind if he read it aloud. Fox agreed with his usual good grace, knowing how important those stories were for his friend. He was very devoted to them; they contained his deeper and tenderer aspirations; with them he suddenly became delicate. And besides, Fox liked to hear them read. They made more sense when transformed into texts. Axel made more sense. In his new role as bard, then, Axel arched his back, drew a solemn breath to compose himself, and began

THE TALE OF SIFT, DARK ELF OF MITHRUM

It came to pass in the days of the Anfauglith that the elves of Fanor, remnants of a once mighty house, hid in the eastern forest of Mithrum, still reluctant to leave their former lands, and their leader, Cerimbrol, drew unto him many companions renowned for their valor in the Illyrian wars. They lived deep in woodland vales, and over the centuries that were to them but moments brief as sunshowers, they became mere legends in the memories of men. The Urlings, ever barbarous, conquering whom they might, in due course came even to the eastlands, wantonly slaying the nomads of the Kargish plateau, hard by the forest eaves. The elves of Mithrum deplored their murtherous cruelty and went forth from secret strongholds to waylay their troops and assassinate their leaders. And when their work was done they withdrew again as they had come, beguiling their enemies with their stealth, until it was said among the Urlings that evil spirits walked abroad.

Now the Emperor divined that these were not spirits but unknown rebels, and he assayed with ever more cunning to hunt them down. Traps were laid for the elven-bands, their ambushes and skirmishes went awry, sometimes those sent out did not return. It happened that, on one such foray, the Urlings, clad all in dark raiment, surprised their assailants with an unlooked for strength, and Cerimbrol was slain on the downs of Peth Beor.

Great was the lamentation in Mithrum then, for all hearts were turned toward Cerimbrol. Some among them resolved to leave for the land of Faerie, where naught faded nor withered. But others would not forsake their life in Mithrum, and it was said of them that they were mortal in their hearts and half in love with death. And as the years lengthened ever more sorrowful, many of the Fanorians did depart for the west, and their

numbers dwindled. Of these, the last was Sift, son of Cerimbrol, who loved
the streams and glades where still the feeling of old Illyria clung like faint
mists, and he could not leave them. When even his most steadfast companions had departed on the westward path, yet Sift remained a solitary
outcast, friend of bird and beast, an intimate of the forest in all its seasons.
Thus he lived for generation upon generation of men, and wheresoever he
passed he restored for a while the grace and beauty of the Hexis.

But it happened that the empire of Ur slowly encroached even upon
Sift's immemorial domain. Settlements and towns grew up on the borders
of Mithrum, and woodsmen ranged farther and farther into the forest. Oft
times he would encounter them standing still on the subtle paths he had
worn through the groves of birch trees and along the babbling streams. It
seemed to Sift then that almost they felt another presence than their own
and, struck with wonder, endeavored to discover it. And though they could
not see him, and even looking full upon him, still they saw but leaf and moss,
stone and bough; though he was to them but a spirit of the wood, always
on the other side of grasping, still Sift thought he surprised in their looks a
need which might lift the veils of their unbelief and draw them back into
Hexical space. Then there stirred in him a sorrow mixed with gladness, for
he remembered Illyria and all that had been, and dared to hope yet again
for a land renewed to its former glory.

But in these latter times the dawn is brief and the day full oft belies its
promise, and such a hope could not take hold in Sift's heart before the sympathies he read in men's faces turned to shadow. They came into the forest to
cut down the trees and cart them out; they dammed the streams and built
roads; they quarried the earth and poisoned the air. And through all these
changes Sift saw the same curious reflection of himself in their eyes, twisted
now into strange shapes of hatred, and a great shuddering came upon him
when he saw in the things men did but the same wonder on an elven path,
the same desire to discover the mystery of Sift.

Now he grew afraid at their incursions and hid in the heart of the forest.
The trees fell beneath men's axes, and wherever he tarried they followed after,
defacing the land, extending their kingdoms of death. And as the fruit fallen
from the tree, past ripeness, will bruise and grow soft, and rot around the
seeds that worms eat at, so the forest of Mithrum diminished around him,
until one day, seeking out yet another place of concealment, Sift found at
last that no such place remained. He looked around him and saw only the

ordered habitations of men, fields and hedgerows, farms and mills, fences and fortresses. Then Sift wandered as in a daze, feeling the shock of this life that had made no other possible. And although most people looked through him unseeing, some there were who paused as he passed, and strove as it were to recall things they had forgotten, the gleam in their eyes softening toward dream, and it seemed to Sift that they drew him by dint of their desire into the glare of a mortal day.

So he hurried on, mistrustful now of that dream in men's eyes, and he did not stop, hoping for a yet more inaccessible hiding place. But the more he sought, the more complicated and engulfing became the world of men. Streets led into other streets and towns stretched into other towns without end. One day, a man dressed all in black, with a huge pointed hat that dwarfed his tiny head, looked into his eyes and said: "Are you not of the Body?" Sift, terrified, fled away without answering while the man turned in puzzlement to watch him go.

He ran in headlong flight this way and that, and some of the people could see him while others could not. On he ran, and the further he went, the deeper into the world of men he penetrated, until at last he came to the great city of Archolon gleaming vaporously on a broad plain. Its towers rose to the heavens in dizzy spirals of glass and beam, sheer as the faces of crystals. All around lay numberless factories with belching smokestacks, and the sooty haze was smeared with jets of flame. Dread seized Sift then, dread at the hellish works taking place there. But the more he tried to flee, the more some malignant force swept him up in the crowds of brazen-throated men creeping in reptile flesh. Ere long he passed through the city gates into the boulevards where they plied their trades and the markets where they sold their wares. He wandered into the warrens of busy sidestreets where they gave way to pleasure, the palaces where their princes vied for power, the cathedrals where they worshiped their god. Those who could see him gasped: "He is not of the Body!" and they whispered among themselves about the stranger. Then some began to follow him, overcome by fascination, and he ran stumbling into a vast hall where a host of men chanted: "Treb! Treb! Treb!" And still they followed him like hunters after prey, tracking him through the ranks of chanters as they raised their arms in unison and dropped them back again to their sides. At length they cornered him and brought him by force to a centurion, who stood on a raised platform before the congregation. And Sift in despair cried out: "Why, O mortals, have you lived as thralls under Treb's cursèd sway, plying your engines of destruction, killing all you love?"

The hall went silent when they heard his voice, for it leapt with the strength of the wind and set their hearts racing. Yet many among them knew not whence it came.

And the people answered: "We are not thralls, but free in the grace of Treb. For Treb is the world, and never has there been another."

"Nay, my children," he implored. "Would that I could show you another world, one that used to be, folded in the deeps of time. Nay. The world is but a finite thing, a world within a world, and we are meant for an infinitude."

"Who speaks?" some said in terror. "We cannot see him!"

"He is not of the Body!" the people wailed.

"I am Sift!" he cried. "The last of the elves to survive the wars of Treb."

His words filled them with confusion, for wrung through ages past they rent the fabric of mortal existence and undid all their certainties. But the centurion said in fell tones: "Seize him, and he shall know what thralldom be!" They bound him in chains and took him to a dungeon, where men in hooded cloaks injected him with a liquid substance called hyleada. He felt a seeping cold, and then a fire that streamed like molten ore into his legs and thighs, his arms and fingers, his throat, his belly. His limbs became heavy, and his sinews throbbed. Convulsions shook him, pangs made his skin ripple and plunge, and out of a torso that opened like a wound another body unfolded, another Sift stepped into the world. He was separated, split in two. He was of the Body.

Now all could see the stranger in their midst. They put him in a cage that hung in the Great Hall of the Emperors, and many people came to gaze upon the Dark Elf of Mithrum. Barkers poked through the iron bars to make him stir, for otherwise he would sit as still as stone and stare vacantly into space. They laughed and called him stupid, feeling their own freedom all the more in the contrast. But Sift would lift his eyes, and from beneath the drowsy lids a great depth of years would dart, striking panic in their hearts. And all the while Sift would see himself as if from a great height, set apart, divided in himself, and all the world of men seemed but a dumb show of shadows in his mind.

The time of Ur turned like a vast spoked wheel around him, season after season, year after year, and men marveled at his unchanging visage who were boys when first he arrived in the city. But they had not been able to *learn the secrets of his immortality, and Sift could tell them nothing that would alleviate their pain or prolong their happiness, so slowly the people of Ur forgot about him. Only the men who brought food and injected him with hyleada had any dealings with him in the end, and one in particular, named Axalax, took pity on Sift, for long he had ministered to him and watched him languish in his cage. He dared not speak to him, for it was forbidden by the guards who kept watch in the Hall of the Emperors, but each time he drew near he would feel a joy that lingered afterward, and all within him a world would open into which he could walk and speak with words full of longing such as never passed his lips among men.*

At last Axalax set out to free Sift from his bondage. He lessened the dosage of hyleada commanded by the emperor himself, and he waited while Sift's strength returned. Then, one night under the watchful eyes of the guards, he left the door to the cage unlocked, and as he withdrew he gripped Sift's arm in a gesture no man had ever before made, rousing him from his torpor enough to understand the meaning of this sign. So it came to pass that Sift slipped from the cage and escaped from the Hall of the Emperors, struggling mightily within himself. For his body craved the hyleada with which he had lived for so long, and all the city of Archolon seemed to flash that craving back to him, and each step away grew heavier on the paving stones until at last he came to a desolate place. There he fell doubled over and shivered as one in fever, and he dreamed of old Illyrian copses nestled in the shadows of slag heaps and swans with misshapen heads floating on poisonous green ponds. And then, more utterly abandoned than he had ever felt, he wanted to die, to pass out from this world of madness and horror, to spread himself thin upon the winds and vanish forevermore.

But Sift did not die on the outskirts of Archolon, and he awoke from his dreams freed somewhat from the urges of men, wandering back into the world of which he formed no part. He lived again as a solitary outcast, keeping to the places where men's eyes did not fall, the neglected places in between men's destinations and decisions. He lived without hope in the vales that could not be used, the deserts where nothing grew except weeds and dragons, the broad plateaus made only of stone and ice, the riverbeds winding through great reaches of empire. And so he lives still to this day, on the edges of attention, like a word we try to remember or a thought that teases us, always on the other side of grasping.

8

Angel

Angel was a critical person by nature. She never let people get away with anything lazy or mean. No lie, no hypocrisy, and no excuse escaped her witnessing eye. It all went straight into those dossiers she kept on the subject of man's inhumanity to man and to nature, about which she could be admirably tough-minded not least with herself. This protected her against the temptation of excluded middles. The world for her was never black and white. Vortex was its proper state, and vertigo the most normal form of relating to it. Principle of this kind, of course, useful as it might be for anticipating and coping with life's vicissitudes, tended to leave the people who knew her unsettled in their more secure beliefs and so prone to attributions of uncanny hoodoo. She was as a result quietly shunned, kept at a distance that was respectful but safe.

Fox was no exception. After the near run-in with Julio he avoided Angel whenever possible, fearing to violate codes of honor whose mystery kept him always on the alert. She remained curious about him, however. She stared from across the school courtyard as he skulked by, tried to catch the title of another book he might be reading, and cracked jokes in class at his expense. He resolved to be yet more nimble and secretive. He began by running in and out of Pedro's class right at the bell and cutting PE every day. Angel was dismayed. Then she was indignant. One day walking down the hallway he saw her approach. He merged toward one wall. So did she. He looped back into the stream of people. She looped back, too. She swerved where he swerved and stopped him in his tracks.

He had no choice but to meet her gaze. Glitter gleamed on her cheekbones and at her temples. Like a lot of Latina girls, she had shaved her eyebrows and painted in replacements that arched higher than normal and trailed off onto the temples.

"I don't understand," she said.

"What?"

"We have to become friends, but you're not helping. Why is that?"

People breezed by their shoulders.

"You act like I'm going to murder you or something."

"Well—"

"I'm not a murderer." The grave manner with which it seemed she wanted him to believe her was not reassuring. He could see her mind-reading. "Julio was a joke."

"A joke!"

"I was just fooling around. I would have told him not to hurt you. Why are you so touchy?"

"Touchy!?"

"Yeah. You're ignoring me."

"I'm just minding my own business, Angel."

"You act like I'm not worth getting to know," she said, sounding hurt. "I think I'm pretty interesting. I'm a staff writer for the yearbook and I have a high GPA. Last year I organized a student protest against the mistreatment of child migrants on the border. I want to go to Berkeley for college, or at least UCLA, and after that I want to be a lawyer. I'm going to help people who don't have anybody, the poor who don't count, who don't have any rights or luck. What are you going to do?"

He drew a blank.

"You haven't thought about it, have you?"

"I guess not."

"It's not too early, you know. The PSATs are coming up."

The second bell rang and they hurried off to class. Another brief conversation like this one took place the next day, and she began to see how he might at last be drawn into friendship. By slow degrees he did relax in her company and even look forward to seeing her. He returned to PE class for the talks they would have sitting on the bleachers. She probed his anxious nature with an impertinence that didn't bother him as much as he expected it would. She drew out a desire to let his guard down and trust others for a change. Of course, it was frightening, too. He could never be sure, after all, whose property he might be trespassing on, or what lay in wait behind the next bend, or what trap she might be setting for him in the final analysis. Angel laughed at such baseless fears. To her mind they betrayed a fundamental misunderstanding of the human condition. Clearly she was going to have to set him straight on a few things.

"Compañero," she said, liking to address him by this estimable noun, "the world is not a place you can get out of. Never forget that. It's a labyrinth. An infinite labyrinth. The more you try to get out, the more in it you get."

"That means there's no escape," he inferred. As this was an intolerable situation for a fox, he explained to her the need always to have an escape route planned out, whatever the circumstances might be.

"But that's what everybody's doing!" she cried. "Escaping! We escape from the maids who clean our toilets for us. We escape from the guys who blow the leaves off our yards or the pool cleaners who don't speak English. We escape from the illegal immigrants who crawl through miles of sewer pipes to wash our cars for us. We escape from the homeless person. We escape from ourselves. We don't see what's happening right in front of our eyes. We don't *want* to see what's happening."

He looked past his feet and down the descending rows of bleachers to the gym floor, and thought for some random reason how they might be sitting on an Aztec pyramid, if it wasn't for everything else. "So?" he said.

"That's the problem, compañero! That's how we become part of the problem. We're all part of it. We're all. . .involved."

She seemed to take this word in a more expanded sense than ordinary usage required.

It struck an unexpected chord in Fox. With a sudden interpretive leap he asked, "Do you mean we're all guilty?"

"Well, yeah, I guess. . .that's one way of putting it," she answered with an evasiveness that seemed out of character for her.

Angel was complicated all right. She chewed on things until Fox hardly recognized them anymore, and because of this they became relevant in new but confusing ways that forced him to work his thoughts out more logically than usual. What she was saying about being part of the problem made a lot of sense to the person who carried shame around with him, for instance. But at the same time

it didn't make sense as a reason for him to stop watching out or taking care, even running away if the occasion was perilous enough, and
it often was perilous enough. He may not have thought too much
about the guy with the leaf blower and why he had to do what he
did, but that didn't mean he was bad because the world was a nightmare from which he tried to awake. If he couldn't elude predators
with his twisty feet, he had a hard time seeing what kept him from
being, okay maybe not eaten, but still in other important ways elim-
inated from the scene. In that nightmare, he averred, everything was
dark and no one had any fur or spots or definable features to speak
of. To struggle out of it was therefore to protect a sense of oneself
as distinctive or different in that featureless darkness.

"Do you feel 'different'?" she asked when he had tried to explain
all this to her.

His face went slack.

"No," he admitted.

"I do," she affirmed. "I'm 'different.' You're 'different.' We're all
'different.' *But we're all 'different' in the same way.*"

"That means nobody's different," he said uneasily. "Everybody's
the same."

"Everybody thinks they're exceptional anyway."

"How can you live like that, knowing you're really. . .not
exceptional?"

"Compañero, it takes a lot of imagination."

Just how much, and what his friend actually knew when it came
to living in her infinite labyrinth, he wouldn't find out until she related to him two key episodes in her moral education.

The first happened when she was eight. It began one day with
her sitting on a flag of grained sandstone in the side patio of the
Melendez family home, her attention split between a lizard that
Julio had just cut in two and a ceramic cantaro with faded blue
flowers painted around its neck. The cantaro was filled with water,
and the sweet vanilla smell of it made Angel's senses reel. The gray
scaly lizard writhed in its two halves, trying to turn around and see
what all the fuss was about, as if it didn't understand that they were
not connected anymore. Before Julio headed off in search of other
occasions for sport, he told her that lizards couldn't die unless you

squished them whole, and that they grew another tail or another leg to replace the one's they'd lost. Angel found this hard to believe, but just to make sure she waited for signs of regeneration in the still twitching halves. The big question was which half would grow a new lizard, or even if both halves would grow new lizards, in which case there would be two instead of one, and Julio would be like God.

Through the open aluminum sash window above her head she heard her mother and two aunts going on about her little sister Lucia in the living room. The clear notes of their adoration buzzed around her like mosquitoes she would have liked to swat. She hated how they played favorites. It was always Lucia this and Lucia that, beautiful Lucia, good Lucia, perfect Lucia. Her mother's eyes lit up for no one more than for Lucia, and all because of one thing: her luxuriant hair. It fell in copious quantities down her back, in sumptuous swirls and eddies of buoyant curls. It glowed when you brushed it, and her mother was always brushing it, hundreds of strokes a night before the television where everyone gathered after dinner, until Lucia dazzled like the sun. Even her father and brothers, who suffered no less than Angel from her mother's neglect, would on these occasions bestir themselves to fits of lusty praise for Lucia and her superior hair. Meanwhile, Angel would lie forward on the floor, close to the television and set apart from the others, kicking her heels together above her knees, holding her chin in her hands and blowing thin, stringy, unlovely hair out of her face.

The lizard showed no signs of growing back, and the vanilla smell of the water was no longer enough of a refuge from the fawning sounds within. Angel was about to get up and go looking for her brothers in the front yard when she heard her mother bark her name.

"Angel!" she cried. "Come into the living room and see your little sister. She's so pretty."

Angel considered a quick escape around the side of the house, but her mother poked her head through the window and ordered her inside. She scrambled to her feet and glumly sidled into the living room. Her aunts, Wanda and Wendy, expansive middle-aged twins in lacy white dresses, white stockings, and patent leather pumps, sat in identical armchairs flanking a rosewood coffee table surmounted by a vase of red tulips. Above that a huge crucifix with an agonized Christ almost as big as Lucia herself dominated the wall and indeed the whole room. "Cristo es la Respuesta" and "Cristo Te Amo" were woven with gold thread into tapestries that hung from the crossbar on either side.

Angel headed for a chair opposite the crucifix, climbed onto it, and sat with her hands wedged between her thighs. Lucia's hair had been braided into a thick cable down her back, and she was now modeling it for her audience in a style as close to haughty as a six-year-old could get, prancing about on the wood floor in a full-length lavender satin dress with white lace frills, bows, and a nosegay of plastic camellias. Angel watched steadily, struck by the unusual symmetry of the scene before her.

"Isn't she darling!" gushed her mother.

"I could eat you," said Wendy.

"I could lick you like a lollipop," said Wanda, and reached over to kiss Lucia wetly on the cheek.

"Don't you think so, Angel?" said her mother.

"Yes," she replied.

"She's just a. . .an. . .," said Wendy with a quick guilty glance at her other niece, blushing because she'd overextended herself, the word burst so from her tongue that Wanda couldn't help but say it for her.

"An angel, do you mean?"

"Yes," she respired.

Angel's nose wrinkled, and that quizzical expression somewhere between a smile and a frown crept into her face. Behind it a decision formed its white-hot nucleus and burned like a new star.

For the rest of that day she marveled at the rare absence of annoyance or pride that left her magnanimous all through dinner. Insults didn't rankle, and random but imperious orders to pick up this toy her brothers had left or that mess her brothers had made only intensified in her the euphoria that comes from unshakable resolve. She did everything asked of her without complaint, gladly, out of "respect and love." She waited for bed, and once in bed she listened to the tick of the clock in the hallway until she was sure everyone had fallen asleep. Then she got up, tiptoed past her snoring brothers Jaime and José, and went to the kitchen. It was like sleepwalking.

In a drawer she found a pair of heavy-duty steel scissors, which she brought with her into her sister's bedroom. She sat on the bed where Lucia reposed in a halo and gazed tenderly upon her. She did feel tender, that was the weird part. It wasn't Lucia's fault her mother loved her so immoderately. It was her hair's.

She took the braid and applied the scissors to the thickest part, careful not to awaken her sister by pulling at it. Sometimes she had to saw at it strand by strand and that took a while, but in the end she managed to cut the braid off altogether. How heavily it weighed in her hands afterward! It was like a snake she'd just killed, its corpse still warm from the life that had so recently pulsed there. She felt almost sentimental escorting the dead thing to the garbage cans in back, burying it in the sludge of last night's dinner. But then she rejected sentiment, felt steely like a bullfighter or a criminal, and returned to her own bed to fall at once into a deep sleep. She dreamed. In her dream her brothers were dressed like bankers in black suits with white collars and top hats, and they floated instead of walked. The house had grown into an infinite labyrinth of twisting hallways and forbidden doors. She ran away in fear, but her brothers floated after her, and no matter which door she opened they always followed behind, on and on. She could not shake them all through the night.

The next morning she awoke to the screams of her mother and Lucia as they discovered what had been done to her hair. A few seconds later she heard the name of Angel taken in vain. "That little bruja," her mother snapped. "I'll kill her!" Angel reacted alertly by leaping out of bed, throwing on some clothes, and climbing through a window to the back yard. There her uncle Opulencio's mango tree, planted as a seedling more than thirty years before and tended lovingly until his death, afforded the only sanctuary she could find. It stood tall and tropical in the back of the yard and was laden with plump fruit. Angel flung herself at the trunk and climbed to the highest point possible. At first her family, surging into the street out front, assumed she'd run off into the neighborhood. It was only when her brother Juan, grown bored with the search, walked to the back yard to pick a mango and espied her eating one of her own, that she was discovered.

"She's in the mango tree!" he cried.

They all ran to the back yard and crowded around. Her mother shook her fist in the air.

"How could you?" she called up to her, clasping Lucia to her bosom with her free hand and kneading the cropped back of her head. "What has Lucia done to deserve such spite? Lucia, have you ever hurt your sister?"

"Never," she sniffed.

"See! And what is Angel doing? Eating a mango like nothing's happened." Her mother appealed to God, away up over Angel's head. Angel even turned half around, in case He was there. "Tell me, what have I done to deserve so vindictive a daughter? Why are you punishing me? Why? Why?"

Her father ordered Angel to come down. She said no.

"What do you mean, no?"

Angel weighed her response. "I mean," she said, "that under the circumstances I'd rather not."

Her brothers offered to storm the tree and pull her down, and her mother considered this a generous offer. But her father, out of regard for his dead brother, whose heart would break to see his mango tree become the scene of internecine strife, decided against it.

"What are you doing?" she taunted her husband now. "Letting her off the hook? I knew it. You're soft. You should flay her alive for this, but you won't. You've always been soft."

"She can't stay up there forever," said her father irritably. "She's just a little girl. As soon as she's hungry and cold she'll come down. Why destroy Opulencio's mango tree, when sooner or later we'll get her?"

"And then what?"

"And then," said her father, "I will flay her alive."

With that they went back inside to eat breakfast. Angel remained in the tree all that day and into the evening. Her mother, by way of strategy, decided to cook a lavish meal, thinking the smells would waft into the yard and smoke her out. But after dinner she was still in the tree. The Melendez family recongregated in the back yard.

"That molé chicken was sure good," her father said. "Are you hungry enough yet?"

"Not at all," she replied. "There are plenty of mangoes to eat. I think I'll stay."

"Stay?" snorted her mother. "You'll starve to death. You'll die from exposure."

"It's not cold at all." A way Angel had of speaking back to adults as if they were equals unnerved her parents.

"Tomorrow we will eat out here," vowed her mother, "right under your nose."

"Fine with me."

"She'll be down anytime now," her father said.

But Angel didn't come down that night either, except once to pee and sneak a drink from the cantaro. She arranged a comfortable enough perch in the angles formed by the tree's branches, and its lambent purple leaves provided more than adequate cover.

The next day her parents' tactics varied little, and it was clear from the stubbornness that had set in on both sides that a war of attrition had begun. Angel stayed up in the tree and family life returned to normal, except that no one was allowed to speak to her or give her food. Day after day went by like this, and Angel managed to survive on mangoes, sucking their stones down to bare white lozenges and dropping them to the ground. Forays under cover of night turned up a warped piece of plywood that fit into a groin of branches and served as a workable bed; she also stole a knife for better mango peeling and a blanket one Sunday when everyone was at church. She dug a hole in the very back of the yard to serve as a latrine. Getting to it posed a problem, as it meant running the risk of capture by her brothers, who loitered beneath like shrewd tomcats with twitching tails, waiting for a bird to land. But after a while they grew bored with this and pursued other distractions, leaving her pretty much alone.

She settled comfortably into the life of a tree-dweller and in fact came to prefer it. Horizontality, she decided, was not for her, because the habits of earthbound people became ridiculous when observed from a height of fifteen or so feet. She watched her brothers prowl, scurry, or stalk through the back yard, and they seemed to her as savage as prehistoric men. The principle of propulsion that governed the putting of one foot before the other, or the swinging of arms by sides, struck her as hilarious, and sometimes it was enough simply to glimpse one of her brothers through the leaves for her to burst into laughter. This confounded the culprit in question, whose face darkened with embarrassed fury because he didn't understand what she was laughing at and felt nonetheless guilty. From the mango tree, Angel realized, you saw not just the usual indiscretions and crimes of earthlings; you also saw the crime of purpose itself, the weird presumption that goes with just being a person. She spent a lot of time mulling this presumption over, not having much else to do up there, and pretty soon she was deep in the paradoxes of original sin, weighing them against a skepticism born of her brief but bracing experience with Catholic devotion and its many hypocrisies.

But still another insight was to be granted Angel before she left the mango tree, and that came a week or so later when she discovered that she'd eaten practically all the mangoes in her reach. Now a new paradox presented itself, unfortunately at a place lower down in its claims than the others. Hunger began to disrupt her meditations and to resolve before her the ultimate impossibility of her situation. A raid on the kitchen that night turned up two peaches, tortillas, and some salsa, which she took back into the tree with her to eat, but somehow it wasn't the same. She didn't see herself scavenging for long like that and still keeping the moral high ground.

She waited a day from the time she consumed the last mango before at last deciding to come down. That evening before dinner she quietly presented herself to her mother and father in the kitchen. They looked at her as if a ghost had just walked into the room, their eyes blank and dilating. A long pause filled with the sound of water dripping from the kitchen tap. This lasted long enough to fool Angel into thinking they might have lost interest in punishing her, but not a microsecond past that, since before she knew it her father had her over a chair and was taking off his belt, preparing under her mother's remorseless direction to beat her within an inch of her life.

This incredible story didn't exactly set Fox easy about Angel when he heard it, but it did illustrate well enough what she meant by inescapable involvement and feeling exceptional when you really weren't. It had him wondering if that shame he carried around without understanding was just of emotions he didn't care to admit he had. Possibly, he granted, but a part of him resisted the idea, too. He might be no stranger to envy, rivalry, or the loneliness of being overlooked, but he didn't necessarily think such emotions controlled or drove him except perhaps in evasion. He just always considered it better not to want things than to let frustration and disappointment twist his heart into the monstrous shapes he often enough observed in other people. Struggle in that nightmare darkness was a survival strategy on many levels of one's personality. That didn't make it a sin or a crime.

But Angel was no monster. Even if she sometimes did monstrous things, she had a heart that in fact Fox was beginning to appreciate for its warmth and candor. At least he thought he was until she told him that second key episode from her life, which threw her, and him, wholly into the vortex and vertigo of the world.

It involved her grandfather Prudencio, a sour old man confined for the most part to a wheelchair. When Angel was thirteen he moved in with her family because his rest home had expelled him for mistreatment of orderlies, nurses, other patients, and various pets. Angel's mom took her father in until another arrangement could be found. And because of some obscure rule of filial succession that was never explained to Angel, but which was strictly adhered to by everyone around her, responsibility for Prudencio fell almost uniquely to the eldest daughter. One day her unenviable task was to wheel him the long seven blocks to the Lucky Dog Cigar Shop after she got home from school. Prudencio loved Cuban cigars, big fat one's that took hours or even days to smoke all the way through. Angel hated them because the reek spoilt the smells around the house she savored most—peppery tomatoes on the vine in her mother's garden, cilantro simmering in a pan in the kitchen, sweetshade from the tree out front. She felt invaded by his cigars and looked upon him with a colonial resentment. But such was the power of family duty to enforce submission that even Angel didn't complain, although she was always testing the limits of her compliance and looking for places to take stands.

On that day it proved too much for her to bear. She pushed Prudencio along the sidewalk as gamely as she could, but it was an arduous task since the street sloped at a slight but steady grade for blocks and blocks. The harder she tried, the angrier it made Prudencio. The unfairness of this preoccupied her as they went, until at length he told her to stop.

"Did you see that crack?" he asked, pointing the cane he kept laid across his lap back up and over his shoulder.

"What crack?"

"The one behind you, where the cement lifts over the root of this acacia tree?"

She looked up at the tree, all tricked out in yellow blossoms, and down behind her to the seam in the sidewalk where, indeed, the pressure of a root had canted one of the cement blocks out of its berth.

"I was trying to be careful," she said.

This only made her grandfather angrier. "Do you know what it's like to be an old man?" he asked.

"No!" she cried, petulant.

"Everything in the world gets bigger," he told her, "and hotter, like in a magnifying glass when you hold it up to the sun. To go from your bed to the toilet can feel like traveling from Chihuahua to Juarez in the back of a flatbed truck in the middle of summer. To ride over that crack with you pushing behind me, do you know what that feels like?"

"Crossing the Sierra Madre on foot without water?" she asked.

"Pendejo de mierda!" He writhed in his seat and attempted to get up, but he was too infirm even for that. She waited until his rage had spent itself and continued on. She pushed him up the gently inclining sidewalk until they happened on another crack. Angel hesitated, looking down at the back of Prudencio's head sunk between skeletal scapulae, and proceeded to ease the wheelchair over the impediment. They went on like this for a while longer, until Angel noticed a slight shift in Prudencio's weight. Then:

"My boot," he said, pointing at his feet.

"What about it?"

"It needs to be tied."

"I can't reach it from here," said Angel.

"The laces will jam in the wheel," he said. "Come around, to the front."

She set the wheelchair brake and took a look at the boot he held out. Sure enough, the laces dangled loose from the top eyelets.

"Tie it," he commanded.

"No way, you old cabron!" she cried, backing off. She wasn't about to come close enough for him to get her. "You think I'm crazy?" But in the moment she reached down to release the brake, fibrous fingers darted around his shoulder like an eel from riprap, grabbing her forearm. She squirmed, but he held on with an unearthly strength. He pulled her around the wheelchair to grip her shoulder and yank her face up to his. She saw repellent yellow teeth and thin lips hover into close view. The smell of acrid tobacco on his breath nauseated her. He took the cane in his other hand and thwacked her as hard as he could twice across the back of her thigh, laying down a livid bruise that would take weeks to heal. She let out two bloodcurdling screams.

"That will teach you to mess with Prudencio," he said, shoving her away. "Now push."

Angel fought back tears as she returned to her position behind the wheelchair. It was all she could do to keep before her the sense of justice on which she relied for her bearings in situations like this one. She took her place on the bench of its august tribunal, donned her white wig, and convened a trial. Defendants crowded around, and she listened to them. Her mother said, "Have mercy on poor Prudencio! He is a broken old man and lonely. All his life he worked in the vineyards and the orange groves, and when I was a girl he was already old. He grew chili peppers in vacant lots all over Orange County, and he stole avocados from the back yards of white people, just so I would not go hungry."

But the plaintiffs demanded a voice as well. Her aunt Wanda said: "When I was a girl I loved a sailor from San Diego, and my papa forbid me to see him. He beat me black and blue and locked me in a cellar for a whole summer to keep me a virgin, and when he let me out again, he swore he would kill me if I so much as spoke to my beloved. No, I for one have no pity left for Prudencio."

As this scene played itself out in Angel's imagination, the sidewalk rose and Prudencio in his wheelchair filled with gravity. She pushed at the handles, muscles straining, leg throbbing. Prudencio accused her of laziness and threatened to "caress" her with his cane one more time if she didn't watch out. It was when he laughed at this remark that it became too much. Angel didn't want to be responsible for this weight, this gravity, any longer. For as long as she could remember it had been there holding her in place, the gravity of tradition, of respecting your family, your race or even "your roots," when all it really boiled down to as far as she could see was power, brute power, exercised without pity or remorse and often for its own sake, just because you could. Nobody was honest about that. How easy it would be to let go, she thought, to deliver her verdict in that courtroom: "Prudencio, you are a mean old man with no kindness in your heart for anybody. Because you are a bully, and because you picked on Angel when she didn't even do anything to you, I hereby sentence you to cart your own damn ass to the cigar store." A voice in fact commanded her: "Let go."

She did. She stepped aside and watched as Prudencio rolled backward down the sidewalk. His eyes widened at the same time as he receded in her view, and for an instant they stayed exactly the same size even though his body shrank. Angel felt a rush of adrenalin, and sweat broke out all over her body. There was excitement, she discovered, in listening to your conscience, refusing to be abused. It could even become a way of life. Back and back Prudencio rolled, thirty feet, forty feet, the whole block long until the sidewalk evened out before an intersection and the wheelchair tumbled him ass over head into a crosswalk. There was danger, too, she realized with more shock than any teenager should probably ever experience: for people rushed out from houses and cars into the street at the sight of her grandfather's calamity, and Angel, amazed by freedom, hobbled down to hear the news that her tormentor, prone on the asphalt and staring fixedly into the sky of his deliverance, was dead.

9

Mimema

Santa Ana winds blew torrents of desert air down the riverbed. Palm fronds shook, willow withes swayed, nettles grown up out of cracks vibrated like freshets. Fox and Axel fought their way through stands of weed and shrub, pants plastered to scissoring legs, cheeks and jowls deformed to bony caricature. Axel kept his cap crushed to his skull with his hand as he went. A high arsenic content in the dust that splattered Fox's face made his skin sting. His T-shirt clung to his torso, and his nipples stood out erect. The feeling was almost sexual. He couldn't help wondering if in the kaleidoscopes of wind and light there might be a human attempt to caress.

But Axel, intrepid, pushed forward as ever into fantastic realms. There was in his staring eyes no pupillary reaction to light. Fatigue, it seemed, had no effect on him. He was as indomitable as a giant lumbering over continents. Fox would have liked to stop, to let the wind drive him back. Why didn't he? The question took on a new significance now. It combined with other questions he was asking himself in the wake of his provoking conversations with Angel: how did one escape from escape itself? And why would one want to when there was no such thing as escape?

Presently they clambered up a bank to investigate an empty construction site. Inside a flimsily erected chainlink fence they found stacks of green pressure-treated wood, pipe and cabling, cinderblocks, piles of crushed rock and gypsum. Fluorescent pink ribbons fluttered from wooden stakes driven willy-nilly into the ground. A grapple loader and a crawler excavator had been left frozen in gestures of titanic frenzy. A mountain of old two-by-fours, serrated sheet rock, bent metal and broken glass dominated the scene. A huge black tarp used as a cover billowed sideways from the bricks that anchored it, beating percussive shadows upon the gashed earth.

Axel drew as close to the tarp's flapping edge as he dared. Powerful quantities of energy flowed through it, and Fox yelled out for him to be careful. But the wind carried his words away. When Axel tried to touch the tarp, it gusted and snapped at his face. He staggered back, holding his cheek with the palm of his hand where a metal eyelet had struck the skin.

"Did you see that?" he called out. "It hit me. It's alive. Globigerina is alive!"

Abandoning caution he started to batter his new adversary with his staff. Each time it parried his blows and repulsed him. At one point it actually wrenched the staff from Axel's hands and flung it across the dirt. He stood astonished.

"I am unmanned!" he cried.

He lifted his hand above his head with a graceful flourish and addressed the tarp. "Good my Lord, vanquished as I am, I grant you all the spoils of victory, yea even unto my life. Take it! Release me from these mortal coils. But ere you destroy me utterly," he added, "promise not to blacken my name among the living and the undead. Say of Axalax that he was valiant to the end. Grant him his place in the pantheon of mighty warriors who die for glory and great deeds."

He listened to the wind rolling through the folds of tarp.

"Gramercy, O Glob," he replied. "If you will but tell it me, I will cogitate upon it and give you straightaway my answer."

Fox heard the wind spend itself in a deep vibrato roar, but there were no syllabic inflections that he could tell. He wondered if one could go too far into fantastic realms. Were there in them secret places it was better not to visit or explore, better to let remain secret? Where was the point past which even Axel could not come back? Did it resemble this construction site? He wanted to shake his friend free from his illusions for once. There were, after all, no dragonlords on their winged steeds blotting out the sun above, no marauding Urlings on their Plain of Jars. Down in the riverbed a dust devil swirled, but there was no trace of a goblin troop come to waylay them on their path.

Axel returned. "Friend Fox," he said, "that hellspawn has presented me with a riddle, which forthwith I must answer truthfully, or die."

"What is it?"

"A question of fiendish nicety. It goes: 'Can the light by which all things are seen, itself be seen?'"

Axel seated himself upon a bale of hay and cogitated. Fox, having nothing better to do, turned the question over in his mind, too. If there were no light, you wouldn't see anything. You would be in the dark. You saw things because there was light to see by. But could you see the light you see by?

"How can you," he remarked, "when light's not a thing?"

"Indeed," said Axel. "Light is not what you see, it's sight itself. It's. . .you! Seeing!"

"But how can you see yourself seeing?" This gave him pause. "You have to stand outside yourself."

Axel leapt up. "I've got it!" He rushed over to the tarp. "Yes, good Glob! The answer is yes! For light is only a word for the angels that throng the universe, and they are as common as houseflies, and perfectly visible, if you know how but to look for them with your Third Eye, which is Imagination!"

Your Third Eye? It loomed up before Fox with cyclopean menace. Did he have one? Did he want one? Maybe not. He fought an impulse to cry out: "Come back, Axel!" The tarp billowed, but that's all it was, a tarp! The riverbed was made up of elements, rock and silt, even smoke, vapor, or bubble, it hardly mattered. Still it resisted, still it burned, chafed, reminding the body that it was perishable. Why wasn't that enough for him? Why see angels in it? Why make a universe out of wind?

It was decreed: Axel had solved the riddle and Globigerina would spare his life. He picked up his staff and ran with a whoop for the crawler excavator. It sat canted over a misshapen ridge of dirt. Its fanged shovel hung petrified over a pool-sized hole, and the hydraulic steel cylinders stretched at the joints as taut as sinews. Axel jumped onto the cab housing, turned almost at right angles to the dirt-caked planetary gear wheels, and communed with its machine soul.

"Do you hear it growling?" he asked. "Do you hear the pistons in the chambers compress air and explode? Can you see it crawl over basalt deposits in dry lakes? Fox! It's like a dinosaur. It makes everything around it primordial."

Fox looked around him. The construction site stretched to a subdivision of coral-pink two-story homes with red tile roofs.

Through a cyclone fence topped by concertina wire he saw dirigible-shaped tanks of liquid gas next to a salvage yard. Overhead, a massive vertical billboard displayed a smiling forty-foot-tall bald man in a suit advertising a real estate company. Across his chest it read: "We sell the hills!" At the foot of the billboard, by its massive steel supports driven into the ground of a vacant lot, there was a caravan of shopping carts filled with cans, bottles, pieces of rug, books, old DVDs, and other miscellaneous items. He couldn't see the nomad to whom it belonged. He couldn't see anybody. The place was deserted and in that he supposed Axel was right, they could just as well have been on some primeval steppe before even there were humans. But when he looked up at the depthless white sky, he saw no pterodactyl flying overhead.

The land was empty. They were in the middle of a void. The problem was that Fox, too, felt empty in the knowledge of it, as if the pith of his own being had dried up and left him as hollow as the white stalks of cow parsnip they were soon afterward passing through on their way up the riverbed once again. He sneezed. The wind drove him back. Its ferocity reminded him of energy's tendency to fill and saturate. Axel pulled ahead, loping on the edge of vacuum, rapturous Axalax in search of—what? Something definite in all that nebulosity? Some mechanism for bending light rays, some particular ice crystal dispersion that he could replicate and so produce at will his own more and more complete mirages?

This had Fox thinking again of the possibility that one could see oneself seeing. Something about Axel's answer bothered him.

"I don't get it," he called out.

"What?" said Axel over his shoulder.

"If light isn't what we see, but seeing itself, that means the person who sees is made of light."

"Right."

"And angels are made of light."

"Uh-huh."

"But if that's true, then we're all angels. Can a person be an angel?"

"All people are angels," said Axel, "but hardly anybody knows it."

"Why not?"

"They've forgotten what they are." He glossed this unfortunate lapse in terms of the riverbed metaphysics he'd invented. "People are emanations of the Hexis, the hologram of the world. But the Hexis has been modified, and we've been separated from the projector."

"There's a projector?"

"Yes."

Fox didn't feel like a projection. He was pretty sure those were real lungs gasping for air in his chest, and real blisters starting to form on the soles of his feet. But if he were just a beam of light, a hologram made by someone's laser, then. . .

"Who's the projectionist?"

Axel frowned. "It's not that kind of projector." He pushed still further into his metaphysical construction. "The Hexis is a space or condition in which we live, but it's also in us as a capability or disposition, a quality that synchronizes with a deeper reality, a hidden world."

"And this. . .'synchronicity' is what makes us angels?"

"It's what we forget when we're separated."

Axel was distracted as he spoke by the sight of a vitreous rock countersunk in the dirt. He knelt to pry it loose. It was a piece of quartz, pentagonal in shape, an inch thick and three or so inches long, with a smoky color.

"Cool," said Fox.

Axel thrust it toward the sun and cried, "Eledhil!"

"Eledhil?"

"A talisman, woven with spells of powerful magic. It will be useful against the sorceress Mimema, whose diabolical influence in this very spot I detect as we speak."

He pocketed it. Around them stretched a forest of buffeted spiny horseweed and salsify. Fox's eyes were drawn to the only motionless objects in his view: ellipsoid white stones scattered in amongst the thrashing plants. In their repose it seemed they really could be stones in a holographic river, both visible and invisible, solid and ethereal. He was about to ask Axel if he thought so, too, when he saw with a start that there was a scrawny roadrunner standing stock still at the center of his vision.

"Look," was all he could say, pointing.

He found it hard to believe it wasn't a weed, so perfectly did it blend into the wash. A few feathers fluttered out from its crest, and it stared as though panic-struck, ready for flight. A lizard lay limp in its long bill. Something seemed to fall into place for Fox then. He thought he understood why Axel saw adversaries in tarps and made a universe out of wind. For imagination didn't connect points within a single dimension but across dimensions, things of a different nature, past and present, space and words, humans and animals, humans and gods. The roadrunner was mythical to him not in the sense of being a fantasy but, more profoundly, in belonging to a reality penetrated by this volatile creative substance. . .a creation, *the* Creation.

Axel abruptly blurted out:

"*Beep beep!*"

The roadrunner dropped the lizard, lowered its head, fanned out its tailfeathers, and bolted in a slashing diagonal across the riverbed. The moment of revelation, if that's what it was, ended as suddenly as it had begun.

"What'd you do that for?!" Fox complained.

"It was evil," Axel said. "A demon, a fallen angel. Sent by Mimema to do us grievous harm."

"You ruined it."

"Ruined what?"

All he could think to say was, "The Creation."

One might have thought Axel would find this notion appealing. But he surprised Fox by shaking his head. "No," he remonstrated. "*We are uncreated.*"

We are uncreated?

"What does that mean?!" cried Fox.

"We aren't born, and we don't die," Axel said. "We're not part of the natural world. We don't change, like a seed or a germ or a gene. We're eternal."

"But we are born, and we do die," Fox objected. "We're not *really* eternal."

"Yes, really we are. There's no such thing as a self, which isn't to say the thing we take a self to be is eternal. That's just a way of fooling ourselves."

"So what's eternal then?"

"Nothing," Axel said as if it were something.

They moved on again, coming at length to a pile of worn concrete fragments, remnants of old freeway beams and piers that had been dumped down the bank. Masses of tangled rebar snaked out from their torn apart surfaces like the wiry hair of decapitated titans. Their leeward side offered a good shelter from the wind, and they paused to rest. Fox was still puzzling over the idea that he both was and wasn't eternal. Axel, observing in his confusion how seriously he was taking the problem, wondered if another story about Sift might help. He had written a new one. Leaning back on one of the piers, he took a notepad from his jacket pocket and opened it. Fox tried his best to listen over the wind that feathered dust into long rolling waves down the riverbed. This was what he heard:

THE LAND OF SALAMANDRINE MEN

For a great length of years Sift hid in Ur, dwelling nowhere long. And often would he recall the days before the Twilight of the Elves, before Illyria was dimmed and his heart broken by the ways of men. A great hunger arose in him then to depart this world of war and weeping, to follow his brethren westward to the undying realms of Faerie. But he knew not how to go nor where to look. Long had it been since the last swan-prowed ships had come to take them away. There were no harbors where he could go to meet their mariners. He knew no magic for calling them hither. And there was no vessel made of mortal hands that could sail where he would fain go.

Of old his only companions had been the animals who alone reminded him of the ancient woodlands of Illyria, but even they in the end did not know him and slunk past whenever he drew nigh. Yet in the wildest places there were still rumors, noise in the howl of the wolves or the bark of foxes, that spoke to ears that might hear of the Dark Elf and his despair. And so it was that these rumors came to the sorceress Mimema in her high redoubt, hard by the desmesne of Roche Dur. She was not of mortal born, yet neither was she one of the immortals in Faerie. From the Aerial Void she came, having no substance but that of the fair semblances she wrought with devious charms. Black was her heart in its exile, and blacker still the craving for vengeance and destruction.

So it was that soon thereafter Sift lingered by the Coromar Cliffs and waited for an end to his torments. And lo! a ship appeared, like to a meteorite that had fallen to earth and left a trail of stardust on the wide sea. In sudden and unlooked for joy Sift ran to the shore and met the shining vessel. He saw a beautiful woman at its prow, and she wore a circlet of diamonds, and her eyes glittered with celestial light.

"Fair lady!" cried he in the ancient tongue of Elvennesse. "Beyond hope thou hast come to me. Long have I waited."

And she answered in kind: "Perilous was my journey, and far have I traveled, over waters and fields of space and aeons. But thou hast been my polestar, and I but thy longing made manifest. Come, fair Sift, may thy life be not sundered from this moment on. Bid farewell to the fallen world. 'Tis noontide in the blessed realms. Faerie awaits thee."

They set course at once, and a sailing wind bore them far away. Foam sprayed off the breasting prow, and water rippled like liquid quartz beneath them. Sift spoke to the lady as one starved of speech, as one whose tongue from long disuse had turned to stone, and she told him of the Vala's bliss in Faerie, and his kinsman who dwelt there in joy and contentment. And all these glad tidings stirred in him a deep love such as he had never hoped to feel again after the many centuries of desolation. On and on they went though the sea might lash, or howl, or heave with unrelenting force. They passed enchanted islands where sirens' songs echoed in the crash of waves, but they heeded them not. At length they happened upon a vast well of darkness in the midst of the sea, and it was as a funnel of air thrust down into its depths, a hole that reached even as far as the center of the earth. In its sea-green walls Sift could see strange leviathans lurking.

Then it came to pass that a windless calm descended upon them, and the sea fell into a fitful unquiet. Arms of kelp floated in the obsidian waters, clutching at vague shapes. The sun was blotted out by shifting auroras of rainbow hues, and they no longer knew by what stars to plot their westward course.

"My lady," said Sift, "what is this place?"

And she answered: "The edge of the world, my lord." For they had come to the Aerial Void where naught may pass and live. Sift's heart misgave him, and he would ask the fair lady more, but she turned and laughed, and her face became as ice fissured by tiny cracks, and he watched as she melted before his eyes. Suddenly he was alone.

For eleven days, if days they were, the swan-prowed ship drifted upon that dead sea, past more of the funneling holes. And on the twelfth day Sift came to a tall platform built on massive pillars. Figures could be seen on stanchions and scaffolds, turning winches or welding steel, and they were strange to Sift, for they had the bodies of men but the faces of salamanders. In the distance he now saw a multitude of these platforms glimmering in the opalescent light, and they seemed all to point toward a distant low-slung shore. And as Sift drew nigh, he saw a citadel of gray stone surmounted far above by a peaked tower, and from the window of this tower a single red lamp gleamed. Many-piled piers snaked out to meet the ships that crisscrossed the waters between. Portions of the water were closed off with dikes and filled with dirt brought by swarming trucks, and pile drivers pounded steel beams into the new earth.

Here it was that Sift's vessel left him, and he passed into a land of nightmare. The salamandrine men lived in wastes of reddish-brown sumps, poisonous leachates standing in ditches, and acid fogs. Their children gasped for air. Animals sickened and withered away. The birds trembled piteously and could not fly. There were no fish in the streams. The strawberries in the fields were big and radiant, but alas! without taste. All day the sala-mandrine men worked in dark mills or on the platforms out at sea, and they knew nothing of ease or pleasure. Sift wandered amongst them, more bewildered than ever he had been before, and all the suffering around him he suffered, too, until he became as one delirious, raving to himself and to the salamandrine men, who listened without sympathy or understanding.

In the hour of his greatest peril he came to a mere flecked with tufts of foam like clouds in its black sky, and he sat by its muddy shore. And behold! he saw reflected there the face of that fair maiden who had lured him to this forsaken land. She was remote and lovely beyond words, and Sift wanted to take refuge in her folded arms, but her eyes glittered treach-erously, and her smile was full of wiles.

"Fair Sift, wherefore hast thou come to such a pass?" she said, and her voice was mocking. "Dost thou think I hath led thee astray? Deluded elf, thou art only where thou seekest to be. Think not thou hast entered the Valley of Death. Behold, thou art in paradise!"

Sift reached out to her where she floated on the still surface of the mere, and he teetered on the brink and fell into the water, and he sank and sank into ever-during darkness, past suffocation and feeling and even the will to live. A red light appeared in the deep, and it grew larger until it filled all the blackness around him, and he passed into a bare chamber hewn of gray stone and opened all around to opalescent skies. It was the citadel and its high tower that first he had spied from the swan-prowed ship, for by *a parapet the same red light shone over the land. He went to the opening and looked out, hearing naught but the moan of wind and the distant echoes of salamandrine industry far below. But skillfully woven into these sounds he began to hear a voice, and that voice grew more distinct, until it seemed to be no different from his own, a voice deep inside that he lived with as he lived with himself, even though it came to him from without.*

Of a sudden the sorceress appeared behind him once more, and she was dressed in a flowing gown that changed color as she moved. She glided to his side and wrapped herself around him as if with mothlike wings, and she kissed him long and long.

"Welcome, lord, to thy kingdom," she said. "As far as thy eye beam travels, so far shall thy dominion be."

"But I want no kingdom," said Sift.

And she answered: "But it is thine, my lord. The figure of thy deepest dream is here made manifest."

"There are no dreams here," he sighed. "Here all is lost."

Then Mimema laughed, and her laughter shook the citadel to its foundations.

"Indeed, here all is lost, yea, all, even loss itself. But what can this mean, unless it be here thou art not lost, but found. Here thou art no stranger, but most at home. And I, am not I thy lover, and are we not mated for eternity?"

Terror seized Sift at her words. He recoiled from her and tried to flee, but there were no doors in the chamber.

"To escape thou wilt have to fly," she said, and with a glance she turned him into an osprey fierce and proud. His terror blended with the raw hunger of a bird of prey, and his heart was savage, and his feathered body burned, and his beak tore the air like flesh. With a loud keening cry he leapt through the window and stretched his wide wings upon the expanse. And he flew, as hard as he could, straight out over the holey seas of the Aerial Void, swooping down upon the waters to feed his frenzied soul and screaming on through the auroral light to the enchanted islands. There was no exhaustion he did not push past, for primitive fear moved him, and above aught else he desired to escape the land of salamandrine men. Waves scudded on the ocean far below for what seemed an age, but ere long the stars wheeled across the sky, and the light of day broke upon the horizon in front of him. And at last, when the spirit of the osprey had so overmastered him that he hardly remembered he was still Sift, he saw the coastlands of Ur once again. There

were the wide beaches and the deep winding fjords, and there the coastal hamlets of the Urlings, and there the Coromar Cliffs where first he'd spied the delusive vessel. He flew hard by the bluffs and hovered, and amazed he saw the body of Sift sleeping beneath a linden tree, and he descended into that body and awoke to the dawn breaking over the shore.

And so he learned that all his journey had been but a dream, and he was glad despite his heavy heart. But when he looked up again to the skies he had in his mind traversed, he saw an osprey, and all the fierce desire for flight came back to him, for its eyes glittered like diamonds, and in its piercing cry he heard the mockery of Mimema.

10

Model Houses

Fox and his mother went one day to the Carbondale subdivision in Irvine, to see the model houses. For years this had been a pastime of theirs. They'd revel in the sumptuous appointments and imagine what it would be like to live in a world as full of promise as they intimated. Sylvie wanted very much to own her own home, to have an escrow account such as she made out for buyers at the company where she worked and mortgage payments instead of rent. But on her salary even a modest townhouse seemed forever out of reach. She'd thought of getting her real estate license and taking her chances as a salesperson, but life as a single mom made frightening the prospect of giving up a stable salary for a sketchy commission. The risk of losing what foundation she and Fox now had in this world, coupled with the memory of having next to no foundation at all, kept her locked in a status quo she found simultaneously unsatisfying.

It was this undertow of frustration in her that diminished the pleasure for Fox. For some time now the ritual had stopped being so fun. Model houses used to be places where he felt less lonely, where in fact he felt his mom's frustration less acutely, but now they only reminded him of how much she'd had to sacrifice in their life together. In particular he was aware of how much she missed the companionship of a partner and the comforts of a normal family life. He felt a little responsible for that. She'd had a few boyfriends over the years, men who stuck around more or less depending, but she never found the right person, either because he lacked the maturity or the patience to deal with a stepson or because of her own insecurities where love was concerned. She resented Fox's father for a lot of reasons, but most of all for the wound he gave her self-esteem.

His name was Kenny. He and Sylvie had run away together in high school, alienating her dour Pennsylvania Dutch parents in Phoenix, who never forgave her recklessness. Kenny was an aspiring artist with dark good looks and a trusting nature. But he turned out to be a little too susceptible. He looked to others for an authority he never had since his parents died when he was just a kid. He grew up in foster homes, feeling like a black sheep shunted here and there, not wanted by much of anybody. As a result he liked to have answers to things all worked out in advance. This made him prey to charismatic people too sure in their sense of right and wrong.

His relationship to Sylvie had already deteriorated by the time he took up with a disabled Vietnam vet who owned a garage full of automatic weapons and considered himself a religious messiah. They were living in a teardrop trailer on the outskirts of Riverside then. Kenny started going on about the holy triumvirate "God, Guts, and Glory," ranting about government conspiracies and the end of the world. Slowly he changed from a charming young man with dreams to a redneck buried deep inside his prejudices. Sylvie never forgave herself for getting him so completely wrong.

One morning she woke up to find him gone, off to some secret compound in the woods of West Virginia according to a letter scrawled in his child's hand, there to hunker down for the Apocalypse. She didn't know whether to laugh or cry. She cared enough to fly out there and look for him, but he didn't want to be found and she gave up in the end. Neither she nor Fox ever saw him again, and not even a photograph remained. The only memento they still kept was his name, Solis, which Sylvie decided was better than Bemesderfer, her maiden name.

Fox had no love for this man who had left him behind, unless the pang of feeling abandoned and the wish that he'd had a father betrayed love at some deeper level. He knew they took after each other, and that did make him curious and wonder if knowing his father might at least help to understand himself better. But he believed his mother when she told him there would be less to learn than he thought and little use in trying to find out. Character was destiny, she told him more than once, and Kenny's real problem was that he had none. While this didn't always reassure Fox of the difference between them, he wasn't so lacking in confidence as to doubt that, whatever else was true, his experience of abandonment meant he would never, ever put someone else through it—not if he could help it anyway, and from what he knew his father could have helped it. For that, indeed, he would never be able to forgive him.

His mother was completely on her own after Kenny left, since her stern and morally uncompromising parents decided to teach her the lesson of a loveless world by locking her out of their lives without an apparent glimmer of regret. Between taking care of Fox and working jobs, she had little time for herself, and the drudgery wore her down. She compensated by nurturing an optimism that allowed her to keep her anxieties in check and go on believing in the future. As Fox grew older this gay affability had become a barrier between them. He didn't blame her. He knew she was coping the best she could with old habits that were hard for him to break as well. But he needed, and he supposed that meant he needed her to break those old habits in a different way now. Positive thinking just didn't work for him. In fact it only drove him deeper into his foxhole. It twisted the heart into those monstrous shapes he preferred to evade.

One of these for his mother showed in an excessive concern with social status. She could be effusive in her appreciation of successful people she had little in common with and dogged in aspirations that put her at odds with herself and her actual prospects. She was always trying to overcome limitations and iron out flaws. She read books on etiquette, took voice lessons, and enrolled in evening art history classes at community colleges. Self-improvement became an obsession that made her quicker to judge, more prone to catty comparisons, more willing to make others feel as bad about themselves as secretly she did about herself. A stranger might conclude she wasn't all that nice a person, selfish and snobby. Only Fox knew how much the cultivation of these traits cost her and how much they worked as hedges against an inner loneliness. All her self-conscious adjustment of character had that as its basis anyway.

She was as excited as ever about the model houses, but the moment soon came when the euphoria wore off even for her. On this occasion at Carbondale, Sylvie's home of choice was Model D, the second most expensive on the cul-de-sac, a Californian ultramoderne with steel frame and clean cubiform volumes. To get to it you went up a walk lined by iceberg roses and crossed a short bridge over a moat. There were outsized concrete steps leading to the porch that looked like the chunks of stone used to make breakwaters and a large door of beaten brass. For half an hour she'd been wandering through a living room with stone fireplace in the round, a recessed seating area enclosed by slanted out Palladium windows, and a large kitchen with granite-topped island and space age appliances from the 1950s. She walked several times up and down a curved stair with stainless steel rails and mahogany treads, then went to linger in the toast-colored sunroom off the master bedroom. Meanwhile, Fox sat on the French neoclassical sofa downstairs, fiddling with an Aubisson pillow and fairly dying of boredom.

Across the room he could see a curved wall of translucent glass blocks, and the gray light welling through them put him in a hypnotic trance. He'd just turned the wall into a huge shining monolith that had descended from outer space when his mom flopped down beside him, glancing around with all the acuity of an appraiser. She pointed to the floor. "Oak," she said. "All over the house. And that's a Turkish silk rug. Nice, huh?"

He shrugged. She got up again for one more sweep of the living room, pausing to finger iridescent fabric curtains and catch her reflection in a gilt-framed mirror. The look she gave herself was a little too penetrating. For an instant only Fox knew with any familiarity she was completely undone, plunged in that well of worry and care she kept so tightly lidded. At once she recovered, her eyes searching the depths of the mirror to see if anybody behind her had noticed this small lapse. Fortunately, it was only him she saw.

"Let's go out back," she said then. "Come on lazybones. We're out of here after that."

She was gone in an eyeblink. He lifted himself to his feet and walked out to a broad parterre where she stood surveying the yard.

"Plenty of scope for landscaping," she said with a wave of her hand. Before them was a column rising from a square pool, surmounted by the marble torso of a Greek god.

"I'm tired," he said.

"Okay, okay, Speed Racer. Let's just sit for a sec in that gazebo over there, and we'll be done."

Sylvie was a petite, compact woman with all but inexhaustible stores of energy. Her brown hair was dyed with henna to hide the premature gray, and her shoulders were toned and broad from working out at the gym during lunch hour. She had little of Fox's dreaminess about her. When she did things it was with quick gestures, and she spoke with the clipped tones of the practical person, eager to get things done. She reminded him of a fugitive the way she moved and thought so frenetically like that, as if she were always about to be captured. He felt responsible for that, too.

They sat in the painted steel gazebo and watched the other visitors wander around the yard, lifting up hand shovels half as if they'd planted the flowers themselves, calling out to loose toddlers to be careful in the glass-enclosed garden room.

"I could sure get used to this," she said. "I'd put a sundial right there by that weeping willow tree." She took in the whole house and pointed at the roof. "There aren't any overhangs, see that? They can extend the walls almost to the property lines that way. Make the most of a small lot."

Fox slipped his fingers underneath his thighs, straightened his back, and fidgeted. "You like it?" she asked.

"I'd live here," he said with another shrug.

"Which bedroom would you want? The one with the shell collection, or the one with that wiggly mirror?"

"I don't know. Whichever. I guess I don't like to think about it much."

"Yeah. I know what you mean." She sighed. "Well, let's get going."

They walked through a carport to the cul-de-sac where their station wagon was parked. Sylvie groaned at the sight of it. Wrecked plastic molding around one sideview mirror disclosed the colored wires inside. Nothing electronic worked the way it should anymore. Recently the automated voice warning system went on the blink, and they had to drive it for two whole days while a monotone woman's voice told them over and over again, "The key is in the ignition, the key is in the ignition. . ." This was one thing a recent raise at the escrow company allowed Sylvie to change. She was shopping around for a new car.

They went afterward to the mall at Fashion Island. Fox sat on a bench outside a store called Italian Country and waited while his mom looked at furniture. People milled around the chambered open-air promenades and the echoed sounds of their voices bloomed into eerie indistinction around him. He caught sight of a poster-sized photograph in a backlit marquee. It showed a bright red and yellow forest through the middle of which ran a rutted dirt lane. The ground under the trees was coated in leaves, and the scene was meant to suggest fall on the east coast. He'd never seen foliage before, and the picture held his gaze. Above the treetops a woman's head tilted back into the sky as if it were falling, and her ecstatic eyes were shaded red and yellow like the leaves. The caption said "Fall In Deep." He ran the phrase over in his mind, trying to figure out what the ad was for. Fall, falling, falling in deeply, falling deeply in love, falling in too deeply, in over your head, drowning in the red and yellow leaves of fall, which was just the same as. . .love?

His mother appeared in the window of Italian Country. She scrutinized a champagne green crushed velvet recliner with ottoman on a display platform while a salesman gave her the lowdown on it. He could tell by her quizzical expression that the price he was telling her meant she wouldn't be buying, but she listened anyway. It was a game she liked to play, and the pleasure it gave her betrayed a strange desire to pretend, to merge herself with spectacles she planned out much like those model houses were planned out for her, with an outsider's eye for the gorgeousness of belonging.

They finished their tour of Fashion Island late in the afternoon and decided to go watch the sunset on the coast. They headed to Newport Beach first, but it was crowded on account of an arts festival on Balboa Island, and Fox suggested they drive instead down Highway 1 to Crystal Cove State Park—Axel's Coromar Cliffs, where Sift had left his body behind for the land of salamandrine men.

The sun was already setting when they parked by a meadow just off the highway and walked along a wood plank path to the edge of the cliff. They decided against the trek down to the beach, finding instead a driftwood bench to sit on. An onshore wind blew at their backs. It shook the surrounding stands of wild radish into pink frenzies and feathered the waves as far as they could see into crazy whitecaps. Fox could well imagine a few iridescent swan-prowed ships out there, delusive though they might be.

"Sure is nice, huh?" said his mother. "Makes all your troubles seem kind of small and petty." She put her arm around him and hugged him to her. "Sometimes I feel lucky."

"You do?"

"Yeah," she said. "Like life is just fine. I wouldn't want to have it any other way."

He smiled at that. He felt closest to her when she said such things, acknowledging however indirectly that she, too, grew tired of the pretense to be more, or different, than she was. It brought out a native sympathy. Whenever Fox saw weakness or fragility, he wanted to go slow. Everything that failed in this world made him tender.

11

El Caballero Blanco

Fox sat in his social studies class listening to someone named Tucker Smallwood recite an essay entitled "My Mercedes."

What a ridiculous name, Tucker Smallwood, he thought. No one should have to take that name seriously. He found himself rearranging the sounds into phrases like Fucker Smallwood, fuck her in the small wood, Tucker's small wood*pecker* (in the small wood), etc. How could he believe in the person to whom such a preposterous name would belong?

"My Mercedes," read Tucker, "first entered my life when I was a mere lad of five and my dad took me to a car dealership in Costa Mesa. That's when I saw it: a 500 SL Mercedes Benz. I was stunned by the beautiful lines on the car that shone in the parking space as if it were meant for me alone. It floated independently of the other vehicles people dared to call true automobiles, and I swore that one day I, too, would own one."

Fox shivered with an animal fright. Feet, he said, do your thing. And they might have, if the whole class didn't lie between him and the door.

"Never did that beautiful car leave my mind," Tucker rhapsodized, "until the sunny morning of my sixteenth birthday, when my dad handed me a piece of paper. I knew at that shining moment that it was a sale's slip for my new pre-owned chestnut brown 500 SL Mercedes Benz. I thrilled to the thought of that happy portfolio of memories I would soon have driving to Disneyland, to Big Bear, to Palm Springs with that special someone. We rushed to pick it up right off the showroom floor. The dealer's list of options was too long to read in the split second before I eased into the leather and woodclad interior. I thought it must surely have been tailor made for me, because my knees fit perfectly beneath the steering wheel and my hand gravitated naturally to the handle of the automatic transmission."

Fox had the feeling he was watching Tucker on a television. He was a kid inside an ad for Mercedes Benz. His presence was measured in pixels, not ounces or pounds. And worst of all, he made everything around him virtual, too. Reality became reality television. Tucker even had Fox wondering about himself.

"You may think it's wrong to be as passionate as I am about a material object," Tucker read, "but I disagree. My Mercedes is much more than a status symbol to show other teenagers who drive VWs or Toyotas just how average their cars truly are." He paused, pinching the skin around his Adam's apple. "No. It represents hard work, commitment and excellence, three virtues necessary to be a success in life. I remember a banner at the dealership which read, 'Engineered like no other car in the world.' So simply stated, so elegantly put. That's what my Mercedes means to me: the drive to be the best that I can be. Thank you."

At this Pedro Freyre rose slowly from behind his cluttered desk and squeezed his T-shirt right where "is" fit in the sentence "A tautology is a tautology."

"That's great, Tucker!" he said. "That was a...a heartfelt response to the assignment, which, people, remember, has to reveal something about the world you live in and the values you hold, whatever they are."

The next presenter was skate punk Ivan Kolesikow, lean and raggedy-headed, with two nose rings like little silver horns that curled from the sides of his nostrils. He held up his skateboard to show its worn polyurethane wheels and scuffed axles, veteran of numberless assaults on curbs and retaining walls throughout Orange. That was to be the topic on which he preferred to riff without reading from a text. It wasn't a requirement.

"When I'm skating," Ivan said, "there's always something I find that isn't meant to be skated. A ledge, a hill, an embankment, or a staircase. That's when it's time to let my artistic abilities flow. My skateboard and I become one, attacking the concrete jungle yet working with it to pull whatever trick there is for me to pull."

Fox groaned. He was in Angel's labyrinth now, no doubt about it, everything different and the same at once, and the idea that there was no way out but in appalled him more than ever. In fact it left him feeling a little indignant. Things just shouldn't be this paradoxical.

"When I ride my skateboard I become submerged in a state of totally relaxed concentration," Ivan explained. "It's not only what the skateboard brings to me but what I bring to the skateboard. Together we feel free from the world and its troubles to conquer the urban landscape—"

Right then a rooster crowed in the hallway. Ivan wanted to forge ahead, prepared to scale mystical heights on behalf of his skateboard, but the sheer weirdness of this rural sound reduced him on second thought to a puzzled silence, and he stared at the door. *Whaaaaaat?* The door opened, disclosing Angel, dauntlessly late for class, and an ancient Mexican man who cradled in his arms a speckled brown and white pinto rooster. It cast dark paranoid glances about the room, its crimson comb flopping this way and that against the man's throat, while he smoothed its hackles gently with his fingers.

Angel's idea for an oral report, it turned out, was to bring to class her great uncle Fulgencio (Prudencio's brother) and have him tell the story of the legendary gamecock El Caballero Blanco, winner of fifty-eight fights straight and a fortune for Fulgencio before they ran afoul of the evil Juanito del Muerto, who drove El Caballero Blanco at last into the sandpit of paradise and left his master penniless once again. He stood by the door and locked his gaze on some far majestic place until Ivan had finished his report and it was Angel's turn, whereupon he shuffled to the head of the room and sat on one corner of Pedro's desk.

Angel, meanwhile, was opening out the three panels of a black trunk set on its end so everyone could see what was inside. It was a shrine to El Caballero Blanco. The central panel, lined in blue velvet, was dominated by an oval headshot of the leghorn rooster, its beak raised in a gesture of pure bravado, its eye gleaming like Fulgencio's into eternity. A wealth of memorabilia had been crammed into the two side panels: yellowed newspaper articles, trophies, feathers, ticket stubs, and handbills. There were also numerous metal blades, some curved and others spiked, all razor-sharp. Some had been set in square patches of chamois leather and featured like jewels, others dangled from waxed string like necklaces of death.

"I want all you homeboys to listen up," said Angel to the class, "cuz my great uncle's gonna tell you about this chicken he used to have—"

"Un *gallo*, Angel," corrected Fulgencio, "un *gallo*."

"Right," said Angel, "He lived a long time ago, before any of us were born, and everybody called him the White Knight. I guess that's because he was pretty badass for a chicken—"

"*Gallo*," sighed Fulgencio, shaking his head in exasperation at his saucy grandniece. Angel pretended not to notice, her lips pursing into the merest quiver of a smile.

The room quieted down and the old man had everybody's attention, which made him a little nervous. But he soon got into the swing of it. "I was born in Jalisco," he began, "in Iztlan del Rio, among the agave and the cimarron, the woodsmoke and the voices of women singing in the town plaza at dusk. I was a quiet boy who kept to himself. I preferred to spend my time wandering alone in the barrancas or picking out constellations in the night sky with an old atlas I had found in a trash heap. My mother was an Indian ragpicker, and my father toiled in the bean fields of Don Sancho Martinez, the richest man in all Iztlan del Rio. I knew that when I was old enough, I, too, would have to go and work for Don Sancho. But I made the mistake of believing that I had only to want the world, in all its splendor, badly enough, for it not to matter that the world didn't want me."

He turned his head aside and coughed. The rooster yawed forward, spooked, so the old man took the time to soothe it back to its previous quiescence, stroking it from the head all the way to the tips of its tailfeathers. The whole class looked on in gape-mouthed awe.

"When I was sixteen, just as I thought, Don Sancho made me help around the farm," he resumed. "I moved into a corrugated tin shack next to the barn and began my new life as a bracero. They treated me like dirt, and I responded by nurturing my illusions in secret. At night I would sit on my stoop and watch Don Sancho's hacienda with its bright, bustling air. I would listen in at the window while Don Sancho and his family sat down to dinner and pine to be included in the warm circle of their loves. In particular I pined for Don Sancho's daughter, Josefina. She was the most beautiful girl I had ever seen, and in the solitude of my heart I adored her even though I was nobody, just a field hand who dug out her father's garlic, who poured her father's salt into piles so it would dry in the sun. Just a pair of arms under a sombrero, working in the hot sun."

His eyes bore holes into the past, intent skin around their edges spasming back through the long years of hope and disappointment.

"Around that time I first noticed El Caballero Blanco scratching around the barnyard. He was just another mongrel rooster, not good for anything but stews really, or dog food. But I saw something in him, maybe then I didn't even know what: some brush of an angel's wing, some hint of a future impatient to begin, or maybe only my own desire that mongrels, too, might find their place in the sun.

"Every day I brought him maize, beetles, worms, even grasshoppers to eat. I built him a roost out of tires piled on top of one another, so that he had to jump and work his legs. That way he got good and strong. I shaved the feathers of his neck, back, and belly so he would not suffer from the heat, and I cut away his crest and cheek flaps so none of the other gallos could peck at him."

He reached into his coat pocket for a handful of birdseed and held it out for his rooster to devour with hectic jabs.

"Meanwhile I could not hide my love from Josefina," he said, "even though she never once considered me a suitor. I brought her wildflowers from the barrancas, but she took them and forgot about me. I serenaded her with a rusted old Supertone guitar, but she stared at the moon and thought of someone else. Finally, I discovered that she had fallen in love with Hector Montoya, the son of a cannery owner in town. I had known him in school as a bully who taunted me with names like "Mestizo the mosquito." He was the kind of boy who tore the wings off butterflies and threw cats into wells. But Josefina saw nothing of his true nature, or if she did she didn't care. Maybe she even liked him for it. She ignored my warnings and ran away with him anyway. Sure enough he took her virginity on a beach at Acapulco, stole her money in Guadalajara, and abandoned her pregnant to the whores and pimps of Mexico City inside of a month.

"What I knew of hate I summoned to curse the man who had dishonored my beloved Josefina, and I swore one day I would squeeze," he leaned forward and grabbed at the air in front of him to illustrate his point, "*squeeze* his cojones until they were crushed to a pulp."

Pedro laughed nervously.

The old man continued. "I asked Josefina to marry me, but she was too proud. 'I would rather marry that gallo,' she said, pointing at El Caballero Blanco where he was busy chasing hens in the barnyard, 'than a spindly muchacho like you.'

"I stared hard at El Caballero Blanco. 'Who can tell what fire smolders in the breast of a no-account rooster?' I said, but she only laughed, rejoining with a sneer, 'You and that bird, pito and pajarito, but not a real man between you.'

"I hardly heard what she said. I was beginning to suspect that El Caballero Blanco was no ordinary gallo. Just after his first moult I pitted him against a veteran gamecock from a nearby town. When he destroyed his foe with the force of a hurricane, I knew he had it: the grito that comes from within. In a flash of inspiration it came to me what I had to do: leave Don Sancho's farm, leave Ixtlan del Rio, and with El Caballero Blanco go out and make my fortune. Once I was rich, I would return and again ask Josefina to marry me. And I felt sure, with the sense of destiny that surrounded El Caballero Blanco like the halo around a saint's head, that she would finally see the noble heart that beat in this breast of a ragpicker's son, and love me at last. The thought made me drunk with joy. Soon after, I tucked El Caballero Blanco into a shabby wicker basket and stole away into the night.

"But what did I know about this rat-trap of a world?" He glared for no particular reason straight at Fox, as if expecting an answer. "Just what you know. Nada. Naa-da. It would be many years before I understood that I would never be Don Fulgencio and never marry Josefina. Life, alas, has no pity for what you wish for. But if there is a God in Heaven, his emissary in this vale of tears was El Caballero Blanco, for with his beak I pecked close to the true heart of the world where love is infinite and cruel, even if, once there, El Caballero Blanco pecked the life right out of it and left me with nothing but dreams.

"He was a headhunter, the kind of gallo that went for the eyes. He hated when he killed. Fast as lightning, lean and elusive, he had the gizzard of an eagle and the asshole of Quetzalcoatl."

Fulgencio turned toward the oval photograph in the shrine and paid his respects. Fox had a sensation of sublimity here, looking at that rooster, mysteries disproportionate in that haughty beak and supercharged eye. A kid named Noel Funsterbusch wanted to know who Quetzalcoatl was, and Pedro went on about the Aztec deity, half mortal and half immortal, a serpent with feathers who stole maize from the gods and presided over human sacrifices—in short, he said, "kind of everything all at once, if you know what I mean."

"We entered a derby in the town of Jiquilpan de Juarez," Fulgencio went on. "Without breaking a sweat El Caballero Blanco took the championship and prize money worth thirty thousand pesos. In Zacualpa, El Caballero Blanco was pitted against the famed Pepito de las Aguas Bravas, the most feared gallo in all Michoacan. A hundred people gathered to witness the battle, but Pepito fought like a fat gallina and El Caballero Blanco carved out his liver. For that I took home one hundred thousand pesos.

"His fame began to spread. We won in every town we came to, and pretty soon people began to say that El Caballero Blanco was bewitched, nothing could kill him, and I was getting rich because I'd made a pact with the devil. Then they refused to fight us." This injustice incensed Fulgencio all over again. "Cobardes! Mariquitas!" he cried, gesturing wildly across the throat of his gallo. "But so it was. Wherever we went fear of El Caballero Blanco preceded us, and people ran away like jackrabbits. All we could do was keep moving deeper into the rainforests, higher over the mountain passes, to places more and more remote. In Nochixtlah El Caballero Blanco cashiered the bird of a dimwitted Oaxacan and won five hundred thousand pesos. On the outskirts of Oxitlan some mojado with a head full of horseshit laughed at El Caballero Blanco, insulting the strength in his godlike legs and his savage beak. But he stopped laughing when El Caballero Blanco tore out the guts of his bird and spread them across the pit, and I walked away with the one million pesos staked on the fight.

"After that there was nowhere else to go except into the Lacandon jungle, among the strange Indian peoples of Chiapas. They lived with nothing, but they liked to gamble, and I won in village after village. By the time I came to San Cristóbal de Las Casas, I had four million pesos sewn into the lining of my coat. We were driving a gaff into the brain of Mexico, and no one knew it but me.

"Perhaps I got too cocky. The world felt small, and all the people in it just popos, just little fleas jumping around in the raised hackles of a gigantic gallo. In the back of my mind I knew I should have stopped. By then I had more than enough money to return to Ixtlan del Rio as the man my beautiful Josefina deserved. El Caballero Blanco would never have to fight again. He could have a barnyard of his own and a harem of plump gallinas to stud his immortal offspring. But I was drunk with greed, with grandeur, I don't know. Nothing could have stopped me.

"And then I saw him, one moonlit night under the biggest matesano tree I had ever seen in my life: Juanito del Muerto, wings outstretched and crowing malevolently, held high above the head of that coño Hector Montoya, my mortal enemy. He strutted around the ring, a clown, a panaso in tight puto jeans, bragging about his bird's conquests. He even had the nerve to say Juanito del Muerto beat the mighty El Caballero Blanco himself, the god of all gallos, in a riverbed near Comitán.

"I wanted to destroy him. And before I did that, I wanted to destroy everything that mattered to him, his manhood, his mother, the dark duende of his blood. I stepped forward into the lamplight and opened the wicker basket in which I still kept El Caballero Blanco. I said, 'Hector Montoya, you lying son of a bitch, I hear your hen singing.'

"And he snickered, 'Aye muere, compinche, gimme a break. Put your money where your mouth is. Abre las piernas!'

"I took all the money I had won, laid it on a table, and said, 'Tomorrow you'll be digging ditches for your dinner.'

"I should have kept my word. I should have left and bought that barnyard for El Caballero Blanco. But I didn't. Instead I tempted fate one time too many.

"I remember the smell of serrano chilies that a man who sold burritos was sauteeing behind his little stand. I remember a radio playing a bolero, *Nosotros*, above the full-throated cries of the bettors. And I remember the leering face of Hector Montoya grow pale when El Caballero Blanco sank a gaff into Juanito's shoulder and he squatted, bloody and panting, so tired he couldn't hold his neck straight. A sudden beatitude filled the space between us. I thought, now El Caballero Blanco will peck at the red eye in Juanito's wobbly head, and El Caballero Blanco did. Now the knuckles of Hector Montoya's hand will turn purple where it gripped the bench he sat on so hard the wood might snap, and the knuckles of Hector Montoya's hand turned purple and the wood snapped.

"It's still hard for me to accept that it didn't happen as it did in my mind. Even now I can't quite believe it. How time cheats! How it takes with one hand what it gives with the other! For as I reveled in my triumph Juanito regained his strength, went back on his tail, and flew at El Caballero Blanco in a rage! They slashed and ripped at each other's underbellies with their spurs, crouched beak to beak. Before long El Caballero Blanco had broken his wing, and blood flowed down his alabaster breast. Still he fought on, and even then it wouldn't have been too late, even then he might have held the day. But something went wrong. The nineteenth round ended and I pulled him from the pit. I took his battered comb in my mouth and blew the blood back into it. I rubbed his legs with alcohol and licked his eyes clean. But as I did, I looked down and saw that his beak was turned crazily sideways. I blinked, but the vision remained. Sound melted like wax from a candle with the moon as its flame, and I heard nothing but guttering breezes in the jungle around me. I reached out with the fingers of a child who does not believe in what he touches and gently plucked the beak of El Caballero Blanco from his cheeks."

Fulgencio retrieved from the shrine a small cardboard box tied with gold elastic string and took out the very same beak, sooty in texture and tapering to a blunt point. He held it out for the class to see.

"This beak is light as balsawood," he said, "but it was all that stood between El Caballero Blanco and certain death, and all that in the end made the difference between a rich man and a poor man."

He hefted the beak, weighing its other, more cosmic substance.

"That's a pretty big difference," nodded Pedro solemnly, "for such a little thing."

"What happened next?" said a rapt Dae Dae Zwernemann from the front row.

"We started the twentieth round. El Caballero Blanco was still game, dragging his broken wing behind him. In the bleachers men crouched forward in poses that seemed to me all the same, screaming 'Vamos, como tu padre!' and 'Picale en el corazon!' In my mind I was far away, walking alone in the jungle of lost desire. Then Juanito rose up with a flurry of wings and rocketed down, burying his spurs deep in El Caballero Blanco's back. He squawked, fell flat, tried to get up, and sank in a heap. Juanito tore out his eyes and stood over him crowing his victory to the heavens, while by my side Hector Montoya, grinning like a weasel, was already pawing at the money on the table. When at last I picked El Caballero Blanco off the sand, he was just a lump of skin and bones, not even good for the frying pan. But as I was hungry as well as poor, I cooked him up anyway and had him for dinner under the matesano tree. The next morning I got a job digging ditches."

The bell rang just as Fulgencio's demeanor reverted to that stony blankness he'd come in with, a little to Fox's eye as if he were this wind-up doll that had just stopped. The rooster in his lap didn't like the bell or the commotion of people shuffling past, so the old man cradled it firmly in his arms and stroked its feathers, waiting the exodus out. As Angel closed up the shrine again, she asked Fox for help carrying the trunk to her car.

He cast a furtive glance toward the door and the chance, strangely lost, at escape. Instead Angel handed him the trunk, and he followed her and Fulgencio outside to her brother Justo's souped up Datsun 510 station wagon. She opened the back hatch and said something Spanish to Fulgencio. Fox lifted the trunk in. Fulgencio, by the open passenger door, reached his hands over the seat as if to guide it toward him. Fox glanced from him to Angel, who waited.

"Push it forward," she said. "He wants it up by him."

"Why?"

"I don't know. Just do it."

Fox leaned in, Fulgencio beckoned, and at last he had to prop his knees on the edge and crawl into the cabin. Angel matter-of-factly slammed the hatch shut behind him. He pressed his hands and forehead against the side window as she went around to the driver's side and got in.

"What are you doing?"

"I'm taking my uncle home," she said.

"But—"

He looked over to see the rooster and Fulgencio staring at him from around a domed headrest.

"She's a good girl," the old man intoned. "Muy bonita."

Before Fox knew it they were off. "Where are you, um, taking *me*?" he asked.

"Nowhere," said Angel, as if it were a place.

He tried to keep calm, telling himself that everything was normal, it was okay if Angel was a murderer and he was getting the evil eye from a rooster in some strange car. It was okay that he'd been whisked away from school unbeknownst to anyone, or that strictly speaking he was being held against his will and that usually implied kidnapping. Fulgencio watched this train of thought transpire in his head.

"You have a time problem," he said. "I can see it in your eyes—a cloud of unknowing. Yes. The future is dark to you. It fills you with fear. It hunts you."

Angel drove.

"You do not understand that the future has only ever already passed and *that* is what hunts you. The future is not dark, it's just not there. And what is there is only a bright emptiness. Amigo," he said, "there are no mysteries. Don't you see? *Everything is happening all at once.*"

A sensation of torque inside Fox's head made him think inexplicably of the Mad Hatter teacup ride at Disneyland, whipping him around bends of his own character.

Upon depositing Fulgencio and his gallo in front of the Melendez house, Angel skidded away down the block.

"Don't listen to the old fart," she cracked over the roar of Justo's engine. "You can't trust what he says."

"Why not?" he asked, watching the orange pointer in the speedometer rocket above 40 mph.

"He lies."

"You mean it's not true, what he said about the White Knight?"

Angel sighed impatiently, as if what he did not understand were right there in front of his face.

"Have you ever noticed how guys like to tell stories?"

"Well—"

"If you're a girl it's clear as the Crystal Cathedral. Guy's get off on telling stories about themselves, their cars, their cocks, whatever."

She swerved into Chapman Circle, the quaint hub of the Orange metropolis, lined with used clothing and antique furniture stores.

"It's hella fucked up," she went on, and changed the subject: "Did you know it's not cool to say 'hella' anymore in So-Cal? Now people make fun of you for saying it." She puzzled over this whim of fashion, a clear light of decision breaking in her eyes. "That's why I'm gonna say it from now on."

"We have to get back to school," Fox observed casually.

Angel bore left around the circle. "Why? We don't do anything at PE anyway, and then it's lunch period. We've got two hours at least."

"They'll know we're gone."

"Where do you want to go?" she asked.

"Anywhere but in a circle," he pleaded on the second loop.

"Hey!" she cried, craning her neck to take in the sight of a kid named Ryan Dodge, dressed in a lime green dinner jacket to match his dyed hair, bright rust red jeans, and a fedora with a feather in it. He walked sullenly across the little circular park. "He's playing hooky, too." She turned a corner. "He's all right, Ryan. He's like a leprechaun, did you notice?"

"Kinda, yeah."

"He'd be good looking if his nose wasn't so long. He needs to grow a few inches, too. But he's not so bad. Once he loses those braces, he'll be okay."

She tooled with seeming aimlessness through Orange until at last pulling into the parking lot of a church. She got out and headed for a fence. All at once it dawned on Fox where they were.

"The riverbed!" he exclaimed as Angel scrambled over the fence and dropped down into that weedy interval he knew so well. The smell of wild licorice filled his nostrils as he followed after.

"I've always called it the Ditch," said Angel.

They cut down a concrete bank to a bar of finely sedimented silt. Their shoes made perfect imprints, dark gray on umber, and the powdery dirt rose in soft billows as they went. Angel had taken out a yo-yo, with which she was performing numerous tricks. Fox let himself relax.

"I didn't know you came here," he said.

"I don't, much. But my brothers are always hanging around in it."

"They are?!"

"Don't ask me why," Angel said. "I told them about the radio-active poisons."

"The what?!"

"Poisons," said Angel. "Well, at least in the Santa Ana River. This military contractor, Aerojet General, used to set off explosives—mustard gas, depleted uranium tankbusters, things like that—in the Chino Hills. When that got too hairy they dumped all their shit into mucky creeks and split. The problem is those creeks feed into the river, where the chemicals sink into the groundwater and give people leukemia and kidney disease."

"Didn't they get into trouble?"

"No way, dude. Not in Orange County. They cart off a few loads of contaminated dirt and build a 250-home development with an 18-hole golf course on the bomb range, that's all."

Fox didn't want to consider what all this meant for someone who spent as much time in the riverbed as he did. Ahead he saw the same stand of willow trees where he and Axel had encountered the crazy man who went on about a whirling wheel. Angel seemed to know the place, too, because she headed straight for it.

"I've been here before," he said.

She sussed out one of the many entrances. They crawled through the network of tunnels, coming at last to the inner chamber where the moldy sofa sat.

"This place is a safe house for my brothers' gang," said Angel. "Los Fuckers."

Fox was stunned by the news. It violated some principle of separate worlds that he had always considered ironclad.

"This river used to be the boundary between two ranchos, way long ago," related Angel. "Actually it was just one, pretty much all of Orange County, but after the Mexican War they split it up between two different families: the Yorbas on one side and the Peraltas on the other. The Peraltas ended up getting rich, and that's why there's so many streets and schools and shit named after them. But the Yorbas screwed up, didn't keep things in order, and sold off the land for a song to the gringos. They ended up living in shacks, and everybody thought they were losers. They still got a lot of things named after them, though."

Angel bounced hard twice on the sofa, and the springs pressing up out of the vinyl squealed loudly. Then she leaned back, waiting for him to say something. But he didn't.

"I sound like a boy," she said. "You ever notice that? When I talk it sounds just like a boy."

Angel let her voice expand to fill the arboreal cavity around them. "I don't know why it is. . .a boy. . .a boy. . .boooooooy."

Fox picked up an empty carton of rolling papers, left there he imagined by some Los Fucker when he'd rolled his last reefer before a rumble.

"Maybe it's because I have five brothers," Angel said. "I've always hung around boys too much. You don't hang around much of anybody, huh? Except Axel."

We keep to ourselves," he said.

"He's pretty weird, that guy. *Hella* weird. In fact, he might be crazy."

"He's not crazy."

"He *acts* crazy."

"You don't know him, that's all."

"Have you ever noticed the way he nods off in class?" she went on, miming an appropriately loony distraction. The likeness was apt enough for him to recall examples of what she meant. "It's like he's hearing somebody talk who's not there."

Fox felt a sharp pang of fear. The question swung like a pendulum through his mind: *Is he crazy?*

Angel could tell this bothered him. She cocked her head, observing him with squirrelly eyes. At length she said, "You're funny."

"I am?"

"Yeah. I don't know any boys like you."

"No?"

"You don't care about any of the things they care about."

Angel's nose wrinkled, and she drew up the corners of her mouth into a mischievous smile. "For example, you're the only boy I know who never talks about sex." She leaned forward. "Why is that?"

Fox caught a distinctly vixenish look in Angel's face. Feelings of paranoia came streaming back, a multifaceted way he had of seeing himself from all these different points in space at once drew suddenly taut the fibers of his being.

"I mean, everybody else has that on their mind. They couldn't think of anything else if they tried. Sex is an obsession. Why not for you?"

"I don't know," he gulped.

"It's hella bizarre."

I'm trapped, he realized. Angel was coming across that sofa now, her dark murderer's face looming up toward his, her lean body stretching closer and closer. Of course. It made perfect sense. Angel's insinuating questions, her overtures of friendship, the talk about labyrinths and those crazy stories from her past—it was all part of a diabolical plot. How could he have been so stupid? *She was a minotaur and she was going to kill him!* Panicked, he tried to worm his way back and off the sofa. But she was on top of him now, pinning him with her legs, digging her shoulder into his chest.

"Sometimes I can't think of anything else but boys," she said dreamily. "I can't help it. It just comes over me. It's a gland thing. My body has a mind of its own, you feel what I'm saying. . . ?"

All Fox could feel was alarm for the delicate organ of his affections, now thumping and throbbing against his ribs. Would she cut it out of him? Was it something he could afford to lose or do without if she decided to keep it? Terrified, or with the attention that terror brings, he noticed Angel's drawn eyebrows trail off toward her temples. Now why would she go and do a thing like that? he wondered as she wrapped her arms around his shoulders and planted a kiss. Strands of hair, smells of faint sweat and breath, engulfed him. His lips had never felt so used. Their knees knocked together. Her bony hip ground into his stomach. Over her cheek he saw patches of sky in the tangled willow trees. They were enclosed. Hidden. Nowhere! His fingers gripped the sofa or waved at the air, too modest to touch her or to believe she'd want him to or even to know if he wanted to.

But Angel laughed, right into his mouth, and that laugh made some baffle inside him fall away. There was no getting around it. She liked him. And it didn't matter that he was self-conscious to the point of catatonia. As Angel herself might put it, that was just the way he was, his way of belonging to the vertiginous world, of wandering in the infinite labyrinth. She liked *that* about him. The thing to do, he thought as calmly as the circumstance would allow, was to hold on, just hold on for dear life if need be, whatever might happen after. In the end that's exactly what he did.

12

Axel at School

Axel walked down the hall toward his human development class feeling solitary. People gave him a wide berth and soon that solitude wasn't a feeling but a fact: it welled around him like a nimbus. In it he felt magical, majestic, striding through meadows of asphodel. He wasn't a teenager but a man-killing hoplite, a battle-hungry myrmidon, a famous breaker of horses stepping out of song and legend. People turned away, he thought, not repelled but dazzled by a shining brightness, a flash of inner grace.

He entered the classroom and squeezed his big frame into a molded plastic chair affixed to a metal desk. Ms. Overton, his human development teacher, was already holding forth by the chalkboard on the concept of "personality." "Personality," she said with a falsetto voice resembling the sound of door hinges squealing, "comes from a combination of heredity and environment. It is a set of core characteristics that make for an identity that is unique at the same time. A good, strong personality is the result of a healthy development through childhood and adolescence. A good, strong personality *grows* and *changes*. A good, strong personality avoids fear and anxiety, thinking hopeful thoughts for the future. Now, psychologists come to understand the good, strong personality by studying the bad, poorly developed personality. These personalities do not *grow* and *change*. They *repeat* themselves over and over again. They are not able to see, touch, smell, hear, and taste because they have shut the world out of their awareness. They develop low intellectual capacity. They don't do normal things like exercise or date or invest in their human capital. They spend most of their time closing themselves off from experience. They live in fantasy worlds, deny reality, and take on other identities rather than form one of their own. . ."

Axel looked around the classroom: sparkly and attentive faces hung on Ms. Overton's every word. For some reason this was the only class he had where such rapture could be observed. Suddenly he felt afraid. He closed his eyes and remembered a day his teacher in the academy for prophetically gifted children made the kids play a game of musical chairs. There he was again moving around the circle. He heard a waltz lilt and swoon from a boom box the teacher had brought from home. He lost himself in the music, wondering what era it belonged to and who was meant to hear it. He turned and turned through elegant halls with double-helix stairways, crystal chandeliers, cut-glass goblets, dapper men in black suits and women with crinoline dresses and sumptuous floral hats. Then the music stopped, and before Axel knew it everybody had sat down and there was no chair for him. He'd been left standing. And he remembered thinking, *Everybody has a place except me.*

"Axel? Axel?" Ms. Overton said, intruding upon these thoughts. He roused himself to find all eyes upon him. He blinked and sat up in his chair. "Are you with us, Axel?" she asked. "Are you present?"

Axel thought about this. "No," he said, trying to be truthful. "I'm more absent."

Titters all around. Ms. Overton's smile was wise and complacent. "It's time to come into the moment," she gently remonstrated.

"Where's that?"

"Where's what?" she asked, distracted by Sally Hammer, a bouncy blonde girl with pigtails and a winning smile, who'd been urging her raised hand on Ms. Overton's attention for some time now.

"The moment that I would come into," said Axel.

"It's now."

"But now's already then," he said.

"Now's always now, Axel."

"Now's never now, Ms. Overton."

Sally could barely keep from squirming out of her seat, so burning was her desire to know. At last Ms. Overton turned to her.

"Yes, Sally?"

Sally raised her button nose just enough to appear condescending. "Ms. Overton," she inquired, "how many calories does sperm have?"

Axel could see it was going to be a long day. Mornings were especially hard because after Ms. Overton came Benny Nordquist, his civics teacher. He had suffered from cancer of the mouth for years and could only speak through a voice box that he held to his throat. He weighed about five hundred pounds. Everything he said was a rant.

"Three inalienable laws govern our social existence," he began when the second bell rang and all his wards were seated. They listened uneasily. His mouth contorted into a dumbshow of grimaces, bereft of its voice. It was like watching an effigy in a wax museum. "The first law is obedience and the second we call survival of the fittest. These laws come from nature. When the wolf hunts the caribou, he takes out the weak and the sick because they are slower. The strong caribou survive for longer. They create more offspring, they broaden their genetic heritage. The weak caribou die out. In this way, the *health* of the herd is preserved."

Axel daydreamed. He was walking alone through the empire of Ur. He came to a shore where a large city lay in ruins. Untold numbers of beaked and jackal-headed ships lay broken along the strand. A sated dragon had coiled its massive body around the towers of a dead fortress. Its glittering head ranged high above, and a forked tongue ten times longer than a man slithered out from its tight-lipped mouth.

"Likewise, we humans form a herd," droned on Mr. Nordquist. "There are strong humans and there are weak humans. But how is the *health* of the herd preserved? Through competition. Competition is the third inalienable law. It separates the winners from the losers, like the wolf does. It functions in exactly the same way. Of course, we don't kill those who lose. We're not allowed to do that. But we can separate them off, so they always remember who they are and don't go getting any ideas about their rights and entitlements. Is this clear? Am I going too fast for you?"

Timid nods, shrugs of shoulders. Axel called out to the dragon: 'O wise and woeful worm!' he said. 'Destroyer of men's dreams, vanquisher of men's sturdy arms! 'Tis said your eyes can see even into the darkest places. Tell me! Have you spied the fair Sift, last of the immortals to grace this dreary land?' The dragon spoke but its mouth didn't move. 'Sift is quick as a moonbeam,' it said. 'He arises like vapor. He vanishes in rays of glare. Where he wanders, none may know. . .'

"You have to keep your place," Mr. Nordquist was saying. "Nature demands it. Survival and obedience plus competition, that's what counts. And all three laws come together in the marketplace, which is like a steppe where the herd lives. There your value is tested against the values of others. Again, it's like the wolf. Weak humans are eaten and disappear. Strong humans are rewarded and brought along so that they can help society become more efficient and secure. The marketplace ensures that the human gene pool remains strong in the face of whatever comes along to threaten it. I don't just mean viruses like AIDS or Swine flu, but, more in the spirit of my academic discipline, civics, those groups of poor people who get ideas, who don't keep their place. They delude themselves into believing they're winners when they're really losers. Or, to put it another way, they try to be masters when they're really slaves. Do you know what happens when slaves try to be masters? They become like a plague or a swarm of locusts. They invade the herd of healthy people. They attach themselves to us like leeches or they burrow into our stomachs like parasites. Do you know how many parasites live in the average healthy human's stomachs? Thousands. Millions. They get in there and fatten on you, and then you know what they do? They copulate, that's what. And they lay eggs. Inside your stomach. Think about it. Whole colonies of wormy aliens. We are constantly being invaded. Don't you see?" He banged the table with his free hand, startling everyone. "*Invasion is permanent!* We have to be vigilant or the herd will be annihilated. That's why competition is important. It instructs us in the art of vigilance. That's also why obedience is important. Obedience to the herd on the steppe of the marketplace. So that it will survive."

Axel longed to be in the company of the sylvan Sift, to wander with him beneath the incandescent eaves of some fair woodland grove. The situation in Ur had become desperate. Soon there would be no relief from imbeciles like Mr. Nordquist. Already it may be too late.

At lunch Axel went to the cafeteria to eat a peanut butter sandwich, alone now that Fox was smitten with that enchantress Angel and spent the hour with her. Down the table a gaggle of ninth-grade girls were whispering to each other, ignoring him. The light in the high windows welled into the room and bounced blankly off the marble floor. There was a din of indistinguishable voices in the background. The peanut butter cloyed in his mouth. He felt his food balling up inside his stomach, heavy as a stone. The girls were talking about boys. Axel wasn't a boy. He was Axalax, walking through a dark forest copse. There he came upon a monster that was half goat and half lion. A chimera. The kind of animal that had the two parts of its body crossed in an X. 'Begone, foul hell spawn, back to the Aerial Void whence thou came!' he cried. He took his sword and raised it over his shoulder, just as the chimera raised its sword over its shoulder. Axel glared into its lion's eyes, only to see his own eyes reflected in them. He stuck out his tongue, and behold! it stuck out its tongue, too. 'You beguile me with symmetries,' he said. 'But I will not be fooled." He unsheathed his longsword. 'Take that!' he cried, and with a single jab gored the monster. Then he took a trudgeon from its noose in the cinched belt of his halberd and pulped its vile head.

He put his half-finished sandwich down on the table, squinting into the light. He felt a headache coming on. He balled up his fists and pressed them into his eyes. He rubbed for a long time, seeing in the phosphene the corpse of the monster he had pulped. He felt his head moving away from his shoulders. When he looked up again he saw little translucent infusoria floating in the air. A look of beatitude came over his face as he watched the motes fall like gentle snowflakes around him.

He heard laughter from the other end of the table. The girls were watching him. "He's so weird," one of them remarked to the others. Axel wanted to say, "Look! Look at the motes!" But he knew they wouldn't understand. Even if they could see them it wouldn't change the fact that he was weird. *Sssoooooooooweeeeuuuuuuuurrrrrrdd!* He'd heard it more times than he could count. He'd heard it whispered behind his back, muttered like a slur, shouted by people who took his weirdness so personally they were indignant about it. The travails of Axalax had been passing hard. They weighed on him like the world on Atlas's shoulders. But there the motes were still descending, even as the girls picked up their trays and went to sit at another table. Right in front of his eyes. It made Axel mad. Why didn't they see things that weren't there? What could be so interesting about the things only everybody saw? He wanted the courage of his convictions here: it was those girls who locked themselves away in their minds, who locked themselves away from life in the very life they found with one another. He thought, *If only we could bear our immortality!*

Axel finished his lunch and let these musings carry him who knew where inside the dark confines of school, until it was time for his next class. He wandered out to the track with its joggers wearing headphones and over to the parking lot where people were smoking cigarettes. He thought, *Nothing I see can be trusted. Not those girls with sky blue eyeliner who take swigs of Bacardi 151 in the backseat of a Camaro. Not the rockabilly guys combing their pompadours back and talking about '57 Chevys.* Axel wasn't alone, solitary; they were alone, together. He put this paradox into its tabernacle to keep safe and guard against the desecrators. It inspired him with a sense of mission. He had to attest in the face of complete indifference to the presence of parallel worlds. That was both his glory and his cross to bear. It was a thankless task. It required the stigmata of all ostracized people, fools and desert saints, madmen and prophets, nobodies banished to their lonely outlands. Sitting in Pedro Freyre's social studies class next period, he supposed it wasn't all that surprising. He shouldn't mind being cast out and despised. What was that, weighed against this witness he made, and in fact made only because he was stigmatized!

Pedro was telling his students of a grandmother he read about in an old book. "So this guy, his name's Marcel, talks to his grandmother on the phone for the first time," he said. "This was back when they first invented phones. Before that the only way you could talk to somebody was in person. Anyway, he talks to his grandmother, and he hears only her *voice*, right, without her being there. This makes Marcel sad, because for the first time she loses for him this magic aura she always had when they were together. He imagines her stripped down to nothing but a. . .a body, you know what I'm saying?"

"No," snorted Jaime Melendez, Angel's brother, slouched way down in his chair and lost in the billows of his LA Dodgers sweatshirt. A big *F* had been shaved into his nearly bald head.

"I mean, just hearing her voice makes him imagine in his," Pedro pointed to the big *F*, a little disconcerted, but he continued, "his head, right, it makes him imagine just her body, which is old and raggedy and about to die. Every other time they'd talked he could look her in the eye, connect up what she was saying to the person looking at him, and this meant he could see her *personality*. But now, all that personality gets stripped away and she's just this body, this thing, something you cart away like a sack of potatoes."

"Maybe you cart *your* grandma away like that," sneered Jaime. "But not me. My abuela's going to Heaven in a stretch limo."

"The point," Pedro went on, "is that it's the *phone* that causes Marcel to see his grandmother like a sack of potatoes. It's the *phone* that strips her of her humanity and makes the way she's only a thing clear to old Marcel. And once that happens, he says, there's no turning back. You can put the person back into the thing, but you can't take the thing out of the person. And that's what I want to talk about today: How communication technology dehumanizes us."

A wave of noisy protest washed over him as the students all raised their smartphones into the air. They'd already pegged Pedro as an old hippie from the days when nobody could pinpoint their exact location or win a contest by calling in from the boulevard or share a photo of the burrito they were having for lunch with their friends, and they felt obliged to set him straight about the virtues of information.

"I haven't got anything against information," said Pedro. "I'm just wondering how it changes things when you can separate off your voice from your body, make it into little pulses of electricity darting through cables, or tag it onto light waves that shoot up to satellites in space. What happens to the person whose voice travels ten thousand miles in a microsecond?"

"Nothing," said Jaime. "He stays a person. Now he can get down with his homeboys in Nepal, if he wants to, that's all. Get it on with a little of that Nepalese rap." He turned and high-fived his friend Anselmo, who had the exact same *F* shaved onto his head.

"In the old days, we lived in what were called *hot* societies," Pedro said, trying to add more dimension to the topic. "That meant we burned wood, coal, copper, whatever. We used industry to change the materials around us, like refining crude oil into gas or iron ore into steel. We still do that, but now we live in this other kind of society, too, where everything's about communication, 'getting connected.' It's all about transmitting voices, images, meanings."

"So?" said Jaime.

"I don't know," said Pedro, confounded. "It's strange, that's all. It's. . .unreal. Airy, somehow, ethereal. Like floating in space. . ."

"Like angels," observed Axel from the back of the room.

Pedro puckered his lips and rubbed his goatee. "Yeah, right. . .I guess. What do you mean?"

"Angels float in space," said Axel. "In clouds, in crowds, in the hallway, here in the classroom. They transmit things, too. They're God's ambassadors. They carry messages between immortals and mortals. That's why they're always going up and down Jacob's Ladder."

"Been seeing any angels lately?" cracked Jaime.

"They're easy to see," Axel said, ignoring this provocation, "if you know how to look or. . .*what* to look for."

"What do you look for?" asked Pedro.

Axel reflected. "Sound," he said then.

"What are you talking about?" scoffed Jaime. "You can't *see* sound. That's illogical."

"No," said Axel. "There's such a thing as visible sound. That's what angels are. When you see sound, you're seeing an angel."

"What does sound look like?" asked Pedro.

"Everything," said Axel. "Me. You. School. The sky. The angels are all around us, and also in between us. They're us, between."

"Are you making this up?" asked Jaime.

"No."

"Between what?" urged an attentive Pedro.

"Just between."

"I get it," said Anselmo.

"So the angels are. . .relays between one thing and another," said Pedro. "Like the postal service, fiberoptic wires, satellites, transistors."

"Teenagers," said Anselmo.

"Teachers," said Pedro.

"Silicon chips!" piped up Willie "Wired" Dunleavy. "Integrated circuits, semiconductors."

"Microprocessors!" shouted Sarah Meinert.

"You're all loco," declared Jaime.

"But there's something I don't understand," said Pedro, frowning. "I mean, sound is vibration, resonance in a body, right? Is that what angels are?"

"Angels don't have bodies," said Axel.

"But how can there be a sound wave without some sort of mass?"

"They don't make a sound you hear. An angel, when it comes, negates sound."

Pedro tried his best to square the two sides of this paradox in his mind. "Like the phone," he said, thinking aloud, "when it separates Marcel's grandmother's voice from her body, while at the same time stripping away her personal voice. Is that the voice of the angels—the voice that's not a voice?"

A burst of static on the intercom system interrupted this conversation, and Principal Castranova came on to inaugurate a school-wide exodus to the gymnasium. It was time for a pep rally. People gathered their belongings and scuttled off, glad to be out of Pedro's clutches. Axel merged with the stream of people making their way down the hall. Abstractly he sensed he was being followed. At length he turned to find himself staring into Pedro's eyes. He wasn't done yet. He asked: "Can there be bad angels?"

"What?"

"Angels who seem like angels, but they're really not."

"Yes," said Axel. "Devils."

"Right," nodded Pedro. "But what's the difference exactly? What's a devil?"

"A fallen angel who tries to become God."

Pedro brooded on this theological conundrum with the look of a kid fitting together pieces of a puzzle he suspects have gotten mixed up with some other. They were standing like rocks in the river of people. "Because, if angels are telephones," he continued, "or newscasters, or the media, or data streams, why is Marcel so depressed when he hears his grandmother's voice? Isn't he hearing the voice of the angels?"

"I don't know," said Axel. "I haven't read the book."

"And if he is, doesn't that, like, mean angels are bad news?"

"They can be good or bad, or even good and bad," Axel explained. "But really that's just a manner of speaking. They're not one thing or another. They pass between and through all things, closed doors, school windows, prison bars, palace walls, and also people: kings, ministers, long-haul truck drivers, housewives, bankers, lunatics. They're everywhere and nowhere. Limitless, beyond number, dazzling. They appear and disappear, like a light set on strobe."

"Like information," said Pedro in fell tones. "Binary numbers. Zeros and ones." He gazed upon his student with a kind of wonder. "How do you know all these things?"

"It's what they tell me," said Axel.

"Who?"

"The angels."

Pedro was about to jump in again when he halted mid-breath, mouth agape, eyes narrowing into portals of perplexity. Parallel worlds, thought Axel. The trembling tone. In the beginning was the Word, and God was with the Word. People just didn't seem to understand that they were in the grip of a demiurge. He wished there was more he could do to help.

The entire student body had gathered on the gymnasium bleachers to watch varsity cheerleaders do an elaborate dance routine. Loudspeakers played the song *Material Girl*. All male eyes in Axel's vicinity fluttered and wowed each time the girls kicked their legs high or bent over.

Static fields of perception began to flow. Things seemed to be losing their consistency. Now that the cheerleaders had ended their routine at centercourt by forming a human wall, atop which the tiniest member of the team had joyously vaulted, Axel observed a row of fat boys without shirts rush onto the court, jutting out their legs like toy soldiers in a marching band. They carried identical frame drums which they beat willy-nilly, and they were singing *Deutschland Über Alles* at the top of their lungs. Principal Castranova held a child's wand with glass dust swirling in its liquid stem. He waved it in the air as if he were a conductor.

"People, people," he said. "I'd like to indulge in a little etymological speculation on the origins of my name. Castration. Do any of you know what that means?"

Everyone except Axel pretended not to hear this question.

"It comes from the Italian *castrato*. That's their word for a member of the male sex whose spermatozoa have been removed from his scrotum. *Castrato*, castration. Then there's Casanova. You've all heard of him. *Castrato*, man with impaired sexual organs. Casanova, famous lover. Do you see the connection? I do. I have been seeing it all my life. I am a castrated Casanova."

Things were turning bizarre. Folds of fat jiggled about the marching boys' middles or drooped over their cheeks, their sensuous red lips leered as they yodeled away, eagle feathers dangled from their frame drums.

"Who's number one?" cried Principal Castranova over the madcap scene, his amplified voice booming off the walls.

The students replied: "South Orange High!"

Principal Castranova cocked his ear and said, "I can't hear you!"

The students, louder: "South Orange High!"

And again: "I can't heeeeear you!"

"South Orange High!"

"And who do we despise more than anyone?" the principal asked. "With such nauseating bile my stomach turns just thinking about them?"

The student body replied as one: "North Orange High!"

"That's right. What do we say to them?"

"Fuuuuuuuck youuuuuu!"

He'd worked the crowd into near apoplectic enthusiasm now, and Axel detected in it what could only be called mass hatred. That's all anyone really wanted at South Orange, all that in their zeal to be good they asked for in return: to hate collectively. Axel held his hands to his ears and closed his eyes, trying not to hear the streaming words and phrases of that hatred in his mind.

The senior class president was now at the podium addressing the assembly. He outlined in detail the preparations for an upcoming Spirit Day, where various compulsory patriotic activities would be combined with D.A.R.E. seminars led by Officer Palin and experimental gymnastic tests designed to establish the physical coordination IQ of every student in the school. People nearby were giggling at the way Axel stuck out his elbows as he pressed his hands to his ears and clamped his eyes shut. The world was roaring. He felt prickles and spikes in his stomach, his lungs, his throat, the bones in his ears. Everything jumped in an intensifying frenzy.

He opened his eyes and looked up into the rafters to see a breach in the roof. A mass of monstrously misshapen figures funneled down into the crowd. Here and there shining white angels were blowing trumpets or battling the monsters with swords. He saw bloated birds with gills and fins, a frog with wings, floating pigs' heads, butterfly snakes, stink beetle girls, ferrets with arms. One of the angels sliced open the gut of a lizard-dog, and maggots swarmed up out of the wound to sprout the opalescent wings of dragonflies. As Axel looked more closely, he noticed the angels begin to form, with their bodies, white letters in the midst of all the hubbub, *Y*'s and *W*'s and *H*'s and *E*'s mostly. In fact, there were letters and parts of words everywhere, tattooed on the scales of snakes with bull's heads, branded into hides of griffins, disgorged from the mouths of balrogs, chaining like double helices around the tails of dragons.

People were swirling off the bleachers around him. Dimly he understood that the pep rally had ended, even though everyone was inexplicably still screaming. Axel stood up and followed the crowd onto the gym floor. Coagulation by the doors caused milling to occur. Axel was surrounded by leathery arms, scaly feet, entrails vomited from fish mouths. A tall skeleton with blank eye sockets came before him.

"Do you have any calamine lotion?" asked the skeleton over the din.

"What?" said Axel.

"Calamine lotion."

"No, I don't."

The skeleton clattered and clanked as if encumbered by invisible armor. "I have to get me some lotion," it said. "I have to."

"But you don't have any skin," observed Axel.

"That doesn't matter," it said. "I've got an itch I can't scratch."

More lanky skeletons appeared herding people toward the doors with long scythes. Several of them dragged a net in which numerous pesky freshmen had become entangled. They writhed and wailed helplessly. In the distance, high up on the farthest tiers of the bleachers, Axel saw student corpses hung by the neck from the rafters. There were skulls everywhere. A skeleton in a white toga unsheathed a sword and swooped suddenly down upon him. He took out his truncheon and with a mighty swing smashed it to smithereens.

Once outside he discovered that the world had changed. The parking lot stretched a barren achromatic desert to the broad central courtyard of the school, where trees and bushes had fallen blighted across the walkways. Fires sent black smoke curling toward a dun-colored sky. On the roof of the main building skeletons held students by their feet and dangled them over the side. Others were engaged in executions. He saw a sword slash across the horizon in the instant of teacher decapitation and knives slit the throats of hall monitors. Varsity football players were being drawn and quartered. Their shrieks and moans clotted the air. Sound knit itself into no rhythm but that of shivaree.

Pedro Freyre was standing next to Principal Castranova by the flagpole. They both followed Axel through the crowd with their eyes. Pedro leaned toward the principal and whispered. Axel knew he was the subject of their exchange. They watched him lope by and issue into the courtyard, where he paused to ponder the safest route to his trigonometry class.

The hallways were packed. People disintegrated around him into currents of hair, lip, eye, scale, blood corpuscle. It might have been hell. But Axel knew better. It was still the earth, *Urrrrth*, with its sheer towers and mazey boulevards, its overlapping systems of transport, passage, bridge, berm, skyway—the ductile utterances of industry in their schoolyard phase, vowels of resistance fusing with consonants of conformity, strings of disciplinary phonemes, strokes of letters mashed together into no meaning at all.

As he fished a math book from his locker, he again glimpsed Pedro with Principal Castranova by the newel post of a stairway down the hall. This time they were pretending not to notice him. He thought, what a waste of time to spend it dodging the obsessions of teachers and principals, while all around them Fall and Creation merged! It was dispiriting. People missed too much. They lived too much in the obvious, shoring up its rules and revenging the slightest infraction of its common sense. He wondered how far they would go in their quest for unanimity. Perhaps as far as it took. The thought gave him pause. He'd better watch it. The risks were high. He had to walk a fine line. Never irrational, he had to confound them with their secret insanity. Without giving them any power, he had to embody that high tonality of soul in which the shared nightmare of the moment resounded. Truth was dispossession, he reminded himself, and insight always alien.

But it was hard work to be a voice crying in the wilderness, and sometimes Axel wanted a reprieve from the responsibility. He worried that he was too alone in all this revelation. He skulked down the hall to where it tee'd and halted before a bottleneck, on the verge of apostasy.

At that moment a hush ran through the crowd, and where the clog was acutest people relaxed, ceased to jockey, and stepped back in unison before the marvelous Sasha Dobrovolsky. Dressed as usual all in white and with that chalky complexion making him look like the ghost of a lord from Versailles, he didn't walk so much as glide into their midst, gazing before him with an expression of mad euphoria. It was an impressive performance, Axel had to say. He felt chastened by his example, John the Baptist to his Jesus, and also moved to new resolve. He took Sasha as a reminder that in this shared nightmare he was not alone after all. He was not without allies.

Sasha felt the same, it appeared, for passing by he shot Axel an unmistakably conspiratorial glance. He hesitated as if unsure of his own sixth sense before turning, with jerky motions reminiscent of a marionette doll, full upon him. Axel, transfixed, watched him pad forward in his satin slippers until the two of them stood face to face. After a long pause Sasha raised a slender powder-white hand to draw away his veil. Dimly Axel became aware that everyone in the hall was looking at them, waiting to see what would happen next. And what happened surprised him most of all. With the poise of a planet moving degree by degree along the path of its silent orbit, Sasha leaned in until their lips were almost touching and whispered "I love the horror of being virgin." Then, eyes fluttering to a close, he kissed him with all the sweetness of a first time.

13

The Book Burning

Blaise Acher was out of ideas. He'd tried to be a good dad, tried to guide his son toward responsible adulthood, tried to sympathize with his problems along the way. Nothing worked. Axel didn't want sympathy. He didn't want to be guided, especially in the ways of the Lord. He didn't want to break down the wall separating him from a true and upright relationship with His Father.

How could Blaise sympathize with that? If Axel were a normal teenager, prone to normal teenage angst, it might be easier. Blaise would understand if Axel wanted to go to the Rendezvous Ballroom, or wherever it was kids went these days for fun, on a Saturday night. He'd understand if he wanted a new car they couldn't afford, and they got into fights about it. He'd understand if Axel wanted to be in a rock band. Hell, he'd even understand wanting to get a Mohawk or dye his hair purple. He wouldn't like it, but he'd understand it. But Axel wasn't interested in any of the usual temptations Blaise remembered from his youth. He fell outside of that essentially social dimension in which rebellion had always happened for him, that magic Ring of Fire in which we put off falsehood and spoke truthfully to our neighbors, our camaradoes in Christ, members one of another, one body and one faith. Axel wasn't a rebel any more than he was a straight shooter who placed his trust in Jesus. He wasn't much of anything except a loner, and God said it wasn't good to be alone. It wasn't good to hide from Him. The number one rule of grace was that the stranger make himself at home. Something had to be done.

Through the telephone at Blaise's ear came a muzak rendition of *I Will Survive*, and even his annoyance at this gross bastardization of a great song he wanted to blame on his son. He knew that was unfair.

It may even have betrayed a little perversity on his part. But Axel annoyed him in the same way, with the same blend of exasperation and grievance. It was as if the difference in time, style, and risk between rock-n-roll and elevator music was somehow his son's fault.

But behind these scattered thoughts Blaise shared a deeper anxiety with his wife Maude, who stood at his side trying to listen in on the line even though he was on hold. Yesterday on her way to the local Albertson's she saw Axel, walking home from school, engaged in an animated conversation with himself, just like a street person who'd lost his marbles. That shook her up, and afterward she and Blaise openly considered the possibility that their son needed professional help. Not knowing what else to do, they decided to consult Pastor Arkwright, their authority in all matters spiritual and not a few of the mundane variety as well. One morning a week he hosted a live phone-in advice show on Channel 518.

Blaise watched him on their television with another caller. He reflected with some timorousness on the ordeal it always was talking to the pastor directly. For the most part he talked to you, or at you, and you listened as respectfully as you could. Prone to fits of temper, gregarious as a hyena but just as fierce when need be, he was like one of those patriarchs in the Bible who lived into their hundreds and was difficult to approach even in his best moods.

When Blaise was a kid he knew the pastor personally. He and his dad were rivals for the hearts and minds of the Orange County populace and just wacky enough to like each other. They shared a stress in the gospels on the inescapability of sin. Jesus Christ may have said He was the way and the truth, fulfilling the law that it might become incarnate, but that didn't mean every Tom, Dick, and Harry in his tent of human flesh had to pretend he was perfect. It didn't even mean Christ's emissaries here on earth had to lead irreproachable lives. Nobody was perfect; everybody sinned. That was the point of *faith*, and the reason why it was all right to have a little fun on the road to righteousness.

Growing up in the heady atmosphere of pretty big-time evangelism, where the stake in souls was high, Blaise had great respect for the spiritual calling. His dad was a minister of the fire-and-brimstone variety, chasing Satan all across the Southwest with a Pentecostal charisma that had people moaning in the aisles. Blaise had some of that same charisma himself. But he never lived up to the Acher standard. He was torn between preaching and music, Jimmy Swaggart and Jerry Lee Lewis, idols both throughout his youth. What it took him too long to figure out was that he had to choose between them. There wasn't enough electron density in the metal of one body to conduct so much heat. He tried to combine the two worlds, sermons on Ezekiel with rock-in-roll. But the result was that he'd never really learned how to do either very well. It wasn't easy at the hoary age of thirty to realize that fidelity to two idols made for twice the mediocrity, but he weathered it, accepted his limitations and moved on to more responsible pursuits, a family, a job, a house, all acquitted with a basic good humor and soft touch he'd never managed to outgrow, even when it seemed he might be better off showing more gumption.

The word "Hello" came booming down the line.

"Pastor Arkwright," chirped Blaise.

"Who's this?"

"I'm so glad—"

"Hold on!" he barked. "We got a feedback problem. Go to another room. I can hear me on your television."

Blaise moved a little into the adjacent hallway, while Maude turned the volume down to a murmur.

"We were hoping for some counsel about our son, Pastor."

"What'd you say your name was?"

"Blaise Acher."

"Right, right, Acher's kid, I remember. You play a mean banjo."

"Thanks, sir," beamed Blaise. "Thanks."

"What can I do for you?"

"Like I said, it's about my son. He's behaving pretty strangely for a teenager—"

"There is no other way for a teenager to behave, Acher."

"Right. Only, well, our Axel's a little stranger than usual."

"How so?"

Blaise's wits unaccountably deserted him here, and he found himself at a loss for good examples. "Well, for one thing, he doesn't eat much, especially not cooked food."

"Why not?"

"He says we're trying to poison him."

"Oh."

"Getting him to sit down at the dinner table with the family can be like pulling teeth," Blaise said. "When he does eat, it tends to be raw or canned things, nuts and seeds, roughage, sprouts and hummus, things like that."

Blaise panicked at the thought that the pastor might not find all of this sufficiently unusual.

"He also reads too much," he added, "all the time in fact, and he starts believing he's like the characters in his books, and he starts acting it all out—"

"What do you mean?"

"He pretends he's a knight or an elf from medieval times. He even talks like one, with funny words no one uses anymore—like 'yeoman,' or 'herborowed.' Sometimes he fights dragons in the living room while we're trying to watch you on TV at night."

"Don't let him do that."

"Well, Pastor Arkwright, it's not as simple as that, since Axel has a mind of his own—"

"Get him out of what he thinks and wants," declared the pastor. Maude wrote that down on a yellow legal pad. "That's the first step. God pulverizes the ego so that he can resurrect the true self. The ego, Acher, is a power generator, a PA system for the soul. But it tries to take the place of God. A man without an ego is no man at all. But a man without God is a godless man, and a godless man is infidel scum."

Static on the line, as Blaise assumed there was more to come and waited for the pastor to continue. When he didn't, he blurted out: "Sometimes Axel won't answer to his own name. He claims to be somebody called Axalax. This will go on for hours, even whole days."

"Acher, you know the Arkwright Ministry is a top-down organization," the pastor gruffly reminded him. "What God's minister ordains is law, period. If some idiot tried to worm his way up onto my platform without asking permission, do you know what he'd be singing? Glory, that's what. I don't care if he's Joel Osteen or the pope, I'd rip his heart out and feed it to the lions. Do you get my drift here, Acher?"

"I'm not sure, sir."

"He who separates himself from his Father is nothing but an ungrateful son who causes shame and brings reproach. He's unworthy in the eyes of God. The word for 'worthy' in Greek is *anaxios.*

A-na-xi-os. It means to be fruitful, ripe, ready for the picking, a complete thing. He who does not ripen, does not grow into a complete thing. *You* have to make your son grow, Acher. Break his ego down as if you were tilling the soil and plant the seed of godliness until it blossoms in his soul. Teach him to be worthy."

Blaise was stirred by the pastor's words here, but not immediately clear how he was going to till Axel's soil or plant that seed. So instead of respond he fleshed out for the pastor the full gravity of the situation. "Things have gotten really bad in just the last day or two," he said. "My wife saw Axel talking to himself when there wasn't anybody around, just going on about something or other, but to himself. This kind of brought it all to a head."

"The bringer of pain is the angel of delight," said the pastor cryptically.

"What kind of pain did you have in mind, sir?"

He thought for a second. "You say he likes to read?"

"That's all he does, when he's home. His room's full of books. We can't even get into it unless we go through the window. It's practically a fire hazard."

"And when he reads these books, that's when he starts acting funny, like he's somebody else?"

"Yeah."

"Well, there's your answer, Acher," said the pastor. "Throw the books away."

"Throw them away, sir?"

"Right. If the eye offends thee, pluck it out."

That's how they left it. Blaise was heartened by the prospect of decisive action. Maude, more level-headed, worried about the consequences once Axel found out what they were going to do, but she was a woman much cowed and untutored in self-trust, so the confusion and shame of seeing her son talk to himself on a public street eventually outweighed her scruples. She was as desperate as Blaise to find a solution to their problem.

They had to be careful. It was going to be hard finagling the time they needed to carry out their operation. Fortunately, Fox came to their aid by inviting Axel to his house for a sleepover marathon of Monty Python episodes. After a small show of resistance that made Maude feel like a bluffing poker player, they let him go.

That afternoon they borrowed their friend Bernie's truck and began the laborious task of removing the books from Axel's shelves and piling them into boxes Blaise brought from the factory where he was a foreman. The two of them lingered long in his gloomy bedroom, so little visited by either, feeling sad at how far apart they'd grown from their son. The books were musty emblems of that separation. The titles seemed all so unrelated. Why was Axel interested in *Women's Bodies, Women's Wisdom*, for instance, or *Nigger and the Narcissus*, or *Combat in the Erogenous Zone*? Blasphemous books! They found themselves looking for clues to their son's psychology in the wildly disconnected subjects. But the books almost seemed chosen to prevent deciphering. *Doing Time on Planet Earth, The Golden Ass, Chicken Soup for the Teenage Soul, The Nibelungenlied, The Human Agenda: How to Be at Home in the Universe, Abuse Excuse, Redwall, Creating Union, Back to Eden, The Blind Watchmaker, Cain: a Mystery, Wake Up to Your Life, A Brief History of Everything, The Bohemians, Through a Speculum that Shines, The Furies, Horoscope for the New Millennium, Cosmos, Chaos and the World to Come, The Last of the Barons, Cum Gravity, The Knot in Time, Between Heaven and Earth, The Child Within Us Lives!* Neither Blaise nor Maude could recognize in these books the boy they had brought into this world, swaddled and cared for, encouraged when he shone with promise, held when others hurt his feelings. But, of course, Axel was never exactly that boy. He always seemed so much more adult, like the infant Jesus in those old paintings, before they figured out how to draw children—a tiny man with five o'clock shadow and the weary eyes of someone who'd seen it all, which was confusing because at the same time Axel hadn't seen much of anything and could still confound them with an almost perfect innocence about the world. Maybe they'd never really had a sense of who Axel was. Or, maybe, and this was the fear that gripped them now, there was no person who survived the haphazardness of these books, no essence of Axel whose consistency lay like a pearl of great price at their heart.

Yet neither knew how to hate the solitude the books recorded, not least because both in their own way knew more about solitude than they would care to admit, and more about the real chances for reconciliation and community in this life than was good for much of anybody. The Achers had had their fair share of the pain that came with being misfits. The price of faith for them had been high even in Orange County. Although the Arkwright Ministry was one of the largest around, mostly because of its shrewd exploitation of new media to gain converts across the country and around the world, it had a reputation for idiosyncrasy. This was due in large part to the pastor himself, who, apart from unconventional views on such topics as sin and resurrection, also gave occasional credence to phenomena like astral projection and UFO's. He was a confirmed eccentric, prone to playing his mandolin from the pulpit, hiring trained monkeys to perform circus tricks on his stage, and dragging out a sermon on one verse of the Bible for days. The Arkwright Ministry was as a result looked down upon by more settled denominations like Methodists, Mormons, and Church of Christer's. In a world of people who understood themselves as "chosen" or, more bluntly, misunderstood and ostracized amidst an enveloping perdition, the Achers felt doubly "chosen," and so freaks among freaks. They'd tried to put a brave face on the condescending snubs their aspirations for mainstream acceptance received from snobbier acquaintances, the not-so-subtle disregard for their feelings, the insulting associations made to New Apostolics, Vineyarders, and others on the neo-charismatic fringe. But a feeling of injury remained, just sharp enough to prick. They "kicked with the pricks," as Saint Paul famously put it, the way they lived with their assumed election in Heaven: humbly and without too much curiosity about what God might in the end have in store for them.

They filled the bed of Bernie's truck with the books and drove them to the dump in the Santa Ana Canyon, neither quite as certain of themselves as when they started. Blaise backed the truck up against a mountain of garbage and started to offload the boxes when he noticed an incinerator nearby. Since it was more than likely that Axel, on finding out, would want to salvage the books before they could be disposed of, and he could be very insistent when angry, Blaise decided on committing them to the fire instead.

"Are you sure?" asked Maude. "I mean, do we need to go that far?"

"What's the difference?!"

"It seems excessive, that's all."

"Courage, Maude, courage," he said as, slipping into the driver's seat, he repositioned the truck close to the incinerator. "Remember what Pastor Arkwright said about Joel Osteen and the pope."

Maude started handing the books to Blaise, and he threw them into the fiery maw. Now he saw why she hesitated: it was worse actually destroying the books. It made what they were doing meaner somehow. Maude grew more and more uneasy with each volume she handed over, lingering over particular titles as if to weigh their worth in the scales of sin.

"*Believe and Achieve*," she read. "That's a Christian book, Blaise. We shouldn't burn Christian books." She placed it to one side. "I'm going to start a pile for those that are okay to keep."

Blaise glowered.

"Oh and look at this!" she cried, holding up a *Davey and Goliath Picture Book*. "Axel learned the Bible with this. We have to keep it."

"We can't start making exceptions, Maude!" cried Blaise. "If we do, we'll end up carting the whole damn load home again!"

"Just some of them," she assured him. "We have to discriminate, that's all. We don't want to burn them just because they're books. What would God say about that?"

She scrutinized *Every Saint Has a Past, Every Sinner a Future* and decided it, too, should go on the saved pile. She opted against *Moses and Monotheism* after a quick perusal of its densely worded pages.

"What about this: *Direct Path: A Spiritual Audit of Corporate America?*" she asked.

"No!"

"Or this: *The Hypostasis of the Archons?*"

"Burn it!"

"But it looks like a Christian book, Blaise!"

He grabbed it from her hands and scanned the cover. "'Hypostasis!'" he read with a sneer. "I don't even know what that means!"

"It must be science fiction."

Blaise threw it into the fire. "Books like this are the reason we're in this mess to begin with, Maude," he said. "Axel's head is stuffed with this bull crap."

He had to be steely in his resolve here. He must not backslide. There'd been too much of that in his life. Discipline was a belief he held rather than a trait he demonstrated, and he hated that about himself. He could spend hours (years!) trying to figure out how Mississippi John Hurt laid down those bass lines on his guitar with only his thumb, but ten minutes of concentration on a tax form sent him reeling for the icebox and a beer. A lack of mental toughness had kept him from believing in himself, kept him from blowing his own trumpet when he should have and even asking for what he rightfully deserved. It made for a false humility too willing to pass itself off as honor. It wasn't honor, just an excuse for self-pity, a corruption of his fighting spirit, the worm in his unclean flesh. If he had truly stuck to his guns, who knew where he'd be today—pastoring, in all likelihood, running his own congregation, tirelessly trumpeting the good Word of the Lord! He needed opportunities to be decisive, to take stands, to be the example he's always wanted to be and admired in people like his dad or Pastor Arkwright. This was why Axel could be so frustrating: he made it impossible to take stands or to know where you stood around him. He left no way for authority to happen.

But that was why Blaise had to hold steady to the course. He was going to do the right thing for once, as a father, as a man. Axel needed him to be strong, needed him to be worthy in the eyes of God. If it had to be here before this incinerator that he drew his line in the sand, so be it. It was as good a place as any. He threw the books in with more gusto now, and each was like a resolution made, a new leaf turned in the sorry life of Blaise Acher.

"The...Dark...Night...of the Soul...and the...Cloud of Unknowing," read Maude perplexedly.

"Never heard of it!"

"It's by a saint."

"Maude!"

"All right, all right," she said, handing it to him.

It went on like this until they had reduced Axel's collection to a single box of books all related to wholesome Christian values. They returned to Orange as dusk settled in. The evening, together with the lightened load and their general weariness, purged and renovated their spirits. They felt hopeful that now they could begin to take charge of Axel's life, lead him away from the shadow where Maude saw him on the street that day. A moment of tenderness passed between them. Blaise and Maude had always been too sensitive for this world. This was what drew them together from the start: a finer attunement, a higher-strung sensibility similarly braced by the shocks of coarser life. It was hard to trust yourself when that was true, when your own weakness was so obvious to you. It made the need for God all the more beautiful, even if also more private, less avowable. But what was God after all if not the guardian of that inner sanctum where words could not reach, and experience, too subtle even to be itself, became this way a kind of prayer? Maude reached over to squeeze Blaise's hand where it gripped the gear stick between them. He flushed, smiling sideways at her. High up on a freeway viaduct and close to the shimmering sky, they felt as if they'd just caught a glimpse of Galilee.

Axel returned with Fox the next afternoon. They passed down the side yard to climb through Axel's window as usual, but they found it locked. Strange gauzy white curtains immediately alerted Axel to the new dispensation at the Acher ranch. They went around to find Blaise and Maude seated with Leonora in the living room, watching Pastor Arkwright's evening sermon, which he punctuated with stern exhortations to send in this month's tithe. He was in the midst of a fund drive.

"Who's been in my room?" were Axel's first words.

"I was," said his father. He glanced guiltily at Maude. "We were."

"Nobody is allowed in my room without my permission."

"You're going to find things have changed around here—"

Axel dashed into his room. A second later a moan, a howl, filled the house. His parents followed him out of the living room, and Fox was alone with Leonora. She informed him what had happened.

"They took all the bookshelves out, stripped away the skulls from the ceiling, and even painted the walls," she said, with her bone white hands laid palms down on the sofa by either side. She wore the same black dress with the blood red rose on the yoke, and she peered at Fox through horn-rimmed glasses that shrank her eyes. "It's a clean room now, airy, bright during the daytime. Neat and tidy. Like a room in a show house."

Axel's screams continued over his parents' attempts to settle him down. "Where are they?" he shrieked.

"We threw them away."

Fox followed Leonora's gaze to the omnipresent television. Pastor Arkwright spoke with leaden cadence into a camera trained in closeup on his fish-like face. The impression was of a man calmly giving voice to the babble, the echolalia, of his innermost thoughts, on the assumption that what bubbled up in so haphazard a fashion would be interesting and useful to his auditors.

"Where are they?" Axel demanded a second time.

"Nowhere," said a distressed Maude. "I mean—"

"We burned them," said Blaise.

Pastor Arkwright was smoking a fat cigar. The lit tip glowed so luridly that it left a contrail of pink light across the screen whenever he took a drag. The whole room around him, to judge by what Fox saw of it on the screen, was filled with smoke. Long pauses studded his speeches, and no attempt was made to fill them with anything except a phone number that flashed from time to time across the bottom. Fox could see pockmarks on the pastor's cheeks as if he were inches away.

"You burned my whole collection?!"

"It's for your own good, son," said Blaise. "Those books were getting—"

"Demons!" yelled Axel. "Serpents! Censors! Inquisitors! You murdered the Word!"

"Now hold on—" said Blaise.

"The Word of eternal life!"

"We think you're too wrapped—"

"The sincere milk of the Word!"

"—up in your own head—"

"Killers!"

"The Lord says you're not supposed to worship false idols—"

"Maniacs!"

Fox listened to the television. "This ministry will conquer the world in the Last Days," said Pastor Arkwright, "but only with your commitment. Make a vow. Right now. Channel 27 in the valley, Channel 518 in the harbor cities, the big Christlife Transmitter up on Old Saddleback. We're riding the airwaves. Soon my voice will carry all the way from Iceland to Antarctica. Pick up that telephone. . ."

Music started and it cut to the aerial view of the red and white radio tower. The shadow of the helicopter rippled on trees, a tin shed, and a cyclone fence.

"We think it's important for you to be more. . ." Blaise couldn't think of the word he wanted.

"Outer directed," suggested Maude.

"And I don't mean out in that ditch either. It's high time you learned to socialize with other kids."

"Fox is another kid."

"I mean *lots* of other kids."

"Why?"

"Why not?!" said Blaise. "What's wrong with a little fun?"

"I have fun!"

"I mean good, clean fun."

Pastor Arkwright appeared on the screen again. "There are people all over the world who commune with the Holy Ghost by listening to my telecasts, did you know that?" he said. "People rely on *your* participation to get the Word out, and what are you doing? Waffling, that's what. Sitting on your hands. Our worldwide mission of Messiahship is to take the Gospel to everyone through cable, over satellite, on the internet. That's our calling, our destiny. But it takes *sacrifice*. So all of you, put down that beer, shake out the crumbs from your shirts, and get off your duffs. Pick up that telephone! Make good on the debt you owe to God. . ."

Fox looked around the room and understood something of the loneliness of Axel's family. It came through in the little details, the Bible with gold leaf lettering on its leather cover and blood-red page edges, the bouquet of plastic flowers, the quilt tacked to the wall with the commandment "Trust and Obey" embroidered in it, Leonora spacing out to Pastor Arkwright's droning voice, which had no warmth except that of anger and intimidation.

"Get out of the flesh and into the spirit," he exhorted. "If you don't you'll end up like that skinflint Philip. Remember him? Jesus asked him how they were going to buy bread for five thousand people, and Philip counted his two hundred pennies. He didn't believe Christ could do a miracle. Why didn't Christ just show him the error of his ways? Because you don't count pennies, that's why. He set Philip up to see if he wouldn't fall back into his miserly old human nature, and he did! He was trapped in his natural perspective."

Something was screwy about Pastor Arkwright's logic here, but Fox couldn't quite put his finger on what. He wanted to leave now, to escape the strange gravity of this other Christian world, about which he knew only that it rested on darkness.

"What sign are you?" asked Leonora out of the blue.

"Sign?" he said. "Oh, Virgo I think."

Leonora nodded sagely. "Modest and shy," she said. "But you tend to worry a lot. Five planets are converging in your fifth sector now. That's the sector for romance and love. It's ruled by the sun, giver of strength and life. Are you in love?"

He gave himself over to fresh wonder at Leonora. "How did you know that?"

"It's in the stars," she said with a shrug.

In the next room they heard Blaise complaining to Maude about Axel. "He's loony, loco, bugnuts. We've got a nut for a son, Maude."

"Don't talk about me as if I'm not here," cried Axel.

"You're not, really. You're never here, even when you're here. It's like Saint Paul said, speaking in tongues. You're always speaking in tongues. I never understand what the fffff—"

"Blaise!" gasped Mrs. Acher.

"—heck you're talking about," Blaise corrected himself.

"That doesn't mean I'm not making sense."

"Like hell it does," Blaise said. "You're the most confusing kid I've ever met. Nothing you do makes any sense. Do you do one thing a normal fifteen-year-old would do? One thing? No! When friends down at the box factory ask me about my son, what can I tell them? 'Well, Sid, he spends most of his time messing around in that riverbed with rats and coyotes, pretending he's in the Middle Ages. When I try and talk to him about normal things, like God or music or baseball, he looks at me like I'm crazy and spouts words I've never even heard of.'"

"That doesn't mean they're not words," said Axel.

"It's nonsense to me, that's all I know. That's why I burned the books." Blaise paused as another thought about his son took shape in his mind. "I know what your problem is. You think you're special. You think you're better than the rest of us. Isn't that right? Admit it! You should be down on your face praying if you think you're special, Axel Acher. Nobody's special! That's what Pastor Arkwright says. Get down on your knees."

"No."

"Get down on your knees!"

Alarmed, Fox sought refuge in the television, following the devious paths of Pastor Arkwright's pitch. "God tests people's faith by setting them up," he explained. "That's His way of setting up His flock. That's what I'm doing, too, setting up *my* flock. Because there's no bank account in eternity except for faith, and God wants you to have a nice tidy little discretionary income in Heaven. So do I. But to get that you've got to make a sacrifice here on earth. You've got to get out of your natural perspective. God has no obligation to help free you from your sloughs of despond, your miserable parsimonious prison houses of flesh. You've got to do it by casting out the demons in your heart. Come on, do it, right now. Cast out those demons. Make a vow. Believe in the miracle of Jesus."

The complete possession of the room that Pastor Arkwright seemed able to secure with only his voice unnerved Fox. To steady himself he moved over to a Barcalounger and put his hand on the headrest.

"Virgo's ruling planet is Mercury," said Leonora, who followed him. "Same as Gemini, which is Axel's sign. Mercury is the planet of youth and childhood. It's also the planet of quicksilver. It rules over communication, exchange of messages, signs and signals." She sighed. "Mercury's been retrograde for weeks now."

"What does that mean?"

"When a planet is retrograde, it looks like it's spinning backwards in the sky. When that happens, things fall apart. Information gets scrambled. Computers crash, you miss appointments, cars break down, checks get lost. Nobody connects." They both listened some more to the argument in the other room. "Don't sign any documents right now or you'll be sorry."

Why don't you spend time with us tonight?" entreated Maude. "It's Sunday."

"We'll do a service with Pastor Arkwright," said Blaise, "sit around the television and read the Bible together, like we used to. I miss those days."

"I hate those days," screamed Axel. "I hate Pastor Arkwright and I hate you, too."

"Axel!" said his mother.

Fox watched Pastor Arkwright's hand writing the words "flesh" and "spirit" side by side on a white board. Beneath the word "flesh" he then wrote "natural perspective."

"To pass up the chance to give an offering," he said, "is to rebel against God. Right there you have a choice: stay with the flesh or offer up the flesh to Christ." He wrote the word "Christ" under the word "spirit." "Do you understand? *Offer up the flesh to Christ.* Don't hold off from transacting with the Lord, because he's setting you up. Invest for a return of faith in Heaven—"

"Then you're not leaving," said Blaise. "We'll stay home tonight. Pastor Arkwright's on until nine."

"Aaaaaaagggghhhh!" cried Axel. A door banged loudly.

Silence.

"Make a vow," said Pastor Arkwright as he wrote the word "miracle" on the white board and circled it. "Right now. Feel the coursing abundance of life in Jesus our Lord and Savior. Believe in the miracle. Present your bodies as a living sacrifice, holy and acceptable to God, that is your spiritual worship."

The front doorbell rang.

"It's Axel," said Leonora.

Fox turned to the door and back around to see Blaise and Mrs. Acher emerging from the hallway. Blaise, peevish, stalked by hiking his pants up around his hips, and Mrs. Acher, impassive in her gray linen dress, glided behind him to the door.

Axel stood in the verge of light. His features were contorted into a masklike rage, his eyes blinded by livid tears. "I don't want to talk to you anymore!" he screamed. "I don't want to be your son. I don't want to be anybody's son. *I don't want to be human!*"

He lunged between his parents and grabbed Fox by the shirt, pulling him out the door. Then he let go and vanished into the night that had begun to fall by that point, leaving his friend to negotiate his parents, who stood there as if their son's words had turned them to stone.

"Excuse me," he mumbled, slicing by.

Once outside, he paused to look back at Blaise and Maude in the doorway, gazing silently past him. Blaise's body appeared to sag, his shoulders to hump beneath the Hawaiian shirt he was wearing. In Mrs. Acher's cheeks Fox saw a color and perspiration that gave her the startled iridescent look of a large quail. They seemed so sad. He understood that it wasn't easy to stand where they stood in that strange Christian world. Blaise shifted his weight slightly in Maude's direction, and their shoulders touched. The gesture made Fox think of the defenselessness in people just before somebody hit them. They were both shrinking from a blow, or sustaining a series of blows, one right after the other coming at them like radio waves from Pastor Arkwright's Christlife Transmitter.

He was overcome by a desire to comfort them. "Don't worry," he said, and Maude smiled wanly, not really hearing him. His standard blush swelled into being on his face. "I'll make sure he's all right."

"Thanks, Fox," she said.

He took off after him.

14

The Garden of Muted Strings

Axel was inconsolable after that unfortunate episode. It broke his spirit as nothing had before in Fox's experience. He lost his bearings altogether in the world of other people, giving way to an angry forgetfulness. He walked in front of cars, went for days without food, and let his appearance go. A wispy goatee sprouted on his chin. The acne on his cheeks worsened. His fingernails grew long and yellow, caked with dirt. He seemed all but unreachable.

One day in the riverbed he resolved on an expedition through a storm drain. It stretched into a darkness so total it might have terminated in Hades. Fox objected on the grounds that they might encounter radioactive poison or rats, but Axel went anyway.

Fox passed into the fetid tunnel after him. Before long the light from the inlet phased out and the darkness became total. He felt disoriented not only in relation to the streets and neighborhoods above but in his senses. Only his hearing was sharpened. It became sonic and three-dimensional like the echolocation of bats. The scrape of Axel's shoes cascading along the segments of pipe made the space resonate.

Presently Axel's loping silhouette grew more distinct in the soft light that spilled into a manhole. By the time Fox arrived he had climbed to the top rung of a step iron to peek through a curb drain. A car peeled past. Two kids caught sight of his face behind the protective grille. They bent down and peered in at him.

"Have you been imprisoned?" one of them asked.

"Like Gyges the giant Hecatoncheires," replied Axel. "The head you see is but one of fifty, and my arms are legion. We have suffered here for an eternity."

He descended again and disappeared into another pipe angling off toward an outlet a few hundred yards ahead. What Fox would have given to be up there with those kids.

"Let's turn back!" he called out, but Axel didn't listen.

Fox caught up with him at the outlet. His friend stood in the late afternoon sun with one arm akimbo and the other, extended, gripping his staff. He gazed down a rectilinear concrete channel with a grave expression on his face. He might have been wearing a gleaming breastplate and holding a javelin or a pike. He might have been a wizard or a king. Anything now but a teenager from Orange.

"Axalax arose from Tartarus," he murmured as Fox came to his side, "and when his eyes were opened, he saw no man. . ."

As this didn't invite any particular response, Fox said, "I wonder if we shouldn't climb a fence and cut back on the streets."

"I'm going on."

"Why?"

"I haven't found him yet."

"Who?"

"Sift," he said, starting through the channel.

Fox struggled to keep up. The walls loomed high on either side. A couple of crows, loitering, took fright at their approach.

"Why do you want to find Sift?"

"He needs my help."

"What for?"

"He has to leave," Axel said. "He has to get out of this mess."

"How can you help with that?"

"I know where the last swan ship can be found."

"You do?"

"Yes."

"Where?"

"By the Sun's Corona, in the Palatinate of the Albatross."

Fox didn't like the sound of that. "I thought Sift was invisible."

"He's sight itself."

"Then you've already found him!" he dared with some trepidation. "He's. . .you."

Axel strode on.

"How are you going to find him?" Fox pressed.

"By looking."

"But how can you look if he's not there?"

"What is 'there'?" Axel demanded, banging his staff upon the concrete in contrapuntal rhythm with his scissoring legs. "Or 'here,' or 'this,' or 'that'? Abstractions, Fox. Like everything else we sense. This world is a fucking delirium. It's time we came to."

"I don't understand what you're talking about, Axel."

They arrived at a tapered prow of concrete: new walls curving in long aerodynamic sweeps that split the channel in two. Axel went right. Up on the cyclone fence that edged the wall Fox saw a "No Trespassing" sign. A mouse skittered along a telephone wire. Two dragonflies were mating in midair.

"Why that way?" he called out.

"It's the way *he* went," said Axel over his shoulder.

"Are you sure?"

"Yes."

Fox wasn't. All he knew was that where Axel wanted to go he didn't know if he could follow. They were in alien territory by then, maybe El Modena, or Tustin.

After a while the sheer walls gave way to slanted embankments. They scrambled up to a sort of tow path. At one point Axel bent down to scrutinize a possible foot print, lifting his nose and sniffing the air as if he were a scout.

"This track was made within the hour," he said. "Sift is close by, I feel it."

They continued on until the channel ended at a dam. A low culvert slit the curvilinear humps of a spillway. They clambered onto a flattened and notched weir overlooking a sunken circular basin. A tall metal tower stood at its center, crisscrossed by rebar grille-work and surrounded by a few old branches and palm fronds. As enigmatic as a dream sculpture, it turned out on closer inspection to be a barricaded drain.

"Sift!" Axel shouted. "Come out! You don't have to be afraid! We're friends!"

A bird's call, like a bouncing ping pong ball, was the only answer more distinct than the background hum of suburbia.

"I think we should turn back," Fox said.

"No."

"But I want to."

"Then I'll keep my oath alone."

Abruptly he whipped around as if in surprise at someone's unlooked for approach.

"What is it?" Fox asked with alarm.

Axel bounded away, glancing wildly around him. "Sift! Sifffft!!" He took off wobbling down a tributary streambed lined in groined stone.

"Come back!" Fox cried hopelessly.

One more time he set off in pursuit. The stream rose into a canyon that cut up through folds of wild and undeveloped terrain rimmed by cantilevered homes. Axel followed its course until the scrub brush and poison oak thickened into impassable barriers. There the stream split off down another spur, taking the riprap with it. Water trickled into standing pools from the higher slopes, where some natural spring bubbled up beyond hope or credit in Orange County. Axel proceeded along the other streambed into a wash that sliced back into mazes of tract houses and cul-de-sacs. The wash issued into a drainage tunnel, as wide as a two-lane underpass. Graffiti covered every inch of cement, and numerous bottles of Rio Claro beer littered the ground.

"Sifffft!!"

His voice damped into silence. He dashed off. Out the far side of the tunnel he entered another rectilinear concrete channel, its sheer slumpstone walls draped with blooms of passion flower, trumpet vine, and bougainvillea. Fox guessed that this channel was the one they hadn't taken at the first fork and that soon they'd be circling back to where they began. He was exhausted, sucking air. To pace himself he focused on his feet pounding the cement alongside the grooved central channel, more damp than wet. He passed under a balustered bridge, and when he emerged into the light on the other side, beads of sweat stinging his eyes forced him to stop. He closed them tight and saw behind his lids the flash of phosphene. When he opened them again, Axel was gone. He wiped his face on his T-shirt sleeve, shocked by the sudden desertion.

"Axel!!!"

In a panic he sprinted off, only to halt a moment later before a gap he hadn't seen in the wall: yet another tangent channel. Axel was already way down the diagonal cut, still running. Fox forced himself past the thresholds of fatigue into a second wind. The effort made him lightheaded. His eyes skimmed along the blurred walls, and their seams, stains, scratches, and spray paint tags were like petroglyphs. He might have been running into prehistory.

He pulled even with Axel where the channel segued into riprap holding the surface soil around an outlet. They were back at the riverbed, a considerable distance upstream. They gazed upon a wash of hardened silt shot through with polygonal cracks. On the opposite bank stood the carcass of a blighted elm tree. Fences hemmed the place in as if it had been quarantined. Even Axel wasn't insensible to its desolation. Fox thought he caught a look of self-doubt in his friend's roving eyes.

"Nothing here," he observed.

Axel pointed down the riverbed toward a dense thicket of bamboo. "He went through there."

"What if he didn't?" Fox said. "I mean, what if he isn't supposed to be found? What if he doesn't *want* to be found? Maybe he's just . . .a legend. A story."

"But not less real, Fox. He's the only reality." As if he'd just figured it out for the first time, he added: "Material, but other."

He set off across the wash. The thicket was even larger than it seemed, stretching a good hundred yards down the channel it filled. But several paths cut through it. On one Axel didn't take Fox thought he glimpsed a figure slink across. The impression was so fleeting he concluded that he must be imagining it. But then, trailing after his friend, he heard the nearby crack of a bamboo stalk, just purposeful enough to set his heart racing. There was a loud report, and something whizzed through the lanceolate leaves. That was no figment. They were not alone in the thicket. At that point a teenager appeared up ahead. He was dressed in army fatigues, a helmet painted in camouflage, and black goggles. He drew the bolt of what appeared to be a semiautomatic rifle and aimed it straight at them, screaming: "Drop! Drop! Get out of the way!"

Fox fell to the ground just as the teenager fired his rifle. But Axel, fascinated by this strange apparition, ignored the projectile whistling past his shoulder. The teenager withdrew again into hiding.

"Checkpoint Chastity's hot! Checkpoint Chastity's hot!" rang out through the bamboo. "Odland, cover me."

"Roger."

A second armed teenager slid noiselessly across the path behind them.

They had stumbled into a paintball game. Running out of it again, they found themselves moments later at a clearing caught in a crossfire. More camouflaged players, crouched in various positions, shot at each other or up at enemies on the banks. Axel was hit, and skeins of red paint formed a lacey *W* over the breast pocket of his suede jacket. Fox feared the arousal of his anger at this desecration, but Axel rather liked the addition it made to the jacket's cluttered designs. He dragged a finger through the red paint and held it up to the light. The skirmish raged on around him.

Fox managed to pull his friend into the shelter of the bamboo, and from there they tried to return the way they had come. But the enemy was staging a flanking maneuver, and once again they found themselves in the line of fire. Fox took a hit on his shoulder. The impact was forceful enough to raise a welt on the skin beneath his shirt. Trapped, he lifted a rotting piece of plywood free from its network of bindweed and propped it up to form a shield. But when he leaned in against it, he discovered its underbelly aswarm with termites feeding on the cellulose and recoiled in disgust.

They had no choice but to bushwhack it through the bamboo to the other end of the thicket. It was alive with whizzing paintballs now. Through an opening they saw on the bank a row of snipers busy strafing the whole riverbed. As they were pinned down, Fox's inclination was to lay low and wait until the battle ended. But Axel's patience had run out.

He stepped resolutely into the open.

"What are you doing?!" asked Fox.

"I'm going to smite them such a stroke that all of heaven shall look down and weep!"

"Axel, no."

He went back to the first clearing where he'd been shot.

"Hullahullahulla!" he cried, charging into the fray.

He jabbed his staff sharply at one player hunkered down in his dugout.

"Now is your death day come!"

Everything went matte behind Fox's eyes. He lost the thread of events, and the world unraveled. He really didn't know where he was, in a game or in a war, in Orange or in a dream.

Axel served as a lightning rod for the combatants, concentrating their attention into a single bolt of electric reaction. They trained their guns on him and fired a fusillade of paintballs. Axel's body convulsed, struck repeatedly and all over. He crumpled to the ground.

"Stop!" Fox yelled, throwing himself over him. Cries of "Cease fire!" went up, but the more overzealous among them got a few more shots in before lowering their weapons. Fox gripped Axel tight, pressing his cheek against his shoulder. For all he knew his friend was dead.

"Don't mess with the U.S., asshole!" cried someone on the bank.

"Gotta watch it, dude," said another nearer at hand. "We play for real."

"Can't be a terrorist and not expect payback," said a third. "In spades."

Axel held rock still, but Fox could tell by the way he'd curled himself tightly into a ball, pressing his lips together and squeezing his eyes shut, that he had survived the onslaught intact.

Timeout was called for a "paintcheck," and as the players came out of hiding to assess the severity of their wounds and argue about the scorecard, Axel recovered his wits enough to follow Fox out of the thicket. His clothes, especially his jacket, were smeared red all over. Even his herringbone cap had been splattered. He looked half way between a bullet-ridden corpse and a harlequin.

A scarcely less battle-scarred Fox felt pulled in many emotional directions at once, but it was anger that got the upper hand.

"It's not fair," he said coldly. "You just do what you want to do, when you want to do it, without thinking about the consequences."

Axel launched into another peroration. "How trifling the trysts of tiiiiii—"

"No!" Fox grabbed his friend's arm and looked straight into his eyes. "You could've gotten hurt. We could've gotten hurt. It was dangerous. Don't you see?" He wanted to sum everything up with just the right words. "You can't. . .act on your fantasies like that."

"Why not?"

He pointed back toward the bamboo. "Because that's what *they're* doing."

That took Axel aback.

"You have to stay, I don't know, a. . .a. . ."—his eyes darted—". . .a *passerby*." He groaned. That wasn't the right word. In frustration he threw up his hands.

"Forget it," he said.

They walked on in the direction of more familiar precincts. Axel didn't speak for a while, staying inside himself, brooding, maybe on what Fox said, maybe not. He couldn't tell. He did seem a little chastened. Even when his interest in Sift revived and he started noticing clues, kneeling by signs, muttering to himself, it was with less abandon than before.

Miles and hours into that day they found themselves under the elevated Santa Ana Freeway, where they mounted a dirt incline to the crossbeam that supported the deck. Cars streaming by above them could not have been more than a few feet off. In the crossbeam they discovered an opening through which a copper pipe ran. It afforded space enough to crawl to the next segment of freeway and marked, of course, one of Sift's much-traveled elf-paths. Axel squeezed his lanky body through the gap, and with a sigh Fox did the same. They scrambled down another less precipitous glacis and set off through the dark underpass.

Where the Santa Ana met the Garden Grove and Orange Freeways they entered a futuristic landscape of viaducts and spurs that canopied tidy stretches of empty space. Slanted sunbeams cut prisms of shadow around massive piers, irradiating a wedge of shed tire here or the delicate awns and florets of a lonely brome grass there. Colonnades receded into moody gloom, and soaring ramps dissolved in weightlessness. Wherever they went a constant reverberation of traffic attended them, sonic waves surging back from buttress or arch to form their troubled noise fields. Now and then they caught the melisma of a truck's hydraulic brakes or the efflorescent moan of an ambulance siren.

It was all weirdly tensile. The gloom made the concrete surfaces bruise or stand out like goosebumps, so hard and so livid they hurt. The bifurcating spans overhead seemed to hold their involucred shapes with the poise of dancers, and huge skew slabs trembled under their variable loads.

They came at length into the open median spaces of the interchange, surrounded by cars winding along ramps and skyways. Terrain had been shaped around drainage swales and gravel trenches. Flowering ice plant stabilized topsoil, yellow sourgrass grew up in the netting of erosion mats, and azalea hedges formed bulwarks against roadside shoulders. They passed two hoary oak trees hung with bearded moss in the center of a cloverleaf, their root zones protected from fill by a brick well. They harked back to a different time, to the days of the Yorba and Peralta cattle ranchers when this was just an alluvial fan at the confluence of the Santiago and the Santa Ana, whose banks they were then hard by.

That alluvial fan seemed yet easier to imagine when they saw a snowy egret foraging in the ivy ground cover. It was doing what its forbears had done there for who knew how many thousands of years. The only humans they would have known were the native people whose land this had once been.

They disturbed the egret's concentration, and with awkward fan-fare it spread its loping wings, bent its neck into an S, and flapped into the moody late afternoon air. Fox watched it tuck in its talons and fly off over the berm of an on-ramp. The sight was almost splendid enough to silence the traffic sounds.

Axel meanwhile had picked up Sift's scent along a paved runoff channel and tracked it through a culvert in the berm. Fox followed after, emerging on the other side to spy the egret once more, heading for some remnant of a wetland on the Santa Ana in all likelihood. Axel clambered up a grassy slope dotted with tiny colored flags. Recently planted saplings drooped in the straightjackets that had been rigged to support them. It was the embankment of a freeway, Fox couldn't be sure even which one he was so turned around, and it stretched straight toward another hazy overpass in the distance.

Heady in his weariness and anxious now about the lateness of the hour, he lingered on in that ancient silence still exhaling from the egret's flight. It took him the time to gain the crest of the embankment to understand that the hallucination was *too* intense. He still couldn't hear the traffic whizzing by below him. Either he was too deep inside his own interior song for rescue or that freeway corridor really was awash in a mellifluous ambient hum.

He met Axel surveying the freeway by a fence that bordered the back yards of houses. The sky, streaked with high cirrus clouds, took on a pearl luster in anticipation of evening. Axel had in his eyes that same grave expression as hours before, lost in thought and far away from him. But it didn't surprise Fox when, a moment later, he said in a normal voice:

"Do you hear that?"

"There's no traffic noise."

They gazed down the embankment at the freeway in mutual wonder. The cars were right there, but all they could hear was that ambient hum.

"Like wind in a conch shell," Fox offered.

"Or waves."

"The sea."

"The music of the spheres," Axel said in awestruck tones.

They ended up near the shoulder inspecting a parabolic dish that had been erected on a metal stand. It was the source of the sound. The dish was pointed at the freeway and equipped at its centerpoint with a microphone. Speakers built into the stand faced in opposite directions and emitted a peculiar drone. When Axel walked in front of it, the drone fluctuated. He put his face to the dish and said, "Alas, poor Yorick!" His voice, smeared to the merest intonations, spread through the air around them.

Apparently the dish morphed the freeway sounds and projected a beam of tuned resonance up the slope. The higher one went the more distortion the resonance caused, masking traffic noise for those who lived in the adjacent neighborhoods.

Fox took a turn in front of the dish. He couldn't think of anything clever to say, so he just declared, "My name is Fox." He heard his voice reduced at once to mere variations of frequency in a clear overtone series. It had no more complexity than that. He was, as it were, voided out, but also, shifting the emphasis slightly, he was the void his voice made so eerie and strange. He had merged with this place that was no place, where life was spent in tense disavowals of flood and flux and all coordinates ("this," "that," "here," "there") had indeed become delirious. Was this what Axel meant by that "material, but other" reality he sought in Sift's inimitable wake? Were they experiencing synchronicity with a hidden world, the holographic Hexis? Or, Fox thought with a shudder, was it another of Mimema's nightmares? Were they in Illyria, or the Aerial Void?

More parabolic dishes lined the freeway at regular intervals. They worked to perfection. The resonance wavered but never let up the whole way along the crest. At last they sat down and just watched the silent cars go by. The sky with its streaked clouds, catching the light of the westering sun, had condensed plasma-like into a stretched auroral skein, and the metamorphosis seemed complete. Wherever they were, it wasn't Orange anymore.

15

The Happening

Axel sat in the back seat of his uncle Gary's car as they drove into the Santiago Canyon for a weekend happening at the Arkwright retreat. Blaise sat in the front passenger seat gossiping with his brother about events at the box factory where they both worked. Beside Axel lay the components of Blaise's PA system and various musical instruments.

A woman on the radio was exhorting listeners to support the Christian station to which it was tuned. "Family Radio is the number one way to preach the values you and I share to your family," she said. "So the Family Radio family would like to ask you and your family to pledge your support to Family Radio."

The road, winding around the Santiago Creek, seemed to mimic the woman's speech. Both had a fatal quality to Axel, in that car against his will, snared in the designs of his parents, who hoped that weekend to cleanse their son in the pastor's pure baptismal waters. But those pure waters only raged down through the dry riverbed of Axel's mind like a Biblical flood. He felt as if they were all listing toward shipwreck.

"The Family Radio family welcomes your family into the family fold," the woman nattered on. "From one family to another family, the Family Radio family puts your family in touch with other families."

With sudden fierceness Axel burst out: "Family! Family! Family!"

Interrupted in their conversation, Blaise and his brother fell silent. As if in shame they avoided each other's eyes, afraid of just what this outburst implied about Axel's state of mind. But Blaise at least had sense enough to turn off the radio. The deeper into the canyon they went, the poorer the reception anyway.

The hills opened out around the reservoir behind the Santiago Dam, and in the distance they saw the double peak of Old Saddleback presiding over the watershed with a patriarchal grandeur. The road looped around the reservoir and continued departing from and returning to the tonic of the creek. Much of the time one wouldn't think their destination was that peak shifting from quarter to quarter in the car windows, sometimes in front of them and sometimes even at their rear. They might have been driving in circles, skirting the same aprons of sun-baked meadow, slicing through the same folded ravines with the same sycamore trees and the same pair of deer staring back at them as they went.

But gradually the hills closed around them, and they rose in elevation. The peak disappeared around a bend and came back into view closer and more massive, rising in ever higher ridges into the still vaster Santa Ana range. It ceased to be an immutable mountain seen from afar and became up close a shifting landscape of crumbling gorges and splintered ridges.

They turned at length into a lane overhung by dark laurel trees. It led them up into canyon country, past rocky slopes festooned with cactus and sagebrush, then through a forest of big cone spruce. They connected after a mile with another road that led up a firebreak to the crest of the mountain. Their ears were popping as they approached Old Saddleback's horn and cantle. A red and white steel radio tower loomed from the space between—Pastor Arkwright's Christlife Transmitter and the site of his retreat.

They pulled up to the electronic gate and punched their password into the keypad. It slid open for them, and they drove between rocky outcroppings down to a parking lot filled with cars and milling people. A huge banner greeted them with the homily: "As iron sharpens iron, men sharpen men!"

They'd come for a special "guys only" happening hosted by retired brigadier general "Holy" Jim Joplin, commanding officer of the local Christian Bondsmen chapter and regional coordinator for their new "Stand in the Gap" crusade. It seemed like just the ticket to Blaise and Maude when they heard about it, just the sort of male-bonding experience Axel needed to bring him out from his shadows. Maude preferred it over their other option anyway, a short-term outward bound program for troubled teens. It broke her heart to think of her Axel trekking in the Arizona wilderness with a bunch of juvenile delinquents. He didn't fit in that picture at all. When the pastor invited Blaise to be music impresario for the happening, it was decided, albeit over their son's objections, that both of them would go.

Blaise went into a large church with a flying roof to see about their accommodations. On the far end of an adjacent football field a group of men in identical yellow shirts, seated on portable bleachers, were chanting in unison: "I love Jesus, yes I do! I love Jesus, how 'bout you?" Axel drifted to a sort of promontory rimmed by railguards and looked out over the Santiago Canyon. It was too hazy to see much of anything.

The compound comprised, along with the church, two dormitories, a sound studio, a mess hall, and numerous campsites. The centerpiece was the radio tower, which stood on the hill above them, as impossible to ignore as the pastor's maniacal desire to extend his Gospel around the world. He was in fact sequestered in the sound studio even then, recording a live sermon for his listeners in Southeast Asia.

Blaise returned with three of the same yellow shirts, mandatory dress for the happening. "Stand in the Gap" was emblazoned across their fronts. After a futile show of resistance Axel had to take his suede jacket off and put one on. They carried their bags to a campsite under an alder tree next to the outhouse. Blaise's brother took charge of pitching their tents while Axel helped his father lug the musical equipment inside the church to the platform. Blaise devoted himself like an eager kid to setting up for that evening's festivities. He took out his vintage Fairbanks Whyte Laydie five-string banjo and lovingly placed it on its stand. He began at once to strategize with Pastor Arkwright's sound engineer, uncoiling electric cord and setting up speakers.

Meanwhile, a heavily muscled man name Zeke, with full-sleeve tattoos on both arms and a handlebar mustache, came into the hall looking for people to play touch football. He spied Axel loitering at the foot of the stage.

"Hey you!" he hailed. Everyone in Axel's general vicinity turned at once to see who might be calling them, but Axel stared off with the faraway eyes of a deaf person.

"I'm talking to *you!*" he said, striding forward. He stood right up close to Axel and stared him down. "Are you 'available'?"

"For what?" asked Axel.

Zeke, rolling his eyes as if the question was ridiculous, grabbed him by the arm and said, "Come on."

He herded Axel out to the field, where men of all ages and backgrounds were picking teams for the game.

"I don't want to play," protested Axel.

"You don't have a choice," replied Zeke. "You gotta tackle sin like a man!"

Axel found himself standing on one end of the field as the game began and a kicked football wobbled in his direction. He stepped aside to let the dangerous projectile go by, miffing his teammates when it dribbled into the end zone. One of them ran after it and set up first down on the twenty-yard line. In huddle, they concocted a play that involved Axel as a defender of the quarterback. He stood on the scrimmage line, but when the ball snapped he withdrew safely from the centers of contact. Zeke, on the opposing team, rushed up all the same and body slammed him to the ground. Axel lay there in a stupor. A teammate finally helped him up.

On the next play, the ball was handed off first to Axel and then to another man running in the opposite direction. Axel acquitted himself of this task competently and watched the action from the far side of the field. As he did so Zeke knocked him to the ground a second time.

It went on like this. Axel hung back, Zeke knocked him down. His stubbornness was never explained, his aggression never personal yet always aimed at him. It would take the rest of that day for Axel to make sense of the claim in these encounters with bodies and forces to remain solid, capable of hurt, unalloyed by absence. In accordance with one of the rituals that applied during the happening, Zeke had made himself Axel's "point man," which meant it was his responsibility to ensure that his ward stayed on the straight and narrow path toward Christian Bondsmanship.

Later Axel was forced with the other recruits to listen to Holy Jim on the subject of righteous manhood. The retired brigadier general wore a tall U.S. cavalry hat along with olive green fatigues and jack boots, and his voice rumbled up from his diaphragm like an earthquake. In a semicircle behind him stood his Bondsmen lieutenants, including Zeke, who fixed his glaring eyes on Axel through the whole speech.

"I love to see men gathered together," Holy Jim began with a deep, suffusing intake of breath, "standing there in the gap, forming a phalanx for the Lord. It warms my heart to see you all a battalion of Biblical Unity."

Axel stood among the ranks of listeners, distracted by the bracing bark of Zeke's voice inside his head: *Queer!* it said. *Pansy!* But when he looked at Zeke, his lips were shut so tight that the skin around his mouth turned pale.

"But if we want to be soldiers raring for the Lord's fight, there's a few things we gotta get straight," Holy Jim informed them. "First off, we gotta get it through our heads that each and every one of us gathered here on this mountaintop is in reality a dead man—deader than the old possum stinking up your grandma's basement." He lowered his eyes in the respect this homely simile seemed to require. "Yes indeed," he said, "man is dead in his rebel spirit, just in the same way that a son is dead who disobeys his Father."

Wimp!

"It's God who's alive—the Almighty, in whose glory we fall short," said Holy Jim. "And so that we may be born again, we have to become like God. A Son of God, reconciled with his Father. Do you want to be a Son of God?"

An excited murmur ran through the crowd. Axel felt its spontaneous and collective yearning, and for the first time that day he was truly afraid.

Pervert!

"To be a Son of God you have to understand the true nature of Christ. And I'm here to tell you that he wasn't a sissy. Hell no! Let me hear you say it!"

"Hell no!!!!"

"Christ was a man's man," said Holy Jim. "He defeated Satan in the desert, cast out demons, healed the sick, stilled the waves, chastised hypocrites. He was a fearless leader, stalwart and brave. To be like Jesus you have to be mighty. Can you be mighty?"

Pussy!

"Are you capable of leadership?"

Fag!

Holy Jim was hitting his stride now, and he began to pace back and forth before his gauntlet of Bondsmen. "I like men to be men," he said. "If a man's not a man, he's separated from Christ. If he's not a mighty leader, he's separated from Christ. If he's one of those gender blenders, he's plunged in Christless eternity! He needs to be reconciled. He needs to break down the wall separating him from his Father. That's what we're about with the "Stand in the Gap" crusade: breaking down the walls. Reconciliation with Godly manhood. That's why we've come together here: to wake up to the Christ inside us all, to receive Him as our Lord and Savior—"

"Amen to that!" broke in a phlegmatic old black man by Axel's side.

"Now I believe from the bottom of my heart that the best way to wake up Christ inside us is good old-fashioned military discipline," said Holy Jim. "Because it's not enough to be mighty and a leader. You have to learn submission, too. You have to learn how to take orders, to be part of a platoon. You have to learn how to give yourselves over to a higher law and sacrifice so that others can count on you when the proverbial shit hits the fan—pardon my French. When I think of God up there with His angels, I think of an army bivouacked on the great battlefields of paradise, singing in one voice 'Glory Glory Hallelujah.'" He nodded. "Yes, sir. We have to make ourselves fit soldiers for God's army. That's the only way we can do battle with the Prince of Darkness. . ."

After Holy Jim's pep talk, the sacred assembly broke into small encounter groups. Axel found himself sitting in a tight circle with seven other men plus Zeke, who was telling them about his experiences as a petty criminal in Calexico. He used to be the world's worst desert rat, he said, lying and cheating his way through life without a thought for anybody else. He'd stabbed his best hombre in the back, let his kids go hungry, and finally shot a man in cold blood while robbing a liquor store. But in prison he met his first Christian Bondsman, who told him about the true nature of Jesus while they spotted each other on the bench press. The Bondsmen taught him to receive Jesus into his heart and imitate him in all things. But that didn't mean he had to be perfect. No way, José.

He had to acknowledge his sin and put it off on the Cross. Because sin was a prerequisite for faith, he said, the first step toward righteousness was to admit his imperfections. He had to make himself "available" before God. That's what the encounter groups were for: to help other people become "available," too. With that in mind, Zeke began soliciting confessions of sin from the other men in the circle.

The first to speak was a middle-aged balding man with the startled look of Caspar the Ghost. "I'm a husband and a father," he said, "and I've sold automobile insurance for over twenty years. Never been out of the ordinary in anything all my life, but I. . .I tend to get jealous of my wife. I worry about what she does home alone during the day, or whether she thinks about other men. I torture myself imagining her with. . .other men. I take the littlest sign and make a whole world out of it. The worst thing is I know none of it is real, that it's all in my head. I just can't stop. It's gotten so bad we fight about it all the time. She says I smother her with my jealousy."

"It's all right, Homer," said Zeke. "You're 'available.' There isn't any escape route here. God requires manhood of all men."

An old man with a shock of white hair and tanned skin of a texture that made Axel think of cascading ash, raised his hand. "I've been married five times. I can't seem to stay faithful to one woman. I've got a wandering eye. I admit it: I've been something of a Don Juan."

"Get it out, Willie."

"I think I need to keep it in, Zeke," he said with a smile. "The truth is I'm a sex addict. I've slept with. . .why, it must be hundreds of women, one right after the other, and I've hurt a lot of people along the way."

A young man with severe acne took his turn. He was a compulsive masturbator. "I do it ten, twenty times a day. I can't stop, even though I know it's a sin."

"It separates you from God."

"I squander all my energy, all my precious life fluid, instead of going out there the natural way and finding a girl. I get so frustrated I could scream."

"Go ahead."

"Now?"

"Be 'available' to God all the way up there in Heaven!"

The young man screamed. The sound was piercing and impressive. He did it again, straining tears from ducts and falling to his knees inside the circle. He writhed in the exquisite torture of his shame. The others patted him on the back and told him it would be okay. Zeke reiterated how important it was to admit your sin as the first step to overcoming. Then he turned to Axel.

"What separates you from God?"

Jolted from a state of sidereal abstraction by the eyes that were turned on him, Axel couldn't think of anything to say. The rest of the men in the group awaited disclosure with an earnestness so keen he felt it drawing words from his mouth, but still none came.

"Don't hide from the Lord, son," said Homer with a kindly pat on his shoulder.

He jumped, resenting the small liberty. "Unhand me!"

"All he wants is your manhood."

"I'm not a man."

"Are you queer?" asked Zeke.

"No," said Axel.

"What are you then?"

Axel looked from face to face, seeing in them a desire to trap him in their self-fulfilling prophecies. But they couldn't fool him. There was no such thing as the sin they were sentimentalizing. Imperfection was just a way of returning to the same gross existence he had long since ceased to believe in or trust. It was all so boring—the same dull round, like spokes in a turning wheel. *I am I.* He couldn't bear it anymore. He stood up and cried: "Nothing! No one of you! I am Axalax, raised by orphans and wolves, and where I go none may follow!"

With that he pushed his chair out of the way and tried to break from the circle. But Zeke came around to catch him full on in a bear hug. Axel squirmed to no avail, and Zeke pulled him back in.

"Sit down."

He sat down. "Brethren as you be mine," he swore, "never shall I love you nor draw you to my fellowship."

"You're going to be 'available,' buddy."

But Zeke underestimated how mulish Axel could be when cornered. From that moment on he refused to speak another word, and he stuck to it through the end of the group session, through the compulsory steeple chase, through the volleyball game. They might have his body, but they would never get his mind.

Even Blaise couldn't make him speak, to his embarrassment when the pastor emerged from his sound studio for the barbecue. Short and slight, he looked so much less imposing in person. But he took your measure with a shrewdness that could unman the most confident spirit. Quick to judge, and intolerant of fools, he had about him the protean quality of a bull, placid enough until incensed, but when incensed beyond any earthly power to subdue.

Blaise greeted him with a smile that stopped just short of being servile. "How's the good fight coming, Pastor?"

"I just finished a simulcast to Malaysia," he informed him with a glance back at the Christlife Transmitter. "We're making disciples across all the nations."

"This here's my son, Axel."

The pastor fixed him in the steel trap of his gaze. Disconcerted, Axel turned away.

"Say hello to the pastor," urged Blaise.

His son responded by prodding a stone free from the dirt with his shoe.

"Axel!"

"It's okay, Acher. Does the clay talk back to the potter? Not on your life. It's in the nature of clay that it hold its form and keep its place. For God we are a bowl or a coffee pot, only the time for glazing is in eternity. I expect you brought your banjo?"

"Yes, sir!"

"Good!" The pastor moved off toward other members of the congregation, who were apprehensively awaiting their turn for an audience. Axel picked up the stone.

"What did you do that for?" complained Blaise. "He's going to think you don't respect your elders."

Axel threw it at a couple of cottonwood trees. The fact of this dogged silence was too much for his father. It reminded him of that frog in the cartoon, which only sang when no one was there—a wicked irony since the usual problem with Axel was getting him to shut up.

"Jesus H. Christ!" he exclaimed finally. "You're impossible."

After the barbecue, people assembled in the church to hear a special sermon by the pastor. Two video cameras, one situated on a tall tripod at the center of the hall and another at one wall, had been trained on a chair at the front of the podium. Before it stood a pedestal for an open Bible, and behind it a wheeled out white board. Microphones hung from various angles and a bright arc lamp bathed the chair in light. Two television screens had been set up on either side of the large cross at the back of the podium, where Blaise was plugging his banjo into an amplifier.

The hall was packed by the time the pastor appeared to sit in his chair. Lights were dimmed. A hush fell over the crowd. The pastor fidgeted to find the best position from which to peruse his Bible, whose gilt-edged pages he was flipping through. His face appeared in a tight closeup on both television screens.

"Since the Bondsmen are here, and I expect Holy Jim doesn't want to hold down the fort of Godly Messiahship alone, I thought I'd preach tonight on the subject of making bonds and keeping them." He cleared his throat and began to think aloud. "Now what is a bond? The dictionary says it's a 'binding tie between people.' It's an oath, a promise. It means agreeing to do a certain thing at a certain time. It says I won't change between what I do now and what I will do in the future. I'll be *faith*ful, full of faith. A promise stalls time, it makes time stand still. It simulates eternity. The miracle of Christ's rebirth is God's Promise to us and the promise we make to God, the foundation of belief. But it's also tithe-time"—here he addressed a technician—"so put the number on screen and let's get some callers. I want to see that switchboard light up. We got some live music for a change: Blaise Acher's here to play us some old standards."

Blaise stepped into the verge of light and nervously took a bow. He let his Whyte Laydie hang from its strap and bent his fingers a few times, limbering up. Then, on a one, two, and three, he started in with a spirited rendition of *Crow Black Chicken*. The cameras focused on the instrument and Blaise's dexterous fingers picking out the melody.

Axel sat next to his uncle near the massive tripod, lost in the ranks of heads and shoulders, not lost enough to avoid the entirely too forward looks of Zeke, who sat like an irritated guardian angel by the edge of the platform. Over and over again Axel heard his telegraphed voice say: *Wake up! Wake up!*

At length the pastor signaled Blaise to stop, and the sermon resumed. "I've been preaching about Bondsmen keeping their promises, pledging their bonds to the Almighty. It's just the same thing as holding up one end of a contract. It was the French philosopher Rousseau who said that the social contract is an agreement between people who feel the same way, on the same wavelength, who converge or come together at the same time. Do you understand what I'm talking about?"

Murmurs of assent from the crowd. He scratched his nose and pulled his chin in to assume a brooding pose. Way back down the canyon of Axel's mind he could hear a clamoring, tinny and out of tune, above pitch.

"At the heart of a promise is the idea of substitution, of 'one-for-the-other'—that is to say, equivalence, or *exchange*. I got ten chickens, you got one hog. That oughta just about be right. A pair of Pumas cost seventy dollars. I pay market rate for that Ford Bronco. Without exchange we'd still be living in mudhuts and believing God was a graven image or a blade of grass. The concept of worth, value, is rooted in *staying the same*, remaining true to your word, to the Word. It's eternity all over again, God's Promise of eternal life. And we need to testify to that Promise. What that means is we need to make testaments of worth to the congregation of the faithful. Because a contract needs other people. It needs membership. One of the biggest mistakes we fall into is that the exchange of money plays no part in the spiritual adventure. Nothing could be further from the truth. Money is the *soul* of every decent Christian. Money is the vehicle by which we make testaments of worth. Though rich, Christ became poor for our sake. That means He gave everything He had. Why is it we don't give everything we have? I'll tell you why. It's not money, it's *love of* money, that some have coveted after. Greed is the root of all evil, and it comes with pestilence. Pick up that telephone."

Blaise took the stage again, this time to play the tune *Home Sweet Home*. It was nothing but jarring noise to Axel. . .grapes of thorns, and figs of thistles. A few minutes later the pastor came back on.

"Do you know why man is greedy?" he resumed. "Do you know why it is that he doesn't make surety on his bonds? I'll tell you why.

He doesn't believe in the miracle of Christ, that He arose after He was crucified, and that He is coming again, and that when He does, we too shall be reborn and meet Him in the air, raised in a twinkling. It's Resurrection we testify to, Resurrection that fills us with faith, Resurrection that we promise one to another. We have to believe in Christ's rebirth. We have to pierce through the veils of time to find the eternity that lies behind. 'Bring ye all the tithes in the storehouse, and prove me that there may be meat in mine house, and prove me now herewith, and see if I don't pour out a blessing upon ye.'"

Axel felt Christ stirring in his breast. He wanted to overturn his chair, raise above his head the scourge of cords, and pour out the changers' money. He wanted to wreak havoc in the hall, storm the platform and denounce all Pharisees and false teachers. Resurrection had nothing to do with faith or promises! It had nothing to do with this long chain of will we forged link by link. Resurrection did not happen once upon a time, it would not happen at some time yet to come. It was always happening! It was a reeling of the self, a fractal in the heart opening an inner world through which we walked alone and without succor. *Danger,* he said to himself. *I'm in danger.* He looked longingly for the doors. It would take all his wits to get away unscathed.

The pastor had meanwhile gone on with his sermon, driving home the importance of his "collection for the saints." At one point he stood, forcing panicked adjustments on the part of his television crew, and went to the white board. He wrote down the words *ecclesia* (the "Called Out One's") and *kuriakon* (the "Lord's Church") by way of grounding his exhortations in the authority of Scripture. A camera zoomed in on his hand, throwing it up in duplicate above him. "Called out by the Caller to support what belongs to Him, your gift is an ecclesiastic article of faith. . ."

A row of knees stretched between Axel and the side aisle, but even if he could manage to get through there was still the problem of Zeke, lying in wait as if he expected Axel to try something funny. His uncle sat on his other side, but beyond him lay another barrier, the tripod. He had no choice but to wait the sermon out. The pastor continued to play on the etymologies of words, second guessing biblical translations, zeroing in on the unimpeachable rightness of his text. But he was not so much the egghead scholar that he forgot his audience altogether, and he wisely let Blaise's musical interludes stretch longer and longer. He even started one segment by asking Blaise how he did bluegrass turnarounds on his rendition of *Foggy Mountain*, and the sermon sidetracked into a music lesson. The pastor ordered the camera trained on Blaise's banjo as he demonstrated the technique.

"I saw Chet Atkins do that once," remarked the pastor.

"I learned it watching him on TV," said Blaise.

"The miracles of the Lord are many. If the high and lonesome bluegrass sound isn't enough for you to have faith, then you might as well hang up your spurs and pack it in."

This gave the pastor an idea. He stepped off the stage while Blaise went into a brief solo, picking out more and more complicated licks and rolls. The pastor came back with a mandolin. Blaise segued into *Orange Blossom Special*, repeating the first few bars until the pastor found the beat and started playing harmony. The camera framed the two of them in a full shot and the sermon became a concert. The church vibrated to the raggy, open-stringed banjo's staccato notes and the mandolin's mellow tremolos. The crowd relaxed, and many even stood up for a little footstomping. The solemnity of a minute before had vanished.

Axel took this opportunity to slip out. But as he shuffled along his row of men twitching to the music, there at the end stood Zeke daring him to break ranks with the fellowship. He headed in the other direction and squeezed past his uncle. Over his shoulder he glimpsed Zeke trailing up the aisle and around to the other side of the hall. He pressed on. But as he went he didn't see an electrical cord snaking between the two chairs he attempted to step over. He tripped and fell athwart the men in front of him, crashing into one of the tripod legs that held up the camera. It bent, the camera whipped backwards and toppled over. The image on the two television screens flitted away from Blaise and the pastor, swept across the roof, jerked through a sudden chaos of shoulders, arms, and knees to settle at point-blank range on Axel's face pressed cheek down on the floor.

The hall was thrown into confusion. Some tried to retrieve the camera, some to help those who'd also fallen, others just to get out of the way, but they all ended up stepping on each other's toes. The pastor roared his displeasure from the platform. Axel slunk away, hoping to elude notice long enough to reach his tent. He made it as far as an exit door before Zeke accosted him.

Half an hour later he found himself led like a truant child into a back office, where the pastor awaited him behind a desk. On the wall over his head were numerous framed photographs of him standing beside famous politicians, including Richard Nixon and Ronald Reagan. In each he was grinning as if at the punchline of the same broad and slightly off-color joke. Blaise leaned against a bookcase crammed with biblical reference books, and Zeke took up a position at the door. Axel sat in the hot seat right before the desk. The pastor, still trying to tame his wrath, was in the process of settling on an approach to the inquisition he had in store for him.

"Nobody's perfect," he said presently. "I know that. We make mistakes. I *preach* that. If anybody tried to tell me he was perfect, I'd send him straight to the nuthouse. Only Christ is perfect, and we only perfect ourselves through faith in His Miracle."

He hesitated, not quite sure the distinction he was drawing between the two kinds of perfection worked as he hoped it would.

"I hate people going on about the sins of others when they haven't cleaned the sticks they use to beat out rabbits from the brush," he said, stretching his theme. "We *are* sinful, period. End of story. We have to accept that as a fact and get on with it."

He drummed his fingers on the desk.

"Hell, once you do, it becomes your duty to enjoy the good things in life: meat and music, that's my motto! Satan doesn't want to see us make merry in God. That's why he sits in the corner and broods, the naysayer, the mockingbird, the grumbling guest who won't sing along."

He at last turned his attention full onto his silent interlocutor, who'd set his face in adamant.

"There can be no quarter given to old Timothy Tempter, or to any of his hirelings—to any and all who make themselves foreigners to the covenant of God's Promise, who set themselves apart from a family relationship with the Father. And from what I've been hearing, son, it doesn't sound like you're in much of a family relationship with the Father. Is that true?"

"Answer the pastor," ordered Blaise.

Axel took out a notepad and pen from his leg pocket, wrote "Divinity of Hell!" on it, and reaching across the room handed it to his father, whose face went white as a sheet as he read it. The pastor looked on with an expression somewhere between forbearance and dyspepsia.

"It's a funny thing about the sinner," he said. "He doesn't think he's sinning! That's what it means to be one of little faith. He holds to the idea that he *is* perfect, like the Prince of Tyre. He thought he was the mightiest of men until the king of kings came and laid his kingdom low. Or Enoch, the Maccabean heretic. He rode a chariot up to Heaven and argued with God, who rebuked him with strokes of fire." The pastor used the ensuing silence to let this lesson sink in. Then he said, "He who thinks he doesn't *need* God, plays at being God. He holds himself up as a paragon, dividing the nation. He doesn't think he has to close ranks with his brethren, or play by rules, or be a responsible member of the community."

The pastor rose from his seat and came out from behind the desk. He halted by an open Bible on a portable lectern and bent over it, idly scanning the page. "When Abraham departed from the ancient city of Ur and took the Israelites to Canaan," he said, squinting, "he went looking for the principle of one God. He called it 'Yahweh-alone.' What he discovered was right up there with the invention of the wheel: the simple truth of *identity*, of resemblance in what is, of universal self-similarity.'"

Holy shit holy shit holy shit, Axel thought, looking straight ahead at the photographs on the wall.

"Blaise, I'd like you to step outside for a minute," said the pastor. "I want to talk to your son man to man."

A lump formed in Blaise's throat at this request. He feared what would happen if he left them together. But he lacked the courage to cross the pastor, so he murmured, "Yes, sir," and left the room.

All at once Axel felt the pastor's iron grip on his shoulder. He pulled him roughly forward until he was splayed face down over the table. Axel struggled to get free, sweeping various papers and books to the floor.

"I'm going to need some help here."

Zeke sprang forward. He sat squarely on the table and pinned Axel there the way a wrestler might, knocking his cap off his head, which set him squirming all the more. Zeke lay his chest over his back and held his arms in with the strength of a vise-grip. The pastor pulled Axel's pants down around his knees.

"I wonder if you really know what it's like to be afraid, son," he said, with a nerveless composure. "Really afraid. So terrified your insides turn to liquid. Sometimes it seems to me that's what it takes to remind us why faith is important. We always remember what hurts." He started taking off his belt. "Crisis is what makes possible the glory of affirmation. Raw and arbitrary power, with no reasons and no excuses, demands our confidence in God."

He took the two ends of the belt in his hand to form with it a more effective strap, and struck Axel hard across the butt. He cried out in pain. "When I was a kid," the pastor went on, "my father used to beat me whenever people sitting on my pew fidgeted during a sermon. I told him, 'It's not my fault they fidgeted! I didn't fidget!' But he didn't care one bit. He beat me anyway."

He hit Axel a second time, and again he cried out.

"It took me a long time to understand why he did that," the pastor continued. "I remember when it finally dawned on me. I was in seminary, reading in the Bible about King Josiah. He discovered a sacred book, and in it were all the rules and regulations that the Hebrews had failed to follow. They were too busy worshiping golden calves and passing seed to pagan idols. Josiah called his people to the Temple, the least to the greatest, and he read to them the words of that sacred book. He renewed the Covenant in the presence of Yahweh and made all the people pledge themselves to the one, true God."

The bungler God, Axel thought. The pastor hit him again. *The bungler God!*

"In that pledge I saw for the first time what the bonds are that hold the Lord's church together. I heard the Call, and in it the Called Ones, a congregational brotherhood, a family in the service of its Father."

Hot tears streaked Axel's cheeks now. Sobs caught in his throat like hiccups. The pain radiated through his mortified flesh.

"I understood that it was in God's nature to be withdrawn," the pastor said, "remote and unfathomable, and that the deep paternal voice of His Law was only an echo across a void, a copy, a *text* to be repeated, blindly if necessary, by us sinners here in the lost world.

And I'm talking to you from one sinner to another, son. Believe me. I'm no saint. All I do is stand in for the Law. I'm a vehicle, like King Cyrus. I represent its deep mystery. And that's why I want to hear from you now. I want you to admit your imperfection like the rest of us. I want to hear His Law vibrating in your perversity. Make a pledge. I know you feel the calling—"

Thwack!

"Send a word, a *real* word of sincere repentance, to the fellowship of the faithful, sunk low in wretchedness. Feel what fear of God can do for you. It's like an old friend you haven't seen in years, reminding you you're not alone. It's what you feel when you really count on other people. It's what makes you *need* other people."

Thwack!

"Come out from your separation and accept your bond, your binding in the sacred book. For that you will regain the citizenship in Israel, that you have lost by your presumption, and the covenant of your brethren, that you have forfeited by your pride. . ."

Axel's mind roared with a thousand voices by this point, but for the life of him he could not sift through them to find the one that mattered now.

16

Anti-Earth

A light went on in Axel's brain after that. He knew with the clarity born of shock that he had to get out of this world in which, unconsenting, he had been born or it would confine him forever in the prison house of its dumb death-wishes. It would mire him in its sublunary muck. He had to escape before it was too late.

Blaise and Gary were asleep in their tents when late that night he donned his cap, put a sweater on under his suede jacket, took the money he found in his dad's wallet, and slipped away. The haze that hung over the mountain during the day had evaporated, and a gibbous moon cast a selenium glow over the compound. He cut across the football field to the promontory. The distant sea was spangled with light, and the glassy film of the reservoir hovered in its slip of earth below. A sulfurous Orange County pulsed like a sleeping giant over the crest of the El Modena grade. He worried it would wake up and one more time try to hurt him.

At his feet an escarpment descended to a broad meadow funneling into one of Old Saddleback's many canyons. It echoed with rasping insects and croaking frogs. He slid down to where the terrain leveled off enough to walk. The Christlife Transmitter, with its red winking light, loomed behind him.

Where the meadow creased to form a small gully, a spring bubbled off an underground rock shelf and wore a muddy channel through the dirt. He followed it across the broad meadow until it dipped into a forest of spruce trees. It was black as pitch in there, and more still than a crypt. A yammering of coyotes rang up the canyon. Bracing himself, he plunged into the forest.

The gully cut deeper and more steeply into the hillside, and the ranks of spruces grew dense up the slopes. Later he found himself scrambling over debris that had tumbled down from high cliffsides. He came to a mammoth boulder covered in a layer of lichen so soft it felt like fur to touch. He skirted its circumference to a ledge that afforded a view of splintered crags across a plummeting gulf. There was no question of following the creek into that. His only option was to mount a steep chaparral slope behind him and reach a ridge he could make out in silhouette against the sky. He went off at a diagonal through the heavy mat of brush, soon discovering trails made by deer and other wild animals.

After a hundred yards or so he seemed no closer to the ridge than when he began. The slope curved parabolically toward the three stars of Orion's belt, glimmering at the rim like, he fancied, figures in a dance of death. He lodged his foot in the angle afforded by a half-buried rock and grabbed an exposed manzanita root to rest. As he did so a swooping shadow frightened him. The rock collapsed beneath his foot. He glanced at an owl pouncing on some nocturnal creature, lost his grip, and began to slide down the slope, down, down past a gnarled white oak and a Balm of Gilead tree, past an owl's silent wingbeat and all rapturous announcing.

He landed at the foot of a scrub madrone on the canyon floor, his cheek pressed heavily upon the earth. The fall left him woozy, and he had trouble piecing together the events that had led up to this moment. To his astonishment he appeared to be gazing at point-blank range into the bell-shaped muzzle of a blunderbuss. He sat up, looking curiously at the firearm. Rust mottled the barrel, and the scrolling silverwork inlaid in the rotted wood stock was tarnished. Hammer, lock, and trigger still appeared perfectly intact. It looked as if it had lain there for centuries. Reverently Axel tried to pick it up. But the blunderbuss, held together by a tension no stronger than that of a waterdrop, disintegrated at his touch.

He felt very alone then. Everything seemed displaced, or out of place, like orphan trees, and he the strangest orphan of all. Only the fortunate discovery of his cap snagged in a branch recalled him to the present enough to consider moving on. He wobbled to his feet, wincing in pain at his bruises and scratches.

He stood on the brink of the creek again, across from a rock alcove that had been scoured out by the pressure of seeping water.

At its base he was surprised to catch the glimmer of a campfire. He forded the stream to investigate further and came upon a Native American man tending it on the floor of a cave. The man wore nothing but a short feathered skirt, and his face was striped black and red. He, too, seemed very alone sitting there absorbed in the dancing flames. This impression grew sharper still when Axel crept to the cave entrance and saw to his shock that the man was covered in ants. They were crawling all over him, and worse, he did nothing to stop them. In fact he seemed to be trying to ignore or, rather, endure them like it was a test or rite of initiation. He was clearly in the throes of some dramatic inner struggle—one, moreover, that took him far away from that cave. Axel would have liked to find out how far, but at that moment he discovered that the man wasn't alone after all. Just visible on the edges of the firelight were four animals, a coyote, a fox, a turtle, and a raven. They looked on with great concern for the man in his ordeal, as if the outcome were in doubt. Axel gathered from hostile side glances that these very cerebral animals also didn't appreciate being interrupted. When the fox growled at him, he decided it was better to withdraw.

He returned to the creek and followed the watercourse through a flat of maple trees, wondering at what seemed like the sound of crinkling paper around him. He sensed turbulence in the air; all points in space were moving like gnats in a swarm. He was entering a realm of precise perceptual distortion, where above and below, forward and backward, mind and matter were as if all run together. The creek trickled through steel radio towers, brain waves formed rivulets in gravel beds, leaves floated in words, and text filled the strata in canyon walls. The world was a sacred book, but not the one Pastor Arkwright read—it had not only the words and lessons of his fluky terrors but letters and the spaces between them, from which angels sprang. It had the vapors, the tiny fluxes, the volatile transmissions of imperceptible things. No doubt about it, Axel thought. He was surrounded by inklings of a deeper divinity than the pastor would ever be able to vouchsafe.

He heard an eerie squeal in the distance, wood straining in some ghostly fluxion of wind or weight, and a resounding crack. That gave him pause. What made him so sure of himself? He wondered if he truly knew what these bearers of code were trying to tell him or what wilderness of implication he was heading into so recklessly. Thousands of years, and much accumulated experience in the vicissitudes of faith, hung in the scales of Axel's courage now, balanced only against his own imagination. Was it not after all in fear that people made an image, and called it God? Should he be afraid?

He halted in a forested canyon flat, lost in these irresolute thoughts, when a plangent voice giggled near at hand. It trailed off into silence, and a second masculine voice expostulated:

"You *are* a saucy girl!"

Axel swung around to confront a nude woman coming up a path toward him. She giggled a second time, darting past and vanishing into the trees. A second later the man appeared behind her, also nude, with the massive frame, bright eyes, and goatish hooves of a satyr.

"Where is my chaste Diana?" he wondered aloud, taking no notice of Axel. "Just wait until I get my hands on you, my elusive huntress!" He trotted off in pursuit.

Axel felt a pushing in his bones. There was sorcery afoot all right. He cautiously resumed his journey down the canyon. A bank of foliage forced him toward a gently sloping meadow dotted with daffodils. There he encountered the couple again. She was perched precariously on the gray bough of a contorted cypress tree, while he reclined upon a bed of serpentine just beneath. They stared fixedly at some mystical point in the middle of the air, both glowing like polished marble.

Axel heard the beating of drums lower down the canyon. He left the couple to the perfection of their oddly self-conscious idyll and walked on, coming at length upon two Doric columns flanking a gap between hedges. They formed an entranceway into a grove lit by torches and colored lamps. He heard the festive murmuring of many people within. He was greeted by a man dressed in a bearskin jacket with gold nuggets for buttons, a sombrero, and gigantic top boots.

"Do you know the password?" he asked.

"No."

"Are you devoted to the Seven Arts?"

Axel considered this.

"No matter," said the man impatiently. "It's High Jinks time. All sprites, fauns, and breezy vagabonds are welcome. Do you have a map?"

"Of what?"

"*Bohemia*," said he, handing him a slip of parchment. On it were indicated a number of vague regions with names like "Isle of Idleness," "Pays de la Jeunesse," and the "Hills of Fame." Nothing was drawn to scale or seemed particularly helpful if he wanted to find his way.

"Yonder is the Fortress of Philistia." The man pointed over Axel's shoulder toward the serpentine outcropping. "It borders the Great Philistine Desert. Is that where you hail, my friend?"

"I came from the Arkwright retreat."

"Just as I feared."

"What is this place?"

"The Forest of Arden," the man said, stepping aside to let him pass.

Axel headed down a rock-lined pathway, encountering on both sides dioramas lit by candles, with life-sized plaster-cast figures that represented mythical scenes. Salmacis embraced Hermaphroditus in a pool, Perseus cut off Medusa's head inside her cave, and Jupiter ravished Leda in the form of a swan. At the far end stood a brass statue of a man with the head of an ox. Its hands were outstretched as if to receive something, only the palms were turned inward so as to suggest dropping what it received. As Axel passed this ambiguous figure by, it bent down with sudden animation and whispered: "This game at being gods is tiresome indeed."

Axel halted as the statue resumed its former rigid pose. There was no expression at all in its ox-eyes. He touched a fold of its gown, as solid and smooth as brass.

He turned to see a girl with a frank elfin face standing beside him. She laughed at his confusion. "Don't worry," she assured him. "Inside it's all fire."

She wore a pleated gauzy chiton cinched at her waist with a golden sash, and her voluminous blond hair was crowned by a circlet of intertwined daisies. She seemed encased in a column of light, and when she moved, she blurred as if projected by a laser. "I'm Ada, daughter to the Crown Prince of Crudelitas. What's your name?"

"Axalax," said he with uncharacteristic bashfulness.

"Are you a man?"

"No."

"A brainchild, then? A moon-calf? A cockatrice?"

"An errant knight."

"Strayed to our High Panjandrum's Nonesuch World!"

She curtsied. He took his cap by its short rim and, sweeping it from his head, made a grand formal bow.

"I am forever at your service, noble dame."

"You are most welcome here, my lord," she said with equal solemnity. "Come." She took his hand in her own and led him into a long and wedge-shaped woodland glade. Many people stood around tipping wine cups and conversing over the sound of beating drums. They were dressed in things like three-cornered hats and Tyrolean capes. One dark-eyed and melancholy woman puffed from an opera-length cigarette holder and blew smoke rings up over the eaves. She tilted her head as a very refined gentleman bent down to whisper in her ear.

"That's Helen Modjeska," the girl informed him. "And her husband, Count Bozenta. Our gracious hosts. They have just arrived from Paris, where Madame played Salomé at the Théâtre de l'Odéon to most enthusiastic acclaim."

They came to a table where half a dozen boisterous men jostled one another for turns at the spigot of a beer keg. They bent their heads back and opened their mouths wide to receive the stream of foamy lager, which just as often missed its mark and soaked into their shirts. Two middle-aged men with dyed black mustachios, linen suits, and bowler hats looked on haughtily.

"Wildheads," observed one of them.

"Babbitts and blasé boozers," said the other.

"Rich amateurs and armchair artists!"

"Are we to truckle to that troll Respectability?" asked the first man of his companion. "Are we to pass our days in the sober industries of sheepish shopkeepers? Filling our purses, buttoning our greatcoats against the cold, scared of our own shadows?"

"Never!" they roared in tandem, and threw themselves into the fray.

Axel looked on in dismay. Ada led him deeper into the glade. Things became more and more phantasmagorical. He passed a juggler in motley, two dusty cowpokes resting under an English yew tree, a horse caparisoned in white drawing a cart full of mournful children. He watched a procession of medieval flagellants in hairshirts carrying a heavy wooden cross on their backs, whipping themselves with bunches of thistle and moaning miserably. Two kneeling Native American girls received communion from a Franciscan friar, with bells tolling the angelus in some invisible campanile.

Further on he noticed a second friar engaged in a heated exchange with that same Native American man from the cave. His face was still striped black and red, and he still wore only a feathered skirt. No ants, though. They were debating whether Yahweh was a god or a demiurge. The Native American swore he was not a god and had botched his Creation as no demiurge ever had before. His work was pathetic, he said. The friar scoffed at such blasphemy and alleged that the Native American was trying to pass himself off as Jesus Christ. His interlocutor burst out laughing. The idea was simply beyond credit.

"I saw that man in a cave," Axel told his guide as they passed them by.

"He wasn't really there," she returned. "Or, rather, he's not really here. He's a star-chief. His habitation is above."

Axel followed her upraised finger with his eyes, but nothing in the darkness relieved his bewilderment. "I don't understand what's happening," he said.

"There's nothing to understand," Ada replied. "This all comes before words."

Just then a company of Dionysian revelers swept them up in their train. Waifish women danced with fey grace, sylvan men skipped along playing their dithyrambs on rural pipes and timbrels. Before Axel knew it they'd arrived at a hooped wooden vat filled with grapes. Everyone began taking off their clothes and climbing in. Laughing, they gathered around, lifted him off his feet, and divested him of his tennis shoes, his pants, his sweater, finally his suede jacket. Then they placed him into the vat. Each time he tried to jump out, many hands pulled him back in again. He was forced to press grapes with his feet. More and more revelers joined in, and at last the vat was too crowded for anyone to move except in tandem with everyone else. They surged this way and that. Losing his balance, Axel slipped and fell to the bottom of the vat. He tried to fight his way up again. Panic set in as he swallowed draughts of the pulpy juice slowly rising up the sides. People kept kicking him, and he heard their gleeful shouts. If he didn't do something fast they were going to drown him with their heedless happiness. He lurched upward and gurgled out:

"Heeeeelp!!!!"

In a twinkling he was walking side by side with the elfin girl down another rock-lined pathway. Everything was as it had been before. Stars shone in the bent intricacies of live oak trees. The moonlight was blank as ever. They were alone in a far reach of the canyon, and the drums were a distant clamor. Ada held a yellow violet in her hand.

"This is an ordinary flower," she observed placidly. "It does not ask to be plucked and admired." She gave it to him. "To appreciate its loveliness you must meet it on its own terms, in the absence of any person who might find it. You have to step out of your own mind."

He let it rest upon his palm. In his imagination it turned into a white dove, and behold! It was a white dove and flew away into the night.

"It is you who blurs the contours, Axalax," she smiled.

Her words filled him with gladness. "We're in Illyria!" he cried. "On the Plane of Indwelling."

"Where nothing is what it seems."

She pointed down the path at a grove of redwood trees so towering their crowns might have touched the heavens.

"There you will find whom you seek above all others," she said. "Sift?"

She nodded. "Go to him," she urged. He trailed off toward the entrance to the grove and passed within. It was perfectly dark, and he waited until he could make out the sentinel outlines of the trunks and the spoked aureoles of branches above him. He sensed a presence that wasn't just that of the place, but an effluence concentrated in a particular figure. He thought he could make it out, seated with drawn up knees in amongst bracken fern and skunk cabbage. Axel took a step, needles and dried cones that carpeted the ground cracking under his foot. The figure vanished. He ran forward crying, "Sift!" He glimpsed what may have been two scissoring legs flit behind the bole of a tree. "Come back!"

He gave chase through to the other end of the grove, where a glint in his peripheral vision led him out into the live oaks again. He saw a glow worm some distance off and, in its meager phosphorescence, unmistakably, Sift's fleeting silhouette. He sprinted through the trees after it, arriving at a vast house just in time to see his quarry flit within a cavelike entrance overhung by dripping crystalline stalactites.

The house, originally of white wood siding with gables and Palladium windows, had been added on to in every direction and in so many different styles that it looked as if it had passed through a kaleidoscope. It rose numerous stories high and sported stone turrets with thatched roofs, wood pagodas, onion-shaped domes made of purple glass, flying buttresses, balustered sleeping porches, and oculus windows. Axel passed under the stalactites but found the riveted metal door locked shut. He walked around, following a wall built in vaguely Mayan design of ornamental concrete blocks to a Chinese pavilion with massive pier-pinnacles at each corner. A long gallery stretched through the pavilion into a court enclosed by beige stucco arcades with cream salmon caryatids for columns. A round basin with a smooth stone lip stood at the center of the mosaic floor, and sphinx heads stared down at him from tapered piers.

At the far end a marble stairway took him up into the house, where he tracked Sift through a maze of rooms and hallways. They seemed warmed by human presences, intimate and lived in, yet not a soul was to be seen. He passed coffered vaults, lotus friezes, niches holding sculpted busts, finials with little saints or beasts figured in them, stiff-backed leather chairs with twisted legs, and cabinets opened to display painted landscapes and still lives. After a while he began to notice a strange chicanery at work. Cozy log fires were intensified by the use of red tinfoil. Bouquets of white roses were made of paper. The luscious fruit in an epergne turned out to be wax. A spittoon looked like a treasure chest, an umbrella stand a knight in shining armor, a bootjack a stag-beetle, a coffee table an orchestrion.

At one point he discovered that a framed portrait of King Ludwig of Bavaria was not framed at all, but painted right onto the wall.

At last he came to a room located high in a clerestory. In it he found a massive telescope that jutted through a slit in the domed ceiling, and it revolved on a disklike dais. On the round walls was a black-and-white panorama of Constantinople in the nineteenth century. Axel looked down from a high hill over rooftops to the Bosphorus, cluttered with tall ships. On the far bank the city rose up another hillside, and in innumerable balconies he could see tiny men dressed in dark suits and women with picture hats shaded by umbrellas gazing out over the water.

On the dais sat a bizarre man with a falcon's hooded head. His body, lithe of limb and torso, was covered in a smooth coat of feathers. He had his hand on a lever with which he rotated the dais, looking fastidiously through the telescope at the stars and recording what he saw in a ledger book on a table beside him. When he sensed Axel in the room, he rolled his beaked face in the opposite direction of the rotating dais and froze, gazing at him without feeling or surprise, as if he'd been expecting him for a long time.

"*Idril hyarmentir oredreth osgiliath,*" he said as if Axel would know what that meant. The unusual astronomer waited for a reply, but when Axel didn't answer his eyes drifted and stared. Axel sensed that he had let him down somehow and that this had not been the first time nor would it be the last. He would go on letting him down until he understood the strange language he spoke. Axel had the feeling this bird-man existed in the room uniquely for him, imprisoned as if in his own personal destiny, and that only he could free him finally from the burden of what had been an interminably long and patient labor. But before he could do that, Axel had to push himself past some limit, some marchland where he had often enough gone wandering, but where he had not as yet been able to find his way.

Sensing that the moment was still not ripe, the bird-man returned to his stargazing, and Axel stood there listening to the lonely scratch of his pen as he wrote the symbols of his observations into the columns of his book.

Presently he made his way back down through the house. Doors slammed as he came upon them, only to turn out not to have been doors at all, but painted facsimiles. Stairways led him straight into ceilings, windows opened onto light wells that reached endlessly up and down. At length he looked into a library, finding there an old man with a gaunt face. He sat on a baize green leather armchair dressed in overalls like a hayseed farmer, squinting through bifocals at the ranks of volumes that filled the shelves.

"These books aren't real," he informed Axel in a Russian accent. He tapped on a spine and listened to the resonant knock it made. "It's a fake library, or my name is not William Williams." He picked up a Gutenberg Bible lying on a deal table. He shook it, and it rattled. He couldn't pull it open until he undid a metal clasp, whereupon he discovered it to be a work-box filled with tiny glass unicorns.

"See!" he cried. "A fraud, a ruse."

"Did a rather tall elf come through here?"

"All of it," he went on. "This place. *Me*. My whole life. Nothing but a swindle."

Axel started to move on again, but the agitated old man called him back. He was in a retrospective mood. "Even as a child I dreamed of coming to California," he told him, "growing up on the tundras of Siberia. All I thought about was sea and sunshine, orange groves, the land of opportunity. I lived inside that dream for half a century and stopped at nothing to make it come true. When I finally got to Laguna Beach, I lived in a shack and painted sunsets for tourists until I could afford to buy my land. Since then I've homesteaded up in Williams Canyon, tending my vegetable garden, raising my bees, coming to Helen's parties, pickling in my solitude. But it's all been a sham. I've not lived. *Nothing has been realized except a dream.* I'm no different from this library. Open me and I will be hollow, too."

Axel didn't know what to say to that, and as the man seemed now completely absorbed in his lament, he slipped away to find a door leading to the outside. On a lawn he heard the crackle of burning wood. Heading through some trees, he came to the same glade as before only at the extreme other end, now the scene of a vigorously stoked bonfire. It burned before a raised stage and a back-cloth with a desert painted on it: a saguaro in the foreground, mesas and buttes, a blue sky with the superimposed words "Ordo Templi Orientis." At the front of the stage stood the brass statue Axel had earlier encountered, staring impassively over the heads of an audience composed entirely of weird costumed creatures: hoof-stamping centaurs, evil-eyed basilisks, sphinxes, ogres, and xiphopaguses. To one side sat three bare-chested men with grass skirts, beating the omnipresent drums.

From the other side of the stage a group of robed figures wearing wooden masks came into view. They formed the chorus in some sort of theatrical performance, and everyone was waiting for it to begin. One of the figures, detaching himself from the mass, stepped forward to address the crowd. All at once the drums ceased.

> LEADER OF CHORUS
> The Great God, who through perils grave brought
> Light and life to the Carthaginians,
> Who once held by its nostrils the proud bull
> And plunged his knife deep in sacred blood—

He stretched out his hand to indicate the statue. The rest of the masked figures spoke in toneless harmony:

> CHORUS
> They called him Mithra then, mediator
> Of gods and men, but he had other names,
> Wanderer through divers lands in guises wild,
> In Moab a mystery they worshiped
> With burnt offerings, and festivals
> Of flame. Achaeans called him Kronos,
> Devourer of his children.

Count Bozenta appeared on the stage dressed in a long druidic robe, followed by Madame Modjeska, who led a small boy by the hand. They were acting the parts of a priest and a priestess, and Axel understood that it was not so much a play as a ritual of some sort. The leader yielded his spot to Count Bozenta, who raised his arms in a *V* above his head and spoke in his turn.

PRIEST
　　　　　　　Betimes
in Zidon he walked with Ashtaroth,
A star of the sun. In saturnals they drove
The people to crazed vociferations,
Excitements unnatural.

PRIESTESS
　　　　　　　O Nimrod,
The Hornèd One, I hear the Great Red Dragon
And Ninus the child, yet father of all
Babylonian deities, come with news
Of rumors rank and spread by Canaan law
That you abomination are, idol
Of the Ammonites and the Phoenicians.

CHORUS
They thought they carried the Shekinah glory
In their holy tabernacles, yet saw not
How the cruel star of their rejoicing
Shone with Baal-fire.

Madame Modjeska lifted the child and placed him in the arms of the statue. The crowd grew restless, looking on through the forked flames and billowing smoke. Axel noticed Ada, come out of nowhere, standing beside him. Although she wore no costume like the others, a decidedly more saturnine expression now animated her features.

PRIEST
Protecting Ruler,
Remphan, Milchom, Molech—

CHORUS
(to the beating of drums)
Moloch the King!

PRIESTESS
Spirit of flame and all that consumes,
Molten law of capricious youth, conceived
In darkness, soon spent, receive this offering,
A child beloved and only-begotten,
In holy sacrifice for our souls' sin.

CHORUS
Moloch the King! Moloch the King!

The crowd erupted, crying in unison "Moloch the King!" The drumming, fiercely polyrhythmic, grew to a deafening hubbub. Around Axel, people began to shake, their eyes rolling up into the backs of their heads and their limbs writhing as if possessed by unruly demons. They pulled at their own hair and shrieked, fell moaning to their knees, tore off each other's costumes and incited themselves to frenzy. Even Ada turned on Axel with a feline rage and began clawing at him.

Terrified, he fled through the grove, confused and without direction. Branches caught at his face and arms. He careened through cobwebs and felt spiders creeping in his collar. The moon darted through the foliage as if frantically tracking his movements. Space pressed in on him, forcing him into more tortuous turns and ever finer transports. He had the impression that he wasn't running at all so much as sinking into a delirium. He had to keep firmly before him that he really was moving, that there was reason for flight, and that he must not lose the way now or forget that this was no dream. Imagination was not a trick of the mind or a passion of the soul, but a friction with the world, giving rise to a strange decision's heat and spark.

As he went he once more saw Sift going before him, winking past salmonberry bushes, stirring so slightly the moss that hung from tree limbs, leaving no imprint in the soft carpets of miner's lettuce. This time he sensed the elusive elf wasn't running away so much as guiding him with sure step toward a safe place. As Axel tore through the brush, he felt himself closing the gap between them.

Suddenly he stumbled upon the bank of a more robust stream. He was in a juncture with still another and larger canyon, at a node in the network of flows draining the uplands of that supernal mountain. The stream ran furtively down the center of a gravel-filled arroyo, and the braids of water shone like quicksilver. It was the Santiago.

And there by the water's edge Sift turned to confront him at last. Tall and slender, clad in a gray elf-cloak with silvery runes woven into its fabric, he gazed steadily through the darkness at Axel, his hand resting upon the upturned root system of a fallen cottonwood tree. His golden hair fell around his shoulders, and a diadem of sapphires encircled his brow. He brought that place into vivid relief around him. He claimed it with a prerogative older than years and beyond the power of ruinous nature to diminish. But if his immortality could not be destroyed, since it had not exactly been created, Axel knew it could be scarred past hope.

"By the Coromar Cliffs I saw a swan-prowed ship," he blurted out to that marvelous creature. "Opalescent and graceful it breasted the foamy waves, and on it was a pilot with a helmet of wings, and he was made of light!"

Sift remained silent and brooding.

"I can take you there!" he urged. "We'll go together."

But Sift pushed forward and cried: "O Axalax, why do you persecute me?"

This shocking question whirled through Axel's mind, the words scattering like leaves in a funnel cloud. He heard a devastating roar, and volatile lights started careening down the canyons. He watched in horror as Sift's eyes became glazed and lidded, filled with unsuspected malice. A red gleam welled through his skin, which shriveled into the ghastly hollows of the skeleton beneath. His hair writhed like snakes combusting into hot flames. Comely Ada appeared in his fair visage, only to morph at once into a grinning harpy. Then he knew it was not Sift he had encountered by those far-feint shores of the Santiago, but the sorceress Mimema. There were two powers at work in that dark night. He closed his eyes to steady himself and felt a teeming as of molecules in the viscous medium of his spirit. They turned into ants infesting his brain. He fell thrashing to the ground, flung this way and that. He detected a new gravity in his imaginary kingdoms then. There were consequences to his moon-pulled wanderings. Isolation in the absolute could bring its own form of terror. All at once, and with the anguish of his helpless revulsion, he yielded to a despair that may always have existed on the far side of pride, opened there like a secret wound, a hemorrhaging desire to be real again, human, subject to time's homesick sorrow. Behind the prophetic struggles, the high vicissitudes of so much standing apart, he was just a kid from Orange after all, with pain receptors intact, longing for love and consolation. Mimema laughed derisively.

"Behold a Son of Man!" she cackled.

"Noooooooooo!!!" he cried.

At that the ground shook beneath his feet. The roar became a flood. It cascaded down the wash and swept him away past glittering submarine palaces and towers. The water became a host of galloping horses with crowned riders clad in bright chainmail, their solemn faces, made of quartz, glowing with a cold blue schiller. They trampled out of him every last ounce of willpower, until he was nothing more than a piece of flotsam pushed here and there. So complete was the tumult that he lost the sense of what was happening, or if anything was happening. All elements, earth and sky, water and air, blended into a single substance of which he too formed a part, swooping with its convex vortices, spiraling in its languorous nebulae. The riders began to fold out into more and more complex polyhedral shapes, refracting through the axes and planes of a crystalline symmetry. Once more he heard the laughter of Mimema, and the hard, gemlike sound of her scorn cut sharply, in twinned cruciform anguish, through his body.

A strange history flashed before his eyes then. It told of realms of unfailing abundance—seventh heaven, octad, pleroma, waters above the firmament—and a material from which everything else was made—phlogiston, quintessence, apeiron. It told of a universal mind and a prime mover, of luminiferous aether and infinite space extrapolated from the moving earth and the pockmarked moon. But it was all false, all lies and spells, all mere variations on the same delusive theme of the Cosmos. The Cosmic Egg. Fall and Creation merged. Genesis. *I am I.* The giant Adam rivaled God and shrank into human form. The angels blew their braying trumpets and fell like autumn leaves to meet their shadows on the dappled ground, east of Eden.

He noticed that the cataclysmic flood was slowing down. The purling water, the pebbles and leaf-veins, the loamy claystone and fascicular roots aswarm around him came gradually to a standstill, and he was frozen like a man in ice. He might have stayed this way forever but for a light, faint at first yet brightening and resolving into a most wondrous vision. He saw a vast turning chariot wheel high above. Inside it were four sparkly angels each with four wings, and their faces were fourfold, disclosing the likenesses of a man, a lion, an ox, and an eagle. They surrounded five concentric spheres, each a color of the rainbow, and each accompanied by another angel busy turning the crank by which its sphere revolved. At the center of the wheel was a golden throne where a celestial spirit sat. His amiable face was the color of amber, and his loins were fire. He said he was Metatron, the Angel Christ, the Divine Man who, beholding the unendurable face of God as the human Enoch, burst into showering sparks, dying not once in time but for all time, over and over again in perpetual Resurrection. And he told Axel that there was a boundary to the fallen world, a crack in the Cosmic Egg, and that if one pushed into it at just the right place and with just the right pressure, one could squeeze through to the other side, and escape.

Axel started awake, surprised to find himself curled up on a gravel bed of the Santiago. The sun had just cleared the saddle of the mountain high above. Its rays were tilting through the branches and needles of tall conifers. He sat up blinking and smacking his webby lips. His clothes were wet all the way through. The pen in his pocket had burst, and a black ink stain ran down his pant leg. He rose to his feet and stood for a time gazing about, listening to a nearby mourning dove make its placid iambs and anapests in the soft folds of its throat. He was back among the living, the only place where imagination mattered. But he knew also that he was not mortal, not a fallen man, not caught in selfhood and sin and the dark dream of sacrifice. That he would leave to Pastor Arkwright and his myrmidons. He was different, or other, wholly other, complete only in this emptiness that surrounded him, present only in this vanishing to which he gave himself. Firm now in the knowledge that this meant he would have to go alone, without any guide, without any authority, he took another step deeper into the hidden world.

17

Gay Moloch

Fox was beside himself when he heard of Axel's disappearance. He waited frantically for news from the search parties organized by his church and local police, busy combing the Santa Ana Mountains. There had been no word of him at all. No one had come forward to say they had seen him on roads, passing through yards, wandering down trails. The suspicion hung in the air that he might be lost in the wilderness of the Cleveland National Forest, hurt, starving, who knew what else? Fox clung to the hope that he had hidden out, right under his pursuers' noses, in some safe place after all. It would be like him to surprise everyone by turning up where they least suspected.

But then one of the Christian Bondsmen found his cap in the bed of the Santiago Creek, a couple miles above the reservoir. It was covered in mud and looked as if it had been wrung like a wet rag. That was too much for Fox. Axel losing his cap was like anyone else losing his head.

It did, however, afford a first clue. Axel had gone down the northern side of the mountain and followed the Santiago Canyon. The search parties concentrated their efforts around the shores of the reservoir and the hills roundabout. Fox guessed he was making his way back to the riverbed below the Villa Park Dam, but the authorities thought it better to confine their search to the canyon for the time being. Angel convinced him to mount one of his own. She even helped by enlisting the aid of her brothers and their gang, Los Fuckers. They gamely scoured the hiding places that they, too, had sussed out in underpasses, storm drains, adjacent storage basins, and tributary flood channels. They even searched the Santa Ana River all the way down to Huntington Beach and up to the Narrows.

Fox made his own forays with Angel to the places he thought Axel might go. They found nothing, but he had the feeling, or at least he wanted to believe, that Axel was there, watching them from a distance, hoping through all the choices and wrong turns that they would discover him at last. One day in the riverbed Fox swung impulsively around to see if he might catch Axel out. This startled Angel, who followed his roving eyes to another humdrum wash, networks of millet grass creeping over cracked dirt, hoary spikes of dead mullein, the wingwall of an overpass. It had her wondering, not for the first time, about the appeal vacancy had for boys, that still empty point they fixed on while watching their dumb ballgames on TV, pursuing their blood sports on mean streets, or mixing beats on their turntables at tribal dance parties.

"Compañero," she said, thinking Fox might need a little refresher here, "nobody is an island."

"Huh?"

"The smallest unit of any human being is always two people."

These words reminded him of what deep down he was looking for in the riverbed—not anything he could *see*, not a thing or a person even, but friendship, fellow feeling, the sense of belonging that Axel more than anyone had given him over the last years. With a sudden leap of the heart he reached out to Angel and hugged her, glad she was there by his side.

Later everyone regrouped in the Melendez back yard. The Los Fuckers had returned empty-handed. They found any number of hobos, hippies, teenage mutants, visitors from Mars, but no Axel.

"The dude's not there," Julio said with a shrug.

"We have to keep trying," urged Angel.

Juan and Jaime were preoccupied with some sort of poem handwritten in heavy black ink on a page torn from a phone book. They'd retrieved it from the riverbed. "What's a 'trollope'?" asked Juan.

"A kind of hoe," said Julio.

They burst out laughing. "Listen to this!" said Juan. He read from the page in the rolling cadences of a rapper: "'There was a sly girl with a polyp/Who grew to be somewhat a trollope/When all hope had fled/And desire was dead/She gave all her coins to Gay Moloch.'"

"That's some crazy-ass shit!' sputtered Jaime.

"Who's Moloch?" inquired little Jacinto, the youngest Melendez, his arm wrapped around Julio's leg and his head tilted to touch his hip. No one knew.

"Hey, wait a minute," said Julio. "I remember seeing that name 'Gay Moloch,' too, more than once."

"Yeah, some kind of graffiti," said Jaime.

"A tag," said Julio uneasily.

"Maybe it's a new gang," augured Juan in fell tones.

"Invading our turf, man," said Julio darkly.

Fox, meanwhile, had taken the torn page to scrutinize the handwriting. It might have been Axel's. In tone and style it certainly fit him. But who knew when it was written, yesterday or last year? He had no memory of Axel depositing poems in the riverbed, but that didn't mean he hadn't.

Fox and Angel went back to look for more clues. They didn't need to search for long. "Gay Moloch" appeared on piers, boulders, slumpstone fences. They came upon another poem scrawled on a sheet of old plywood. It went: "There was a gray geezer whose dollop/ of spittle proved most melancholic/His wife washed it clean/but it maintained its sheen/thanks to the slime of Gay Moloch."

They found two more in the same vicinity, one about a retired bassoon player and another about a circus clown with a devil's backbone. Fox rested easy for once. At last some signs!

"They're all the same," observed Angel, comparing the poems over lunch at a Fatburger. "They have the same rhyme scheme, and the lines have the same numbers of syllables in them, more or less."

Angel pulled out her phone and discovered on the Princeton Encyclopedia of Poetry website that the form was called a limerick. But it also said that a limerick was a nonsense verse. It wasn't supposed to mean anything at all.

Fox wracked his brain looking in them for hints as to Axel's whereabouts, but nothing struck him. The characters resembled no one he knew, and the only link between them was "Gay Moloch." They looked up that name and discovered that it belonged to a pagan deity who seduced the Israelites of the Old Testament into idolatrous worship. Moloch demanded human sacrifice in particular of children, whom the worshipers referred to as "seed" they would "pass" to the frightful god.

That gave them both pause. If they weren't mistaken, "passing seed" sounded a lot like the act of procreation.

"Why would, like. . .*sex*. . .be equated with sacrificing kids?" asked Angel. "That's how you *make* kids!"

"'Archaeologists have uncovered infant skeletons in burial grounds around pagan shrines all over Palestine,'" Fox read on Angel's phone.

"Mierda!" she exclaimed. "I can't believe it. They made kids by killing kids."

"What I want to know," said Fox, "is why this Moloch guy is so *happy*?"

They had both agreed that this was the sense in which that qualifier should be taken.

Answers would not be forthcoming. They kept a watch in the riverbed, finding still another limerick even, but no Axel. A week went by, then two weeks. They began to suspect that he hadn't written them at all and they were wasting their time.

Maude and Blaise, at their wits' end, had meanwhile given in to their worst fears. Maybe Axel was not coming back. They had pushed him too far, and he had left them behind for good. They felt rejected—an old feeling, way too familiar, reminding them of that sensitivity they needed the help of ultimate answers to shelter from life's storms. They felt like such washouts as parents. The truth was they'd never liked laying down laws. Authority always scared them. Dogmatism just made them clumsy. Deep down their tactic as parents had been to guard Axel against their own limitations by sacrificing them on the altar of Christian godliness. It therefore hurt all the more to realize that they may have driven him away.

The police gave up their search and remanded Axel's case to the missing person's bureau. His name was entered in a database along with hundreds of other children and teens who had disappeared without a trace, and his picture was put up on websites, post office walls, and library bulletin boards. The first time Fox saw one of these pictures he wanted to cry. Axel's mug had been juxtaposed with three others on a poster making them seem like criminals, with statistics listing height, weight, age, when last seen and so on. Some of the others had been missing for months.

Angel proved resourceful in expanding their search. She began by asking kids she knew at school if they had heard anything. This led them to various haunts and lairs frequented by Straight Edge punk rockers, video game addicts and *Rocky Horror Picture Show* devotees. They made a flyer with a photograph and description of Axel to distribute to people they came across. Invariably someone mentioned another place they might try. In this way they cast their net wider and wider. Justo let them borrow his Datsun 510, and they spent most afternoons after school driving around to community centers, boys and girls clubs, churches. They went to malls and talked to the kids who loitered in them. They visited the cafes where disheveled teen literati liked to go and read their paperback novels by D.H. Lawrence and Ayn Rand, pretending it was Paris. They asked around at rockabilly drive-ins, Mod gallery spaces, glam-rock space stations, New Wave discos, rave warehouses, and hip hop street jams. They didn't find Axel in any of them.

Some of the kids they encountered were runaways themselves and knew the rounds of youth welfare services where others who might have heard something could be approached. They met kids sleeping rough in back alleys, spare-changing in front of 7-11s, or donating at plasma centers for money to eat. Some related stories that chilled them to hear. One boy was kidnapped off the streets of Modesto by a strange man and raised alone in the woods; when the authorities finally caught up with him, he'd changed so much his real family barely recognized him, and before long he just took off again. Another boy was sexually abused by his foster father for years, and one girl found her mother hanging by a telephone cord in the garage when she was only five. Compared to where many of them had come from, living on the streets didn't seem so bad, although Fox and Angel would never forget how bad that was after they met one girl, named She-Ra, who had an infected boil the size of a lemon on her neck and a bad case of scabies.

Slowly they moved into the alternate universe of homeless people, the full extent of which shocked them both. They went to municipal shelters where battered women and disabled people slept doubled up as though stacked in warehouses. They went to welfare hotels, emergency hostels, board-and-care facilities, single-room occupancy buildings. Through their questioning after Axel they came to learn more about the habits of the homeless: how they lived constantly on the move, kicked out of one park or beach after another, riding public transit busses all day long or watching the same movies over and over again in theaters to pass the time. Some were crazy, inmates released from state mental hospitals who muttered to themselves while picking through garbage cans. Others were crack addicts with yellow eyes, searching for hidden messages in dirt and twigs. All were hardened by adversity, deeply pessimistic, and desperate for some small share of the ordinary life everyone else took for granted.

These experiences made Fox and Angel a lot soberer about the many social problems that beset them. Angel, of course, tied it all in with the other examples of injustice she had collected in her bursting clip files. She regaled Fox in the car between their various destinations with accounts of maquiladora workers exploited in Tijuana, day laborers living in cardboard boxes, refugees forced into camps, or not even refugees, but people treated as if that's what they were right in their own neighborhoods and towns. She expanded on a theory she'd developed that more and more people were becoming exiles uprooted from any home or identity. Exiles, she said, had no rights, not those of citizenship, work, or law. They floated between cultures and states. They were people who were not people, disposable people who could be used, abused, even killed with impunity. And it was a local as well as a global phenomenon. They were living in our midsts like ghosts.

This took Fox back to the time when he and his mother weren't that far away from homelessness themselves. He remembered what it felt like having no settled place to call his own, the worry so intense it made him want to jump out of his skin, the nightmares he had of patterns in gaudy wallpaper no one he knew chose. Dispossession was his friend back then, even if not particularly a kind one. It kept him company amidst the ghosts. He played with it like lumpy stuffed animals bought at garage sales or used Lego. He wore it like shirts with stretched sleeves smelling of a strange boy's sweat. With it he performed the lonely rituals of first days at new schools, holidays without friends or family, afternoons spent by himself while his mother was away at work.

These feelings and memories came to weigh on him more as the days passed with no new developments. They gave another painful twist to the thought that Axel was one of those disposable people he saw living on skid row, waiting in line for soggy burritos at a food bank, or loitering in bus terminals because they were warm and had bathrooms.

Angel grew alarmed at this darker turn in Fox's mood. She understood by now how deep his insecurities ran, and she wanted him to know that he didn't have to feel so precarious anymore. He wasn't an exile or a loner or a ghost. He belonged.

"Cheer up," she said as they made their way to a Salvation Army depot in Anaheim one day. "Axel will turn up. He can't stay lost forever." She spoke with a brave face, though. The truth was she wondered now. All their efforts were beginning to seem futile. It occurred to both of them that they might soon have to give up the search. It was like sifting on a beach for one particular grain of sand, and only lunatics did that.

Axel had become his Sift, Fox realized with a start. He imagined that sad elfin figure passing through the gas stations and mini-mall parking lots he saw through the window as Angel drove. He wasn't likely to hear the appeals mere mortals like Fox made. They would only push him farther into the overlooked margins where he lived. He wondered if the same was true for Axel. Could it be that he was avoiding them on purpose? That he didn't want to be found the way, or for the reasons, Fox had assumed or hoped he would? That there was something wrong with those reasons? Axel had never been that interested in the sense of belonging when it came down to it. Even friendship and fellow feeling could seem incidental to him and his more private, personal projects. Axel was all idiosyncrasy, but he didn't always connect that with a communal concern. Fox even reproached him for it sometimes. The minor chord it struck in his own shaky past hurt his feelings. It was as if Axel was the one abandoning him rather than the other way around. Now, he supposed, that betrayed a certain selfishness mixing up those reasons, a certain neediness coloring his judgment of Axel's nonconformity. Maybe he should just let his friend go in that ghostly exile if that's where he found the permission and courage to be himself. Let him shamble on forever in his overlooked margins, always on the other side of grasping. But Fox, of course, would never do that. He couldn't. However mixed up, he did connect idiosyncrasy with communal concern.

"Hey, compañero!"

Angel pointed through the windshield at a startling change taking place in the air over Orange County. Even though it was the middle of the day, sunlight had dimmed. Buildings, telephone poles, bus benches, and billboards were all thrown into shadow. A partial eclipse of the sun was underway.

Angel stopped at a park where people had gathered to witness the event. Some were holding small black cardboard squares up to the sky. Others had set up Dobsonian telescopes on the grass, with their tubes, of various sizes, mounted on squat rocker boxes or spidery stands. People stood bent over to look in the eyepieces while others spoke excitedly among themselves or to friends on their phones.

They both got in line and waited for a turn at one of the telescopes. Nearby, kids made pinhole cameras with their fingers and projected upside-down crescents onto the sidewalk. A man dressed in a midnight blue robe dotted with white stars and a conical wizard's hat held up a large round mirror covered with thick perforated paper. It reflected a perfect little cosmos of eclipses on the wall of a recreational playhouse. Several people were gazing at the dopplered light in the shadows of two rosewood trees, where myriads more scalloped images were traced.

When Fox's turn came before a telescope, he saw the filtered representation of the sun projected into the dark interior of the tube. The edge of the moon's silhouette was jagged, and it seemed he was looking at actual flares of burning hydrogen on the sun. He wasn't, though. It was a shimmer in the eyepiece, like the kind one saw in old silent movies. Behind him he heard a man, the owner of the telescope, explaining the phenomenon to Angel.

"It's distortion caused by temperature differences in the air," he said. "The more air you look through, the more distortion it causes. It's like the sheen over a barbecue grill, only of course on a much grander scale. Astronomers call it 'seeing.'"

Fox wondered if that meant the distortion was itself a 'seeing,' that 'seeing' was a noun. He supposed Axel would have said he was seeing 'seeing.' He was seeing the light you see by.

The eclipse presently came to an end and the afternoon returned to normal. It felt much later in the day than it was, as if an extra hour had been added. Fox and Angel didn't exactly know what to do with it. They got back in the Datsun and drove, going through the motions of their original plan to visit the Salvation Army depot. There they ran into She-Ra, busy working her way through bins of used clothing for any decent pair of jeans or raggedy coat that happened to fit. She told them about a benefit concert put on by Straight Edgers that evening.

"It's going to rock," she predicted. "Some cool hardcore bands are playing. The Bad Marks, Stroke, Gouge—The Gashes are headlining. A lot of kids'll be there, from all over."

Fox didn't want to go. It seemed they really were abandoning Axel now, and the thought left him feeling abandoned. But Angel insisted they check it out anyway, just in case something new turned up. "You never know what's going to happen," she said. "And besides, if we don't find anything, at least we can have a little fun."

The concert took place at a derelict movie theater in Garden Grove, not far from the Santa Ana River. The facade was all boarded up. A door in an alley, formerly an exit, led them into the dark auditorium crowded with teens. It was one of those old theaters with molded plaster, fake balconies flanked by swirling columns, frescoes framed in between pilasters and tympanums, and trompe l'oeil paintings of stained-glass windows. Big cracks ate through the flaking plaster on the ceiling, exposing triangles of red brick. All the seats had been removed.

On the stage a band was screaming out a song that made the whole building shake. Fox followed Angel through the crowd. They saw people they'd met in their quest for Axel, and also people they recognized from school. There was Ivan Kolesikow with his skateboard and Ryan Dodge in his lime green coat. Angel went over to say hello. Fox hung back. He gazed over jumping heads and shoulders at the singer on stage, a girl with a Mohawk and piercings all over her face. Above the heavy reverb action of the guitars and the thumping beat laid down by a maniacal drummer, he picked out the words to the song.

DON'T MEDICAAAAAAAAATE,
CELEBRAAAAAAAAAATE!
DON'T PROCRASTINAAAAAAAAAATE,

DEDICAAAAAAAAAATE!
DON'T FORNICAAAAAAAATE,
VINDICAAAAAAAAATE!

Fox had never understood how Straight Edgers could be so into abstinence and nonviolence when their lifestyle was so transgressive and violent. Many of them were even Christian like Axel. He wondered if they felt transgressive and only wanted to divert that into constructive channels, or if transgression was something they only admired or cared to experience at a distance, without risks or consequences. That would make it more like a fantasy they acted out. . .again like Axel.

He saw Ryan pull Angel down to the mosh pit, where she fell in with those busy slamming their bodies together. A concessions girl, dressed in a strapless black leather getup that pushed her boobs into pale exaggerated melons, approached shining a blue penlight onto a tray she carried. It was arrayed with various candies that looked stale. She didn't seem all that concerned about selling them. But she paused and inquired with an arched eyebrow if he wanted anything. He said no, and she moved on with the forlorn step of someone who'd been selling stale candies for an eternity.

More people pressing toward the front drew him nearer and nearer to the margin, until at last he stood alone by one wall like a stuccoed angel he glimpsed sitting humped beneath the weight of its wings on a ledge way up near the ceiling. His heart sank. He was back in old precincts now. Back in the old vulpine habits of withdrawal and fear. He fancied that the angel's eyes, which must have been painted white or made out of glass because they shone with a queer brightness, were picking him out of the crowd for some sinister purpose.

At length he went to the front lobby in search of a bathroom, which he found down a stairway in a musty basement. He entered a stall and sat on the toilet, feeling the floor beneath his feet vibrate to the music from the stage. He didn't really have to go. He was just hiding away as usual. He remained there struggling once again with this shy side of his character. At the same time he tried absentmindedly to make out the graffiti that swarmed on the stall. It reminded him of

Axel's jacket, not least in its indecipherability. No, he wouldn't find his friend here, he thought with a sigh. The scent was definitely cold.

Then something attracted his eye in the dense intaglios of competing letters and symbols. His breath caught. Just beneath an arrow-pierced heart enclosing "Hannah, UR My Angel," he read, crudely etched, the words "Gay Moloch."

18

The Aleph

One morning soon after the concert, Fox and Angel drove to an elementary school to pick up Axel's sister Leonora, who was in the sixth grade there. She'd called Fox the previous day with an idea. She wouldn't say more about it than that she wanted to take them to see a friend who might be able to help find her brother. When Fox remarked that it was a school day, she said that couldn't be helped. It was the only way she could do it without telling her parents.

"Why shouldn't they know?" he asked.

All she said was, "They wouldn't understand."

She cut an arresting figure alone before the school in her same black dress with a red rose on the yoke, narrow-chested and pale, her eyes beady in the horn-rimmed glasses she wore. She looked like an orphan escaping to the circus, an impression made yet more striking by the resolute way she opened the back door, got in, and told them to drive down Tustin Avenue as if she wasn't twelve but twenty-five.

"Where are we going?" asked Fox.

"To see Madame Dobrovolsky," she replied.

"Madame *who*?!" exclaimed Angel behind the wheel.

"Do-bro-vol-sky," Leonora enunciated. "She has. . .unique talents."

This made Angel suspicious. "What kind of unique talents?"

Leonora pressed her lips together, composing an answer in her head. "In Belarus, when Madame Dobrovolsky was a little girl, it was common for dentists to use mercury instead of lead to fill in cavities. When Madame Dobrovolsky moved to London as a young woman, she began to notice that she heard things—weather reports, newscasts, parts of songs. At first she thought it was just because more people listened to the radio in London than in Minsk. But pretty soon she saw that no one else heard them in the same way she did. It wasn't until she met an elderly Hungarian toymaker with the same problem that she figured it out. It was the fillings inside her mouth. The mercury acted as a signal receiver, tuning radio waves."

"Come on!" said Angel.

"She must have eaten a lot of candy as a kid."

"You're shitting us!"

Leonora scratched her cheek and looked out the window. "But radio waves weren't the only thing she knew how to hear."

"Wait a minute," said Angel. Stopped at an intersection, she twisted around to face her precocious interlocutor. "Do you mean to tell me you're taking us to see a psychic?"

"She prefers to be called a medium," explained Leonora. "A channeler. The light's green."

"Oh brother!" Angel drove.

"How do you know her?" asked Fox.

"When people share certain. . .rare sensibilities," Leonora replied cryptically, "you tend to find one another."

Fox spent a moment arranging scattered details he knew about Leonora into a more definite picture than he had thought to form of her before. It also raised an adjacent question. "Is Axel, um, psychic, too?"

"No," Leonora said. "He's too obsessional. He often gets things wrong. But he is very intelligent. He corrects himself in the end."

"What's he getting wrong now?" Angel asked with a touch of sarcasm.

Leonora answered directly. "The doctrine of the fall of the angels."

Angel, knitting her brow in sudden leeriness, located the little girl in her rear view mirror. "What's that?"

"The question of why they gave up their divinity."

"Why did they?"

Leonora shrugged. "Just because they could, I suppose."

Angel, struck by resonances she felt more than understood, chewed on that for a block or two. It had her assessing Leonora in a more wondering light.

Fox wanted to know exactly what Axel got wrong, but there Leonora was less certain. All she did say was that he had underestimated the problem of evil. "It runs deeper than he imagines," she said. "But I think he's learning better."

After a while she pointed out an ordinary storefront with a pink neon sign in the window. It said "Madame Dobrovolsky's Mystic Temple." On the window were the words: "Encounters with the Other World. Expert Guidance. Courteous and Discreet. By Appointment Only."

They parked in front and knocked on the door, which swung open to reveal Sasha Dobrovolsky from South Orange High, in his ubiquitous all-white costume. He looked at them as if from a great height, serenely remote and beautiful.

"You're playing hooky, too," observed Angel as they passed into an antechamber.

"I'm here to assist my grandmother," he informed them. "She's waiting."

"Is this going to be a seance?" inquired Fox.

"Madame Dobrovolsky calls it a 'sitting,'" Leonora corrected.

"It's not a sitting either," said Sasha, opening another door. "My grandmother doesn't talk to the dead."

"Because the dead don't talk!" said a voice from within. They stepped into a larger room to meet an old woman with a narrow face grooved with wrinkles, kindly blue eyes, and a wry trembling mouth. She wore a dellarobia blue voile dress trimmed down each side of the front with wide loose bands of lace. A necklace of pearls graced her breast, and numerous rings crowded her knuckles. A fragrance of rosewater exhaled from her person, just a little too strong to be agreeable. Her regal bearing made Fox think of a queen in some far off time.

"That is one of the many misperceptions lesser practitioners of the divining arts have allowed to go unchecked," she said. "There is no such thing as death. Death is the end of things." She went to Leonora and greeted her with a kiss on both cheeks. "How are you my dear?"

"Very well, Madame Dobrovolsky. These are my friends." She introduced Fox and Angel. As the old woman was a little deaf, she listened through a curved wood funnel inlaid with silver arabesques.

"Welcome to my temple," she said warmly.

The room was lined on all sides with books. A round table with chairs stood at the center, and on it a glass vase held a splendid bouquet of blood red dahlias. The only other object in the room was a free-standing marble column about waist high. The column tapered rather grotesquely into a face that stared back at you with an anguished expression.

"Do you know what that is?" she asked Fox as he regarded it curiously.

"No," he said.

"It's called a *herm*. In ancient Greece it was very common for people to keep one in their homes. The face is that of Hermes, the messenger god. He was said to bring good luck."

"Why does he look like he's caught inside the column?" asked Angel.

"Ah! Good question. The relation between matter and messages has been a vexed one for thousands of years." They waited for her to say more, but instead she turned away and said, "Please sit, around the table, with me."

They did. The old woman listened gravely through her hearing trumpet as Leonora explained the problem of her missing brother. "And you want me to help you find him?" Madame Dobrovolsky said when she had finished. "I'm afraid I can't make any promises. I'm only a very ordinary sensitive. I don't foretell the future or solve riddles. I don't grant wishes or even give advice. I'm only a vessel, a vehicle. Like a telephone line," she said, doubting the aptness of the simile. "But that's too conceptual. I cannot say what I will find on the other end, or whether it will be useful or not."

"Then what's the point?" Angel couldn't help asking.

Madame Dobrovolsky eyed her sideways. "You're quite right to be skeptical, my dear. There are many frauds in my line of work. You know them by the petulance with which they deny it. So I won't. I won't try to convince you that I speak to spirits, stones, fairies, cetaceans, even 'energies,' 'higher powers' or 'multidimensional entities.' None of it would be true, or all of it would be as true as any other words. What are words? What do they hold in place? How?" She raised a finger. "Ah, now that's interesting."

She instructed them to close their eyes and join hands. "We must all try to be as still and quiet as possible. Sink into yourself. Breathe very slowly. Meditate. Feel your hips, your bellies, root themselves in your chair. Imagine your chair sinking into the floor. I want you to try and hear something for me. It's a ticking sound, hard to isolate, but there." She paused. "Do you hear it? It's not a clock. I keep no clocks in my temple."

After a while they did detect a murmurous mechanical sound, like a metronome. It might have been silence itself, they had to be so silent to hear it.

"It's a water meter," said Madame Dobrovolsky, "ticking in the pipes that run through the foundation of this building. It's always there, like a heartbeat. It drives me up the wall."

She let them listen to it for a minute more.

"Yes, words," she said at last. "How curiously they catch us up. In my native tongue, there are so many things I can express that I can't in English. In Russian I am sleek and slippery, like an eel darting through coral reefs. I'm tricky, and not to be trusted. I say what I don't mean, and I mean what I don't say. After all I'm not an eel. I don't live in coral reefs. Do I exist apart from these things I am not? Or is it rather that *I am only what I am not?*"

That made a funny kind of sense to Fox. Angel groaned inwardly. It was all mumbo-jumbo to her.

"This is why so many of my fellow spiritualists are fools," Madame Dobrovolsky went on. "They think that what we attune ourselves to lies beyond language, in some sort of transport or passion. But it's just the other way around. It is language to which we attune."

In the darkness behind his eyes Fox saw slender radiographic filaments like hairs float by. It seemed they were the shapes of her words in his mind.

"I prefer to think of language as a house—a ticking, creaking, rustling house. You dwell in it. And it is in you as much as you are in it. Of course, that is still but a metaphor—and metaphors are not static. They are metamorphoses, transitions from one state to another. That's why at the same time you are not at home in language at all. You must never be at home in it. Nothing is more foreign than this state of being at home. Within the limits of what is known, the foreign is already there in the form of a disquieting familiarity."

She fell silent. After a while she began twitching as if she were asleep. It was a bit disconcerting. A long time passed like this before she said, "Give me paper and a pen, Sasha dear." He broke the circle to retrieve the implements from the waiting room. When he returned and handed them to her, she resumed her monologue.

"We don't simply move through language," she said. "We are taken up in its movement. We are *plunged* into it, as if into a vortex. It absorbs and subsumes." They heard her writing very slowly. "It *consumes*. Like an obsession. I am feeling this obsession now, but with such pressure that I lose the sense of it as an impulse or a desire that comes from me. It is more a gravity, enveloping me, holding me to my chair, to this table, in this room. It describes a space the way a bird in flight describes a curve. In that space I see a meadow under a vaulted sky, streaked by moving clouds. The grass undulates in the breeze. It terminates in a high cliff. The sea lies far below."

Angel squeezed Fox's hand and ever so softly whispered "loooneeey" in his ear. But he wasn't so sure.

"There is a man," she said. "A tall man. Dressed in black. He stands at the cliff. There are children in the grass. . .playing. No, they're not playing. They're being led. . .or herded, for the tall man holds a shepherd's crook. He seems to be bringing them to the edge of the cliff. Yes. And they are jumping off. Oh dear. One after another, they jump into the sea, to be dashed against the rocks below."

All of a sudden Fox realized that she was talking about the near-death experience Axel had when he turned fourteen.

"There is a ship, floating just beyond the surf. It appears to be made out of shell, because it is nacreous like mother of pearl, and its prow curves into the proud head of a swan. There is a man. . .no, two men, standing on the deck. A brilliant radiance is in their faces. They are hauling in a large net. I can't see what they've caught. Not fish. No, nothing like that."

Again she lapsed into silence. Fox wanted to leap out of his seat.

"Ah yes!" she said then. "I see it now. They are catching the souls—no, that's too psychological, too rational, too. . .*Platonic*. They are catching the sparks, the *pneuma*—of the children who have fallen from the cliff. That's what it is. They are fishing their spiritual flesh out of the sea so they do not drown. They're rather like fisher kings, sea-gods from empyrean isles, belonging neither to heaven nor to earth. How very exquisite. I wish I could speak to them. They look so princely standing before the mast. I wish—OOUUUCCCHHHH!"

There was a powerful flash that dopplered through everyone's optic nerves. Madame Dobrovolsky jerked in her seat and raised her arms as if to ward off a blow. Eyes popped open. "I'm sorry," she said through the liver-spotted hands that now covered her face. "I went too far. You must never be insistent. Beings of Light do not like impertinence." She sighed, lowering her hands to regain her composure. "I lost the connection. The 'line' went dead. Even after all these years I can't control it. It comes and it goes."

"Is that it?!" Fox asked, dismayed.

Madame Dobrovolsky took up her hearing trumpet. "What?" she said.

"*Is that it?*" repeated Leonora.

"I'm afraid so."

"But nothing happened!" said Angel uneasily. She didn't know just what to make of that flash.

"Quite," said Madame Dobrovolsky.

"What about Axel!" Fox cried. "Was he in the grass, too? What does it mean?"

"Mean? I'm not sure." She patted his hand. "Things always mean more or less than you can be sure of. That's the one thing you *can* be sure of. Nobody knows. Not me. Not you. Not anybody. It's all hints and inklings. Here," she said, tearing a piece of paper out of the legal pad and giving it to him. "This is what I wrote down while the channel was open."

Fox looked at the piece of paper and read this constellation of letters:

$$
\begin{array}{cccc}
B & E & R & T \\
E & V & E & R \\
R & E & V & E \\
T & R & E & B
\end{array}
$$

They seemed to come at him like missives from a dream, revealing a knowledge he shared with no one but Axel. Madame Dobrovolsky had ambushed him in his own memory.

"It's an acrostic," observed Angel over his shoulder. "It's the same across and down."

"Why yes, it is," said Madame Dobrovolsky. "I hadn't noticed." Suddenly a nostalgic glow enlivened her features. "I remember a queer psychiatrist I used to know, in Paris. He once said the best remedy for a broken heart was crossword puzzles."

"I've never heard of *reve* before," said Angel.

"In French it means *dream*," Sasha translated. His dad was a comparative literature professor at UC Irvine.

Angel frowned, drawing the syllable out in her head. "*Sueño* sounds dreamier to me," she opined after a few seconds.

As the encounter appeared to be over, they prepared to leave again. Leonora handed Madame Dobrovolsky a wad of money she'd saved up to pay for her services. The old woman accepted it with the bland look of pleasure taken in unspoken things. Angel noted this look with an eagle's eye and wasn't sure she liked it.

"Don't these sessions usually last, like, an *hour*?" she tartly inquired.

"My grandmother doesn't limit herself to such arbitrary lengths of time," said Sasha, taking offense. "Her encounters have been known to last through the night. Sometimes they end before they begin. Once I saw her slam the door on a pastry chef from Palm Springs before he even came into the temple. But her clients rarely go away unsatisfied."

Angel wasn't sure just what that proved, but she decided not to push it.

Fox, meanwhile, stood by worrying the acrostic, hoping by some excess of concentration to force from the letters their secret divagations. Why Bert? What did this person he hardly knew and liked even less have to tell him about Axel, or about anything? He didn't want to care about a dumb bus driver who once called him a "little shit," even if he was the Dark Lord of Illyria. *Bert, Treb, Treb, Bert.* He ran the names over in his mind. Bert becoming Treb, Treb this imaginative transposition of Bert. *Ever*, forever. *Reve*, dream. A dream that lasts forever, a dream you don't wake up from, a *real* dream. . .a hallucination. Damn! The whole world was becoming dyslexic!

"I can't do it by myself," he murmured.

Madame Dobrovolsky, who apparently knew how to hear when she wanted to, heard this and tried to reassure him. "But of course you can, my dear. It's the only way. It's easy—as easy as picking up a book, or making a cup of tea, or holding the bow of a violin in your hand. That doesn't mean it isn't hard," she said, a little smile of understatement playing upon her lips, "to be easy, to be ready for aptitude when it comes. But the way to that readiness is always a return." She pitched her voice one conspiratorial octave lower. "You already have what you need to find your friend, Fox Solis. It is simply a question of looking into yourself."

"But when I do, all I find is. . .nothing!" he exclaimed.

"Exactly," she said. "You find space, and with it internal stars. We humans carry heaven and earth within us. The parts of our bodies have their counterparts in the sky. In that analogy we find grace."

She was leading them out to the street by then. Angel was already in the car, and Leonora stood with Sasha on the sidewalk.

Fox faced her for the last time. "I don't know how," he confessed.

Madame Dobrovolsky nodded sympathetically. "It takes time," she acknowledged. Then she had an idea. "I have a friend who might be of more help to you than I." She took a moment to assess the wisdom of the course of action she was about to recommend. "It is a risk," she said at length. "My friend is not an entirely, how shall I put it, even-keeled personality. I don't say he's dangerous. Oh no. But he's unpredictable, impulsive, not half so cautious as he should be, knowing what he knows. His name is Theodore. Theodore Von-Koch. He runs a shop in the Crown Regency Center. . .that ridiculous mall somewhere up by Downey, I think. I would never be able to find it on my own, but it should be easy enough for you. Go. Tell him I sent you. You'll know him by the name of his shop: *Imago Mundi.*"

Afterward Angel declared herself against driving to the Crown Regency Center, which was all the way in LA County. "We're not going to find Axel like this," she complained while merging the Datsun into boulevard traffic. "We'd be better off going door to door, pounding the pavement, mixing it up with people."

"But Madame Dobrovolsky's a person," countered Leonora. "Sasha's a person. And now there's this other person we didn't know of before, who might be able to help."

"It's too esoteric for me," said Angel. "That's all I know."

"I think we should go." Leonora looked at Fox. "What do you think?"

"I think we should, too," he admitted. "You never know what's going to happen."

"And besides," said Leonora, "if we don't find anything, at least we can have a little fun."

Angel eyed the strange girl in her rear view mirror for the second time that day. "How did you know I said that?"

"Said what?" asked Leonora innocently.

The light turned yellow and Angel speeded through it, swerving up a ramp to the Garden Grove Freeway and reflecting on the sometimes hazy difference between coincidence and fate. Exasperated, she wrinkled her nose. "Man, with you guys I feel like I'm swinging at a piñata I know isn't there," she cracked.

None of them had ever been to the Crown Regency Center before, but it was impossible to miss: a massive pyramid the color of amethyst at its deepest, looming to one side of the 605 Freeway. They arrived at a parking lot and marveled at the building. It was constructed out of steel beams and thick translucent glass flecked with fibers that produced star-shaped rays of light in its depths. They had to walk halfway around its base before they found anything like a way in. They might not have seen even that if they weren't frustrated enough by then to notice a narrow slit into which a semicircular driveway looped in and out. It was just high enough for people to walk under without banging their heads.

Once inside, they passed through a massive circular door swooping round and round like a windmill laid on end. It issued into a lobby cramped with air conditioning ducts and bulkheads. It felt more like a bunker than an entrance. There was an escalator that took them to a landing, where they confronted nothing but plain white walls.

From there, however, things changed completely. A second escalator took them into a spectacular atrium more than two hundred feet high. They floated up through a serene pond encased in glass, where shoals of tropical fish hung in eerie silence. The lozenge-shaped chassis of a glass elevator, covered with amber lights, zoomed down from above and came to a stop almost right on top of them, crashing into the water. Another shot up in soundless ascension toward the roof.

At the center of the broad atrium stood a forty-foot-high armillary sphere made of steel beams curved into Möbius strips. A creek ran through a marble channel beneath it, forming braided rivulets over a bed of jade pebbles and feeding the fish pond. Real palm trees followed the watercourse, planted in tubs that had been countersunk into the marble banks. They saw fountains of the most ingenious construction all around them: sliding in sheets of liquid glass over obsidian ledges, shooting in segmented spurts timed to the muzak that seemed to be everywhere, purling into convex silver basins to disappear without a splash.

The mall took up five floors on all sides, with terraced promenades overlooking the atrium. There were the usual stores, food courts, a twelve-theater cinema with an IMAX screen, and even a merry-go-round for very young children. Angel, Fox, and Leonora wandered awestruck through the crowds, going in circles and losing all sense of direction except for up.

Finally they stopped at an information kiosk, where a chipper woman dressed for some reason in the livery of a hotel bellhop told them how to get to Imago Mundi. It was an unprepossessing shop tucked in between a Z Gallerie and a Kenneth Cole shoe store. They went in to find it filled with numerous small fountains featuring minerals and rocks of various shapes and sizes, some in bowls, others nestled in geodes, still others upholding revolving spheres. Some had bonzai trees in them and looked like tiny landscapes. The sounds of bubbling water, calming yet strangely cacophonous, filled the room.

At the back, behind a counter, stood a rangy man of middle age with long stringy hair, leathery skin, and little burst blood vessels flecking his nose. His most conspicuous feature was a purple stain that ran across his forehead to one temple, bisecting his left eye socket. Somewhere Fox had seen that before. . .

"Fountains of wellbeing!" the man called out with the excessive joviality of one trying too hard to be a good salesman. He came around the counter, stubbing his toe on an electrical floor outlet, and greeted them while nervously attempting to smooth the wrinkles in his T-shirt with the palms of his hands. "That's what I call them. Soothing and refreshing reminders of pristine places in these fast-paced times! Good for home or office!"

"We—" Fox began.

The man cut him off, carried away by his pitch, which it seemed as if he'd only just memorized and was trying to get out before he forgot. "Masks computer hum and unwanted street noise!" Noticing that his customers were three young people, he added, "Good for schools and libraries, too."

"Are you Theodore?" asked Fox.

The man's hands froze on his shirt. He backed into the counter, surprised to find it still there, and launched into nervous denials. "No, that's not me. No way. You got the wrong guy. Theodore? Don't know the man. Never been any Theodore here—"

"Madame Dobrovolsky sent us," Leonora thought it merciful to interject.

He stared, not quite prepared to believe in this owly little girl speaking to him so forthrightly. "Oh! In that case, I am Theodore." He crossed his arms against his chest. "Who are you?"

One by one they said their names.

"And you're friends of Julia Dobrovolsky? Great old lady. I always liked her. Her dad was a count, or a marquis, or something. He and my dad used to hang out. They were pals, way back when." Embarrassed at a sudden lack of new topics for conversation, he blurted: "You guys want some pop?"

He opened a refrigerator just inside the door to a back storeroom. "I've got Hawaiian Punch, Coke, Pepsi, 7-Up, Orange Crush, Dr. Pepper, Sprite, Mountain Dew, Fanta, all with diet and zero options. Help yourself."

Their shock at so wide a range of choices required some explanation. "It's what happens when I can't have any alcohol," he said sheepishly. "I keep hoping for a substitute."

Only slightly less mystified, they took what they wanted while Theodore gathered stools around the counter. He seemed to relax once they all sat down. "Oooh boy, you guys had me scared," he confessed. "I'm not very good when the unexpected happens. I startle easily. That's why I prefer it when people are customers. It's simpler that way. You know who they are, they know who they are. No surprises. It's almost comforting. Everyone honest, clear, distinct, assumed into the consumer ether."

"Haven't I seen you somewhere before?" queried Fox.

"I don't think so."

Then Fox remembered. "I know. It was in the riverbed—were you ever in the Santiago Creek?"

"Me? No." The earnest expression in Fox's face shamed him. "Yes," he admitted. "All right. I was."

"You were talking to yourself," Fox shyly recalled.

Theodore's face reddened.

"You were saying something about a vision you had."

The older man tried to shrug it off. "Oh it was nothing. You know"—he wiggled his fingers dismissively—"*delirium*. I was at a rehab center in a nearby Mormon church. I couldn't hack it. I escaped—with a duffel bag full of confiscated opiates. Boy was it a blast. I hid out there for, oh, four or five weeks, until my stash was gone. But I got my act together. Dried out. Got straight. See!" he said, holding up his arms. "No tracks!" His interlocutors weren't sure what to think about that. He changed the subject. "Now I've got this job. It's tough, a tough business, fountains. Did I say they've been proven to reduce stress by several prominent psychologists and crystallomancers?"

"No," said Fox.

"Especially the gemstone one's—chalcedony, lapus lazuli, the opals."

They sipped their drinks.

"Madame Dobrovolsky said you might be able to help us find my brother," said Leonora.

"Why would I know anything about him?"

The three of them exchanged uncertain glances.

"Aren't you psychic?" asked Angel.

"Are you kidding? I'm as sensitive as a rock. The world is a total enigma to me. And people? Shades, ciphers, nullities. I haven't a clue why they do the things they do, or think the things they think, or go in for all the crap they go in for. I just want them to leave me alone."

"But Madame Dobrovolsky wouldn't be mistaken," said Leonora.

"There isn't much that old lady gets wrong," agreed Theodore. "What's your brother's name?"

"Axel Acher."

"Acher? That means 'other,' or 'stranger,' in Hebrew."

"It does?!" said Leonora.

"It was the code name of a rabbi, Elisha ben Abuya, a compadre of Ishmael. He messed with this patriarch named Enoch, who had a mystical experience and transmogrified into an archangel, Metatron. Acher accused him of trying to play God, mixing up the human with the divine in a way that the keepers of the faith considered heretical. Metatron ended up getting sixty—"

"Lashes of fire," interjected Fox.

"That's right."

"How do you know that?" said Angel.

"Axel was telling me about it once."

"Metatron came to be known as the Heavenly Scribe," Theodore continued, "recording the things that happened in the celestial spheres and reading the face of God, which of course no human is supposed to be able to do without dying. But he didn't die. Or he did die, over and over again, and that's how he kept on living. It made him a sort of intermediary between gods and men. Other religious traditions picked up on this and assimilated him into their systems. He was the top angel in the Zohar. Egyptians called him Thoth. In the Koran he went by the name Idris, and the Sufis associated him with a Greek god, Hermes. Certain Gnostic sects thought of him as the 'Angel Christ.'"

"But I don't get it," said Fox perplexedly. "Why did Acher accuse Metatron of playing God, if he was Jesus Christ?"

"Metatron was a daemon, which made him *daemonic*, like Satan—dangerous because he was ambiguous, mortal and immortal, angel and devil, everything and nothing. He was a trickster. He liked to steal, and steal away. That's why he ended up going by a lot of names."

They all turned this information over in their minds. At last Angel, more sarcastic than she maybe wanted to sound, remarked, "Well, now we're really getting somewhere!"

Fox told Theodore about the various clues they had gathered: Gay Moloch, the limericks, and the acrostic.

"Let me see them," he said. Fox gave him the limericks, which he could make as little of as they did. Then Fox showed him the acrostic. As Theodore studied it, Fox told him who Bert was and how Axel had turned him into Treb and made him part of his private mythology.

"He takes a real person and makes him unreal?"

"Treb causes a war between the elves and men by stealing these magic jewels. Eventually he's defeated and banished to a place called the Aerial Void, but after it's over the world is changed. Elves and men don't understand one another anymore, and they can't live together in the Hexis." The solemnity with which everyone tried to see the relevance in all this made Fox blanch. "The elves start to go away, sailing over the sea to the land of"—he gulped—"Faerie."

It sounded silly even to him, and he hadn't even gotten started yet on Axalax and Sift. Everyone referred once again to the piece of paper with the acrostic, hoping there might be another way to understand it.

"Treb is Bert backwards," observed Leonora. "And each word has four letters. That's sixteen letters in all. Four is the square root of sixteen. Sixteen is four squared, or two to the fourth power. Two times two times two times two. A series of identical elements."

Theodore brooded over the page. "It's also a double acrostic," he noticed. "It doesn't just scan across and down, but up and backwards . . ." As he said this a dawning look of discovery crept into his face.

"Like a mirror image," said Angel solemnly. "Symmetrical."

"If we could just find the key," said Fox, "the one thing that would connect all the pieces."

"I know why Julia sent you here," Theodore announced. Half to himself he added, "But I don't know why she sent you here. She doesn't approve of the Aleph."

"What's the Aleph?" asked Fox.

"Nothing," he said. "Or rather, something. I don't know." He stood up. "Come on."

They went out to the promenade and Theodore locked the door behind them, placing a sign on it which read, "Mañana!" They proceeded to catch a crowded elevator, pushing through to the window in back as they rose over the palm trees and the armillary sphere. They saw the creek winding through to the pond and people shrinking until they seemed like plastic figurines in a toy mall.

"It's a world inside a world," marveled Leonora, gripping a handrail as if she might fall.

"Yeah," sighed Theodore. "Architecture has become so introverted these days. It's a shame if you ask me."

The upper floors, lined with greenish windows, had been given over to corporate offices, where men in suits sat in cubicles and stared forlornly at computer screens. At the very top they stopped at the entrance to a restaurant, where the last remaining passengers exited.

Theodore took a card from his wallet and inserted it into a slit beneath an LED screen on a panel. Then he punched in a code and pressed a knob with the letter *A* on it. The elevator rose through the roof.

"Where are we going?" asked Fox as everything around them went dark.

"The Apex," Theodore replied. "Where I live."

The elevator took them to a fancy A-frame penthouse with shiny wood floors, tall sloping windows, and trussed beams through which they glimpsed the very tip of the Crown Regency Center, made of quartz. Free-standing walls partitioned a living room appointed with biomorphic furniture in bright primary colors, a kitchen with island stoves and countertops, and several adjacent rooms. There was a platform suspended by cables and accessed by a ladder, where a futon and twisted up blankets could be glimpsed.

"You live *here*?!" said Angel.

"Yeah. Have to sell a lot of fountains for this, huh? Fortunately, I don't have to pay the rent."

"Why not?"

"My dad was Ernest Von-Koch."

That meant nothing to Angel.

"He was the Howard Hughes of Orange County," Theodore explained. "He made his first fortune with oil. Many fortunes followed. He had his hand in pretty much everything: real estate development, defense contracting, aerospace, water companies, freeway construction, fast food franchising, payday lending, home mortgages, movies. This was his mall."

"You must be pretty rich then."

Theodore snorted. "Rich enough to kill off any desire I might have had to make something of myself. That's why I'm such a loser. I know, I know," he said, warding off the anticipated chorus of their disagreement with his hand. "No need to spare my feelings. That's what I am. A failure. I have no willpower. I don't finish things. I wiggle out of responsibilities. I run away at the first sign of trouble. I don't stand up for my principles. I lie, I cheat, I cozen, I connive— and all just because I can."

"I don't think you're that bad," said Leonora.

"Don't be fooled!" he warned her. "I am the soul of addiction. I was born from its seed. Believe me. The Von-Kotches are nothing but a gang of pimps and pushers. I bet you're wondering about this birthmark on my forehead."

Angel and Leonora hesitated.

"Don't bother to deny it. It's very noticeable. It's a curse. A bane. You know what this is?" he said, pointing at his forehead. "It's the mark of Cain."

"You're too hard on yourself," said Angel. "It just makes you different. I bet it's a reason why, whatever else is true, at least you're not a pimp or a pusher, right?"

This brought Theodore up short. "I guess that's true," he said. "But I live by their good graces."

"Nice of them to let you stay here anyway."

"It's not out of any generosity, I can tell you that. Von-Koch Enterprises lets me stay because the place is haunted, that's all. My brothers and sisters would rather boil in acid than step foot in here. It's where my dad lived before he died. He went completely bonkers at the end—like Colonel Sanders. He became a billionaire anchorite, growing slowly more bizarre in his twilight years, brooding over his empire, nattering at God like a modern-day Lucifer. The minute he gave up the ghost the heavenly choirs must've sung, because he was one sour mean-ass son of a bitch."

"Weird," was all Angel could say to that.

Fox had drifted over to one of the windows. The pyramid cut just above the smog line, and the coastal plain of Orange County beneath him was cloaked in a brown diaphanous sheen. The only thing he could see clearly was the twinned peak of Old Saddleback far in the distance, floating like an island on a sea of molecular fluorocarbons. Finding Axel in all that seemed beyond hopeless.

He turned back into the penthouse. "What's the Aleph?" he asked Theodore a second time. They sat down on the funky biomorphic furniture in the living room.

"Well, the answer is not so easy as the question." Theodore excused himself for a moment, returning from another room with a *Business Week* magazine. "I don't subscribe, by the way," he said as he held it up. "They just keep sending them, in the event my dad, who's been cryogenically frozen, might one day come back to life and need a quick update on the financial scene." On the cover was a hexagonal headshot of Bill Gates, composed of smaller hexagons containing identical headshots of Bill Gates. Beneath his effigy it proclaimed in bold letters: "Only Connect."

"This is a representation of a hologram," he informed them, "which works on the same principle as a transfinite number. Each part contains the whole. The Aleph's like that, too: a point in space where all other points converge." He held his breath and shifted uncomfortably in his seat. "And it's in my basement."

"This *point*?" said Fox.

"Yeah. You see, my dad was quite a collector, back in the day. The Apex used to be filled with priceless things—Zurbarán paintings, an original Stradivarius, two-thousand-year-old Buddhas, a caliph's rubies, Saint Augustine's annotated copy of Plato's *Republic*, King Charlemagne's plumed casque, Napoleon's toothbrush, you name it. Of course, all of that was taken out after he died. Only one thing was overlooked: the Aleph.

"My dad bought it for a fortune off some guys named Zunino and Zungri in Buenos Aires, who'd found it embedded in a stairwell after demolishing a house to make room for their restaurant. My dad stored it here in a sixteenth-century *Wunderkammer*, or cabinet of wonder, along with an ostrich egg, a unicorn horn, and a stuffed phoenix first collected by August I, elector of Saxony. Now that I think about it, it was right around then that my dad started losing his marbles. I was only a kid at the time. I never connected his deciding the Apex was a ship sailing the Pacific Ocean, stringing up rope from all the beams and pretending he was Thor Heyerdahl, to the Aleph. It was only when he died, and I was fighting my venal brothers and sisters for the booty he'd left behind, that I happened on it. The experience, let me tell you, blew my mind. I knew then that the thing for me to do was to hide it. It turned out to be easy. My brothers and sisters took the *Wunderkammer* and never thought to ask what the rotted out plank inside it was. So I got to keep it."

"I still don't see what this has to do with anything," said Angel testily.

"Well, the Aleph, of course, is also the first letter in the Hebrew alphabet. That means it comes at the beginning, right? It's original. Not simply at the origin of language, but of grammar: tense, verbs, and so of time; or nouns, things, animals, people, and so of the space they inhabit. More than that, the Aleph indicates what, coming before, has no time and takes up no space. You can't say what it is, or where it is, because it's not past, present, or future. It's simultaneous, containing everything at once, all-seeing."

"Like God," said Leonora.

"That's the way the Kabbalists thought about it. They called it *En Soph*, the universal godhead."

"Oh brother!" said Angel. "Do you really expect me to believe you keep God in your basement? I thought He was dead."

"The guy who said that was only hoping it was true," said Theodore. "Take my word for it, He's alive and well. He's a predatory old engineer with a stock portfolio that won't quit, and He likes to torture young people."

"So *He* lives in your basement?"

"No." Theodore puckered his lips like a kid who's been caught in a lie. "What's down there isn't the real Aleph," he conceded. "I found that out later, when I decided to do a little research. A very knowledgeable librarian at the National Library in Argentina set me straight. It's a fake. My dad got rooked. The real Aleph is inside a stone column in the courtyard of a mosque in Cairo."

"Then why the hell are we here?!" fumed Angel.

"It's fake, but that doesn't mean it's not interesting."

"It could help us find Axel?" said Fox.

"Maybe. Maybe not. It's one hell of a ride either way. When you look at it, you have all manner of revelations. Everything happens at once. You *see* what's going on. It's like mainlining the universe."

An uneasy silence followed. "So one of us should go down there?" Fox inferred.

Theodore drummed his fingers on the armrest of his chair, growing shifty-eyed all of a sudden. "If you want."

Fox looked at Angel. "No way," she said. "I'm not going anywhere near that thing, whatever it is."

"I'll do it then," he said.

"Are you sure?" said Angel. "Dude, it could be dangerous. It already drove Theodore's dad wacko."

"That's not exactly true," said Theodore. "My dad was always a little wacko."

"I'm not too sure about *you* either," she cracked.

"It's just an enhancer. It takes what's already there and heightens it."

"Leonora." Angel appealed to the other woman in the room.

"She might be right," said the little girl cautiously. "From what I gather, the Aleph is like the One Ring of Power. When you put it on, you see all sorts of things. But at the same time, you don't know what might see *you*. You might be mesmerized by the Eye of Sauron and turned into Gollum."

"But that's just it!" Fox cried, hitting all of a sudden on why Madame Dobrovolsky thought he should meet Theodore. "That Eye already sees me. It's been seeing me all my life, freezing me up inside, making sure I never have any confidence or trust myself enough to . . .to. . .get out of myself."

"The point is not to get out of yourself," said Angel. "The point is to find Axel."

"But if I don't, we might never find him."

This gave Angel pause.

"I feel like I have a responsibility," he said. "I have to, I don't know. . .jump out of my own skin."

Angel pressed her lips together and sighed. Then she went over and threw her arms around his shoulders. "Mierda!" she said, burying her face in the crook of his neck. "Why are boys such dingbats?"

On that note, nothing remained to be done but to go and see what the Aleph might bring. Theodore led Fox to the other side of the apartment and opened a door. A narrow flight of stairs descended into darkness. "I covered all the windows down there. That makes it easier to see. Feel your way to a soft rug on the floor. It's a buffalo skin with a bunch of pillows. Lie on it and wait." He dashed off and returned with a marble-sized quid of rolled up plant matter, which he handed to Fox.

"What's this?"

"Nothing," said Theodore. "A sort of insurance. It's called *Salvia divinorum*. Trust me. Put it in your mouth, chew on it until your eyes adjust to the darkness enough to see a wooden whale box on an ottoman. That's where the Aleph is. Then spit the salvia out and keep looking at that box."

Fox nodded.

"One more thing," added Theodore. "Whatever you find, it won't be what you expect. It's in the nature of the experience that you won't

be ready for it. Just remember that none of it is real, and everything
will be all right in the end."

"Okay."

Theodore closed the door behind him. Fox took a moment to
brace himself. Then he walked down the stairs, groping across the
pitch-black basement until he stumbled over the box and found the
rug. He lay flat on his back, chewing the bitter tasting plant into
a viscous chaw, and watched as things around him slowly began to
take on dim outlines.

Soon he felt a mild nausea giving way to a strange sense of repose.
The darkness became a comfort to him. It seemed old and familiar,
like a place where he had always been. It lulled him into a memory
so primitive it took his breath away: he saw his mother through the
eyes of an infant sitting on her lap, the hills and valleys of her blouse
harboring a flesh that smelled of milk and radiated an inviting heat.
He heard her speaking to someone, maybe his father, off in shadows
Fox had never been able to penetrate. He felt her voice rumbling
in her body and wondered about the hard consonantal stops and
yawning vowels. It seemed as if her words moved ahead of her or
spoke through her things she herself did not understand. It was like
a dream, this sense of language as a question, reaching back to the
child he still was in his deep mind, but also forward to the person
he had become, prefigured in that child.

A sort of force field appeared to be warping space in the room.
Fox could feel it deform his body in smooth, continuous motions,
stretching an arm here, twisting a hip there, folding a shoulder into
itself, squeezing his waist until he was nothing more than a head
with legs. It reminded him of machines for making taffy. This went
on for what seemed like hours, although he had the impression time,
too, could be stretched and squeezed in the same manner. He kept
waiting for a change to happen with Theodore's box, remembering
sunsets in an El Monte park when he was a child and how he would
lay on the grass waiting for the evening star to surprise him already
there in the sky.

He now noticed a tiny crystal sphere hovering through the whale
that had been carved in relief onto the side of the box. At first he
assumed it was just an illusion of his drifting consciousness, but gradually it dawned on him that it must be the Aleph. It glowed and pulsed,

emitting a blue light charged with a force of attraction he saw was the source of that peculiar warping in the room. He stared at it, feeling pulled like kelp by shifting tides into its transparent depths. He felt his eye concentrate as it slid from one scale or order of magnitude to another, until far inside the crystal he could see complex lattices of molecules and atoms. They seemed to form a stable structure at first, but Fox soon noticed the regular arrangements of ions dividing and opening out, contracting by way of an inverse expansion. Soon the interior of the sphere was spacious, vaulted, a microcosm. He saw in it another Crown Regency Center and another 605 Freeway. He saw another coastal plain on which another Orange County stretched between another ocean and another Old Saddleback. He saw another Fox in the basement. Everything had its double, and in seeing his Fox wondered at that person he was, so little able to trust himself. Just what was it that made him tick?

At this point Fox began to understand why the Aleph came at the beginning. As if projected on a movie screen behind his eyes, he saw it in the primordial sea when the first prokaryotic cells developed cytoplasm and nuclei. He saw it when lobe-finned fishes evolved fin bones, when the first vertebrates became terrestrial, when a minor lineage of primates began to walk upright, use their hands, and talk to one another. The Aleph was there among the cavemen he now saw pressed tightly together on some drying savanna, starting at each terrifying sound in the night. It was there the first time a stick became a weapon, there at the invention of the wheel, there when someone first diverted water to irrigate a field. All of human history appeared to Fox as the dream of a controlled and self-contained world, of the world as a perfect little scale model. In it he saw civilization's genius and its violence, its beauty and its unbelievable cruelty. He saw the reasons for its walls and houses, its crossroads and networks, its towns and cities, and also its books and formulas, its rules and codes. And the strangest thing was that Fox didn't in fact see all this so much as feel it in his own seeing. He was a part of what he saw, inside the model that was inside him, a living ideal, a real *image* in his own huge and faraway solar Eye.

The Aleph was starting to blow his mind. It made him a lot smarter than he was, so much smarter he feared it might be too much for him to handle. He tried to anchor himself in reality again by speaking, or at least by hearing himself speak. But he couldn't do it. All he had was the desire or intention to signify. How well he knew its insignificance! It was the principle of his solitude and the deep ache of his love. It ran through his voice like a riverbed. He saw Axel there, too, anonymous and passed over, picking his way through make-believe kingdoms, searching not just for his own hallucinations but for the hallucination inscribed like a petroglyph at the center of their shared world. With a jolt Fox realized that this meant he knew where his friend was. It couldn't've been more obvious. He should have seen it right away. Axel had even been trying to tell him when he scrawled the words "Gay Moloch" on an overpass wall or an embankment. Fox was *meant* to understand. . .

He seemed to be not so much floating now as dropping gently through empty space, and the sensation was exactly the same feeling for what he was supposed to understand, as if his thoughts were physical, massive, subject to gravity. He accelerated. Images, losing their coherence, became drops and icicles of light streaking all around. It scared him to think in this free fall that he might break apart, like the tiny grain of a meteor disintegrating in atmosphere. But somehow it never came to that. By giving himself over to what he could not understand, he felt instead the possibility of a new equilibrium. It soon seemed as instinctive as a bird to him just how he should adjust himself to air and flow, and so find buoyancy in falling. Suddenly he had wings like rainbows, his bones were feather light, and his body blazed all over with brilliantly colored signs and symbols. He was a force of nature, an avatar, a myth. Soaring was his element. He might never have known anything else. He cut through an immense blue sky, seeing glued into the empyrean above him that big solar Eye, bleary and bloodshot and forever watchful. If all his life it had been there tracking his each and every move, crushing him beneath the weight of a merciless inspection, now for the first time it had lost sight of him, and its eyebeam roved like the shadow of a cloud across the earth, impatient once again to darken his joy. But he was too quick for it. He passed it by. He would never let it have such daring as this.

An amazing psychedelic journey followed. He looped and coiled around mountains of cumulus cloud, planed through their white

moraines to plummet toward a green and living California. He caught
bugs with swallows at the moving edge of a shadow. He darted with
hummingbirds through rank upon rank of passion flowers. He veered
with pelicans into the blue sea and swam with dolphins, catching in
their antic sideways eyes his own virtuosity reflected. He rose out of
the water to fly with ospreys up narrow canyons to their high nests.
He circled jagged peaks with turkey vultures, swooping down to
desert plains to feed on roadkill. He followed long arterial streets
to huddled roofs and glided unseen among the people, feeling their
burdens and sorrows with tender fellowship, glimpsing in what they
kept only to themselves, the subtle feelings having no place in the
world, the painful recognition that a life without the sublime was
small and petty and not worth living.

How opalescent intelligence was in him, like scattered light in
a fine summer mist. It made him canny and deft. It sensitized him
to the deep complexity in things. He skimmed the waves that beat
upon the shoreline as they broke down into smaller and smaller
wavelets. He listened to the wind at his cheek and heard messages
of flux and friction it would take ages to decipher, but he could do
it in a microsecond. Anything was possible. He could feel his way
into things of which he had no conception: the insoluble problems
of turbulence, the changeable behavior of a nonlinear equation, the
harmonic structure of a musical composition, the depths of another
person's heart. He could even find Axel. Indeed he'd already spied
him on a distant headland meadow, along with the other kids who
roamed through the wavy grass. That same tall man, swathed in black
robes and a black hood, stood on a precipice that stretched in jagged
lines ten thousand miles and more. He had mesmerized the children
who knew too little of authority to mistrust it, like the animals on
Galapagos Island when they first saw Charles Darwin. Even Axel
had been fooled. He took his place in line with the others, calmly
watching as one by one they leapt over the edge. Soon it would be
his turn. Fox came screaming down to save him.

But just as he neared he felt a deflection in the air, like a magnet repelling another magnet. He veered away again in surprise at
whatever force it was strong enough to withstand him. Wheeling
back, he saw a hideous flying creature materialize over the cliff. It
had dangling legs like a wasp, and paired buzzing wings that kept it

clumsily aloft. Its mammoth tail switched with the force of a heavy whip. It had no face, but inflamed like a wound, a livid asshole turned inside out, it was all gut. Fox knew what it was: the Ur-angel, ruler of the gross and the actual, under whose dominion life had been separated from this shimmering existence and concentrated in itself, made a thing of pure hostility, a thing embittered by its own isolation and obsessed with its own miserable survival.

And it had come seeking its nourishment precisely in what was most alien to it. Axel stood beside the cloaked figure, who made a cross before his chest and muttered words in Latin. The Ur-angel hovered, consumed by hatred and hunger, blotting out the light. A fold opened to disclose a ravenous mouth with rows of sliding and gnashing metallic teeth. Axel bowed his head, submitting himself humbly to the obscene consummation about to take place. Fox in horror watched the archfiend descend, entangling Axel in its life-less legs. He flew straight at it, straight into its magnetic field, and with a resounding "Nooooooo!!!" he swerved along a curve that passed through all points into a night so complete he remembered nothing else.

Who knew how much time passed after that. A while later he became aware that he lay in the basement crying softly to himself, making little noises in his throat and drifting through vestiges of vatic agony. A stray draft cooled the tears that streaked his cheeks. Shivers played on his skin like breezes. One last heave, more automatic than anything, and he was plain old Fox Solis again, alone with his dumb inhibitions and appalled by the discovery of just how mortal he really was.

When he had collected his wits enough to stand, he lumbered up the stairs again and came upon Angel, Leonora, and Theodore in the living room, where they sat around a table playing a game of Deluxe Scrabble. They didn't expect him back so soon. Although it felt as if years had gone by, it had in fact only been a couple of hours or so. He stood haggard and beat, looking over Theodore's shoulder at the board as he laid down the last letter of the word "logarithm."

"You don't look so hot," said Angel.

Fox only shrugged. Leonora took her turn, placing an *M* above the *O* in "logarithm," then an *L* beneath it, followed by another *O* and a *C*, tucked above the *H* of "Holocene." Fox couldn't keep the letters from jumping and transposing in his head. The dyslexia was going crazy.

"Are you all right?" Angel asked, coming to him.

He had trouble knowing how to answer that.

"Did the Aleph tell you where Axel is?" pressed Leonora.

"No." His failure weighed in him like a stone. "At one point I thought I knew, but I lost it."

"Here, sit," said Theodore, standing up abruptly and upsetting the board with his knee. Fox watched as the wood pieces slid into a new configuration. *M, O, L, O, L, O, G, O. . .*

As if a last hallucinogenic flash had been granted him, he saw the letters shift kaleidoscopically into that headland with wavy grass at the edge of a cliff. He saw in swift succession Axel, the tall man in black, his own mythic avatar, a dolphin leaping in the surf, the moon tracing its edge against the surface of the sun, Sift passing through gas stations and mini-mall parking lots, Bert on the beach saying "little shits" under his breath, the horrible Ur-angel. The images vanished right away, but in their visionary wake he felt the ludic advent of an idea.

"Wait," he said, grabbing Theodore's wrist to keep him from putting the pieces back where they were supposed to be on the board. He fished out a *Y* and aligned the letters *G-A-Y-M-O-L-O-C-H* in a row. He scratched his temple and looked hard at them, turning each backward letter very deliberately around again in his mind's eye. After a few seconds he began to rearrange them in different orders, trying different combinations: *H-O-L-C-Y-M-A-G-O. . .L-A-M-O-G-O-H-C-Y. . . L-O-M-O-G-A-C-H-Y. . .*

Then it hit him, with all the zap of a left hook. He might even have seen stars. A final arrangement of the letters confirmed it. *GAY MOLOCH* was an anagram for *LOGOMACHY*, and Axel was hiding out at Crystal Cove State Beach.

19

Ur

Orange County had never struck Fox as much of a place to live in. It didn't seem to grow out of any healthy symbiosis with the land. On the contrary, it fought the land with all its might, hemming it in, carving it up, shifting its contours until it hardly resembled anything natural. Orange County for Fox was like an apartment complex on a terraced hillside. If the developers had grudgingly to forego one or two lots for a butterfly preserve, it didn't mean that in the weedy vacant lot that remained one had a relation to a hillside, or even that there had ever been a hillside. In Orange County there were no hills, just as there was no river basin, no streams, and no desert. Those rare clear days after rain washed away the inversion layer could administer a shock to the system, but it didn't last any longer than it took for the smog to come back. Fox could still have moments of surprise on seeing just how closely the Santa Ana Mountains hugged him in on one side or how Catalina Island floated just off the coast on the other. He knew these features of the landscape did exist, of course, and in fact were only bringing him back down to earth, locating him in a place. It was just that when they presented themselves to him, they did so in such sharp contrast to his ordinary experience that he wouldn't have blinked had someone told him they were the splendors of Shangri-La.

But that afternoon, as Angel navigated the traffic that had locked the freeways and boulevards into their usual rush-hour paralysis, and she tried her level best to reach Crystal Cove before nightfall, Fox realized that Orange County wasn't like he thought a place without dimension or coordinates. Its complex mosaics of low-rise mini-cities, housing tracts, subdivisions, and circumferential collector streets made for a definite form of life. It even had a claim on his heart since it was all he had ever known really. At some level too deep for taking back he loved the abstraction in big-box retail stores, Mission-style mini-malls, and car lots crisscrossed with streamers. He loved that surface foreshortening in people who ducked through a Bavarian castle on a miniature golf course, hit golf balls into nets at a practice range, spoke to the drive-in menu at a Jack-in-the-Box, or walked briskly on treadmills in a 24-hour fitness salon. Nothing could be more endearing to him even than the trophy shop in a mini-mall that hung a huge portrait of William Shakespeare in the window or the funeral parlor that had taken up residence in a Polynesian lodge. He belonged to the commercial strip as much as it belonged to him. He took comfort in the dream it refracted of a life unanchored in place and time, in history, in language.

Orange County harbored its own special brand of chaos, too. And its symbol wasn't just rush-hour gridlock. Maybe especially at its most orderly, in those somnolent neighborhood streets down which Fox's eye flew in intimations of utopia, he sensed that dream had become scarily disconnected and arbitrary, even mad. No more proof of this did he need maybe than the English cottage they passed in Fullerton, painted and trimmed in lavender hues, where an exact replica the size of a shed dominated the front yard, and before which an old woman in a lavender dress, with lavender pumps and lavender-tinted sunglasses, sat on a lawn chair holding a lavender umbrella over her head and watched the lavender world go by. She was charming, eccentric, lovable even, but she was as much in that dream as anyone could be.

Angel attacked the traffic, switching as she drove between stations on the radio for updates and sigalerts. Leonora occasionally suggested an alternate route, but Angel disapproved of backseat drivers and kept her own counsel. She cut down sidestreets, got stuck, doubled back, tried a connector freeway, got off again. She jumped from one boulevard to another, dodging jammed intersections. Through it all Fox watched that mad dream continue refracting itself on all sides. He saw it in a baseball diamond dwarfed by a mountain of stacked containers for cargo ships. He saw it in a tomato field wedged between a freeway viaduct and an industrial park, with its old farmhouse and people still homesteading as if in another century. He saw it in a drive-in called the Big Donut which was itself a big donut. He saw it in the cows that ran through a chute into a dirt corral nestled under an Army radar dish, infested with crows. He saw it in a tract house dominated by an oil well and called "The McDermott Family Oil Company," or a bit later on in the fire that had broken out in a distant oil field, burning as if on some alien planet.

Pretty soon Angel came to the coast at Huntington Beach and turned south on Highway 1. When they crossed Victoria Bridge over the mouth of the Santa Ana River, which extended its straight-line labyrinth back into the interior from which they'd just come, Fox was reminded that the riverbed had been scouring out Orange County for untold millions of years. It was the reason why people had moved there in the first place, the source of their life and livelihood. But all along it had cradled them in phantasms. It had turned them into angels, into creatures who worked or served doing what Axel told him angels generally did anyway: conducting, relaying, transferring, transforming, transmitting flows of energy. Whether people were surfing off some jetty, or diverting tidal water into a recreational pond stocked with Chinook salmon, or refining oil into gas, they made a kind of divinity visible. On the far bank of the Santa Ana stood a monumental electric generating station, all lit up in a gathering haze. As Angel drove past, and Fox craned his neck to take it in, he couldn't help thinking it was a portion of some Heavenly City.

A while later he observed a row of trailer homes backed up against a reclaimed wetland. They'd been raised on platforms so their inhabitants could see over the highway to the ocean, dotted with oil rigs. He tried to imagine what it would be like to live in accommodations so extreme to the angelic labors going on around them. It seemed dismal beyond words. Even when, in Newport Beach, the apartment blocks and Mediterranean villas he saw from the highway assumed a more prosperous air, Fox could only conclude that the dream was not only mad but mean. It denigrated and cheapened what it touched, and every attempt at grace—sculptures of dolphins on lawns, benches set in quaint bowers, topiary trees—only felt diminished by the contrast. In the end that Heavenly City became Archolon, the scene of a strange perfection turning people into things that could be aggregated and regimented, measured and manipulated, without regard for their feelings, their inner lives. And what's worse, people did it to themselves. They were daemons of their own rationalized paradise.

They encountered more traffic where the highway curved around Balboa Island and crossed the marina at Newport Bay, and it made for slow-going through downtown Corona del Mar. The sun started to set, angular rays of light filled storefront windows with glare, shadows of roadside signs stretched into bulging caricatures of themselves. Fox noticed that the neighborhoods were distinctly more affluent. There were beautiful homes on tree-lined streets, and everything seemed in its place, immune to care or envy. Corona del Mar belonged to the archangels, the centurions, the high priests and priestesses of Ur. Fox wondered if they were ever saddened by their own perfection, if they felt it diminished them or wished for something else in their heart of hearts. He didn't suppose he would ever find out. He couldn't very well ask them. But he was also beginning to think he didn't care.

The highway rejoined the sea where it met the Irvine Hills, falling in gracefully aproned ravines to the cliffs and beaches around Crystal Cove. Several housing tracts had sprouted on the graded ridges just off the road to Irvine and above the highway toward Laguna Beach. But the bare meadows and domed crests of the still largely undeveloped hills isolated them like colonies on a desert planet.

Angel turned into the parking lot. No one was around. The three of them walked along the wood plank pathway and down the trail to the beach. The sun glowed a lustrous red over the horizon. A sheet of dark clouds had shot high above Catalina Island. To Fox's eye they resembled the vanguard of an immense ghoulish army.

They followed the shore to the place where Axel had been tormented by Danny Kemp in the eighth grade. Fox showed them the carved word *LOGOMACHY*, now weathered into the sandstone. He half-expected Axel to appear carrying that same spire of driftwood he'd found, but he didn't.

The tide was in, and they had to wait for a retreating wave to scuttle around a cliffside to a further stretch of the beach. It ran a hundred yards to the foot of another cliff washed by the sea. Recessed in a small alcove at the far end they found a crude dwelling made of driftwood and an old tarpaulin. A ring of stones enclosed the sooty remains of a fire, and inside there was an odd assortment of plastic water bottles, potato chip bags, and fast-food takeout boxes.

Leonora crawled into the hovel, searching half-heartedly for clues. Angel looked on with arms akimbo, wondering what their next move would be. Fox drifted to the edge of the surf and looked down the base of the cliff past seastacks and crashing waves. The coast, facing more west where he stood, twisted sharply south to wrap around the rock-girded oval of Crystal Cove, hidden from view. On the far side it swept in a long southeasterly line toward more bluffs in the distance. The highway swooped down almost to sea level before meeting the outskirts of Laguna Beach. Car lights streamed in opposite directions. Fox gazed up at the crest, where the headland tapered to a kind of tented peak just at the point the cove cut into the shore. As he took in the unusual formation a figure appeared there, distracted by something on the water that Fox couldn't see. In the dimming light he was nothing more than a silhouette, indistinguishable from anybody. But when he began swinging his arms as if in greeting, and the shapes of his jacket stood out clearly against the sky, there could be no mistake.

"Aaaaaxel!!!" Fox cried out, but the sounds of the sea damped his voice. Angel and Leonora hurried to his side and looked up as the figure lost his balance for a moment in the enthusiasm of his waving. He stood precariously close to the edge of the cliff.

In a panic Fox took off running back down the beach. He splashed through the waves that crashed against the cliffside and struggled wet in dry sand toward the trailhead. There he forced himself to sprint up the path, wishing with all his might that the supernatural strength of the Aleph would revisit him one last time so he could fly straight through the air. He kicked away rocks as he went, feeling in them how much they kept their forms, mocking his desire for flight. He had never felt so chained to his body, never more aware of the fact that he was finite, subject to forces it took all his wits just to keep from kicking him around, too.

Once on the headland he had to stop and catch his breath. The sun, almost touching the horizon, began to bleed light upon the water. Rapidly it squeezed itself into an hourglass shape. He ran along the crest through the thickets of wild radish, past the bench where he and his mother had once sat, on into meadows of blooming mustard and fennel. He had to ease himself through a barbed wire fence and thread his way through cactus plants half-concealed in tall grass. A heady scent of sage perfumed the sea air. The dark bank of clouds, jutting high into the atmosphere, was streaked a gaudy purple.

Axel teetered at the edge, still waving. Fox saw in quick bows of his head that he was wrestling with an intention to jump. Involved as ever in his own inner dramas, he was dangerously indifferent to anything earthly. He might dash himself upon the rocks below without a second thought. Fox reproached himself for not having had the courage to accept Axel in *his* finitude, as the troubled person he was and not the paragon of his own imaginative construction. For too long he had taken Axel at face value this way, with a blend of awe and timidity that was closer to convenience than conviction, closer to comfort than respect. There it was, he thought miserably, the secret truth about himself and the deeper source of his shame: he had not loved enough. He had not hated his fearful nature enough to remember that we were never alone, that even in defection we formed part of existence, and that for this reason we had to care for others more even than we cared for ourselves and take part with all our hearts and minds.

He ascended toward the promontory. The sun was now contorted almost beyond recognition on the horizon, reminding him of a mushroom cloud. Axel dropped his windmilling arms. Light rays caught the tangled mass of letters on his back, *Ardol, Schwein, Loth, Bluin.* They swirled around a dense point of revelation, all meaning and no meaning at once, *LOGOMACHY* and *GAY MOLOCH.*

Axel hunched his shoulders and raised his fists to his chest. Fox felt a whirling in his brain, as if the rising ground on which he ran kept rising and looping over until he was walking upside down and backwards. Then Axel bent his knees, threw his elbows out, and leapt off the cliff.

At the same time, heart exploding, Fox screamed:
"Noooooooooooo!!!!!!!!!!"

He skidded to a halt at the place where Axel had stood. Just at that moment the last vestige of the sun converged upon a vanishing point and with a green flash slipped away. Fox felt ten kinds of fool. On a ledge six feet below stood Axel, all intact, gazing out over the sea. He had long stringy hair and a wispy beard, his clothes were impossibly ratty, and even from that distance Fox caught a whiff of a month's old body odor. But that notwithstanding, Axel had never seemed more alive.

Fox dropped down beside him. "Are you okay?" he asked, placing a protective hand on Axel's shoulder.

"Sure."

"You scared me."

"Why?"

Sheepishly he replied, "I thought you were going to jump."

Axel shot him an irritated glance. "Are you crazy?!"

But Fox didn't hear this. He was too busy looking gape-mouthed onto the water in the cove below, where a brightly opalescent ship floated on the undulating tide. It had a single mast and a square sail, and a tall neck tapering into a swan's beaked head. On the deck Fox saw two shining figures dressed in silver robes and silver helmets with upswept wings. They were pulling in a glimmering net that filled the whole depth of the sea between them. Fox blinked and wiped away the tears that had sprung into his eyes. The figures remained, as real as his friend beside him, even as real as a rust-red stain beneath a scupper or the slosh of bilgewater inside the hull.

"It's Sift," Axel explained. "He found the ship that will take him back to Faerie." He squeezed the scruffy mane of his hair and shrugged. "Now we don't have to worry about him anymore."

Fox kept staring, but not at Sift. With an awareness pulverizing him to his very core—ribs, eyes, anus, larynx, skull, and gut pulling apart and recomposing themselves in another order than that of being—he saw his and Axel's faces in the two figures standing on that deck. He saw himself by the light of an estrangement so complete he was all strangeness, all anomaly, erring and deviating by nature, yet in that nature, unbelievably, striking a divine spark. Then he knew that the important thing was what gripped and shattered internally like this, the torn, uprooted, misfit parts of ourselves, since it was in those parts that we discovered how to care, and what to live for, in the great winding reaches of empire. Fox had become one of Madame Dobrovolsky's fisher kings, and his role from then on would be to make sure the children at the edge of that cliff did not fall off, and if they did fall off, to catch their subtle bodies in his nets and keep them from the grave that awaited at the bottom of the sea. And with that he felt lifted as if by a buoyant wave over the crest to the headland behind, where Angel and Leonora stood amidst the mustard and the cactus plants wondering what had happened to them—back into the world.